Nocturne
for
Madness

Nocturne for Madness

Robb White

NEW PULP PRESS

Published by New Pulp Press, LLC, 926 Truman Avenue, Key West, Florida 33040, USA.

For information contact:
Publisher@NewPulpPress.com

ISBN-13: 978-0692609026 (New Pulp Press)
ISBN-10: 0692609024

For Joe Zingaro

"No pleasure [in life] but meanness."

- The Misfit, Flannery O'Connor's
"A Good Man Is Hard to Find"

Nocturne
for
Madness

Chapter 1

Winter, Jefferson-on-the-Lake, Northern Ohio

Thomas Haftmann dreamed all night of ortolans. Those delicate birds like sparrows that French gourmands cooked in their own grease and were eaten whole, the birds' feet sticking out of the eaters' mouths. The tiny bills being spat onto expensive plates. He had seen it once like that in New Orleans. They wore sheets over their heads to keep blood and hot juices spattering anyone nearby.

The ortolans were held by tiny strings to their feet and were gently nibbling cracked corn from his hand. One by one he ate them, indifferent to the gore jetting from his mouth as he clamped his jaws around each bird. He could not get enough of them; they were sticky and sweet. In the logic of dreams their feathers would fall away before he ate them so that he tasted nothing but flesh.

He awoke with the taste lingering and his mouth full of saliva. He remembered fragments of his dream and wondered if the juncos and titmice he threw seed and bread scraps to all winter long were playing into his subconscious.

He thought: *I may die in this hellhole.* He cranked himself off the sofa, a red velour job he'd picked up on the cheap at the Goodwill store, went into the kitchen and, out of some masochistic whim, microwaved stale coffee.

Shower, shave, work—another morning's uninspiring routine beckoned. Being self-employed, so long out of harness from Cleveland homicide, had lost its joy. He knew he had to see a woman about her son. How his thirteen-year-old corpse had come to be sprawled across her kitchen floor with most of his brain matter excavated from his skull. Haftmann had an uneasy relationship with the Lake cops and their cranky chief. He was allowed him to poach on their territory from time to time as long as he remembered he was no longer a cop and was (he would say) merely mortal; some in the precinct would say much, much less than mortal. "Gumshoe" and "shamus" weren't altogether passé as slang references to his private investigation career, but "window peeper" and "snoop" were more common among the Lake cops he encountered. Like the crow's-feet around his one good eye or the gray spreading outward and spilling downward from his crown, he was aware that time was passing faster with each birthday. Unfortunately, he wasn't growing a thicker skin with each passing season. His concern that life was shortening as he aged was borne out by science and by the fear that he would never have enough money to live decently in retirement because he intended to jettison his second career as soon as he was able to. Haftmann was forced to define "decently" as having sufficient beer money because he had re-acquired a bad habit from the early years of his marriage to a woman who had decided he was the particular baggage she needed to jettison in middle age.

Haftmann, a self-styled existentialist, wasn't comforted by physicists who say there might exist subatomic particles in the brain released after death and these alone comprise human consciousness. Bright lights, a tunnel, one's kith and kin, not to mention a flaxen-haired Jesus pointing the way to the pearly gates was a construct of our culture, nothing more. The body's last twitch, a gift to the dying, and a little squirt of endorphins to ease the way to death.

Most of what he learned late in life annoyed him, in fact, so he resolved that, that when the time came for him to go into the great blackness of oblivion, he might as well go out as he had come into the world and remain as obtusely stupid to whatever new knowledge the smart ones might try to pour into his head. *In my end is my beginning*, he mused, thinking of his long-ago catechism days, and blew on the steaming coffee. He set about facing the day ahead.

~ ~ ~

Jefferson-on-the-Lake in the wintertime is an eyesore: scabby paint blistered raw by arctic winds roaring down from Canada, desolate and boarded up, the hordes of tourists long gone to jobs and warmer climates, empty lots. The locals brooded during long winter nights waiting for spring, for the lights, the return of the tourists, and, mostly, the money. When America made steel in the Mahoning Valley near Youngstown and the big mills of what is now a tourist stop in the Steel Valley Trail of Pittsburgh, middle-class families, hard-drinking fraternity boys, dope-dealing bike trash from Cleveland, Sandusky, Toledo and points west – even south to West Virginia – all mingled along the one thoroughfare near the Strip.

Three million people passing through the strip every summer, or so the Chamber of Commerce liked to brag. No one knew how much money stayed afterwards because the few people who owned anything weren't about to tell. Everyone skimmed off the top. Just like the 1950s when the swing bands came to town. Only now there were skinheads, the girls had Kool-Aid-colored hair and lip rings, and the music was rock and techno dance, and there was dope.

And crime. Even in the winter, the man who dreamed of ortolans had plenty to do, if, as Haftmann knew too well, you weren't born a child of privilege. Haftmann was

3

nearly always broke, and not only had he doubled-down on his drinking but he had caught the gambling bug. Like most drivers who aren't afraid of snow, he clipped a few stop signs that were meant for summer traffic and cut a swathe through the snow on Route 531. The lake was frozen to the farthest point of his vision, where its blue sheen intersected the gray planes of sky and water. Erie, being the shallowest of the Great Lakes, locked up soonest.

He drove past the old beach where he and his two cousins had once tried to walk across the frozen lake to Canada. They were rescued by a helicopter, all found flat on their faces on inch-thick ice, their names in the paper, bragging in school, and everyone famous for the ditsy stunt. His cousin had his arm ripped off in a sprocket when a belt feeder jammed at the Cleveland Electric Illuminating plant. He bled to death while the dayshift foreman stood by vomiting on his shoes. Spider, another gangly limbed cousin, died after his third operation at the Cleveland Clinic after a crane fell on him at the titanium plant in Ashtabula when he was already short a kidney and one lung from a boating accident two years after the mistimed Canada expedition.

The station house was a mile off the Strip, a two-story cement block affair with energy-efficient windows, the downstairs held cages for the summer season, and the upstairs was partitioned for two detectives. The decor inspired by some ergonomics thinking, bled pastel colors from the three-sided partition walls. The Jefferson precinct, nicknamed JOTL like the resort, had fax linkup to CID in Columbus and computers in the dispatch room, which did double duty as a muster room for patrolmen and detectives. In busy summertime, heads popped up over cubicles, prairie-gophering, just like their big-city counterparts in Cleveland homicide.

He pulled into the lot, scrunching the tires into the same drift he'd used yesterday, showing his offside treads bald, next to the candy-apple red Cherokee. He got brain freeze outside the car while the gust lasted. His exposed fingers burned from the vicious cold. Inside the station, he smelled must like an overlay of cheap disinfectant, a smell of lavender urine cakes that made his nose wrinkle.

The cops here worked twelve hours on and twelve off. He couldn't find the report the detective working the case had been working on because whoever was sharing his desk had put it somewhere, so he took the piece of paper with the number of the woman he had to see and dialed. He got her after ten rings of the third try. She said she had the flu and she could meet him after her food stamp appointment. He said no, not possible, he'd be over in ten minutes and she'd have to be there, the unspoken threat capably transmitted through the waves of frigid air separating them. She whined a bit more in the nasal lower-class tone of the helpless.

"You gonna see that skank this morning?"

Big Steve. Jefferson-on-the-Lake's third chief of police in as many years. The fat lieutenant knew how to make the payola system work. A pig-eyed, bloated careerist whose two forms of communication were rage and silence. Seven bars had burned to the ground during his tenure; all seven owners collected. Probably the same torch all seven times, according to the conspicuous saddle burns the arson investigator noted in his report, and a rumored Youngstown mafia connection.

"She's got my only lead," Haftmann says, making sure his voice stayed even. He despised the chief but he needed to preserve his second-hand access to the station house's technology and databases.

"You must be getting a good dollar to stay on the trail after three years," the lieutenant says.

"About that," Haftmann replies, but he's a cigar-store Indian, refusing to give Millimaki anything he might use down the road.

Haftmann had tangled with Steve Millimaki more than once over bribery of certain Lake cops. Before he tacked up his shingle on the Strip five years ago, Detective Sergeant Thomas Haftmann, ex of Cleveland homicide and on loan to the Lake cops from Jefferson Sheriff's department where his wife had encouraged him to apply, was still part of the brotherhood of cops. He missed the paramilitary organization of a big police department. Micah had clout as a rising star in the prosecutor's office.

"See the new broad before you go out," Millimaki says.

In an era of social networking and Facebooking, Millimaki continued to revel in his Neanderthal chauvinism and was never called out on it.

Haftmann figured Big Steve had put a move on the new dispatch clerk, a civilian new-hire, and she wasn't having any. Otherwise "broad" would have been "pussy" or "gash." Station house gossip had it that Big Steve had been getting regular trim from the blonde, well-lunged dispatcher who hadn't been around since her husband surprised her at home playing a tune on a rookie cop's skin flute.

Haftmann found her getting a machine coffee in the radio room. She was petite, a dishwater blonde in her forties, swimming in her uniform.

"My name's Haftmann. You wanted to see me?"

"Hi, my name's Shawna. I'm the new dispatcher. Lieutenant Millimaki – "

"We call him Big Steve."

She looked at him from a pair of ice-blue eyes. Micah was a dusky beauty but Haftmann was struck by her prettiness and the high cheekbones that accentuated her eyes.

"We call him Big Steve because he's big." She squints, wondering if a joke at her expense is en route – cops and their twisted pranks.

"Big as in big mouth. Big as in lard ass," Haftmann says and cracks a smile.

"I assume you don't have to report to him, Detective Haftmann," she says.

"Just Tom. I'm not a cop. My presence in this place is tolerated but not welcomed."

A smile appears slowly, still unsure whether it's safe to mock the boss to this stranger; her hair is not so mousy, Haftmann sees, the fluorescent lighting dampens its luster, the eyes jumping at you, however.

"Okay, Tom."

"What have you got, Shawna?"

He smiled back and hoped that he didn't look too much the wreck he saw in the mirror this morning. Bags like a baboon under his eyes. A blue-black beard stubble, gut roll with handles. No boyish figure, he. Muscle tone lost with years of bad diet and pounding down the cheeseburgers from the dollar menu on surveillance. It never helped that his ex-wife had a high metabolism and never put on weight.

"I don't know all the officers by name yet, so I didn't know you—"

"I left the force a few years ago," Haftmann says. "I'm a private investigator. You know where Tico's Place is on the Strip? Used to be a palm reader's place. My office is right across the street."

She held out the small package with his name on it.

"I found this in my car this morning," she says. "I don't know if it was put in the lot then or left last night and I just noticed it on the back seat."

It felt like a CD disk wrapped in a cut-up grocery bag with ordinary twine, fist-sized.

7

He saw his name spelled in letters of the same height. The penmanship of a child, you would say, done with a black Sharpie.

"I hope it isn't anything urgent . . ."

Haftmann thinks: afraid of a screw-up her first week on the job.

"I'm sure it's okay."

Those eyes, hard to miss, Haftmann thinks, and notes how her smile lights them up. He knows Micah always preferred working in a male-dominated environment because she had to have the competition. He wonders what this woman's reasons are. Micah despised the sexual attention she drew, but not all women were like her. *None like her*, Haftmann thinks, and despises himself for the weakness.

Without berating himself this time, he wonders why he didn't ask if she locked her car.

~ ~ ~

Into the stinging wind, an ice razor across his forehead. The vineyards stretching into Siberian whiteness all around with ragged clumps of snowdrift pockmarking the expanse. Most of the Mexican grape pickers had gone back or settled long ago; now they're children starred in sports at the high school. The Northeastern part of the state was dotted by a smattering of family vineyards which were turning more profits every year.

One fall after school he and a cousin had picked the grapes for Welch's. His back stooped, his insides all cramped together; the Mexicans were indifferent to outsiders. They seemed like gypsies to him, romantic and exotic. His hands were cut and torn so many times by the constant contact with spiky tendrils that it took most of the picking season to get scar tissue. One job he looked back on with loathing but it left him with an intense admiration for those who could do that kind of shit labor their whole lives.

He slipped the package into his coat pocket and got into his car. The battery had seized up, the Neon's nose pointed right into the wind. Cursing, he got the cables out of the trunk, retrieved his bona fide burglar tool from the wheel well, still cursing, he jimmied the Cherokee's window next to his banged-up Chrysler, hot-wired it with aching, numb fingers and a litany of more imaginative curses, and, finally, with a twist of wires, he jump-started his car. No one could see from the slatted windows into the parking lot, but he was taking up far too much time, and this would not be considered a prank. If caught, he was burning all his bridges to officialdom. About to toss the jumper cables back in his trunk, he knew without looking the Cherokee's vanity plates said NVTHIS1, as the vehicle belonged to the lieutenant; this and the bitter cold that stung his hands so enraged him that he decided to indulge the impulse building up inside—no, for weeks, Micah's betrayal, his failed life, the despair of everything. Haftmann removed the plastic rubber grip from the clip handle and, heart full of malice, he keyed the Cherokee's flank.

~ ~ ~

Haftmann's first stop was Jefferson, five miles southwest. He drove a steady 35 mph, nerves knotted at the hissing and sucking noises of the snow churning under the chassis like synthesized rebop from autotracked dance music. *This is what they play in hell,* he thought.

All stiffs in Ashtabula County went to Jefferson. Doc Harris was M. E., a shortsighted, snappish curmudgeon who should have retired before Haftmann left Cleveland homicide bureau. Another station house joke: Better to be buried alive and awake screaming in your grave than to revive on Doc Harris's table.

Haftmann found the M. E.'s assistant skulking along a corridor.

"Where's Doc?"

Grimace. "He's assisting in Painesville. Ligatures they can't figure out. He wanted in while it was still fresh."

Fuckola. "He say when Detective Stelmashuk's report's ready?"

"Got it downstairs," the creep says; "second desk."

Three pages. *Fuck me.* Forensics jargon, most of it familiar after twenty years of cop work. The boy's spleen weighed 110 grams, his kidneys 200, a mild autolysis on sectioning but a clear cortico-medulliary demarcation. He skipped genitourinary tract, pancreas and adrenal glands, gastrointestinal tract, paused at neck – strap muscles torn, upper trachea filled with brownish-red mucoid fluid, massive hemorrhaging in the larynx – and cut his eyes to MANNER OF DEATH.

There he found the expected postmortem symptoms in clinical terminology for what happens to you when you get within the blast area of a twelve-gauge shotgun. Pompous old Doc Harris, his signature an ego trip. The last sentence an oratorical nicety: "The undersigned reserves a determination of either suicide or homicide pending additional investigation by appropriate agencies and notification of the undersigned as the subsequent data develops therein." M. E.'s used to fear the three centuries' shelf life of paper; now it's the digitized eternity of cyberspace.

He high-stepped it across the street to the diner for donuts and coffee. Remembered the package in his pocket and took it out. He thumbed a serrated edge and the upper curve of a letter, maybe an S, scissored out but probably a shopping bag, the twine featured a square knot. The printing was felt tip, clumsy like a child's, and the *e* and *a* in his name were done the same way – a schwa tipped upwards. No address, no zip.

Inside he found Kleenex wrapped around a cell phone and a cassette tape. He held the tape up to the fluorescent lighting to see where it had been cued: halfway. TDK High Position Type II SA 90, the figure 70 was used to separate the words High and Bias in the lower left corner. *Graphics equalizer number . . . What is this shit?* Haftmann hadn't touched a cassette since he and Micah started dating.

Nothing else to note. The cell phone was a Droid and looked expensive. *Some deadass's idea of fun on a winter morning? Fuck it. It could wait.*

He wondered if the mother had cleaned the blood spatter from the walls by the time he got there. If he had a dollar for every time somebody had asked him when the cops or the city was coming in to clean up the blood in their houses, he'd be a rich man. He finished his coffee, left a dollar, and cursed Stelmashuk for tipping him off so late. If he had been there when the scene was fresh was fresh . . . but that was the old cop brain thinking.

At the corner of West Jefferson and Market he used the last working pay phone in town to call a number at the Cleveland Clinic. The wind whipped his coat open to the neck; the skies were pewter.

Good morning Cleveland Clinic. One sentence in the breathless soprano of receptionists.

"Doctor Matrooshian's extension."

"One moment." *Buzz-whirr-click-ka-chuck.*

"Doctor Matrooshian's office. May-I-help-you?"

"This is Thomas Haftmann. I'm returning the doctor's call."

Doctor of Psychiatry Terd Porn Matrooshian. Haftmann thought he was joking when the shrink first introduced himself. He saw the square face and intelligent dark eyes as soon as he heard him come over the line.

"So good of you to call, Detective."

Snide little bugger. Matrooshian's message on his answering machine was three days old.

"I'm not a Detective, Doctor. I've told you that many times."

"Ah, yes." The *yes* coming over as *yiss.* I have finished with the Minnesota Multiphasic – you recall the last test? – and I would like to schedule an appointment with you again soon."

"That's not going to be possible. I'm working too many hours now. I'm really close to this scumbag." *From here-to-the-moon close.*

"Detec—Mister Haftmann, it is urgent that we talk as soon as possible." All those hissing s's like a basket of vipers.

"I can't get away right now."

Silence at his end. Pondering years of prevaricating responses from scores of reluctant patients like him.

"You *must* schedule an appointment with me. It was a condition of your sent—of your *retirement* from the department."

"Just as soon as I can, Doctor."

The lie as obvious as a nose oyster on a white linen tablecloth.

"You know, *Mister* Haftmann, it would be most inappropriate for me to tell you anything over the telephone and your pension depends upon – "

Haftmann's pulse rate rose. "Right now, I need to find out who blew a kid's brains out all over his kitchen walls—"

Matrooshian blurted it out like a toxic froth of sibilants: "Schizophrenia. Incipient stages but manifest. Your dreams are full of hunting and eating and killing and so far you are the hunter, not yet the hunted, but that will change . . ."

Haftmann hit the toggle button so hard he cracked receiver.

Crazy like my religious nut of a grandmother.

Overhead the sky showed a crease of yellow through its violet like pus in a wound. He scissor-walked through the Courthouse parking lot's fresh covering of snow, found his car's windshield dusted and brushed it off with a hand spiderwebbed with cracks from the cold. He took 307 west to 534 and drove north all the way back to Jefferson-on-the-Lake. The woman lived in a house trailer just outside the township on Myers Road. The hissing from beneath the chassis was louder on the drive back; pinprick holes from beneath the rusted floorboards. *Only three years old,* he thought. Ohio winters and road salt. Too late for a chassis bath.

Too late for a lot of things, he grunted to his face in the rearview mirror.

All houses smell of their owners. Bad houses always stank. This one reeked to high heaven. Acid stink of piss right into your pores. He let the cop he once was take over, noted the dirty gray and white kitchen lozenges, yellow tobacco film on the walls, crud and dirt in the bathroom. Bathrooms brown and yellow, as if Freud needed to summoned from the collective abyss to explain that choice of colors—or was it Jung? Micah, that bookworm, always dinning in his ear about some mumbo-jumbo claptrap or other.

The woman had a tattered godseye in the same colors on one wall and pressed Black-Eyed Susans braided with Flowering Spurge underneath it. He declined a cup of instant coffee when she asked, eager to get the small, wretched courtesies over.

Haftmann knew that the problem was with the splatter. That numbskull Stelmashuk couldn't find his ass with both hands and a mirror. It was simple: the boy had been moved. Most of his brain matter had vacated his skull but the concentration indicated he'd fallen somewhere left of the chalk lines. Like a child making a snow angel, hard-pumping arteries had exsanguinated most of his body's blood, which poured out in streams across the kitchen, crisscrossed midway because of the skewed tug of gravity – the trailer old, decrepit – and still had enough force to cross a tongue-and-groove deck to fall in thick, plum-shaped drops. Haftmann had seen the crusty brown hole beside the porch on his way in.

The foul-smelling, stale air made him antsy, and he wanted to get it over with. *Brace her now*, his instincts said. He had spoken to the boy's best friend yesterday – a scrawny epileptic whose terror shook the dining room table so badly that any experienced cop would have Mirandized him on the spot. They were playing with the twelve-gauge, fast loading and ejecting, heavy metal music for background. The pump lay across his chest when the EMR techs arrived.

This goddam woman. Slurping her coffee and making generalizing complaints about cops "messing with her" and welfare not increasing her food stamp allotment in that whiny lowlife tone he hated. Haftmann was an equal-opportunity hater: white or black, he despised people who lived in filth like this. He imagined a bullet plowing through the shell of her skull and chewing her brains to bits in a wound channel you could put your arm into. So stupid she'd probably still be speaking by the time the slug exited. He interrupted her convoluted story of recent woes – never mind the dead child she shat forth into the world – and asked her why she didn't tell him about the fight he was in at school.

"He always getting' into fights," she complained. "Them other kids tease him because they made him take EMR classes."

Educable Mentally Retarded, educationese.

Haftmann closed his eyes and summoned the words from Doc's report: one of the boy's fists was curled around a 2 & 3/4-inch shell, number 4 buckshot for the Remington eleven hundred. A 28-inch barrel. The neck arteries were exposed. That meant he was probably within three feet of the muzzle because the buckshot would have spread.

Haftmann got up, walked into the living room with his back to the woman. He noticed the notebook sitting on a table.

"You ever catch him watching hard-core porn?"

The question didn't faze her, but her eyes turned to slits. "The cops found some DVDs and magazines beneath his daybed over there. He ain't got money so I don't know where those things come from."

She made a fumbling play for her cigarettes, lit one. Snorted smoke through both nostrils.

"You ain't a cop, they said. I'm seeing you because that detective said I should cooperate."

Haftmann pivoted and glared: "So cooperate."

"Why should I?"

"Because I'll give a good report to the detective in charge for you. It could help with your food stamps. Your boy use dope?"

"First you askin' about porn, now dope?"

"Yes or no, simple question. It's no reflection on you as a parent if he did. Most kids at his age will experiment." *You hatchet-faced bitch.*

"Once in a while. I tried to get him to stop but—"

"Yeah, uh-huh."

"All the kids at school, you know—"

The thought of having to touch her made his skin crawl. The air was rank with a mic of smalls of food, cooking oil, stale perfume; drops of sweat fell from his armpits and hit him in the love handles. The heat in the trailer was enough to smelt iron ore.

"I don't care about kids at school. Did you do dope with him because I know fucking well you did."

The screech erupted from her throat and then, faster than he could have believed possible, she hoisted herself out of her chair and threw both hands toward his face, nails splayed and clawing to gouge and scratch. The caterwaul was lost in the gargling noise of her throat. He forearmed her wrists and brought his right hand around in a slap that knocked her to the floor.

Haftmann reached his left hand out and plucked her up to his face by the hair at the nape of her neck; he waited until her eyes focused and hissed: "That's right, I'm not a cop. I'll slap the living shit out of you until you tell me something that's true!"

Her eyes widened. Reading him now: *a maniac in my kitchen . . .*

"Tell me about Lonnie Dale Nelson because I know you know him."

He led her to a chair and eased her gently down. The storm over.

At the table, his hands folded in front of him to show her no more harm, he listened through self-pitying sobs and a mishmash of lies and truth. He felt it got as close as it needed to make the connection. There was once an 8-year-old girl who, if she were still alive, would be 11 now. Lonnie Dale Nelson, Haftmann was convinced, had been the last to see her before she disappeared.

He pieced it together between the epileptic friend's version and the mother's. It must have happened like this: the kid had come home from school, not having a particularly good day, even then. He'd been kicked in the nuts when a classmate called him "a fuckin' retard" in study hall and his half-on, half-off girlfriend figured she could get the dope he supplied without having to give up the sex for it. He got home and found his mother 69-ing on the daybed with her current boyfriend. The boyfriend was very big and kinky; he liked young boys too, and had tried to get the kid to perform oral sex on him. The mother wasn't resisting the idea anymore because her own dope habit was too big to kick and this slimeball was her source. (She'd already lost one other child to the courts for child-endangering.) The Lake cops knew her well, so she couldn't go back to her real money-making skill: blowing the clientele of a certain bar on the Strip, bikers mostly. Slimeball ordered the boy into the bed. The kid refused. He held her head down on the bed and threatened to snuff her with a pillow if the kid refused again. The boy said he wasn't about to suck his tattooed prick just because his whore of a mother did and took a few blows to the side of the head for showing *disrespect*, her word. More drinking, some grass to mellow things out. Same overtures to the kid that evening but apparently he'd had enough by then. He made the last mistake he'd ever make in his short life: he came out of his bedroom with the Remington and pointed it at his mother's lover, who went all theatrical with pleading and begging, until he got one meaty paw on the barrel, twisted it out of the kid's hands – no great feat considering the kid weighed 125 pounds – and put the barrel six inches from the boy's face and squeezed off a shell.

Knowing that, even in this trashy trailer park for losers, the noise of a twelve-gauge going off in a trailer with tin walls was certain to draw attention, they played a quick game of hide-the-evidence. So a handful of shells got tossed around the room and the telephone cord was wrapped around the boy's legs to make it look as though another domestic tragedy with guns had occurred. He said it would give him time and that she had no choice; they'd both go down together. She'd done a stint at the Ohio Reformatory for Women in Marysville when she was a teen shoplifter-hooker and didn't like it much. *What did she have to lose, really? Besides, he was already dead, wasn't he? . . .*

Haftmann asked her if she'd like him to drive her to the station. She said okay. Haftmann helped her on with her coat, a shabby checkered job too flimsy for the season, and as he was cupping the back of her head out of habit because this wasn't one of the department's cars and he wasn't a cop, a sob escaped from his throat but he covered it with a cough. All the way over, he didn't once look at her.

At the station he gave her to the downstairs desk sergeant and went looking for Stelmashuk to give him the word. They got an APB out, much good would it do them because Lonnie Dale Nelson may be a cretin and a perv of the worst sort, but he wouldn't hang around someone drawing down serious heat in this part of the state. DMV gave them his vehicle's make and a physical description that tallied with the one from the boy's mother, except for the detail of a tacky beard that he insisted on growing despite his light fringe of reddish-blond hair. Criminal Investigation Bureau in Columbus faxed prints and an old mug sheet.

Stelmashuk was upstairs at his computer making up his preliminary homicide report for the murder book; he paused with his fingers over the keyboard.

"Hey, Haftmann. Trajectory got a *d* in it?"

"Fuck if I know."

"How far you think that guy is by now?"

"I don't know and I don't give a fuck. I'm after Nelson, remember, not that slather-assed sonofabitch."

"Canada or Florida. Wanna bet? I hear you're a betting man. I'll go fifty on Florida."

"I only bet off-track in licensed venues, flatfoot," Haftmann deadpanned.

"Ain't what I heard, Thomas. Word is you're in deep. Oscar says you get down on the Browns so much he's gotta keep a separate book all for you. Lays it off to Youngstown. He says you ever hit, he'll be running his bar for you."

"Oscar's got a big mouth."

"Says there ain't much fear in that because you always lose . . ."

Millimaki loomed over Stel's other shoulder. His bad eye keeps fucking up his peripheral vision. "Haftmann, you're here again?" "Yeah, Chief, just chatting with my old pal here," Haftmann says but can't work up even a thin smile to go with it.

"You're just a visitor here."

Wet sound of the unlit Swisher Sweet being hauled around to the other side of his mouth.

He watches the fat cop do the owner's shuffle back to his own office. *You Hunky fuck—*

Before the smoking ban, coils of blue cigar smoke would follow him keeping tempo. Soft click of metal as the door shut.

All other noise in the office stopped. Detectives in their cubicles silent. Then, a little noise and another, back-to-normal sounds: word processors making their soft clacking, the *ker-chug* of a computer being turned on somewhere, squad gossip picking up, the right decibel level for the time of day and the season.

Words danced as if borne on streamers of flying ants, but that one word of Matrooshian's: *schizophrenia* caused a red mist across his vision. Heard in the outside with a wind chill of ten degrees seemed about right. Not a word to hear in a warm room with lights and noise and people all around. *Not passion*, he thought, *but true madness: it has no pity either*.

He drove home, talking to himself, as he always did when agitated. Fuck what the other drivers thought.

At home on his velour couch he watched fat lazy flakes tick the windowpanes of his front room overlooking a scrub and barren wasteland. He had a can of beer in his hand for supper, a meat loaf TV dinner so tasteless he left it untouched. He had stupidly told the shrink in Cleveland that he sometimes heard rhymes in his head and these would stay with him almost to the point of consciousness before dawn. Did he write these words down? *Fuck no, he was a cop, not a poet. Oh, sweet barbecued Jesus, all my thoughts are mine and how can I separate paranoia from this feeling I may be going insane, and everything that comes into my head is making me think I am really going insane?*

He sipped the beer and watched the snow fall and thought of small boy with a blue face running into the house from play. He had been raised by his grandmother whose worst curse was a quietly muttered *Scheisse*. What would she say now, he wondered, if she knew Lady Gaga had a song of that title?

He whipped the can backwards and heard it bounce around the kitchen. He was itchy and bored. It was only 8:00 at night. It was blacker than Toby's ass outside, dark since 4:30 and still bitter cold.

His vig was up to $750. He had to get Oscar a yard by Friday. Oscar must be getting word to Millimaki to put pressure on him. He never once went "on the arm," as cops used to say back in Cleveland, and he was damned if he would ever have done bag work or inform on police operations for some lowlife dope dealer. Before he left Cleveland PD, Internal Affairs and an F.B.I. sting got wind that half the west side cops were showing up on vice reports by the other half.

He had to squeeze Micah. *Maybe she'll kick in more if he tells her he's seeing a Cleveland psychiatrist*, he thinks. The tax lawyer she left him for had a condo in Hilton Head and could damned well afford it.

There was a game of his own to run, too, if he could get up the nerve. That smoothie Artiss Poole had been collared and was doing his full bid in Youngstown. No more medium-security prisons that looked like community colleges except for the razor wire. He had blurted out details Haftmann remembered. In effect, Artiss gave him the scoop on pulling off a pretty good mail fraud scheme while he was bragging away in the interrogation room. Easy money, "the Artist" had said, if you don't get too greedy.

The skag's words from this morning: *What choice do I have?*

He called Micah and whored away any integrity he might have salvaged from their divorce. Somehow he played it right because her guilt at taking another man into her bed while they were separated did the trick. (*Get help, Thomas, you're sick. You let the job destroy our marriage and I can't help you anymore. You won't drag me down with you.*)

He lay back on the sofa and thought about the dead boy's brains on the wall.

Did it matter now?

His mind drifted into those familiar paths memory had carved long ago. Coming back from sailing as a deckhand on the Great Lakes, he buried his grandmother next in the new all-faiths cemetery in Kingsville. When he'd shipped out of Ashtabula in June, it had been a vast meadow filled with Spiked Blazing Star and Yellow Lady's Slipper. By then, she didn't know or recognize him. She didn't know the priest who came to give her Extreme Unction.

Haftmann awoke near dawn; it was going to be less freezing than yesterday because he could hear the sleet make rattling noises against the windowpanes in the semi-dark.

He got up and made coffee. He went to his coat and found the cassette and cell phone he'd put in his pocket. He had to go into a closet to fish out an old Walkman. The reflected glare of oncoming headlights in the windowpanes broke his concentration.

When it came, it surprised him. The voice was small and seemed to float all around the room. Some of the songs were in English and some in Italian. There was rapid passagework between songs and Haftmann could feel the emotions without understanding the words: clear, silver notes, a passionate outpouring here, a shrill vibrato edge there; he thought of the vocal acrobatics of a mockingbird and remembered Micah going on one time about a soprano named Sumi Jo. At the end of her repertoire, she gave one last outburst of energy, and the emotions were strong but mixed and then there was the silence of the tape.

He played the second side and got nothing until the end of the tape and got background noises: water running, a glass breaking, scraping sounds, and then breathing – a slow susurration of breath. Words he cannot make out. End of tape.

The cell phone was something else: a man's veiny cock extended. A large male hand appeared on the screen to improve the erection.

What the fuck?

~ ~ ~

The Cleveland shrink nattering on about dissociation, ego breakdown . . . *So much has been written about this subject, so little known . . .*

"Give it to me in English."

Haftmann is kicking himself for his mad decision to drive to Cleveland just to hear this drivel.

"*Dementia praecox.*"

"English, I said."

"Now, it really isn't that simple. I want you to take some tests. I'll arrange for an MRI today if you have the time. We can see those areas of the brain just as I showed you . . ."

"You mean you can tell if I'm going crazy from that?"

"No, not like that. But a scan can help us see if there are any structural abnormalities that might help us rule out bipolar disorder or tumors . . ."

Haftmann tunes out Matrooshian as the little man launches into a technical explanation. Micah would have been fascinated by it all.

Haftmann stares at him but doesn't listen. The doctor is too enamored of his own explanation anyway. He remembers that word, *schizophrenia*, used that first time. So terrifying he refused to talk about it with Micah when he got home. A department-mandated psychiatric examination because he had put a round in a boy's head, to save the child he was threatening to kill with a hammer. The boy was so jacked-up on crank that the Federal Special round he put into him blew out most of his brain matter before he dropped to the floor.

Now he just wanted to know how much time he had left before the bomb in his head went off. He had someone to catch, someone who was far, far crazier than he could ever become.

~ ~ ~

Nocturne for Madness

He left the house, recalled he hadn't shaved, turned around in the sudden morning squall blown up by warm air meeting frigid air barreling across Lake Erie from Canada, said, to the juncos and starlings eyeing him for a feed. Almost went back in to get seed but couldn't face the inside of his house once he had left it. He'd told the shrink how things in his house seemed to be taking on hard metallic edges, crowding him, so he moved everything out but a few essentials. He didn't tell him that sometimes things looked out of proportion, as if they were secretly taking on a life of their own while he was out of the house. He'd be wearing a Kansas vest if he told him half of what went through his mind every day.

At the station he dropped off the cassette at Lab Tech with a note for Phil to isolate background stuff and try a voice graph on the whispering. Dub the music, all taped stuff obviously, and put a copy on Stelmashuk's desk.

He looked around but nobody would look back at him. Haftmann, the invisible man. *Someone here*, he thinks, *might be playing me . . . giving me this shit and hoping I run around chasing my tail.* Even that newbie Shawna knew cops were jokesters at heart.

Looking down, he noticed his name on a triple-folded letter. He opened it. Sheriff's stationery, informing him that he was *persona non grata* at the Jefferson-on-the-Lake precinct, signed Lt. Stephen A. Millimaki.

On his way out the door he saw Shawna; when he got close he saw her tip her face away from him in a half-hearted effort to conceal a healing black-and-yellow shiner.

"Lemme guess. You walked into a door, or your boyfriend cold-cocked you."

"My husband."

"Jesus, I'm sorry."

Haftmann never expected this. Abused women always covered up, denied, lied for their abusive men. This brutal honesty went against the grain.

Braving it out instead, he thinks. But he knew how much it hurt to be hit by another human being. The humiliation of it. How it degrades you. He heard a growl from Millimaki's office. Snickering in the nearest detective cubicle like little boys' laughter. He hears: "Some asshole keyed his Jeep while it sat in the lot the other day."

He turns back to her. "It looks good on you, Slim."

"Yeah, I bet." One yellow eye lost in folds of puffy blackened skin.

"The kids are right," she said. "Life's a bitch and then you die."

His shame multiplied: he remembered once raising a fist to Micah. *The look on her face.* It fills him with squirmy distress even to this day.

"My grandmother used to tell me that angels bleed for us when we hurt each other so God is distracted from revenge."

"Your grandmother never met my husband," she said.

"True, but my grannie was a tough old bird. She once she stood up to a Russian artillery officer who wanted to arrest my mother for stealing food." *Why am I bringing this shit up to a woman whose husband just beat her?*

"Re-ally?" She said it the way old-time hippies on the Strip used to say "Far out."

Haftmann tries to cover the awkwardness. "She had these old-fashioned ideas about honor and love—" *Fuck me, dumb thing to say. Not my circus, not my monkeys. Why should I care?*

That did it. The dam burst and she let her face turn to silly putty trying to fight it back, be brave. A sob spasmed out of her slender throat and she was gone. Shame burned him all the way out to his car in the body's own alchemy.

25

Jesus-Shit-Fuck. His magic triad, a voodoo curse to keep hot grief down.

He drove south down 534 like a loon, swung east on 90, and found Cold Spring Road, although he'd driven to it only one other time in his life. Micah's tax-accountant lawyer lived there when he was giving it to her on the side, and now they both lived there. Haftmann wanted to do a Rambo, Columbine that motherfucker *good*, hurt him *baaad* – but he lost control of his own face, sobs jerking into humiliating, gagging sounds. The image of Micah nude in his bed with her back exposed to her ass crack was more than enough to steady him to take money from her. He gripped the wheel with such maniacal force that he almost fishtailed a string of cars at a Seven-Eleven.

The lawyer's house had Armington Lake for a backyard; an acre of lawn, manicured and chemically treated when it wasn't under snow.

She opened right away, glared at him with those tawny eyes, a hellcat when angry.

"I need money, Micah."

"Thomas, why are you doing this?"

"Just lend me the money, God damn it, or—"

"Or *what*, you shithead?"

"Or . . . nothing."

She thrust it into his hands. Saw him coming and didn't want him inside their house. "You're a sick, selfish, hateful man. Get help."

He was about to tell her that, in fact, he was doing that very thing. But instead he turns, like a goose-stepping Nazi in a cartoon, and was down the steps. She screams his name, but the wind tears it away, deflects it past him like a ghostly whisper of old sorrow.

You pathetic bastard!

That he heard.

On the ride home, he feels his insides shrivel. He thinks he knew fear as a cop. Has looked the wrong way down a few barrels when he worked Detroit and West 110th in Cleveland, but, no, that wasn't real fear at all. "Pussy fear," his partner called it. The real thing would find him at home in his living room. Things would seem to come to life in the murky quiet and fill him with terror. Sometimes it got him at work in his office, too, but he could fight it there. Not at home. It was too big, too all-consuming.

Lately, it seemed as if a bright hot light, like an oncoming car's headlights, filled the room and everything was illuminated; he sometimes slipped into a prolonged stupor and couldn't move, ignored his work, lost clients. He could barely get out the door to go to his ratty office on the Strip after a weekend at home.

Sometimes he heard voices and he wasn't sure they were inside his own head.

He hears the phone ringing him out of his stupor.

"Haftmann, Phil here."

Haftmann croaks out a greeting.

"If Millimaki finds out I'm doing favors on company time, let alone for you, I'll be working litter patrol."

"Tell me what you have, Phil."

"Am I boring you, so sorry – "

"Phil, fucking Jesus – "

"Awright, awright. You got – nothing. There's nothing there but what it sounds like. Music, opera shit or something, and normal sounds of glass breaking, chairs being shuffled, breathing. You can't do voice prints on a breather."

"Okay."

"I got one thing for you. You'll love it."

"Stop fucking around."

"Flies."

"What do you—"

"Flies, man, flies! The breather's in a room with a shitload of flies."

"So fucking what?"

"So you tell me. Where do you get flies when it's ten below?"

"Maybe he taped it in summertime."

"Nope."

"I'm going to rip out your gizzard, Phil."

"I got a really high accuracy rating on the emulsifier test on the tensile quality of the tape. No more than two to three months tops. When did we have snow? Middle of November?"

"Bullshit."

"He could have bred 'em from maggots. Don't tell me how to do my job, you prick. And I got something else."

"What?"

"Today's Thursday. You lost a day."

Jesus Christ.

The line deader than Julius Caesar in his hand. His cop's instincts told him he was stupid not to have dusted the cassette even if it meant telling Millimaki, just in case it wasn't some shitbird's idea of a joke. Too late now.

He dressed and drove through a blizzard that thumped the Neon's chassis, wind whistling like a lullaby from hell, and had to squint through the gusts that always reminded him of his childhood fantasy of flying a rocket ship and carving a niche of safety through meteor showers the size of boulders.

He heard the soprano's voice again, filling the car with silver notes. A diminuendo of whispered sobs that wasn't on the tape. He seemed to be putting on someone else's knowledge; his scalp tingled and an adrenalin jolt hit his stomach as a Dr. Pepper truck swung too far into his lane – *goddamned icy roads.*

He tasted bile, sour metal. *Like a demon pissing on my tongue.*

Turning into the lot, he thought once more of his first partner, their ten years of patrolling Cleveland's mean streets, an apprenticeship well-served: Frank showed him how to keep the slime from the job from taking over your life and dragging you down. Frank Cunningham, dead these many years of bleeding ulcers. The old cop winking at the rookie: "Well, kid, let's go see what evil lurks in the heart of Cleveland . . ."

From the parking lot in the chill dawn light he could see lights flickering inside the building, both floors, as if some freak outage were affecting each floor at intervals. Off, then on, weird shit in the sunless morning.

Inside he sees men and women, officers, clerks, file workers, cheering and clapping. Lights being turned on and off.

"What's the story, Pete? That clown Millimaki die in his sleep last night?"

Pete, without the usual props of cigarette and coffee mug, actually grinning.

"Better'n that, Haftmann. They fried another one in Florida ten minutes ago, our time. I hope that prick lived long enough to feel his eyes explode out of his head."

Up the stairs, cops and detectives watching a portable hi-def TV; a Cleveland news channel and a live cut-in to a middle-class home where a mother and teenaged daughter are being interviewed by a celebrity reporter. Haftmann looks over the shoulders of cops, dispatchers. A popular TV host with a gap-toothed grin asserts his bogus charm toward a mother and daughter seated together on a studio divan.

"And so you've been corresponding with one of the nation's most notorious killers for the last eight months.

Please tell our viewers about the last letter you received from this, this—"

The mother interrupts the host and his feigned astonishment, which draws a brief curl of disdain from his lips. She wags the killer's letter as if on cue, holding it aloft in her excitement.

The reporter exclaims some nonsense about "words beyond the grave" while the camera zooms on the woman's face. She brandishes the letter once again. Haftmann notes that her eyes were violet-tinted. He's lost in an image Micah once planted in his head when she read a biography of Josef Mengele, Angel of death of Auschwitz. It's a grotesque image of a lab in the female barracks with tables covered with pairs of eyes with irises tinted in Day-Glo colors and iridescent hues. He half-listens to the TV woman's gush.

"This is a letter we received yesterday."

"Jesus," someone nearby says in disgust, "The stupid bitch is proud of her tame psychopath."

Zoom in to the letter itself. Elegant handwriting, the serifs of his capitals a touch of vanity, hiding the madness, but not the ego.

Haftmann tunes out the woman, wonders what it is in some women that could draw them to murderous men. This one let her own daughter in on her dangerous groupie fixation. The daughter speaks now, breaks his concentration, and he sees a pretty girl with too much mascara:

"—but, like, Mom and me, like, were surprised because, I mean, when Mom wrote him last time, right Mom? About what color are his eyes and so . . ."

The reporter jumps in, deflecting her teenage patter: "Alyssa, would you read the last sentence that he wrote to you?"

She holds the letter, scans it for the passage, reads in a sing-song: "My eyes are blue."

A detective grunts noisily. All thinking of a handsome, boyish maniac's last words, embodied through a pretty teenager's voice, the kind he liked to trawl for in his highway forays.

Millimaki, despite his bulk, appeared cat-like from his office: the boss catching his employees goofing off, but he speaks their single collective thought:

"He'd of bashed your pretty head in, too, sweetie."

Chapter 2

Winter Solstice

The man who had sent the cassette and cellphone to Thomas Haftmann at the Jefferson-on-the-Lake precinct came awake gasping like a fish jerked to the deck.

He shook with nervous tremors that were the residual effects of the drugs and the workout. Calming himself, he remembered who he was; he felt powerful, rested, whole. He had enough strength in his thighs to bring himself to a standing position despite the massive overdeveloped torso. He flicked moisture from his fingers like a priest blessing communicants. He sweated profusely nearly all the time because his body's air-conditioning system had to work overtime to expel the synergism of the drugs he ingested during his workouts.

Lonnie Dale Nelson, 39 years old, standing, looked like a beefcake photo: bikini briefs, a crotch bulge worthy of a porn actor, chest span of fifty inches, and California hair, bleached and wavy. He was calling himself Roger Hower these days because of his likeness to the Dutch actor, Rutger Hauer, whom he'd seen in *Blade Runner*. When he discovered a film in which Hauer plays a wandering, remorseless killer who terrorizes the teenager who picked him up on the highway, it was if he had found something he had been looking for all his life.

In the mirror, he preened for long minutes at a time, cultivating the knowing smirk of a man who was free, a man who had the courage to challenge himself to do all that was required of him. Lonnie Dale Nelson believed he was totally free because the System, as he called *them*, wanted him to be.

He liked the lone-wolf image the newscasters were calling terrorists these days, but he did not yet understand why the System, the voices he acknowledged, wanted him to send a memento of his last house call to the private investigator, that cop who had busted him on a two-bit marijuana possession while he was passing through that shitty resort. In those days, he was a teenager drifting on his way to—somewhere else. Sometimes, when he was confused, the System would send an angel to tell him not to worry. The angel's intense whispering was guiding him, keeping him safe from the mumbo-jumbo of clashing voices that used to torment his sleep.

Despite the intense cold, the basement of the house was stifling. The air was rancid with the smell of menses. He took the bag of discarded, bloody meat wrappings into the utility room and tossed them into the middle of the room; at once hoards of flies disbursed about the room. The room, like the rest of the basement was littered with piles of trash, paper wrappings, and food boxes from the incessant eating Nelson found necessary to maintain bulk. Because no one ever got an invitation to enter his home, he didn't have to worry about nosy neighbors. Look at that guy in Cleveland who littered his house with decomposing bodies of crack whores he strangled, the neighbors believed a sausage factory on the street was giving off that foul odor.

His lunch consisted of anabolic steroids he consumed by the handful – recently introduced into his repertoire – purchased in bulk from Mexico through an Internet mailing service. His weight spiraled to 280 pounds, but the power lifting and blitz-eating sessions maintained it. On occasion, the System ordered him to fast to clean the toxins out of his body. The only exercise he allowed himself at those times was a routine of self-inflicted torture: he'd strike his fists into five-gallon buckets of sand, hundreds of times with each fist; he admired the grayish-yellow lumps of dead flesh the size of crab apples at the base of each thumb.

He popped a couple amphetamines to counter the serenity coming over him and crossed the room to a makeshift kitchen area. He took a glassine bag out of the freezer and tapped a small portion of tea into the strainer and lit the burner. Joyless drinking but the chifir's red beverage gave a boost to his system he had to have for his workout; it was a dozen times stronger than tea, so concentrated that he could synchronize his lifting endurance by it.

He had a special workout he called the Berserker, named for the Viking warrior who ran headfirst into battle, oblivious to fear or pain: the berserker died first but he would kill the most enemy. The sight of a berserker advancing was enough to scatter the enemy from the field. It was special to Lonnie Dale Nelson because he only accomplished it eight times, sobbing from total exhaustion on the floor in the greasy light of daybreak. Each time happened just before a house call. It was like an aura that shrouded him and gave him such intense focus.

He did five sets of bench presses with 220 pounds on the bar. His upper arms flexed like albino pythons devouring rodents.

He thought about the couple in Warren, an hour's ride north on Route 11. His great chest heaving with the exertion, his mind made pictures of the couple fondling each other, then him.

Sopping in his own sweat, he thought about the Painesville woman who had him enter her from behind while her stereo played that strange, haunting music so much like the songs his grandmother sang.

Nelson had been born with unusual gifts: a spatial memory that would have made him a chess master, perfect pitch, and total recall. He began to sing the words to an aria in a voice that was pleasant and modulated in the right places despite the huge bellows of his chest.

He squeezed his eyes shut and slipped a hand inside his briefs; thumb and forefinger encircled a spade-shaped glans, but the erection wouldn't come. The steroids occasionally made him impotent, shrunk his testicles. No matter. The System would send the angel to him when the time was right.

Discipline and timing, he knew, were everything.

~ ~ ~

Route 11 passes through the heart of Jefferson and deadheads six miles north, just a stone's throw from Lake Erie – that is, if you've got the arm of Madison Bumgarner. Haftmann stares at the blinking cursor, his hands poised above the keyboard like a pianist about to take on the Goldberg Variations and fuck it up royally. A tic worms a path down his right cheek.

I must be crazy, he thought. *I could go to prison for this.*

He scrolls the text and decides he wants one powerful image to close the pitch: electrically shocked genitalia was a cliché of torture but, hell, it had always worked for psalm-singing muzzlers and kite pushers like Artiss, his best fraud bust when he made detective. The college had been on semester break for a week now and one bored computer science major had obviously drawn supervisor's duty. One other man occupied a terminal in the corner of the computer room. He was fat and had a drunkard's face which a prissy Van Dyke did little to conceal.

The room's drafty but Haftmann is already itchy with sweat. He can smell himself.

One thing a cop learns on the job is writing. A simple lewd vagrant arrest produces twelve forms: four arrest sheets, four statement-of-fact forms, and four line-up sheets.

He's knocked off homicide reports in less time than he's now spending on his scam letter; in fact, he's not struggled this hard with any other report he'd done on the job the suicide – an old man with Alzheimer's had left his clothes in a pile on the frozen tundra of the public beach and walked nude into Lake Erie. The old guy must have walked a hundred yards to the water's edge. Ice fisherman found the bundle under the snow but no note. They'd probably find him in the spring, or, as had happened a few times already, his gas-bloated corpse would bob to the surface or find its way inside air pocket beneath the translucent ice. Pike, walleye, and yellow perch would nibble it down bit by bit and grow fat on the host.

Last night Haftmann dreamed he was stuck fast to the ice, miles out from shore, the gray sky opaque to the horizon. He couldn't tell morning from afternoon, but he could look beneath his feet miles down into the piercing cold water. Then he saw a speck – black and white like the head of a chickadee. But it grew massive until he knew what it was: a killer whale hurtling up through the cold depths at pounding speed to get the speck on the ice—him.

He focused, banished these random memories. He had to be painstakingly accurate because he did not intend to go to prison. The worst part would be the moment when he hung his face out at the post office. If he didn't draw postal inspectors, he could figure on a few thousand bucks. Enough to pay off Oscar, who had left another shadowy message on Haftmann's office recorder the night before last.

Christmas Eve traffic on the Dewey Thruway was another kind of nightmare. He had to get the red cancellation stamp that would identify each envelope with a 20678 zip, a meter number from Albany, and the .071

cancellation mark. The crucial business was the non-profit organization mark. Artiss, a master at "promoting," in prison lingo, holding forth like a visiting lecturer down in the interrogation room; his brown hands and long fingers could wrap themselves completely around Haftmann's fleshy hand.

He couldn't afford to give the New York State Office of Charities time to get wind of him; so he chose to do it right under their noses using postal sacks he'd liberated from the Jefferson Courthouse. His mailing list was ginned up from an Internet search he had Phil do from databases. He told Phil he needed some paperwork from cases involving Ponzi schemes and pyramid confidence games collecting dust in boxes in Cleveland and it was too far to travel. *Could he help him out?*

Artiss, clotheshorse, teenage shoplifter, sneak thief, got himself three deuces jammed in Youngstown pen for his last scam, which conned thousands out of gullible widows. Haftmann knew from prison scuttlebutt that Artiss and Lonnie Nelson were once cellmates, for thirty days, while each awaited sentencing due to an overloaded summer docket.

Before Ohio, Artiss had done a stretch for a home invasion at Jacktown in Michigan. He decided to follow the smell of easy money downwind of I-75 and began ripping off thousands from storeowners between Toledo and Jefferson-on-the-Lake.

The wind howled in the black outside. Over the winking cursor, stuck on the word *compassion*, his mind's eye superimposed the winking, approving face of Artiss, which transformed at once into the walnut-brown Matrooshian's visage.

The expelled air from the machine, where light played among millions of 1's and 0's beneath the chassis, the corrupt, sweet smell of baby oil and bananas tickles Haftmann's nostrils.

It triggers an olfactory memory: he and Micah were in bed; he's hoping she'd put that damned book down so they can have sex. She refused. He asked her what was so frigging interesting in it, and she told him it's by a French priest who believed the universe was evolving. "How?" he asked her. She told him about this Omega Point of the priest's; it's supposed to be outside the universe but irreversible and supremely complex. "It draws all things to itself," she said. "You mean like a black hole?" he asked. "No," she said, and became quiet for a moment; "like Christ." He realized he wouldn't be getting any that night.

Maybe the good father had something there, Haftmann realizes. *Things are getting more complicated every day. One thing for sure: there's no going back from this point.*

~ ~ ~

Fifty miles away at the southern end of Route 11, Lonnie Dale Nelson was cruising the business district of East Palestine. There was a Laundromat he liked. This far south of Lake Erie, they were beyond the reach of the lake effect and were basking in twenty-five degrees Fahrenheit and no wind-chill factor.

He pulled into the lot off Burgoyne once he saw her profiled in the lights, among half a dozen of the neighborhood poor, a few stringy women mostly trailed by their brood. Too poor to afford babysitters or washing machines, he knew. Welfare trash: suitable for his purpose. The angel had spoken to him last night about the plan – so clearly. First, he had to ditch this celibacy. All his life, sex was punishment; now it was to be the way toward the light.

Two hours later he was in her apartment, Seven and Sevens littering the kitchen table, while the baby slept.

He'd met her in a country-western bar three nights ago. She wanted to feel his biceps, talk about tattoos. He was looking at one of hers now, a dripping black rose on her buttock bisected by the elastic band of pink panties. Her butterfly movements were exposing it a petal at a time, a drop of black blood and a thorn now visible.

He didn't like the way she was doing it. Clenching and unclenching her small fist around the root of his shaft; her opened mouth just brushing the head. He looked at his watch. Almost time to get to work. He let her go on in the same way for five minutes, then pulled it out of her mouth, making a plopping sound with her cheek. He gave it three slow pulls until the foreskin showed clear of the purple-velvet head and shot his load into her face. Just like the porn sites he watched, he facialized her with gobs around the eyes. She tried to keep her mouth closed but he ordered her to open it. She obeyed the new tone of his voice and received a last spritzing of his cum on the back of her tongue and throat.

"Show me," he said and encircled her neck with his hands. So easy to snap, he thought.

She opened her mouth to show him.

"Swallow it," he said.

Before she got off her knees, he was out the door, never saying a word, just leaving her there like that as if she were a cheap whore. Although she knew the baby was asleep, something made her want to make sure.

~ ~ ~

Haftmann finished typing out the bill for his last client, this one a simple malicious mischief deal involving a local tightfisted car dealer whose plate glass windows were broken Christmas Eve. Someone had sprayed green fluorescent smiley faces on the hoods of five new Lincolns. It was rumored by the locals that Youngstown mafia bought their black Town Cars from his dealership. Some old-school *paisanos* bought them to give everyone the impression they were made men. When Haftmann asked if he had any suspects, the owner said: "You gotta be shitting me, man. Why don't you start with my staff, and ask, see, I had to cut back on the Christmas bonuses this year . . ."

~ ~ ~

Killing time in his office, Haftmann Googled Elizabethan lute songs and found lyrics identifying the songs on the tape as John Dowland's "Come again, sweet love doth now invite" and Monteverdi's "*Quel squardo segnosetto.*" But the explanations baffled him; what the hell was a "tricky chromatic interval," he wondered. Something else about lutenists of the period, which he skipped over. Some more stuff from the Elizabethan period and one or two pieces of early baroque.

Micah stuff, he thought. It seemed to be all about love and love's torment. One piece on the tape he identified as religious: George Herbert's "Love Bade Me Welcome." *Wikipedia* said Herbert was an Anglican priest.

He called down to the Dana School of Music and finally wound up talking to a senior practicing for her recital. Haftmann played the tape into his cell phone.

"The last two songs, including the Herbert piece," she said, "were done by a male countertenor. He isn't that comfortable in the upper registers and he's not tonally rich enough to carry it off. Like a man with a great natural voice imitating a female soprano."

"So what?"

"Well, Mister Hartmann – "

"Haftmann."

"Sorry. He sounds like a castrato."

"A what?"

"I mean, nobody alive has ever heard one in the flesh."

"You mean a guy without his ba – testicles?"

41

"That's what they used to do to boys on the threshold of puberty to maintain the purity – "

"I see, I see. OK, so could he be a homosexual?"

"No," she said, "I don't think so. It doesn't work like that. He's a man, for sure, most likely not gay, but he's trying to sound like a woman."

"I'm confused," Haftmann said.

"Well, it's the other song, the last one that throws everything off balance. His timbral characteristics are all wrong."

"You're losing me, Miss."

"It's a poem, not a song. It's German. Heine's *Ich grolle nicht*. But the thing is, you see, he seems unsure of himself. Like, say, he doesn't know German at all, the wrong inflections. In fact, my tutor here would say he gives a truly risible performance on those two pieces."

"Ha, yes, risible," Haftmann says. *As if I know what the fuck that means either.*

He drives through sleet to Oscar's Bavarian Chalet on the Strip. His heart is pumping with the memory of Lonnie Nelson, outsized teenager caught with dope, in the back of his patrol car humming to himself in what he must have been pidgin German. Nelson immediately clammed up and didn't speak again through booking. Haftmann had to punch him up through NCIC to get vital statistics. His last glimpse of Nelson was a long stare back at him from the detention cage.

When he told Micah about the punk he'd bagged in the back of his prowl car, he did his imitation of the kid for her complete with the gabbling.

"He's not one of your typical losers, babe," she said.

"How do you know that?" he asked.

"Because," she said, "even with you mangling the verse like that, I can recognize Schiller."

"Micah, what are you talking about?"

"You big dummy," she said. "It's the 'Ode to Joy.'"

There are six cars within a block, most with out-of-town plates. That means high rollers some from Erie fifty miles east, and that was pretty much what he found upstairs: twenty-five, thirty guys, middle-aged, some dago shopkeepers from Ashtabula and Jefferson, a few locals like Chic Ross and Tony Kowslowski, a couple guys not affiliated with the powerful families in town or their backers. All twenties and fifties on the table.

One of Oscar's bar whores was walking around bare-lunged with a tray of drinks. Jiggling tits made you drink more, more drinking made you reckless at the tables, or so Oscar's cunning theory of fleecing his gamblers went. He finds Oscar at the bar, a jerrybuilt contraption that could be disassembled fast, if need be.

"Haftmann, so nice to see you. Heard you was in Florida chasing another runaway. Got my fucking cash, asshole?"

"Carry me another week. I'll get it all, including the vigorish."

"Haftmann, Jesus Christ Almighty," Oscar said with a shake of his head.

"I want in on the Super Bowl, and I want the Vegas line."

"My line or nothing. And only when you pay up the vig."

"You put Millimaki on me, didn't you, Oscar?"

"I don't talk to that fuck," Oscar said with convincing vehemence.

"If I find out differently, I'm going to put your ass in a burlap bag with a dog, a cat, and a monkey and throw it in the lake."

"Fuck you. I want my money, Haftmann."

"Don't try to sic your guinea friends on me, either."

Haftmann was breathing heavily by the time he got outside; he guessed he'd made the act convincing enough. What bothered him, though, was that before he walked into the place he had no intention of doing anything but giving Oscar the money he had sponged off Micah.

~ ~ ~

Lonnie Dale Nelson was lying naked on his living room floor in his two-story house in East Palestine overlooking the Ohio River. He was in the Dead Pose. The bottoms of his feet were soaking wet, and he gave off a strong body odor; his breath was foul.

He concentrated on the Warren couple. From deep inside his mind's zone of agitation, he watched its quicksilver movements and the pictures it made. These would help to relax him if he had a prevision of events soon to come.

His breath was so rank it seemed to have weight and color. He made his breathing rhythmic and expanded his chest, expelling air slowly. He knew of Yogi who had such control over their recti muscles that they could almost massage their insides with their movement in rotation. Nelson considered that a waste.

He did cockstands – bringing his cock to a point of erection and letting it fall back to slap his thigh.

He brought the same image into focus: a close-up of a man and woman paying him homage on either side of him with their lips, and tongues, and teeth. The sweat glistening on their bodies, the musky air redolent of sex.

He brought himself to climax with two quick thrusts; his semen a white ribbon in the air. He rubbed its hot stickiness into his chest and pubic hair until he was matted, then his face, licked it off his fingers; the salty burn stinging his eyes.

The angel was soothing him now, appearing more often, had given him back his virility, and opened all his pores at once. He lost control of his bowels, defecating and urinating at the same time. He writhed on the floor in frenzied pain in his excreta, and the discharge from his nostrils gagged him. His muscles spasmed; the contractions burned like liquid fire injected into his veins. He wondered if this was death.

He contorted in an agony of pain that made him lose consciousness and drift out of time. He felt the angel come inside his own skin and take all the pain out. He lay in a fetal position on his floor for the next five hours, passing into and out of consciousness. He dreamed of peeling the flesh from so many bodies that their skins were dropped, one by one, like finger-drip sand castles into glistening pink piles. The angel came to scold him, told him not to use his hands: *do it like this*, and he leaped, an entrechat, with a knife extended to him, but it was a mirror that showed him his own ripped-away, glistening face.

~ ~ ~

Haftmann stubs out a Marlboro and swallows the ropy phlegm of a cough. He was feverish and achy; his breath was sour from stomach gas and smoking too much. Another loser habit that seemed to fall out of his past and sink its hooks into him. He was like a rock climber trying to hold on to a manhole cover while he climbed. Everything was harder now.

It was almost 11:00 a.m., and he had to see that jerk car dealer again before noon. First, he had to get Stelmashuk's report on the dead kid's mother's interrogation. Nick had called his machine last night while he was out. The mother knew Lonnie Dale because her biker boyfriend brought him over to the trailer for three-way sex. Stelmashuk's tone dropped an octave at the end of the message. "She said he's big, very buffed, and – you'll like this part, Haftmann – she said he's got really crazy eyes."

Haftmann's former partner from that lone summer stint as a Lake cop was another cop on loan from the highway patrol, a *Guns & Ammo* nut, who bored him stupid with his monologues on steel tips or how you can bury an Uzi in the desert and dig it up in perfect condition. Haftmann had once taken MacDuff into a bad fight at a notorious bikers' bar on the Strip that summer and knew he carried a serrated Navy SEALS knife taped to his calf.

"Fuck off, MacDuff."

"Sure, Haftmann. Ex-homicide bull like you tells me to shut up, I shut the fuck up. When a two-bit gumshoe has more rights in my own goddamned precinct . . ."

"Mac, I prefer you to shut your mouth," Haftmann said, this time with a look.

MacDuff gets up, takes a step toward Haftmann and then brushes his shoulder as he passes by. Haftmann watches him wander off.

"Take it easy on MacDuff, Haftmann," Phil says from his carrel. "He can burn me with Millimaki over these goddamned favors you keep bugging me for."

"Sorry, Phil. He just rubs me all wrong for some reason. I never liked that guy."

Phil looks at Haftmann.

"What are you thinking about now?" Haftmann asks him. Haftmann could see that Phil was going down memory lane because his gimlet eyes always got oily.

"Remember that PCP case we had five years ago?"

As if you could forget a mother and daughter on the floor of an all-night convenience store; ice pick holes in their brains.

"I remember," says Haftmann, wishing he didn't.

Haftmann cuts his eyes to see MacDuff still there, taking it all in. MacDuff, eyes alight at the thought of permanent position with JOTL homicide, yearns to end his days on the road camel-jockeying highways and pulling over drunks and speeders.

"What of it, Phil?"

"He played their ear holes like he was conducting the Cleveland Orchestra. Whew."

MacDuff's raw laughter booms around the cubicles. Out of the corner of his good eye he catches Shawna, her pretty face an ovoid blur because his eyes are shut against the image, but the sight of Shawna brings it back in Technicolor. MacDuff, too, catches a glimpse of her shapely bottom walking back to her office. In a stage whisper, he says, "Mmm, sweet. I wouldn't mind threading the needle with her some night," MacDuff says.

"And you've got just the needle dick to do it," Haftmann says before he can stop himself. He sees Phil is frowning, but the others within earshot are laughing aloud or trying to stifle laughter, depending on where he or she was in the cop hierarchy.

Haftmann looks at Phil and tries to make his face sad. "Sorry, pal."

"Here's a copy of the report on the suicide. Now kindly fuck off before Millimaki gets back from the sauna."

~ ~ ~

Back home, juggling a can of beer and a cigarette, he calls the officer noted in Phil's report.

Lt. Mondine tells Haftmann that the suicide, the Alzheimer's victim, wasn't old, that old anyway. Just fifty-seven, but the disease had been creeping up on him steadily over the past few years. The daughter who hired him to locate her missing father said he got to be too much to handle for his wife, who was ten, twelve years younger, a schoolteacher at Riverside High School in Painesville.

"See, I figured we have this much in common, and I should talk to someone at your end, even though you're not—you're not . . ."

47

"I'm not a cop," Haftmann finished for him.

"He's the ex-husband of a woman we found dead in her Jacuzzi. She'd been dead awhile. Pathologist figured since the start of Christmas vacation, but it's hard to tell because of the condition of the body when we got to it."

"So how can I help you, Officer?"

"The drowner won't come up for air until April or May when the water warms up. Everybody I talked to at the county nursing home tells me the guy was too weak, too spacey to harm anybody. He's locked into that nursing home right up to the day he took his walk into the lake. I figured he wasn't coherent enough to write a note."

"That's what cops here figured," Haftmann says.

"His whereabouts put him there." Haftmann perks up at the reference to "him." A cop using "whereabouts" in conversation is a warning sign like a guy with muttonchops sideburns on a blind date.

"Go on, Lieutenant," Haftmann said.

"Here's the thing. The daughter says she, the dead woman, was his second marriage. She didn't elaborate, but she didn't get along too well with her; it was obvious. Had two kids of her own and couldn't take the old man herself. Your M. E. Harris, right? He came over to help with the autopsy. This is a couple weeks back now. She's found in the hot tub, like I said."

"How did she die?"

"Hyperthermia. Just slowly cooked herself into a state of unconsciousness, passed out, and drowned. Blood-alcohol level couldn't be measured too accurately, you know, but we figured she must have been pretty drunk. Broken bottle of Chablis, clothes scattered around. Signs of disorder but nothing major."

"I'm still listening," Haftmann adds, hoping for what's coming next.

"We found ligatures on her neck but not deep ones. Just enough to make your pathologist suspect some erotic sex-play prior to her lapsing unconscious."

Haftmann's hand on his cell phone turns clammy. "Does the daughter know anything?"

"She seemed embarrassed when D'Agostino brought it up. Wouldn't hear of it. Gave us all this ballyhoo about her stepmother's reputation, blah-blah. Said she belonged to Cedars of Lebanon or Daughters of Cedars or whatever. But D'Agostino's a crude bastard. He forgets his manners once in a while. He asks her how come if her stepmother is such a great woman and all, you know, she happens to boil herself to death."

"What did the daughter say?" Haftmann wants to climb the drapes waiting for the answer.

"She was a beauty, the mother, I mean. Forty-four but a tight body. Full body tan. Big rack. Not so pretty when we got to her, of course. She was practically parboiled in the water." Mondine waits half-a-beat for an appreciative reply for his wit, hears nothing, and continued: "It took four of us to drag her out. D'Agostino gets all over this rookie cop who's about to light a cigarette to kill the smell. She had enough stomach gas to blow us all out the door. Like a waterlogged bomb. Then D'Agostino lights up, the asshole.

"Lieutenant, I'll risk your thinking me stupid, but I'll ask it anyway. Why didn't she get up out of the water?"

"That's the fifty-thousand-dollar question, right? Why didn't she get out of the water when she feels it start to cook her?"

Haftmann offers up a cop's response: "She was too blitzed to realize it. This happens."

"No, no," Mondine said.

"What's homicide's angle?"

"She was with a guy. The woman was a three-hole wonder, according to the autopsy. When we drained the water we found the usual stuff in the catch, pubes, not all hers, different textures and colors, some male. The male head hairs were dyed-cheap blond peroxide stuff sold everywhere. The pubic hairs were all black, hers and his."

"I don't hear anything yet to bring your homicide into this," Haftmann said.

"We found a glob of airplane glue on the sideboard. Mass spec pins it down but we don't know what that could mean."

"An old burglar's trick?" Haftmann offers; "airplane glue on the fingertips. No prints."

"Another thing is the water valve," Mondine replied. It's in the basement and it seems to have stuck. Nobody with his fingers is strong enough to turn it. No scars on the metal showing somebody put a wrench to it − "

"The guy could have used a towel and a crescent wrench."

"Our lab tech guys would have found fibers," Mondine countered.

As a detective, Haftmann had never put blind faith in forensics like the TV cops, but he let them do their work to get them out of his way faster.

"OK, I'm going to give you a theory here."

"Shoot," Haftmann said.

"There's this stop-valve assembly on the Jacuzzi. Nothing complicated. Like a toilet tank. You got an adjusting sleeve, some kind of plug insert and an O-ring over that. Washers didn't leak. Trip handle hadn't been touched since she put the thing in. But the thermostat setting said eighty degrees. The water in that tub was one-two-five degrees when we got there. I checked it myself. D'Agostino says somebody in the family should sue the manufacturer. Got a 'watertight' case, he says, his little joke.'

"You said there were two things that didn't make sense?"

"Like I said, she was pretty rank by the time we got to her. Her face was the only thing showing above the water, so the agitation kept her from rolling over on her stomach. But we fixed the time of death two days after her neighbors tell us loud music was playing from her upstairs around three in the morning. Classical music. We found maggots in her eye sockets and flies living in her esophagus."

Haftmann's heart was beating like a bongo now. *Opera again.* And flies.

"Lieutenant, you said classical music. Can you describe the singer's voice?"

"Say what?"

"Was it tenor, baritone – "

"The high-pitched one. Soprano, I think."

A female voice—except not a female.

~ ~ ~

Coming across the Jennings Randolph Bridge from West Virginia, Lonnie Nelson nearly spun his car sideways into the path of a semi. His mind was on other things.

He'd bought hardware at different places, and he owned arc-welding equipment that he stored in the Pet Room. He built a homemade nautilus on the same camshaft principle as the original. He needed to do some stress-testing calculations when he got home. Wire ties wouldn't hold. If he knew what the inside of their house looked like, he'd know if simple butt-jointed cylinders would do the trick.

The Warren couple had emailed back, and he'd called them from a pay phone at a Dairy Mart last night. He was getting ready to make another house call.

He'd overheard a couple of ridge runners talking at the saloon in Moundsville. A rare astrological occurrence was forthcoming: a blue moon had coincided with the winter solstice. That could explain the angel's frequent visits of late.

Last night he was clamping and soldering a few pieces when the insistent murmur from beneath the bench press annoyed him so much that he went to look under it, suspecting rats. In fact, his house was rat-infested from trash. Nelson had often seen pairs of red eyes regarding him from piles he'd shoveled into the corners. The owner was retired in Florida permanently and the club's owner, who got him the place, never bothered to check. Nelson figured he kept the maintenance share, too, without sending it on, but he didn't care as long as he kept away.

The flies bred effortlessly in the stench. He used entire rooms of the old house to throw discarded clothes that he never washed. Whatever he dropped on the floor stayed on the floor – pocket change, food, dishes – and was never picked up. The angel had made that clear, and he seemed pleased by Nelson's befouling his own nest. He marked each room of the house with vomit, sputum, ejaculations, blood, and voidings from every orifice. The odor was overpowering – but no one would ever get the dubious privilege of walking into the house invited and live to report it. From the street it looked forlorn and derelict, nothing worth stealing, no reason to try to sell something to the occupant.

The murmuring voices devolved into a single urgent voice which became a chant in a foreign tongue that Nelson had never heard spoken; it grew louder, ever more insistent with demands that would not drop into words he could understand. Vowels rose and soared around the room like the notes from the tape and the cell phone from her with his dick photo that he had put inside the car with Haftmann's name on the wrapping.

Lonnie Dale remembered Haftmann's arrest report. He assumed Haftmann was still on the force. He had copied those letters from different magazines he'd found at the club, but he could not make the 'e' in the cop's middle name come out right; it looked like a bisected arrow, but that was the best he could do. So skilled with his powerful, adroit fingers around machinery, he could not fathom the inability of his mind and fingers to work together with letters. The sound was all around him now, wrapping him in folds.

Then, all at once, he knew – and laughed from deep in his chest. The sounds were coming from his own mouth.

Another sign, another gift from the angel. *Understanding.*

~ ~ ~

"My name is Thomas Haftmann. I'm a private investigator from Jefferson-on-the-Lake. I was told by the detective in charge that you might have some information for me. I'd like to ask you some questions, if I may, about your stepmother's death."

The woman, Mrs. Wulffson, regarded him from her doorway. "What about my father's death? Doesn't this have something to do with his disappearance?"

"Ma'am, the investigating police tell me it's a certainty your father's death is a suicide," Haftmann said, silently hoping Painesville PD had not tipped her off he was coming. As a courtesy, Haftmann informed Mondine he wanted to speak to the woman "about a separate matter."

"I know," she says. "He couldn't have survived long in the outside air. The ward supervisor said he was wearing just a bathrobe over his pajamas."

She admits him into the foyer. "Listen, Officer, I want my father's body found."

53

"I understand how you feel, Mrs. Wulffson." He wonders if he should allow her assumption he's a cop to continue and decides he has to.

"He tried to walk out before," she says and gives a laugh that was closer to a sob. "He never got as far as the lobby before this. It's a terrible shame that his luck was such that no one saw him leave."

Haftmann blunders into the pause. "I'm looking for a man named Lonnie Dale Nelson. Does that name mean anything to you?"

"No, I never heard of him. I can't comment on any of this on the advice of my lawyer who is looking into the probability – the certainty, I should say – of inexcusable neglect at that place."

"Yes, ma'am, I do understand, but I'm only interested in– "

"His wife, that awful woman, was horrid to him. Slapped him right in front of me once! Talked to him as if he were a baby. God, I never hated another human being so much before."

Once they start talking, let them talk. Haftmann nodded his head.

"She'd divorced him and got the house. His insurance let us put him into the home, but it isn't as though I *allowed* him to be institutionalized."

"Mrs. Wulffson, was your stepmother . . . dating any men that you knew of?"

"After the divorce, she and I went our separate ways. Believe me, by then it was mutual. I suspected she was unfaithful to Dad long before, yet I never had any reason – I mean, Dad wouldn't talk to me about it, of course. I just felt something was wrong with his marriage. He grew terribly depressed, but he wouldn't talk about anything."

"Do you know whether your stepmother's personal belongings have been removed from the house?"

54

"I believe so. None of Dad's stuff was left behind when she took – I mean, when the court *awarded* her the house."

The drip of sarcasm could be heard in the next street, but Haftmann kept his poker face and nodded again as if to agree to the perfidious court's decision.

Mrs. Wulfsson thought a moment, her hand grazing her chin where the tiniest of hairs sprouted. "I know she had relatives from Lockport."

"Thanks very much, and I'm sorry I had to bother you with this."

"What's this Lonnie Dale Nelson done?"

"He may have taken a little girl from her family," Haftmann says. "It's an old case. I'm just following up."

"Oh, how long has she been missing?"

Haftmann said, "Three years."

"That's a long time to be missing, isn't it?"

"Yes." *For her parents*, Haftmann thought, *it was ringside seats in hell.*

~ ~ ~

The ride to Albany took eight hours, and despite the low, purple clouds stretching from Ohio to New York, nothing unexpected occurred to break his mood. He thought: *I am about to commit a felony crime. I should feel something.* Interstate 90 was completely clear of snow or ice except for the metal-and-glass debris of a recent accident outside Buffalo.

The Albany Post Office looked like every ugly Victorian building he'd ever seen. He waited for a few men talking in the parking lot to head toward the loading docks behind the building, and then he followed them with satchels under each arm. A voice from the gatehouse called out to ask him if he needed help. He shouted back that he was all right and joined a queue of men and women waiting for a shift change.

55

He added his sacks to the bulk mail stacked against one wall and walked out. He had a story worked out in case he had to speak to someone, but no one bothered him or looked at him.

Once he was past the line of sight of the guardhouse at the mouth of the parking lot, he felt his lungs deflate like a collapsed balloon.

From downtown he took the spur to Guilderland and then 88; he could pick up I 90 again at Jamestown. His mind was fatigued, stressed out.

By the time he passed the last Erie exit, he was profoundly depressed. It seemed as though he were reading the same Peach Street exit sign in a timeless limbo of driving. Snow fell. Blue-black clouds with incandescent centers like pustules spread across the horizon.

Soon a squall blew up and slowed him to 35 mph. His eyes were bleary from the whiteout. Zero visibility. Long-haulers ruled the passing lane, and he could see their wake cut holes in the whirlwind for a second their roar cancelled out by the greater howl of the storm. He drove for an hour without a single car or truck passing him. He was completely alone in a moving vehicle and continually disoriented by the snow all around. He was greasy and his wrist ached from the pressure he kept on the wheel. He'd eaten nothing except cellophane-wrapped cheese and two sour pickles from a jar at the back of the fridge. He tried to concentrate on the image on the jar's lid, Poland's eagle wearing a crown of arrows and holding nothing but air in its flexed talons.

There was no object ahead or behind. If there had been an overpass, a tree, something to define himself against in this all-white landscape of numbing torpor, he would have aimed the car at it. The image of the eagle returned, something to chip away at the terrible gridlock of hopelessness overwhelming him. At that instant, in the nothingness of a landscape that stretched like a barbed-wire fence from here to the North Pole, Haftmann pronounced his mantra of hopelessness against the blank wall of the universe.

Jesus Shit Fuck. Jesusshitfuck. Jesusshitfuck . . .

~ ~ ~

"Rock her back to me," said Lonnie Dale Nelson.

He had his erection entirely buried in the wife from behind while she made soft noises around her husband's cock. They had been in the same position for a half hour, the couple mellowed out by the smoke, Nelson by his own discipline. He took it out and enjoyed the sight of it. He slapped it against the cheeks of her ass, leaving snail tracks across her buttocks but making her moan all the more. The husband seemed to be in a world of his own; the same plastic grin stuck on his face. Nelson slipped it back into her vagina; her still-distended lips and brownie winking at him – *ha, taking his picture.* Her breasts were big and veiny around the areolae but too floppy in his hands. The husband was still short-stroking her mouth and making noises as if he were close to climaxing. His favorite porn site had categories for every taste; his favorite was rough sex, not the staged punishments of BDSM, but the ones where the girls were surrounded by men and drenched in come and the men would urinate in their open mouths afterward. Lonnie Dale, sexual libertine, avoided one category only: any video which had a white girl servicing black males was out of bounds. White girls pushing strollers with little brown babies in them drove him into a rage so intense he had to bite his arms to keep from going outside and killing the first nigger who crossed his path.

The angel, who approved his bigotry, had not only returned his manhood in a manner that amazed during sex but he was masturbating as often as five times a day now. The angel had whispered to him last night about his transformation. He would be exalted when his work for the System was completed. Lonnie Dale's boyhood brain had discovered in a forgotten book of myths the Japanese myth of the Celestial River wherein the sky princess Tanabata meets her lover Kengyu on the seventh night of the seventh moon across a bridge of magpies. But the angel's whispering garbled "bridge of magpies" to become "a bridge of maggots," most fitting as a mistranslation because of his obsession with flies.

Chapter 3

When he was twelve years old, Lonnie Dale Nelson was removed from his third foster home and sent to the Massillon State Reformatory for Boys.

The letter that accompanied him was from his former foster father, a retired steelworker looking to fill in a gap in his marriage and eke out his pension with the $450 check from the state each month. He expressed his shock and horror at coming home from afternoon errands and finding his wife and this boy having sex. The charge was true but the umbrage was a fabrication; his wife had been having sex with random males, even high school boys, for the most part of their marriage. She had taught, insisted, that he perform cunnilingus on her each afternoon when her husband was out. The boy didn't mind, enjoyed the attention and the moans his licking caused in the woman.

Later, he tried to avoid oral sex with her during menses, but she was more aggressive, wilder in her demands at that time. She would chant for him to "lick it," over and over until it became a single word from deep in her throat. The smell nauseated him at first, but he controlled his breathing easily enough and, given his constant attention to her down there, his tongue was as tough as shoe leather.

Sometimes, after supper when his foster father was snoozing in his La-Z-Boy passed out from a pint of Jim Beam, she would stick her finger in her vagina and jab it between his lips. When her husband passed out, she would devour his penis and testicles in her mouth, terrifying him with the half-mocking threat to rip them off with her teeth. Her eyes were wild, and he did not know if she were

59

serious about this threat. Up to this point, he had never had an erection and did not have any pubic hair at this time.

He experienced pubescence during the two years he stayed at the institution in Massillon, which also served as the site for the state's second-largest home for the criminally insane after Lima. His dorm was dominated by three older boys who routinely sodomized the younger boys in their charge. There was one wide-eyed boy of ten or eleven whose eyes shone with greasy light as the fresh meat was introduced into the dorm by a man in charge who called himself Stinson. The boy knew that the new fish's size would guarantee his replacement.

The first time was in the showers where Lonnie Dale was held by two sidekicks of the largest boy. He rammed himself into the boy's rectum, assisted by the lubrication of Vaseline and a towel held around his mouth and doubled in a knot at the back of his head. When he had finished, the other two alternated position and he was raped twice more. There was blood on the last boy's organ, although his erection wasn't as large as the other two. During the bucking and shoving that went on for a length of time that, to Lonnie Dale, could never be measured, not by any clock. He thought of that time as a fracturing of pain into infinitesimal moments as countable as the grains of sand on a beach. He felt his mind splintering into dozens of points of light. He used to concentrate that he was walking through a door, opening it into a bare room, walking ahead to another door – and so on and on until his mind and body could deal with it. He heard voices in his bunk later that night and awoke in terror but there were only the usual noises of the dorm; one boy was crying softly. He did not realize he was that boy.

He was raped a dozen times more that week. His rectal passage was swollen, bloody, and he could barely walk to breakfast a week after his arrival. When he finally could not leave his bunk, he was visited by a doctor who checked his forehead for fever and noticed the blood beneath the sheets. He spent two months in the hospital and had three separate operations to repair tissue damage. He weighed ninety pounds when he left the hospital and was addicted to painkillers whose names he didn't know and couldn't have spelled anyway because everyone assumed he was clinically mentally retarded. His incredible spatial sense and photographic memory had never come up in those drawings he did of people, trees, and houses.

The first night he was returned to the dorm he noticed that the small boy who had seemed so friendly at first looked at him with hatred. He had been burned with metal buttons held beneath cigarette lighters and burned all over his back and stomach until he performed fellatio on the same boys who had cornholed the new kid. His emaciated torso was bright with circular scars in various shades of healing. His eyes said that it didn't matter that he was back: he could not escape from this hell anyway. He would put a cellophane bag over his own head six months later.

Lonnie Dale never told anyone what happened to him, or about the cries he heard at night. The staff at the reformatory was not indifferent to the care of the boys in their charge in other respects. He had had three foster homes and was considered unadoptable at that point. As a ward of the state, he attended the local grade school, and somehow knew that he was different from the other children. He was rarely left in the company of other children in his class, and had begun to grow in spurts the year of his eighth-grade schooling, so that he was left to himself during recess. He didn't mind. He excelled at music but his teachers despaired of teaching him how to read the notes. Sometimes he found a fierce joy in playing King-of-the-Hill on huge snowdrifts, tamped by hundreds of feet, into small hills that the older boys defended from the rest of the schoolyard. Lonnie Dale Nelson became notorious throughout the schoolyard as the one force atop the hill that couldn't be removed. You would have had to kill him to get him off, they all said.

By the end of his elementary school, he had ceased doing homework and had stopped talking to almost every adult he came into contact with. He drew pictures instead that spoke eloquently of violence. Sometimes he was the King of the Hill with daggers dripping blood or carrying block-shaped guns that rained bullets with tracers showing their paths to the hearts and heads of his enemies. The other children left him alone, and it was a general relief when he transferred automatically to the public high school downtown.

At sixteen, he dropped out. One of the reformatory counselors had attempted to force him with a jocular, assertive humor into continuing his schooling at least until he graduated from high school. Lonnie Dale broke his nose with one hard punch that kept the counselor off his back for the last two months of his stay.

He had begun lifting weights with a passion and dedication that replaced all other interests. By the time he was eighteen he had seventeen-inch biceps instead of the stick-like arms he had brought into the dorm years before. His tormentors had left years ago. The smallest boy, who had a guile and sly charm, had gone to a foster home. The others enlisted together, the 82nd Airborne at Fort Benning, Georgia.

Lonnie Dale had planned to kill them all and kept track of them as best he could. A suspicious staff worker, however, didn't believe his interest to be harmless and shredded all records of the three boys' whereabouts before she left. What couldn't be destroyed was locked into a wall safe in the records office.

Three weeks before he turned eighteen, he was caught by a janitor in the records office, papers scattered all around him. He was unable to read well enough to tell what most of the papers said, but he couldn't find any of the three names except for one letter that noted the exceptional bravery under fire of Spec. 5 Teagarden and Sgt. Davisson. The major who had signed it called them warriors in the service of their country. They died together in a firefight at the battle of Najaf. Lonnie Dale wept with frustrated rage.

It took him one year, eight months, and thirteen days to find the remaining boy who was then living in one of those nondescript middle counties of Ohio, which, to newcomers to the Midwest, all look alike.

The flat terrain of Delaware County is slightly broken by the Scioto River. There used to be a town there called Africa, named for the freed slaves who settled near the border of Union and Delaware. It's gone now, except for the cemetery that once marked an important stop on the Underground Railroad, and, of course, the locals will tell you that two presidents sprung from the remarkable 23rd Ohio Regiment despite the unremarkable and short-lived tenures of Hayes and McKinley themselves.

His foster father had given him an introduction to the man who owned the county's biggest John Deere dealership and he'd developed into what they called down there a crackerjack salesman. He did well enough to buy a white frame house across from the old metal truss bridge that crossed the river. Ox-eyes grew freely in the open fields; swallowtails roosted at dusk in the trees, and red-winged blackbirds darted among the swamp birch and poison sumac.

Roger "the Dodger" Crandall had acquired a wife and baby son by the time Nelson found him. Lonnie Dale decided to call himself Will Rose if asked, inspired by a glimpse at the statue of General William Rosecrans, after being told who the statue honored at a local cafe.

He came down 203 and found him inside the John Deere place talking to a couple of farmers. He watched his gestures from his car in the parking lot to be sure of him; the glare from the plate-glass window obscured facial expressions, but the hands and the quick movements throughout his conversation gave him the final proof. He was broader in the shoulders and inches taller, yet there was no mistaking that it was he who had helped Teagarden and Davisson sodomize him.

Lonnie Dale sat in the car and dropped a tab of acid and listened to the local radio stations weather reports while he baked in the late summer heat. A mosquito had gotten inside the car and found the sweaty salt-flesh of Nelson perfect sustenance. Lonnie Dale listened to the riffs of her buzzing around his head and sat calmly while she feasted on his blood. Roy Orbison sang "Pretty Woman" for the second time in an hour, and Orbison's strange, almost womanly voice, enchanted him.

He followed him to his house across the river. He drove past it as soon as he saw him turn into the graveled driveway and found a dirt road bordered by rosinweed and prairie dock.

He removed the rope and hunting knife from beneath his seat and locked them in the trunk of the car. He had a dot of acid left and some reefer from Meigs County left over from his last buy to help him pass the hours until dark. This trip was a little rough. It was like riding the Scrambler at the county fair when you're the only one riding and the operator's gone off somewhere. He avoided looking in the rear view mirror because he knew his face was melting and he tried to put it back into place with his fingers. Metallica's "For Whom the Bell Tolls" blasted from the bulging speakers into his ear buds. Any passerby seeing him rocking to and fro in his car would have crossed the street.

He had a little buzz left by the time he walked the mile back to the house. He saw that the lights were off except for the phosphorescent glow of the TV set behind the curtains.

He meant to say something, but when the door was opened to his knock, there didn't seem to be anything left to say.

The three bodies, including the infant, were found on the banks of the Scioto by fishermen at sundown. Autopsies revealed that both had been sodomized with a broom handle taken from the couple's kitchen and greased with dish soap. The man's face had been pummeled beyond recognition, but the killer's hands had been padded by a makeshift boxing glove of kitchen towels and electric tape. The eighteen-year-old wife's neck had been broken in three places, and cops theorized that the baby had been hurled against the living room wall at such velocity that they at first believed the head had been decapitated by the time they found the tiny corpse tangled in fronds at the water's edge of the river. The soft skull had merely pancaked into the baby's neck. The manhunt spread north to Marion County, west to Champaign, east to Licking, and as far south as Pickaway. To the conservative, God-loving locals, every bearded drifter in thirteen central Ohio counties was suspect.

People said it was just like what happened out there in California to that pregnant Hollywood actress and her rich friends, by God. Somebody joked about calling Pelican Bay to see if Charley Manson was still in his cell.

Chapter 4

Christmas

By mid-December, the air temperature plunged to an iron-cold ten below zero at nights and barely made it to five degrees by afternoon. Driving down the deserted, wind-swept Strip, you would not believe the JOTL's Chamber of Commerce that one-and-a-half million people would walk past their doors by Labor Day.

Like the anomaly of Las Vegas, America's crime capital perched in the desert like a neon cancer, Jefferson-on-the-Lake hunkered down on Lake Erie's shore, squat between Cleveland and Erie with its smug, middle-of-the-litter complacency, existing in open defiance of all the silo towns in between.

Alone in a draft house Haftmann dreamed of a tropical rain forest: all bright blue sky overhead and scintillating dots of color punctuating the green. It was noisy with the chatter of exotic birds. Monkeys screeched in the canopy. The air was humid, right at the bursting point of water.

The vegetation was suffocating, thick, and pungent with rot; his skin crawled with the itch and flutter of insects. Haftmann climbed a tree to get his bearings and hauled himself upwards with the agonizing slowness of movement in dreams. Finally, he could see the dazzling sky. He sat in the crotch of the tree for a long time, gazing, sweating in the misty vapor until the noises of the forest all around stopped abruptly. Then one sound took over: chewing, millions of tiny mouths were devouring something. He saw an arm fall to the jungle floor, its white bones showing through the red meat; the detail was excruciating: sinew, fingernails, arm hair, a tattoo that had been burned off many years ago, the warped and livid skin still showing the outlines of a woman's name in gothic script: Micah.

Oh Jesus. Oh fuck. His arm. The seething red and brown ants were eating chunks of his own flesh. He looked down at his side and saw the torn and bloody hole of a stump –

Screaming, he awoke to the sound of his own voice boxing the empty room.

The phone was ringing. 6:30 a.m. Christmas Day. "Yippie, fucking hell," Haftmann groans.

"Haftmann, sorry to bother you at home. The daywatch commander gave me your number. I have to tell you that it goes against my deepest instincts to help a private investigator for any reason, but Lieutenant Mondine said he checked you out with Cleveland PD. You've still got friends in homicide back there."

Haftmann, groggy, his head a stew of leftover and ragged dream fragments, said, "Now that we've covered my biography, what can I do for you?"

"I've got something for you that might help explain your suicide, the drowner, or might not. Anyway, I thought I'd pass it along. Suicides without a note are a real bitch. We traced a few numbers for our hot-tub lady and she was a swinger, it seems like."

"Last time I checked, Officer, we lived in America. Fucking is still legal."

"You always this pleasant in the morning? We found an old box of photos. She used an out-of-state photo lab to develop her prints—thirty-five millimeter with an automatic timer. She had an advertisement in a magazine for people who want to connect."

"They still use print magazines for that?"

"No, it's all pretty much on the internet nowadays."

Haftmann remembers a commercial advertisement for one on TV. It claimed God was eager to find you a match. God as your very own pimp. "Was there a photo or a description she used?"

"No photo insert, but she called herself, uh, I'm quoting now, 'White female, mid-forties, great shape, no smoke or drink, looking for compatible couples, select males twenty-five to forty-five, can entertain or travel, send full-length photo, need not be nude.'"

"I appreciate the call," Haftmann said, perking up his antennae now.

"She was an active little cooze, all right, but nobody in her family had any idea. Kept a really low profile. Naturally, being a school teacher."

"You're calling it murder?" Haftmann thinks, maybe, she was too much for the old guy to handle. Brooded about it, going crazy from Alzheimer's can't be a picnic . . .

"We're keeping an open mind. Thought you'd like to know – "

"Thanks. Tell Lieutenant Mondine I'm obliged."

"There's this, too. Something I kept back from the press and you didn't get this from me. We got half the *Plain Dealer* camped out on our steps as it is."

"Go on."

"That house was an inferno when we walked in. I mean the thermostat was stuck on high. No prints except hers. The candles had melted on the mantle and were all twisted from the heat. At first we figure the perp tried to screw up forensics. But D'Agostino got back the VICAP profile analysis from Quantico . . ."

A long pause here, reluctant to say the words, describe the wacko.

Haftmann is already thinking it: *serial killer.*

"Shit," Haftmann said into the phone.

"You got it in one, man."

~ ~ ~

"Mrs. Wulffson," Haftmann says, "I give you my word in the strictest confidence that nothing you tell me about your stepmother will be used in any way to embarrass you."

"Please go away. I'm sick to my stomach as it is." She clutched her robe tighter around her midriff.

"You must understand that a little girl's life is at the end of all this," Haftmann pleads.

It turned out that the Jacuzzi had become a kind of sexual centerpiece for the dead woman, whose liberation from small-town morals was too much for her stepdaughter to bear. Too much for most people in a mostly blue-collar factory town. There were two photos recovered with her father's items returned from the nursing home but so well secreted that it was unlikely they had been viewed. Her husband, whose mind had begun wandering too much for her to cope with, kept them as mementos of his marriage, too important to part with, even though the woman herself had initiated divorce proceedings.

She looked good in her black-and-pink lace teddy – no doubt about it. Color definition was sufficiently good despite the photo's age to show the lavender areolae surrounding her nipples in the cutout bra. Her muscle tone looked good, aerobics probably. She had her crotch hair shaved like current skin models affecting the no-ruff look.

Mrs. Wulffson had burned the other one. ("Was I supposed to treasure it as a keepsake for his grandchildren? For God sake, she had a man's thing in her mouth!")

Haftmann gulped a couple bennies he had swiped from Jefferson Toxicology years ago to help him on the long drive to Cincinnati. He wondered if they'd still work.

He picked up Interstate 71 off the Shoreway in Cleveland and stayed on it, a big artery like a diagonal strap across the state's heart. When the state's tourist bureau began churning out that gush about Ohio-as-the-heart-of-it-all, Haftmann laughed aloud. It meant the brains were somewhere else. His natal state was a black vortex sucking in all the vice and corruption from the coasts.

The road was clear and deserted, too cold to snow, as the local halfwits liked to say. Holiday travelers clustered like shiny metallic bees near Columbus and Mansfield, but the open stretches were like a vast, desert wasteland lying before him.

He had two thoughts in his head on the way down to collect the money from the scam: Would he end his career, possibly his life, in shock and blood and disaster on a post office floor in a few hours' time? He took his snub nose and hollow points because he wanted to make sure of oblivion when he put the gun to his temple, not lobotomize himself, wake up a vegetable in the county nursing home.

The other question: *Why me? Why pick me?*

On his way out the door Haftmann retrieved a copy of the Herbert poem from his overcoat pocket. He unfolded it and read it again, squinting to see its words in the light from his streaked windows. LOVE BADE ME WELCOME. What love had he known that he had not already betrayed? He watched dust motes cavort in the winter light, turned on his heel and walked out the door. Unless they cocked-up Lonnie Dale's biography, he was supposed to be a barely literate cretin like most cons in the joint. *What the hell.*

He had tried to learn something at the Kent State branch campus library by dragging a few books off the shelf, but he found little that helped: Herbert was a mystic who turned his back on money to serve God. That other one, John Donne, seemed to have a story, now: from gash hound to preacher in one cycle. They lost him with their goofy definitions of "metaphysical poetry" and "conceit." *Artsy-fartsy Micah stuff.*

When he saw the first houses looking down at him, those elaborate Victorian structures with gingerbread and gables built by the first families and scions of robber barons, he began to hum about an emerald city and kept it up right to the moment he found Main and the slew of government buildings where the post office would be.

~ ~ ~

Lonnie Dale often dreamed of his mother. She was always naked and her belly was hugely pregnant. He did not know her after the age of four because he was mostly state-raised, although he knew that she had abandoned him about that time. Too many children, he guessed, but was never curious about the brothers and sisters he assumed he had. Sometimes his naked mother was frolicking with another naked woman, bigger-boned and also pregnant, who would pin his mother down and fondle her. But when the other woman had her down, she would find the triple business of the male beneath the beard of her cunt hair, which folded up like a surprise.

His mother and the woman were riding naked on their broad asses down a hill. They were laughing and didn't mind the cold. His mother let him ride on her pregnant belly down the hill. "Wheee!" he said and looked into her bland face for – *something*, he guessed, confirmation, affirmation of his existence but never love – *no, not that, never that.*

He awoke calmly to a new day. He was going to move. The System had decided and communicated to him their displeasure. They were angry about the flies. He should not have taken flies to Warren. It should have been like the Painesville house call – meticulous and precisely planned.

He had brought the flies on his own both times,

At first he thought they approved because they didn't say anything.

He was hoisting iron yesterday when he knew; repetitions of 405 on the bench press he'd designed from *Popular Mechanics*. He had done four (hunh), five (hunh), and brought the bar to his chest when the buzzing began in his ears and the weight suddenly doubled of its own. They were pressing it down. Just before, he'd been snapping it up with crisp symmetry, the Lipidex really cooking in his body, giving him power to do anything – now he was in danger of suffocating, unable to tip the bar to either side. *Can't do it.* His lungs were screaming for air. He started to choke on the vomit surging into his throat. Then, merciful at last, the angel came to spot him; the weight nothing now as he set it into the forks, but his veins and tendons quivered like spaghetti for ten minutes until he had the strength to roll off the bench.

There was a thudding, concussive rhythm in his brain that tortured him all night at work. The bar was busy with serious wintertime drinkers. The heavy metal acoustics searing zigzags across the surface of his brain. Faces demonic under the bar lights. Customers' voices fading in and out; he was certain they were mocking him, speaking in other languages. He tried to focus on faces but noses, eyebrows, and lips were all separate.

One or two customers wrinkled their noses at the acidic smell he was giving off. Two squarejohns at the end of the bar were talking about one of the dancers, a gyrating blonde with sacral dimples. A pink labial lip winked out from her thonged bikini at the male heads in front of the stage. The lights made her look ripped; each dent and cut clearly defined. Hers was the same winter zodiac sign as his: Capricorn, the Goat.

While Haftmann was crossing the state on his return trip, the news about the Warren house broke all over Ohio. Every police agency in the state knew about it.

Murder is not a federal crime unless state boundaries are crossed, yet Warren police didn't hesitate to request F.B.I. assistance once the site was secured. One look was enough: a maniac was loose.

VICAP, as all TV forensics fans know by now, is Quantico's criminal psychology division at the Behavioral Sciences Unit. Every serial killer apprehended in the last decade has had his interior picture taken – that is, his profile, modus, idiosyncrasies, preferences documented, itemized, and logged into a computer network. Sociopaths like to talk about themselves and their crimes; very few decline the opportunity to contribute. Some household names comprised this pioneering effort: Edmund Emil Kemper III, a taciturn giant of a man at 6'9 and 300 pounds: like Ohio's son, Jeffrey Dahmer out of Milwaukee, a head collector. Little Charlie Manson who, of course, made 10050 Cielo Drive in beautiful Bel Aire famous on 9 August 1969; Richard (Night Stalker) Ramirez, dead of liver cancer in San Quentin, Henry Lee Lucas, David (Son of Sam) Berkowitz, Kenneth Bianchi, one-half of the Hillside Strangler tandem, and last but not least, the amiable, blue-eyed, boy, that Young Republican and *pro se* defender Theodore Bundy.

Less well known than Bundy is a kind of twin in the rogue women-hating category is Gary Addison Taylor. Whereas Bundy ended his trolling days in Florida, thence to "Old Sparky," Taylor began his career there by attacking women when he was thirteen-years-old. Like Taylor, Harry ("Harv the Hammer") Louis Carignan became one of those typical wandering serial killers of the 60s and 70s by killing women in six states including Alaska; he had maps with 180 scarlet circles drawn at the time of his arrest. Because serial killers are so mobile (Henry Lee Lucas once traveled across the country with a rotting head of a victim on the backseat), they are usually first confronted with authority in the personage of a traffic cop.

Early in their marriage, Micah had once tried to explain the murder-will-out myth to Haftmann ("This shithead, this guy Chaucer, did he ever see blood spatter, Micah?") and when she got to the part about how a murdered person's retina encased the visage of the murderer, Haftmann interrupted with a guffaw that made her red in the face: "Hey, Micah, the last stiff I found was a fourteen-year-old crack whore named Charisse. I found her where her killer dumped her between two buildings on the Cuyahoga, the part of the Flats. I don't know what was in her eyeballs because the animals got to her first. You know that the opossum will eat its way into a corpse from the anal passage, core it like a fucking apple, right?"

That was the first and last forensics lesson in the Haftmann household.

To return: the accumulation of raw data on serial killers began in September 1984 at the tenth triennial meeting of the International Association Of Forensic Sciences held at Oxford, England. Their report is noteworthy because it construed data from the thirty-six interviewees of the Basic Science Units development of profiles in cases of sexual homicide. In fact, they began by differentiating between sexual and non-sexual homicides on the simple basis of number of victims to period of time in which the killings occurred.

To be sure, the ratios had to factor in homicides of one, double, triple, etc. Mass Murder equals four victims in a short period of time; spree killings are sequential over hours *sans* a cooling off period (a little slang to enliven the dry-as-dust jargon of the trade; Doc Harris always winced at these infelicities and *vox populi* cullings).

Serial homicides mean time breaks between victims; serial killers may take anywhere from days to years to recharge their batteries, but all things begin with names so sexual homicide is itself defined in the report as resulting from one person killing another in a context of power, sexuality, and brutality.

This is what the collating and number-crunching is all about, a recent year's sampling should suffice: 32% white/43% one parent missing/47% no father present by age twelve/72% cold relationship with father/66% domineering mother/41% pre-adult history of institutionalization/86% psychiatric history/36% attempted suicide/80% unsteady employment/68% unskilled workers but good intelligence and mean IQ around bright normal/42% physically abused as children/74% psychologically abused and 70% sexual interest in voyeurism, fetishism, and pornography.

On the morning of the day Ted Bundy was strapped into Old Sparky, Haftmann is up north in the panhandle on the trail of another teen run away. He finds her in a trailer park in Panama City wearing a t-shirt that said CHI-O CHI-O IT'S OFF TO HELL I GO. She told him Chi Omega was a sorority house. On the back it said BURN, BUNDY, BURN.

Even in the midst of hideous carnage, a cop can find humor. But Haftmann was impatient with shrinks and so-called experts for taking their explanations of evil and malevolence from maniacs. "All Klebold and Harris wanted," according to Marilyn Manson, "was for somebody to listen to them."

"Fuck him and all the rest of those narcissists," Haftmann said between boilermakers at Tico's.

The first officer on the scene was Patrolman Arnie Lukačs. At first he thought someone was home because the chimney was smoking. That turned out to be escaping hot air; the inside of the house was a blast furnace.

The door was open, no one responded to his tapping at the window. Lukačs requested permission to enter the house, wanting to be sure in case these were high-minded, litigating types – *maybe Jews on vacation, ya know? Fuck, they'd sue his ass and buy theirselves a new Jew canoe.*

Steam was hissing out of the baseboards. Red smears were crisscrossing the carpet, going up the stairs.

He got the gun out.

He should have been used to the smell because his father and uncles were all meat cutters; he himself had worked Golden Dawn before joining the force.

When he saw what was in the living room, he sent a spume of his stomach's contents onto the congealing mess on the floor, animating the cloud of black flies that were feasting.

He got outside before another gut-bursting spasm sent a mushroom-colored plume in front of him that spattered his shoes and pant cuffs.

He waited until the cold air revitalized him and walked with shaky steps down the driveway to his unit and keyed the mike; he managed to get enough professionalism into his transmission and used the right codes. Dabbing at specks of vomit on his uniform sleeve, he waited by his unit and dreaded the needling from the old timers more than the ass-chewing he was certainly going to get for puking on the crime scene.

~ ~ ~

By the time he headed up 46 for Jefferson, Haftmann was convinced that postal inspectors had put a tail on him. He was giddy at the thought and, when headlights in the early winter afternoon approached too close, panicked and almost tossed the sacks out the back window.

He stopped home long enough to put the sacks on his living room floor and change his shirt before driving at breakneck speed to his office. He left a message for Shawna at the station house; he believed in luck.

The drudgery of cross-checking paperwork on five years of runaways, missing and stolen children in the hope of one detail that might link a small girl to Lonnie Dale Nelson fatigued him: another pang of regret in a lifetime of grieving for lost or betrayed innocence. Unable to stand himself for company, he checked his email: 5 messages, 1 seemed to be a new customer, the others were bill collectors.

At the station of the detectives rolled out of his cubicle in a Santa Claus costume, blitzed from the afternoon's Christmas party, and saw Haftmann. "Holy Jesus Christ," Haftmann muttered. "A-fucking-men to that, brother," said Santa Claus.

He found Shawna at the end of her shift and asked her out for coffee. She looked at him a long time, puckering her eyes, before she accepted.

They found an all-season diner on the Strip, a Times Square facsimile with a mauve-and-pink decor.

He felt a rush looking at her that loosened his tongue. He had bottled up so much since Micah booked. In more ways than one, he knew, because there was talk all over the strip about his drinking. Tico's wife Marta made a face every time he walked into her husband's bar. "Yo, Marta," he often crooned, "so lovely to see you, too, dear."

The secret knowledge of his crime made him feel expansive, happy to look into her eyes. The swelling and discoloration gone, they were restored to that striking yellow with tawny flecks in the iris.

They drank lukewarm coffee in chipped mugs and talked about the job, the weather, high schools they'd attended. We seem to have gone to different schools together, Haftmann said, and it made her smile. There were laugh wrinkles around her eyes. He saw that she was older than he'd first reckoned. They would speak shyly after this of their first date, but each one knew then that that was what it was.

He told her about the day he decided to become a cop and how his grandmother, who had a European's understanding of police, called him *ein grosse Scheissβekopf* when he told her what he wanted to be.

He asked her why she said yes when he had asked her out.

Later she said: "I don't know. I guess I just liked you from the moment I gave you that package. Your eyes smile even when you say bitter things."

Then she said this: "You have a bad reputation. Everyone's afraid of you going postal. They talk about it at the station."

"What do you think?"

"You don't seem to care what anyone thinks about you. I wanted to sit and talk to you because it would make my husband jealous if he knew. Small revenge for this." She tapped her healing eye and smiled. "Maybe I wanted to see what it's like for myself."

"So what's it like?"

"It's a nice feeling mostly. But you're wound up, and it's easy to tell you're fighting something. I've seen you at the station and you look so – intense. As if you could push a button and wipe out the whole world and everyone in it."

"That's a lot to tell from a single glance, isn't it?"

"They say you're . . . a screwball because of your – "

"My divorce," he finished for her.

Haftmann asked if he could see her again, but she said no, it wouldn't be a good idea. He left it at that. He took her back to the station's lot and drove back to the Strip, stopping in front of Oscar's Chalet.

Oscar was leaning against the bar in his usual corner, a pair of bifocals hanging from his nose. Haftmann watches his eyes as he moves up to him. "Merry Christmas, Oscar."

"Shit, you."

Oscar twitches and moves from one foot to the other like a kid with a bladder problem. "Stay away from me, Haftmann."

"Got something for you." Haftmann throws a bundle of cash wadded with rubber bands onto the bar top: "I want Oregon, Vegas line."

Oscar scoops the wad off the bar without a word. Haftmann checks out a poker game in the back room, local high rollers including the car dealer whose windows were smashed before Christmas. One of them sees him, looks up from his hole card.

"Hey, the fuzz is here. Oscar put the fix in for you, Haftmann?"

"What do you think?"

"I think you're full of shit."

"Hey, private eye," someone calls out, "you couldn't find a turd in a punchbowl."

Haftmann leaves with their collective laughter booting him in the ass.

Chapter 5

Epiphany

Lonnie Dale Nelson walked out of the Dusty Armadillo in Rootstown with tears streaming down his cheeks. Terri Clark had concluded her performance with "Pretty Woman," and the audience roared and stamped its feet as soon as the riff fell into place.

Nelson could duplicate Orbison's epicene voice to perfection. Even back in the boys' dorm, he thought the singer looked bloated, pasty-faced – ought to pump some iron.

He located his car next to a pickup with a gun rack behind the driver's seat. Two men and two women were talking about the concert, beer cans in their hands, a Jack Daniels on top of the cab. One of the men had a red baseball cap on that said "I Eat Raw Pussy."

"Hey, homo, you miss the Rainbow parade by mistake? Shee-it, you faggot."

Marvin's blue baseball cap had scrambled eggs without a slogan.

"Hey, girls, check out the big queer. Hey, big boy, you wanta suck my cock?"

One of the women told Marvin to leave him alone. The other woman said he sure was big, but he didn't look like no homo she'd ever seen.

Nelson sometimes bought large, old-lady blouses with billowing sleeves because of his girth and because he could get them cheap at yard sales and Salvation Army stores. The one he wore tonight was pink with tiny blue flowers. He had knee-length army surplus overcoat that he hoped would make him look less conspicuous. Hair, grown out in the winter months, was tied in a pony so tight to the back of his head that the peroxide made it look lacquered.

"Hey, you, I'll kick your fat ass all over this parking lot you don't say thanks to the lady for saving your ass."

"Thank you," said Lonnie Dale absently without looking at the men; he knew the angel did not want attention drawn to him. *You're too close now . . .* He opened his car door to get inside. He was thinking about Terri Clark's repertoire, still felt the music's glow. He had already sized the two men up and dismissed them: rednecks with booze got a little braver. Not worth his time even if the angel said he could. His occupation of choice was bouncer.

He drove out of the lot just as a beer bottle smashed against his right rear fender. He saw the bigger of the two men, Marvin, mouth the word *faggot*, but it was lost in the wind.

He stopped at an Italian diner on 9th Street in downtown Cleveland and ate linguini with clam sauce, tortellini soup, chicken parmagiana with angel-hair pasta, two salads, two slices of French cherry pie, garlic bread, and four bottles of Lowenbrau.

On the walk down Euclid to his car, he was accosted by two black pimps and one desperate, skinny teenager, who threatened to slit his throat if he didn't "give it up." When Nelson brushed his arm with the knife aside, he said he'd blow him for ten dollars.

Nelson also ignored a black prostitute in gold lame hot pants; her melodious voice offered "the best skull in town."

He was in a binge-eating period, and he had to use two shopping carts at the grocery store. He had two pieces of paper in his pocket. He decided to use an all-night supermarket as long as he was in Cleveland, this shithole town full of coons. His diet for the week was written in child's block-letter handwriting, with his characteristic left-handed slant, and each item on his list was phonetically spelled:

2 dozin eggz, 4 loves of rie bred, 2 dozin bannans, 4 loves Etalin bred, 3 pouns dinner rols, 2 pouns Etalin saosage, 2 pouns mazarela, 1 dozin granole barz, 8 ouns creem cheez, 3 pouns of can pineaple, 3 pouns hot dog, 3 cans nacho cheez dip, 2 pouns chille saus, 4 galons orang juis, 1 galon cranbery juise, 2 qts Gatoraid, 1 qt cottige cheez, 6 pouns spaggetty saus, 1 poun bagls, 32 slises American cheez, 4 pouns Ric-a-Roni, 2 pouns rigitony, 2 pouns pez, 1 poun dry frut, 4 pouns frozin korn, 7 gren aples, 4 pouns aple saus, 2 cuekumbers, 2 pouns spaggetty, 14 1/2 pouns stake, 12 orngs, 2 pouns otmeel, 1 poun rasenz, 1/2 gal. aple juise, 2 pouns pork, 5 pouns chken, 1 poun marjaren, 1 gal Hevelee Hash ice creem, 2 pouns MŸslix sereal (he made the umlaut *u* exactly as he recalled it from the cereal boxes scattered around the basement of the house in East Palestine, 2 gals lo-fat milk, 2 boxes of Yummy Mummy sereal, 10 pouns potatae, 2 & 1/2 gals bottled water, a cas of Redd Bul.

He needed the green apples for their laxative effect; sometimes six or seven meals a day were necessary. He added Super Tea to the regimen of eating and lifting because it guaranteed maximum caffeine and 340 calories. He began with the chifir as soon as he was in the door at four or five o'clock in the morning. By dawn, he had broken a good sweat and his leg was thumping between sets from excess nervous energy.

During binge periods, his system was continually flushing; he used the tub upstairs to excrete, and if the smell got too bad, he'd wash most of it down the drain with a hose.

The other piece of paper was meticulously copied out by hand from letters he had traced from magazines. He put the numbers from 0 to 9 above certain letters. His gift of recalling what he read was special but highly selective; mostly the neurons behind the brain cells misfired, or refused to cooperate when he attempted to comprehend what he recalled. He was afraid of one thing only now, afraid of being drowned in the stunning clarity of the System's messages to him. All the words in the world were a secret coda of violence he alone would be permitted to penetrate when the time was right. One day he would design a machine that would cast the letters onto paper, and save himself the trouble he had to take to prevent detection by handwriting analysis. He was a big fan of *Forensics Files* and had seen every episode. He had no idea whatsoever what short tandem repeats meant or mitochondrial DNA testing involved. But he knew that sweat, come, and hair follicles were bad things to leave behind in a crime scene.

The paper, transposed from Nelson's phonetic spelling, said this:

Have you got eyes of blue?
Have you got eyes of blue?
I ask you as a personal friend,
Have you got eyes of blue?

He looked out over the room in the blank mindless gaze of a white-lipped cobra. Hours later he came to humming the words of "The Farmer in the Dell," oblivious to everything else except the steady, reassuring drone of flies.

~ ~ ~

"You heard that F.B.I. jamoke say I can work on the case – "

"Get him out of here, MacDuff."

"Wait a second, Millimaki – "

"Get the fuck out now, Haftmann."

MacDuff scooped him under one arm the way cops have been bumrushing deadbeats for a hundred years.

Haftmann slipped it with ease, turned MacDuff around in a come-along move that amazed him that, in his shape, he could do it the way the academy had taught trainees all those years ago.

"I'll kill you, you fuck, let me go!"

Haftmann released him at once. Cops in this era of cop killing and rioting over the shootings of blacks across the country had put every precinct on age. Not a wise thing to do under the circumstances, Haftmann realizes much too late. Phil rushing up the stairs. There was Shawna watching him from the corner of the muster room. Frozen faces. *Not again, Lord*. Millimaki regarded him calmly while he picked at a carbuncle on his neck. His cell's ring tones broke the spell his move on MacDuff had created. Everyone relaxed. Haftmann expels a deep breath, but he knows this likely to be his last visit to a place where he used to work.

He moves casually to the muster room to take the call but feels the heat of eyes boring into his back for that stupid stunt with MacDuff. He's spoken twice to Commander Vanderhyden of Ohio's Bureau of Criminal Investigation. Vanderhyden tells him that Agent Thorpe from the Columbus field office of the F.B.I. has left messages for him to call.

"I haven't checked my emails today," Haftmann tells him.

"Your office phone," Vanderhyden says, irritation heavy in his voice. "You do go to work once in a while, I assume."

Haftmann is about to apologize but the Commander has ended the call.

Haftmann knows he's got to slow down, take stock of things. He feels like a circus magician with too many spinning plates in the air, not to mention the ones his own vices put there. He knows Big Steve Millimaki is in a tizzy thanks to the tape being in his possession. Hindsight, naturally, makes the cops look stupid, even if they aren't concerned about crime beyond their bailiwick. Millimaki, however, played a hand that might work out for him. He had lied to the feds and said they'd dusted the cassette as soon as Haftmann, citizen and private investigator working a lost-child case, had brought it to the attention of the lawful authorities. He hoped they bought it. Phil said Millimaki's rumbling intestines were heard all over the station. "Stomach acid," he told his troops, while looking in the general direction of Haftmann's former cubicle, according to a smirking Phil.

An F.B.I. factotum from the Cleveland office had already picked up the tape. He wore regulation latex gloves and dropped it into a glassine bag. Haftmann winced at the overkill.

It was made crystal clear by every state and federal cop he had spoken with that he was to have no active role in this investigation. Since the alleged killer had made contact with him, he was to be kept informed of developments – as a courtesy only.

A spit-shined, silver-haired F.B.I. man named Booth had been the last to leave, and as he passed by, he tossed a thumb over his shoulder at Millimaki's office. With his other hand he gave the herky-jerky masturbatory gesture all boys know and winked in Haftmann's general direction. Haftmann's spirits lift: *A feeb SAC with a sense of humor.* Haftmann catches up with him in the parking lot under a sky of titanium. Haftmann senses an immediate appraisal by the F.B.I. agent: unshaven, shirt untucked, high-top tennis shoes, his entire rumpled, unmade-bed appearance; by contrast the federal cop's charcoal slacks had a knife-point crease.

"Yes, Mister Haftmann?"

"Cut me in, sir. I'll get nothing here. I can help you."

He doesn't move to shake Haftmann's hand, however.

"Don't take this the wrong way," said Booth. "Your concern about the missing girl is admirable, but it's small potatoes. I know that sounds harsh but you haven't convinced me that your man is our man in the first place."

"I know that. It's Agent Booth, right? I used to work—"

"Mister Haftmann, I'm not at all interested in your work history here . . . in this lovely little resort town of yours," he says and fixes him with a look.

"Hear me out first," Haftmann says, way too much pleading in his voice now. "I'm trying to explain a feeling I had when I looked in this guy's eyes years ago – when he was just a kid – and saw just how crazy he was." Haftmann is acutely aware of his own bloodshot eyes as he says this.

"Really? Clairvoyance is one of your gifts then. Listen, Haftmann. Try to understand. We'll check out your Larry Nelson—

"Lonnie, God damn it! Lonnie Dale Nelson," Haftmann is boiling now and going for broke.

The agent checks him out again – head-to-toe, as if he's looking at a slovenly woman on the street. "We'll give you every scrap of information from anywhere, from anyone, including you, every consideration possible."

"What about what I asked you?"

"Cutting you in?" The smirk tells Haftmann the question's unworthy of a serious answer." He half-turns, growing impatient to go, and says, "We'll forward you anything we turn up that might assist your own case. How's that?"

Haftmann's glare is cold. "You're shining me on, Booth. You knew after five minutes with Millimaki he couldn't find his ass with both hands and a mirror. Damn it, I can help you."

Booth's face is stern and patient. "You're a private investigator, Haftmann. Stay clear."

Booth gets into a red Porsche, fires it up, and leaves Haftmann standing, unkempt and uncouth, in the lot. The rooster tail of churned snow and gravel he leaves behind puts a point to his refusal. Haftmann turns back and sees Shawna regarding him from the slatted window. The eerie light flattens the sharp planes of her face and gives her a death mask. Suddenly she's gone and his heart aches for her, for him, but mostly for the little girl he may never find.

Haftmann is back in his office in ten minutes and he's calling in every marker he's earned in twenty years as a cop and here as a private investigator.

He speaks to two people at the Warren investigation scene: one is the state's best blood man and the other is the rookie cop who was sent by concerned relatives and employers to check into the quiet house off the Warren-Youngstown strip in its respectable, middle-class neighborhood.

The blood man tells Haftmann that the cop's regurgitation couldn't have loused up anything; gouts of blood patterned the walls in every room of the house, including the upstairs closets. Crazy bastard sprayed it out of some kind of device. "I thought we would be lucky at first, but no saliva, except theirs, to type for DNA."

The rookie has to be gotten to by cajolery, less arm-twisting here, because he's done a lot of business over the years with Youngstown vice, even thought of relocating to a town where there was a wider pool of clientele to tap. What's left of the Cleveland, Pittsburgh, and Youngstown mafia families consider Jefferson-on-the-Lake neutral turf.

The young cop tells him he's still taking some vicious ribbing from the veterans on the force. The blue brotherhood is tough on their own. It can be like a wolf pack sometimes. A male wolf will grip some misbehaving cub and drive his face into the dirt to get him to behave. The problem was, Mike the rookie tells him, he forgot to key off the mike during his last transmission, and renditions of "Jesus, it's a slaughterhouse" were getting yuks from the same clowns who never knew how to be silent in front of a wreck. The guys had begun calling him O'Rourke because of the vomiting sounds and they were starting to nickname him "the Irishman" around the station house.

Haftmann is glad he's sitting down in his office when he learns the details; they aren't pretty:

The maniac had cut off their heads. (Mike uses the term freely; fuck "suspect" or that jargonistically worse term from the FBI, "unsub" for "unknown subject" or "perp" or "actor," or anything else," says Mike. "He's a fuckin' four-star maniac. Period.") He'd used three kinds of knots: bowline, timber hitch, and the common square knot for the contraption in the living room. (Haftmann himself knows knots from his own sailing days.)

The rope was polypropylene cord, no help there either, but they learned that it was manufactured at Lehigh Cordage in Allentown, Pennsylvania, and distributed as far south as Moundsville, West Virginia, and was carried in every Walmart, Sears, and Ben Franklin in three states.

The fiber analysis team was positive he had brought no equipment into the room. The carpet was a soggy, maggot-infested swamp by the time they got there, but there was no evident tearing. That meant he was extremely strong.

He had hoisted the two bodies by the ankles and attached them to a boot-clamp device built for that purpose. ("Jesus," Mike says with both amazement and even admiration in his voice, "do you realize how strong this guy has to be to hoist a dead body weight like that?")

Haftmann thinks about that for a long moment. Most guys in the academy could barely handle the fireman's carry with their assigned partners. It got worse. "He field dressed them. Dropped their guts onto the floor," says Mike and his voice is quavering. He covers it by throat-clearing and continues."

Paramedics who assisted in the removal had to wear masks to keep the flies bolting from body cavities into their mouths.

All the taps were turned on.

Size 11 triple E tennis shoes, crosstrainers, showed walking and running strides all over the place – a mosaic of red smears with a crosshatched design, a clue that soon dead ended: "a generic knockoff from Hong Kong, purchasable in thirty-six states," Mike remembered.

"Another thing," Mike adds, "Lab says he may be even bigger; something about pounds-per-square inch, most of the pressure at the ends of his footprints. Like he was wearing shoes a couple sizes too small."

"A big man – or one strong sonofabitch," he says to Haftmann. The soggiest indentations had crusted over and a conservative guess was over six feet and over, maybe way over, 250 pounds. Big enough to grab a 190-pound man by the ankles and attach him to the ceiling of his own living room.

He'd sodomized them both. Rictus of the man's anal passage showed a separate breakdown after normal decomposition. If you could call "normal" a hothouse atmosphere fit for orchids. *And those flies – what a macabre touch*, Haftmann thinks.

Haftmann has time at home with a few cans of beer to help tamp down his revulsion at this Grand Guignol (a Micah term he treasures yet). He sees it with an old cop's eyes: That grotesque rigmarole on the ceiling. Their headless corpses upside down. Her heavy breasts, absurd looking, a trimmed caramel thatch of pubic hair at the apex of her legs. The clotted neck wound profoundly comic and tragic at the same time.

They found her head jammed in the upstairs toilet. One of the techs who fished it out asked a supervisor if he wanted the banana-shaped turd in the bowl too. Home invaders are notorious for taking a dump in the houses they hit – on beds, carpets, dining room tables. On closer inspection it turned out to be her husband's mangled genitals. "Bag it separately, jerkoff, and stop talking," said the supervisor.

The hatbox was the touch that finally did it. One of the techs found the husband's head wrapped in foulard inside a hatbox in one of the closets upstairs. He was called the Jack-in-the-Box Killer in the tabloids from there on out.

Some kind of genie garage-door opener had been used to power the display, and the light switch was to be the trigger. He'd set the castors at right angles so that their bodies would meet in the center of the room.

He'd even allowed for their differences in body weight, and one theory had it that the bluish-gray intestines folded into the corner of the living room was compensation for gravity – the way a homeowner setting drainpipe would allow for a quarter-inch dip.

Jesus Wheezus. Haftmann thought of his grandmother's heartfelt, broken English: *Mein Gott.*

The F.B.I., however, did include him in its distribution list of the psychological profile. (Haftmann ceases to curse out Booth from that moment it arrived in his office fax.) The psychobabble had been dummied down, but it was another example of stating the obvious in polysyllables. The killer was setting up a pattern of obsessive-compulsive behavior (the running faucets). The flies were clearly a signature, his handiwork, but draining off the blood was commonplace and could have a multitude of symbolic values.

He was self-centered and sacrificial. The report also said his thought processes were not criminal in essence but highly personal, irrational, and delusional. Furthermore, he had an incomprehensible psychological and idiosyncratic gain from the spectacle.

It could be a cry for help, a self-dramatization with a therapeutic trait. (Haftmann wants to gag at this part. *Who gives a shit what these sick bastards think about their mommies or whether they weren't potty-trained right? Fuck them.*) Phil told him that when Millimaki read that part, he belly-laughed and said he'd loan the sick bastard his own gun for a permanent cure.)

In perfect F.B.I. humorless, nose-blind-to-irony style, it noted the unsub's M. O. was "amateurish but high risk-taking."

Like most perpetrators of stranger crimes, he would be difficult to catch, the report noted. But then a flourish from the profiler which startled even Haftmann: "A serial killer who is not a narcissist is the most lone of men."

The report also noted that such killers were prone to suicide; if they survived into their forties, and remained free, their inward directed aggression would "exacerbate these intrapunitive tendencies" and relieve society of the task.

The report ended with an audible thud of unintended rhyme: "The unsub is unstable." ("Holy Jesus Christ, are they absolutely sure?" Stel roared out during muster). The good news was that he (no one believed a woman was capable of this) was certain to be conspicuous through some kind of aberrant behavior. He was overtly sexually disturbed and might have infantile regressive symptoms of a confusing the dynamics of sex and excreting ("Ah, the head in the toilet, I presume," pronounced Stel to the other cops, refining his wit.)

Haftmann doesn't buy into the profiling craze, but he accepts the major premises and conclusions. Their man was predictable and organized within his fantasy life, indifferent to immediate success and frequently imitative. At this point, it wasn't entirely possible to rule out what cops jokingly called "the moon bike," or lunar cycle. If he were, in fact, acting on some astrological motivation or allowing that influence him, he seems to have his own timetable.

Millimaki flipped through the rest of the report. Nothing more to be gleaned from the forensics of the tape. Sony's electronics division had stopped manufacture back in the eighties. "F.B.I. pinheads," he said.

Haftmann was home counting his loot.

Haftmann destroyed everything but the cash, and the money had multiplied gloriously – all three came in on New Year's Day. He was out of Oscar's clutches, and he'd paid Micah back her grand. He built a pyre of checks, almost $1,800 worth, and two notes from generous donors who had sent him their prayers.

He felt like a shitheel.

The morning he received in the mail a restraining order from the Jefferson Courthouse, Western District that, to wit, forbade contact with Micah L. née Sondergaard ("formerly Haftmann") by any and all means of communication.

He calls Shawna the dispatcher to have a drink with him. She says no twice.

He calls Phil and "hires" him at a double-sawbuck a week to be his eyes and ears around the station.

Two days after meeting Booth, he learns this: Someone from one of the supermarket tabloids, a major one based in Florida, called the station for Haftmann and wanted to talk to him about the Warren double massacre. Stelmashuk told her he didn't work there anymore.

"Give me his number, Detective," she insisted.

"What's the matter?" Stel fired back; "Your rag get tired of showing Kim Kardashian's ass every week?"

The F.B.I. had used every test and every sophisticated device it possessed, including a fiber optic laser-scanning test. Nothing, nada, zilch-point-shit, according to Phil.

Haftmann's second big lie to Booth, coordinating the F.B.I. and state's investigation, was that he'd found the tape on the dashboard. Chivalry had nothing to do with keeping Shawna out of it: the handwriting with its slanted block lettering on grocery bag paper was lost forever. He'd made a rookie move when he tossed it out of his coat pocket on the way to pick up the mother of the murdered boy.

"The F.B.I. has to keep a low profile," said Booth. He explained to Haftmann, as though the ex-detective were a cretin to whom one had to enunciate each word, that the psycho was undoubtedly Ohio's problem, not the nation's federal police.

"Fuck them," said Millimaki, "Where'd those flies come from?" Millimaki is furious that Haftmann had been given semi-official status at the precinct. He's been suspect number one for the car-keying for weeks anyway. On a lighter note, MacDuff's desk was vacant. Phil called him right away. "He's got drippy dick. Gettin' his wang checked out at the Cleveland Clinic right now."

Haftmann thinks about the stockpile of messages from Dr. Matrooshian to have him call his office right away; he's added those to the burning checks. Haftmann flashes to an image of the little shrink and shivers as if he'd seen a Peruvian green tarantula walking across the desk.

He boxes up Micah's left-behind books and creates an inventory out of guilt. Part of him wants to blame these inanimate objects and their pernicious influence on her for destroying their marriage. The sad truth is that he read portions of all of them when Micah wasn't around and felt that stirring in his chest every autodidact feels who realizes he's discovered some deeply embedded truths about the world and about himself. In they go, like clowns tumbling into a Volkswagen instead of out of it: 1. Albert Camus: *Rebelling Against the Absurd.* 2. Jean-Paul Sartre: *Inventing Meanings in a Meaningless World.* 3. Martin Heidegger: *Confronting Existential Guilt and Death.* 4. Søren Kierkegaard: *Willing One Thing.* 5. Abraham Maslow: *Becoming Self-Actualizing.*

Haftmann works on writing to his last remaining clients until midnight while a black wind rages outside. Phil calls from the station; he's earning his money by reporting on the annual precinct New Year's party. Haftmann envisions it: The same drunken detective who'd been Santa Claus every year since he was there comes reeling out of the muster room with an arm draped around one of the women from the radio room. He's wearing a diaper and a sash ribbon that had Happy New Year emblazoned in sparkle flake numerals. His hairy belly jiggled as they started to negotiate the stairs; both were loop-legged from the office party. Thinking they were out of Phil's sight, she reached a hand into his diaper and gave a squeeze, giggling: "Happy New Year, sugar. Oh, oh, oh. It feels like you got a baby's arm down there!" "Yeah," grunts the detective, "and it's got an apple in its fist just for you, babe."

As if he were standing right there next to Phil, Haftmann can see them stumble up the stairs for some privacy somewhere, and thinks about the F.B.I. profile and wonders what the hell constitutes "conspicuous behavior" nowadays.

~ ~ ~

Lonnie Dale Nelson, at the moment the two station-house lovers found their privacy for an upstairs quickie, was on his hands and knees in the Lion Pose; jaw agape, throat muscles distended, biceps taut, buttocks tight, and chest puffed, he scrutinized himself in the mirror. He liked what he saw.

He'd first seen a male model in a nudist camp brochure that one of the janitors, a fudgepacker named Jimmy Lee Pushic, had smuggled into the boys' dorm in Massillon.

That man's arms were pipe stems compared to the body builders in *Muscle and Fitness*; even so, he remembered how impressed he'd been. Maybe he really was the homo the others had called him – even while they were screwing his asshole.

He thought of the hillbilly from Bluefield, West Virginia, who traded him a shoebox of baseball cards for a mechanical device he had designed in shop. It fit over the thumb and worked with a double-jointed camber to manipulate thumb and index finger.

He told the hillbilly it was for gouging people's eyes out of their heads. He tried it on while humming Nancy Sinatra's "Boots," a song they used to play all night in the boys' dorm whenever general punishment was on order. He kept baseball cards under his bunk and took them out, letting the glossy feel of each one wear through his fingertips, enjoying the smell of bubble gum wafting under his nose and the sound they made whenever he riffled them.

He rolled off his bunk, tossed the cards onto the floor and methodically ripped each clipping into strips. He took a match from the packet tucked inside the Camels on the nightstand of the bunk next to his, and then he lit the pile.

An alcoholic staff psychologist with a vulpine face asked him why. "Baseball is for assholes," answered Lonnie Dale.

Three years later, on his eighteenth birthday, Nelson was released. He hotwired a beat-up Chevrolet pickup in the reformatory parking lot and left Massillon forever.

Generally, when he was responding to sex ads, he avoided that part of the state.

Before he ditched the truck, he'd picked up a hitchhiker – a runaway with dread locks and beads, sixteen or seventeen. She wanted to go to Calumet City, south of Chicago, and said she'd blow him on the way. He said that was fine by him.

He never left the state; the System had been talking to him for several weeks by then and warned him that if he ever left Ohio he'd die with his mouth open screaming in his own blood.

They were buzzing along at 65 mph, about twenty-five miles from the state line when he asked her to do it.

"You fuckin' nuts, man?" She pointed out the open window at trucks, cars with vacationing families packed inside, silver-tubed trailers whizzing past.

"Now or never," he said. After she went down on him and swallowed his jism, wiping a stringy cord of drool and semen afterward on the upholstery, he pulled into the next rest stop before leaving and state and, cradling her neck in the crook of his forearm, he squeezed until her nose and eyes bled.

He had gained two inches and added thirty pounds from the carbohydrate-saturated institution food. He'd been lifting weights frenziedly ever since he saw that nudist camp photo and the guy doing a Charles Atlas pose, his long, thin dick hanging down.

It was the middle of a sunny summer day; no one had seen anything. It was as if time had stopped and he had become invisible. He felt he could do anything. More: he *knew* it.

He wedged her between two Rose-of-Sharon bushes and drove off. He hadn't thought about her in years. It was the first time he knew that he was beyond punishment, beyond the reach of any other human being. He would never be made to suffer again. He would do the hurting. The System would protect him.

He thought about the man and woman from Warren and how far he had come since that day. He continued to pose, humming "Boots," and scrutinizing himself carefully in the mirror.

~ ~ ~

By sheer accident, rifling MacDuff's desk for aspirin, Phil told Haftmann that one of the reports MacDuff had been working on was a Treasury request for information about a postal inspection scam that had been traced to its pick-up point at the Cincinnati Post Office. Over 3,000 police agencies in the country were being alerted and requested to send information about similar M. O.s involving charity organizations to Cleveland headquarters of the Midwest Regional District of the F.B.I. A contact name and number was listed.

He wasn't worried about MacDuff, who would handle this as routine enquiry, write a report, and forget it. It was the two-time loser on Coitsville-Hubbard Road fifty miles away in Youngstown that bothered him. The convict grapevine, every man a potential snitch, was the unofficial source for much of the criminal activity in America. The prissy Artiss could drop him for the cost of a postage stamp, get a "cooperated with authorities" on his jacket in time for his next parole hearing. Forget that he had been a private investigator, as a former detective sergeant, Haftmann would be using his arms for paddles up that famous creek. Cops had a grapevine of their own, and it was explicit about the fates of ex-cops in prison: every bull goose loon on the tier was obligated to humiliate you, even as far as to get other cons to pack up and sodomize you in gang rapes until you had an asshole big enough to turn a car around in, and then, when you thought the worst was over, arrange for an Aryan Brotherhood member to be your next cellie; he'd obligingly follow orders from the shotcaller in his pod and put a shiv into your heart or a garrote around your neck while you slept.

MacDuff's return to the stationhouse was loathsome to Haftmann. He might have to talk to the man and, worse, listen to him talk about three subjects: his clap, the fifty he'd bet on Ohio State in the first National College Bowl playoffs, and whether the Browns were ever going to get a decent QB.

Even Phil, at Tico's Place over a beer, was getting on his nerves. "Who gives a shit what your tiny mind thinks, Phil? You want to help me find this guy or you want to talk Johnny Football and pussy all day? Let me know because I got work to do."

Grabbing his crotch and moaning in fake pain, Phil goes into his MacDuff mode: "Broads, man. You can't live with them, and you can't live with them. Haw, haw."

"Shut up, Phil. One MacDuff is plenty for a lifetime."

Haftmann did accomplish two things: he found out from the Cleveland Museum of Art Director that a world-class soprano had sung a repertoire of Elizabethan lute songs two weeks before the Painesville woman cooked herself, or was cooked, in her own Jacuzzi.

He spoke to the Western Reserve Psychiatric Habilitation Center in Sagamore Hills, and the maximum security Moritz Forensic Center. He gave a friendly-sounding staff psychiatrist his parameters – white male Cauc (the hairs in the drain were male and female – all Caucasian), big, powerful, and though he supposed it were a redundancy, prone to violence, probably needed psychotropic drugs to control his violence, between the ages of twenty and forty, maybe an outpatient. Could have walked away from Massillon State Hospital or been incarcerated at Lima, where the criminally insane are still housed.

"Got anybody like that?"

"Got any number like that" was the response. "But HIPPA regs say I can't say a word to you about them. Besides, the F.B.I. has already been through our records."

Haftmann drove to the facility that evening as the dayshift staff was trickling out to their cars. He scoped a likely prospect, a fat bearded male with glasses, mid-twenties, and followed down Interstate 90 to TGIF's. Haftmann took a seat at the bar, a twenties-something watering hole by the looks of it, and when the time was right, made his way to the fat guy nursing his third Heineken's. The man was clearly a loner and a guy who had as much chance scoring with one of the bevy of attractive college girls bustling back and forth with trays of food as he had of getting a lap dance in a madrasa. Haftmann got the names of six, "crazy as bedbugs," walking the street right now, according to the guy, who was interning there with his bachelor's of science. "Being an intern means you do scutwork for free," he said, obviously not happy with his low-level position. They were all alcohol and drug abusers—meth, especially, being Ohio's particular scourge, heroin a distant second, and opioid abuse gaining ground every year.

"We let a guy out of here last week," he said with a bark, "who fatally beat his sister, crippled his own mother. Pled insanity. Refused to take his medication, kicked over a nurse's cart, beat another outpatient so badly he's in a nursing home in the next county right now."

"It sounds like the kind of work I used to do, only it was lawyers letting them out," Haftmann says, still cajoling and spending freely on the man whose taste in alcohol had shifted to more expensive beverages. "The patients make decisions about what medicine they want to take. Can you believe it?"

He gave the man his card and a fifty, promised him twice that much, if he's send him a list of "potentials" – Haftmann let drop the magic initials F.B.I. in the hope that this would inflate his ego while he was stoking his greed. He doubted Vanderhyden three-hundred-fifty miles away down in Columbus would get wind he was taking an active part in the investigation and snitch him off to Booth.

He ought to pull Vanderhyden's chain right now, he thinks, see whether they were following up the swingers' internet leads. B.C.I. could seize records in a capital felony murder case. With the Attorney General being squeezed by the governor for results, they had *carte blanche* all over the state. *Christ*, it sounded so tame after the fact, but he could still hear the quaver in the Warren cop's voice, see the blood spatter, the steaming viscera. It's rare to walk in on a crime scene that cops call a full-tilt boogie and not be affected permanently.

The obscenity of murder was that you made someone participate in the act of his or her own death. There was nothing, he felt, worse than contaminating your life with murder's corrosive stain; like having the HIV virus in your bloodstream.

Take down the psycho; get an eleven-year-old girl back to her parents – or find the place where Lonnie Dale Nelson left her to rot. Some peace there, finally, in knowing. Haftmann almost wept when the girl's father reluctantly admitted he and his wife were separating. "Why?" Haftmann begged to know, fearing that his failure to return their daughter was the true reason.

"Irreconcilable differences," said the husband lamely but his were hollowed out by grief.

He sent me voices on a cassette. 'Guilty of dust and sin.'

I'll get you first, crazy fuck.

"Blood on the moon," Frank used to say, after some dark malevolence of the night in Cleveland, of the world, of things seen only in dreams.

Haftmann's own search of dating and adultery sites— never mind the sheer volume of porn, which even a frenzied masturbating teen boy could never exhaust with Olympic swimming pools of jack juice, his cynical aplomb made him conclude that half of Ohio was apparently boning the other half, and both halves pretended that none of it was happening. He wasn't naïve enough to believe that all those emails to men scouting porn on the Internet ended with anything other than a pitch for money. *There have to be dicks at the other end of the terminal,* Haftmann thinks. What a world: black-hat hackers, Russians stealing identities and personal information, and radical Muslims creating acolytes by the hundreds, if not thousands, with appeals to mass murder.

Something for everyone: gays, bi's, fetishes for body parts – toes, nipples, whatever floats your boat – mostly, but not exclusively female, groups, orgies, fantasies involving women looking like little girls, pregnant women with teats squirting milk, cocks squirting quarts of come, fat women, black women, slender Japanese women inserting their entire arms to the elbows in each other's anuses and vaginas. Twisting their closed fists inside so that the belly-button ring jiggled with the motion – an embarrassment of steamy riches, if you like that kind of variety.

The Doc Johnson marital aids site was a hoot – if you could call a double-donged latex penis with roostertail head, a marital aid, instead of the whole show.

Haftmann took an excursion into BDSM; the guy wasn't into ordinary sex, he figures. He found plenty of sites featuring dungeons and domes holding whips. One thumbnail of a man with an S-shaped cock wore a black mask and held an angry-looking whip. His swollen testicles were bound by a leather thong. His specialty, he professed, were couples and women with an interest in B & D and light S & M: "No fatties, white only, light smoke and drink OK."

There was a dark net below that where he found it hard to believe what people posted or enjoyed viewing. Those who trolled those depths were kith and kin to no one he could recognize. He slammed the lid of his laptop shut when he came to website specializing in photos of gore and atrocities around the world like videos of a dozen Iranian men being hanged in public, crucifixions in Syria by ISOL fanatics, a 16-year-old Filipina gang raped, dead in the weeds, curled into a fetal position, her black hair matted to her face, and the rock used to kill her by men from her own village lying next to her face. Brain matter was coming through her nostrils. The site's featured photo of the week was a sample of what lay within: a nude, hogtied Chinese woman with a pole inserted through her anus and extending out of her gaping mouth. Her eyes bulged and her large breasts hung down. Haftmann stared, doubting it was real, hoping nothing like that existed for anyone with fingertips and a key-search term to discover. Computer graphics made this, but it's more a hope and a belief. *You can't unsee this stuff*, he knows. Only cops used to have to carry this awful burden; now anyone can partake of the rotten feast of human depravity.

Haftmann thinks of the Jacuzzi schoolteacher: *harmless fetish*? Or was she a genuine kink treading the cliff's edge with one foot dangling over the brink? Those Sea World trainers all think they're in control but an image of a killer whale came to mind: alone, isolated in a dark, cramped tank, made to perform by punishment, frustrated, denied food if the trick isn't done right, raked by the more agile female's teeth. Wouldn't that make an intelligent mammal crazed? What about a man in similar circumstances—alone, isolated, tormented by bullies? Haftmann didn't buy modern theories of an "evil gene" because it was obvious we make our own. In Copenhagen, Micah told him, you can leave a baby in a stroller while you go inside to shop. "Don't try that here," Haftmann told her, but the very mention of the word "baby" to her was enough to douse the joke with ice water.

He bought a yellow highlighter at the drug store next to the Dairy Mart across the street and went to work. First, he didn't exclude the possibility that the killer was too stupid, too careless, or – contrary to the Quantico profile – too ego-damaged to place his own ad soliciting couples.

He didn't ignore those Craigslist ads from single males with a bisexual bent, but he concentrated on the single-male-seeking-couples theme. He discounted those with photos where the man was physically small (it was true: you didn't know who had a big one), or past the age limits theorized. Murder was like the majority of sports – a younger man's game.

He had doubts about excluding obvious solicitations from women who were prostitutes, or close enough to it, housewives with their live cams, so eager to take a credit card from any man out there. Some would pay exorbitant prices for used panties no doubt worn by hucksters and con artists like the little fraud in Youngstown. He made contact with one dome, a YSU student majoring in

Elizabethan history, who knew how to get men to pay up. She told him about humiliating one client by forcing him to insert his small penis into his own wedding ring.

Jesus, there were a lot of them out there.

Too much for one investigator, he hoped Booth used all his F.B.I. juice to put a team of record sifters on the porn work detail. Someone out there liked music and at least once had tortured a couple to the sounds of a soprano singing love songs accompanied by Elizabethan lutes.

He'd knew he'd have to trade his Big Clue about the Painesville woman's father, the floater under the ice of Lake Erie somewhere, who would have known his wife subscribed to websites she wouldn't want her colleagues to know about.

He also knew that Mondine, the Painesville homicide lieutenant, had soft-pedaled her risky lifestyle to the lackey from Columbus Booth would have sent by now to liaise the double murders – if only out of deference to the stepdaughter's husband, a local big-shot contractor.

When found, with or without the coercion of the feds, would any of these people be willing to talk about something as private as their sex lives, especially when it was being linked in the Cleveland papers with the infamous 1935 Cleveland butcher who was never found and who had brought Eliot Ness's career as public safety director crashing down around his ears? *Not likely*, he thinks. Sport fucking was a middle-class activity everywhere, and middle-class respectability was sacrosanct. The respectable newspapers were starting to pick up the Jack-in-the-Box Killer motif even though the crudity of the name bothered them. (Over drinks at Tico's, Phil reminded him the news media managed to get over their qualms about the girl band "Pussy Riot" in Russia.)

Why had he gone so berserk in Warren? Haftmann wonders for the hundredth time. The blood man told him there was enough in that house to make little Charley Manson weep. Forensics said he'd walked the distance of a mile or so in the house during that night of frenzy. A cop with twenty years on the Warren PD had burst into tears like a baby. That rookie cop would awaken in a cold sweat more than once before he was through, and he'd always be sure why.

So why the missing fury in the Jacuzzi killing? A few ligature marks; she passed out and died by going to sleep. The water seared her lungs but she did drown. Harris may be the most cautious and politic M. E. he'd ever known, but he was too competent to louse up a bathtub drowning.

Did the psycho killer place ads or respond to ads, like the Painesville woman's from her early days of soliciting through swingers' magazines? Or was there some kind of sado-masochistic trigger in the websites themselves he solicited? Something is missing; something held off his maniacal fury. All genuine psychos had a trigger. Could the ingredient still be in that house as well as in his fucked-up head?

Phil jars him out of his reverie with something about new ammo coming in from Columbus.

"Hollow points with liquid aluminum canisters," Phil says, his eyes are bright even in the dimly lit bar. "Devastators, man. Blow you to pieces but they won't penetrate these flimsy walls." Phil taps the near wall for emphasis.

"You Lake cops lost your minds?" Haftmann grunts. "Do you actually think any of you will get a chance to take a pot shot at this guy? That has as much chance as a Hezbollah ten points of negotiation memo to Tel Aviv."

"You never know," Phil says with a wink.

"I've seen you at the range, Phil," Haftmann counters. "You couldn't hit him if he was sitting at the other end of the bar drooling in his beer."

~ ~ ~

"Got any Stones—like, early Stones, I mean, not that later country shit?"

The man's heavy-lidded eyes box Nelson's filthy room as he looks up from his rooting among Nelson's CD collection, mostly illegal downloads on which he had scribbled names or type of music.

"Lookee here, dude," the bouncer said. "You got a 'j' in 'religious,' and fuckin' 'metal' ain't got no *d* in it." He said "metal" again for emphasis, clicking the dental *t* off his palate. "Where the fuck'd you go to school, man? You sure as shit didn't win no fucking spelling bees."

Lonnie Dale Nelson had been cultivating this subhuman waste of skin for a week now; it was his last step in preparation for the move. "Here and there," he said agreeably.

The guest who was pouring down one of the Budweisers he had pilfered from the club at 3:00 in the morning was part-time bike trash and part-time regular trash. He did a little dealing on the side or made loans to the customers of his derelict bar. He'd even tried to pimp out some of the girls who showed up at the place but none were interested. The bouncer envisioned himself as a man of many talents.

He continued to comment on the infelicities of spelling he happened to catch on the labels; apparently, Nelson's block lettering was a source of great amusement in the pre-dawn, unsober hours before morning light restored the world to equilibrium.

He read: 'Mass in F-Minor by Cambridge Tabernacle Choir,' enunciating each syllable. "Hey, man, you got two tapes of the same thing." Nelson informed him that the other was the same Roman Catholic Mass, from "Kyrie" to "Agnus Dei,' but this one was the Elektric Prunes, a group his guest had never heard of. Nelson's phonetic spelling got it right by chance.

"They, like, heavy metal, or what, man?"

Lonnie Dale let the man talk, talk himself out; plenty of time. They shared a joint, Ohio homegrown weed: Meigs County Gold. "Good shit, man," the douchebag said.

Douchebag liked to comment on everything, a know-it-all. An expert on everything despite the fact he was poorer than a shithouse mouse, had nothing to brag about. Nelson's house was so far off the beaten path you never knew it was there, Douchebag said as if that were some kind of statement to write down. His backyard overlooking the dirty Ohio River.

"I betcha you can see tugboats and barges and shit from back here, right?"

The dirt and filth of Nelson's rooms, the piles of clothing, the crap pile out in the yard didn't faze Douchebag whose body gave off a stench like leather. "Nice fucking stereo, though. Bose, eh?"

The smell, however, could not be ignored for long and Nelson worried about that so kept the brews flowing.

The drone of insects from beneath the floorboards was loud. "What the fuck is that buzzing noise, man? Something's fucked up in your cellar. Sounds like the blower fan to your furnace. Want me to check it out?"

If you do, Nelson thought without any emotion, *it'll be the very last thing you do.*

"So we gonna do a deal on 'roids, man?" Douchebag said, forgetting his own offer of a moment ago.

That was the bait. One look at Lon Nelson, and there was no doubt in his mind the big dude was into some serious steroids. The man was just too fuckin' big. "C'mon, man, yes or no? We on, like, because I got shit to do today." He drinks, burps, wipes his mouth. He looked, to Nelson, like a dog licking itself.

Nelson knew the fat bouncer had nothing whatsoever to do but pass out and wake up in time for his next work shift at that redneck, cement-block dump of a bar.

"I gotta tell you, man, as a personal friend. Your deodorant? It ain't makin' it, Jack, no offense."

Nelson stifled another yawn, content to listen to general drift of his prattle until the last possible moment. He might say something worth paying attention; his private douchebag was about to play a very important role in the plan.

Time to head north, he realizes as the first light of pale light cracks the dirty back porch windows.

"I gotta go a little higher than I told you at the club, man, 'cause, see, the heat is on, you know? They don't call me the candy man of East Fuckin' Palestine for nothin', yo?"

They'll call you something else very soon, Nelson thought. He felt it was time.

Douchebag had been chosen by the System. "Here," said Nelson, extending to him the golden filigree cross.

"Fuckin'-A, man. I seen you wearing this around the club. But if we ain't talking cash on the barrelhead, I'm outa here, Jack. Do I look like a fuckin' pawn shop?"

Nelson smiled at him. Gave him the best imitation of the Rutger Hauer smirk he'd seen on his DVDs. Reaching for him, like a great cat, he had him around the neck. He tried to scream, his brain trying to fathom this sudden violence but he merely burbled and drool rolled from his lower lip.

Long minutes passed. It takes several minutes, according to his forensics show, to manually strangle someone to death. The man's bulging face was turning dark with blood, he'd urinated his Levi's, and his legs were still kicking, the boots *thud-thudding* on the floorboards harmlessly. Then Nelson relaxed his powerful arms. The bouncer rolled from him in slo-mo but his left leg spasmed and Nelson reached down to make sure with one last levering motion of his neck caught in the vice of his forearm. A last spasm in the leg. Anger throttled up in Nelson and for a moment he was in danger of going berserk on the bouncer's body—really tearing him up but that would be an unforgivable mistake, and he knew the angel would visit him in wrath if he failed in his mission. He let the bouncer's head smack the floor. All was stillness. The body stared up with that disinterested stare all dead people have.

Sometimes, when he was good, the System allowed him little gifts like the pair of hundred-dollar bills folded in the bouncer's right boot. About three sizes larger, but it shouldn't matter if the next phase proceeded as planned through the frozen January days ahead.

He was sorry about losing the music and the weights he had engineered so carefully. The System was adamant: nothing would go that could indicate a precipitated move.

He felt serene, quiescent. He took out his flaccid penis and let it stiffen outside his pants. Popped a Buddy Holly into his cassette player, and lay back on his ratty couch. The angel could make him come twice in succession without his having to minister with his hand. He was coming now; he shot it in gobs onto the dead man's bluish face. By the time he'd found 11 North, he heard the first sirens, but the conflagration would have been complete; long before he'd doused the trash in the room thoroughly, drenched the body in kerosene.

They'd find a crispy, charbroiled and blackened body in the fighter's pose of burn victims, this one with a gold necklace singed to whatever was left of its chest. His forensics show taught him that the chemical contents of the human body, a corpse's raw resources, are worth about a dollar. But it takes several thousand degrees of heat over several hours to disintegrate a body, so he had no fear that the bouncer would disappear into ash. No dental records to prove that the blackened pile of smoldering garbage wasn't once the man who rented the place under an alias. If the cops ever get close, the angel assured him, this will end their search for Lonnie Dale Nelson.

~ ~ ~

Haftmann was sitting alone in his living room on his faded couch during an hour of the night that mystics call the Dark Night of the Soul.

He was thinking about a song his mother had taken away with her from the rubble of Berlin, a G.I.'s bride nine years older than her gullible husband, had him convinced that a baby was swelling her stomach:

Es geht alles vorüber,
Es geht alles vorbei.

Looking at the wind howling outside the windows, he was not convinced that May would even come. January had locked Ohio, north and south, into its grip, and it was, as every clown on the street loved to remind him, *colder than a witch's teat. . .*

He was gazing at a teat now. A firm pair of them, silicone-enhanced from the gravity-defying angle of the pose. She had sent a photo along with her ad to complement the words, perhaps confirm the unabashed list of enticements she described.

There were three separate photos, a triangular collage of her flesh, as though some layout Artist had decided how to present herself. This is what Haftmann read:

FRENZIED. WF-97556. Turned 40, crazy for cock and first bi experience. Fantasy of thick young males, 18-40, or two males, one to fuck while I jack or suck the other one off, makes me cum. I'm 5'5, 126 lbs., pretty, tanned, lotioned, perfumed, wet, creamy, aching clit and pussy. Have very talented tongue, firm breasts with pink nipples, firm ass, tight hairy pussy with asshole trimmed with hair (when not shaved). Ultrasensitive clit, lacquered nails for tricky hands, long legs, beautiful feet with lacquered toes. Love to lick and suck full balls, work my way up the shaft to the head of your cock, tease and suck till it explodes. Just love the feel, taste, and smell of hot cum. When I climax, my clit comes out of its hood. Very wide and 1" long and erect. Lacquered toes point down, palms, arches and pussy drenched with wetness, leg and pussy muscles snap and tighten to suck the best cock dry. For my first bi experience, a female with desire and physicals mentioned would be nice. Have male friend who would like to watch and/or participate, but not necessary. After all, I'm 40 and truly frenzied. Full photos with phone for reply. Pleasure only! NORTHERN OH

In two of the photos she was arched on the balls of her feet, arms extended to catch a beach ball or hide her face from the camera. There was a circle of white erasing her face from view in these two; no doubt added at her request. Haftmann guessed this was done as a courtesy to advertisers at their request, but it reminded him of the excelsior wrapped around the faces of gunshot victims as they lay in their open coffins.

The third photo was all ass, a close-up with a bird's-eye view of the camera lens pointed right at her puckered anus (it was fringed with light hair). Designed to be more bluntly erotic than the other two, Haftmann felt it caricatured a woman in the abandonment of lust. He looked at her hand with its delicate fingers separating the folds of labia to expose the much-touted clitoris, the boy in the boat. His thoughts were dark; she looked dismembered.

He had waited all day to do this, and now there was no more reason to procrastinate. He had the same fear that gripped him when the little doctor in Cleveland had talked about insanity the way Millimaki discussed his hemorrhoids.

At what hour of the morning was courage most completely drained? He felt the room begin to slide around him, resettle itself in the darkness.

Must do it now.

He opened the envelope Shelia had given him on his way out of the station after the fracas that afternoon. Her eyes weren't smiling. She called his house an hour later to say she found it stuck to the Cherokee's left wiper blade. She made a quip about the irregularity of postal service on the Lake, but neither of them laughed.

Had he opened it? "Not yet," he said to her disembodied voice on the answering machine; the LED light winked at him in the darkened room like a code in semaphore.

He didn't get far into the first stanza before the room spun:

Hav you gott eyez of blu?
Hav you gott eyez of blu?
Oh, Christ. You.

Chapter 6

Spring

Spring in Ohio is the season for suicides. Not winter with its depressing, suppurating gray skies that last until late April in the northern part of the state – or autumn with its melancholy and relentless advance into winter.

Native Ohioans, especially those transplanted from the New Englanders who settled the Western Reserve, have an older memory of spring; a kind of ancestral wading pool by contrast to a Jungian swimming pool from which, they say, we take our characteristics and most ancient memories. Presumably these sit somewhere between our lizard brain with its *eat, procreate, die* motto and the recently-acquired veneer of sophistication that allows us to choose money market options and gear down a Porsche. There were springs in which the first Ohio settlers would come out of their sod and timber shacks, blinking at the frail sun, emaciated by the long winter's diet of cracked corn, twenty pounds lighter, on frames already exhausted from bone-breaking labor, lousy with vermin. Yet you renew yourself with nature as the days grow longer and your diet improves. Spring: Life.

If you found yourself out of sync with nature, unable to renew, there were the many alternatives to choose from, according to Haftmann's book-crazed ex, such as "shuffle off the mortal coil" or "pop your clogs," to pawn your clogs, in other words, or, simply enough, as the very last thing a person would do: to die.

Christ knows old Doc Harris had seen them all by now. His position as coroner and his proximity to Sodom-on-the-Lake (his sole unappreciated witticism) gave him every opportunity to study the manners and means whereby Ohioans took themselves, and on occasion others not so near or dear to them, into that no-man's land we call that black curtain of oblivion, the afterlife.

Haftmann had gone to high school with fellow cop Nick Mantooth's brother, a jock who gave up rock music and fag-bashing to become a mortician. On the day Mrs. Wulffson's father bobbed to the surface, he and Haftmann were having an *auld-lang-syne* session at Tico's Place on the Strip.

"Tommy," he said, "It ain't the ones who lie there who give us the most trouble. It's the ones that walk around."

Haftmann agreed; he'd learned that as a rookie in Cleveland.

"Maybe the old guy really loved her," Nicky mused, "and couldn't stand the idea of other guys walking around in her womb."

Haftmann despised himself for still feeling that way about Micah, in fact. His eyes burned with shame at remembered jealousy. Haftmann muttered into his draft. "It's too bad for the daughter he didn't wait for spring. The marine patrol says the cutter from Ashtabula can't get to him where he is, but you can see him with good field glasses. Just a speck, but he's socked in there, a little pocket, where it's tricky to get to."

"Just need a couple more days of sun," Mantooth said. "Then I get him because he's on my turf. He'll be a gas balloon when he comes up after being under that long."

Haftmann finds a cryptic message from Phil when he returns to his office the next day to try to hang on to the three paying clients he has left. He dials the number from Phil and gets the Youngstown State Penitentiary, Food Services. The little con Artist has made trustee. Easier to puke on someone if you're a warden's man. *Artiss, you miserable rat.*

Not good, thinks Haftmann, *he knows.*

The investigation into the Warren double homicide has lost some of its frenetic energy, but the papers found a new tack to keep it on the back pages by insinuating police incompetence. As if the psycho were wandering the streets in daylight with a bloody ax in his back pocket. Even the liberal Cleveland *Plain Dealer* had found grist for its mill in attacking the cops' inability to track down the killer. They dredge up an article from the 1990's about dead crack whores found in vacant lots scattered around Cleveland's east side. The "strawberry girls" murders, around 20 of them, were never solved. His own county was used as a dumping ground for four of them. But it was nothing like the exasperated editorials pouring out of Warren into their daily when the modest house in a good neighborhood sat on its foundation and said to all passersby: "I was a charnel house for a sadistic sex killer. What are you doing about it?"

Haftmann has failed to get either Vanderhyden in Columbus or Booth, heading his task force in Cleveland, to warm to his charm. They feed him tidbits only after repeated calls to their office staff. He was told the F.B.I.'s own forensics team was flying in to take the Painesville house apart, board by board.

He, however, has a theory about the killer that no one's buying. He does them in pairs, first with banners and bells on, evidence the macabre élan of the Warren abattoir; then a second time with subtlety, the organized fantasy dictating how it should be done.

Behavioral Sciences said in its profile to expect trophies from the kills but nobody yet has a handle on the out-of-control rage. "It's in his dreams," Haftmann emails Booth. But thinks: *How do you deconstruct a dream from the dreamer?*

He taps a source in Columbus and winds up with a thumb drive FedExed to him with fifty-two pages of single-spaced printout: all stranger crimes; all had occurred in Ohio during the past five years. Haftmann studies each one, a monk in his cell at night, follows up the interesting ones with a phone call, often to the neglect of his dwindling clientele and to Millimaki's wrath when he hears scuttlebutt around town concerning Haftmann's doings. He has no idea what muscle the F.B.I. is using on Millimaki, but Booth has him muzzled pretty well.

He concentrates on the women. He divides them by the killer's own pendulum swings: the ones with lots of blood spatter and the others with – *what was it?* – Micah's favorite smartass expression: *Je ne se quoi? Savoir faire?* It annoys Haftmann that you had to talk like a diplomat to get anything out of administrators like McDougal. Even Doc Harris told Haftmann to cease his pestering: "Don't you private eyes have a few chores to look into?"

You prick, Haftmann thinks. *You were inside the house. Maybe you saw something the untrained eyes of the paramedics had missed.* Harris admits to liking one part of Haftmann's theory. "Yes, the drowned woman conceivably could have been the downside of his organized madness."

Haftmann believes her killing was somehow crucial; she was the breaking point, he tells him while the pathologist fidgets in front of a mirror in his lab with his polka-dotted bow tie, trying to get it situated right with his prominent Adam's apple.

"I don't think he was killing them until her," he tells Doc. "He wanted something they were willing to give. Sex, money, whatever. Now he's killing everything in his path, spinning out of control."

"So why contact you, Haftmann?" Harris asks reasonably. "You're a nobody."

Haftmann ignores the jibe. "I don't know why, Doc."

"That would trouble me," he snorts and gives himself a last admiring glance.

"Doc, you have no idea how it troubles me too." *Especially at night in my dreams.*

Either way, the psycho-killer was flipping them all off: *Catch me if you can, but I'm smarter than all of you.*

Thousands of clues have been exhausted through the skin mags, porn stores selling DVDs, and anywhere the killer might have gone. Nobody had anything to tell. Or knew something but wouldn't tell, which came to the same thing.

He makes a short list of the stranger crimes that look good and convinces the liaison flunkey to send these to VICAP for analysis. So far zippo.

The infestation of drugs into big and small cities alike was proving to be another glitch for the F.B.I.'s computer. It didn't know how to handle the rash of prostitute murders, for instance, as more and more young women gave in to their addictions and went into bars or hung out on dangerous street corners to sell themselves.no way to teach it. There were, Haftmann easily reckoned, nineteen to twenty-two murders of young women, mostly black, between the ages of fifteen and thirty-five in Cleveland alone during the last calendar year. They were all found dead on their backs with their skirts up around their waists or their pants pulled down to their ankles. They'd all had sex recently and traces of cocaine were found in all but one of their systems. The majority were involved with drugs, single mothers from the projects, or hangers-on of the drug underworld.

It was first speculated that a serial killer was on the loose, although the city's PR team kept a lid on it. Then a bizarre theory emerged that the cocaine and sex had proved fatal; "coronary occlusions induced by orgasm," even though these young women were mostly trading sex for drugs or money at the same time. Why else would they be found in these dangerous rat holes all over Cleveland's underbelly?

It had first happened in Miami, America's other drug capital after Washington D. C., and it was by now a routine phenomenon in major cities. Frank said to him on patrol that if Jesus Christ were to come back to earth and visit Cleveland he wouldn't be able to stop vomiting on his sandals. Cruising Hough, he'd point to clusters of young men in vacant lots standing on street corners. "Look at their shitty lives," he'd say. "We scrape the shit off society's shoes, but it's like trying to hold back Niagara Falls with your hands."

Haftmann discovers a Micah book he'd missed in his original inventory. He takes it with him into the crapper. She always used bobby pins or anything handy as bookmarkers. He finds one sentence double underlined by a blue highlighter from Jung's *Memories, Dreams, Reflections*: "I exist on the foundation of something I do not know."

"I know just how you feel, pal," Haftmann says and slams the book shut.

~ ~ ~

When the juncos went back to Canada in early spring, dreams of Ante Ente came to Lonnie Dale Nelson at night.

Ente (he spelled it phonetically, as with everything) was the only person he had ever loved. He was a wolf, a Finnish white-blond timber wolf. He had terrorized every boy at the Massillon State Reformatory. Even the staff feared him, gave him a wide berth. If he wanted to leave the dorm in his underclothes, scowling, helping himself to the food in the kitchen while the food service workers were filling trays, he did it and defied anyone to do anything about it.

They said he was crazy. He used to drop from tree branches onto passing cars for fun.

They said he killed someone when he was fourteen. They said he could never go to prison for it.

He ruled the dorm even though he was three years younger than the oldest males; he perfected his own legend, and he even had a boxing tactic the other boys imitated and called the "Ente Dive," where you came up swinging a roundhouse right to your opponent's jaw.

After his last fight, no one bothered him again. He had the last of his contenders in a headlock and was squeezing the sobbing boy into submission. While he talked to the other boys surrounding the fight like a dog pack, insulting his victim with obscenities, he'd spit on his body. The boy's shirt had been ripped to shreds and hung from his waist in tatters, and there were white gobs of saliva on his skin. Ente would add a hawker, interrupting his own monologue, and the boys would *ooh* and *ahh* like a willing chorus of slaves.

Before Ente's arrival, he collected money and sexual favors like a medieval baron asserting his rights of first fruits on a peasant's bride. He had not been back from the hospital long; he was still feverish at night and they made him wear a woman's sanitary pad to keep the blood from staining his bed sheets.

Nelson kept a jagged piece of glass under his pillow in case the bully decided to visit him. He knew from his two tormentors and the smaller one that trailed him like a pilot fish that he was part of the inheritance of ward punks.

Last night they'd held heated buttons under their cigarette lighters' flames and branded the boy whose bunk was next to his. He knew the boy was sucking them off from the gagging sounds he made. He was nauseated with fear and he held the glass so tightly that his hand bled and blood oozed between his fingers. It left a livid scar that arced across the lump of callous along his left palm.

He intended to cut his own throat if they approached his bunk.

Ente saved him from that.

Just the image of the saliva glinting on the boy's skin was sufficient to bring him off. At night in the bunk he could see Orion's Belt through the grilled mesh window and he thought of Ente and his cock grew stiff, doubling in size until it felt like the business end of a baseball bat. His most erotic thought was spitting into the blond boy's mouth while he came.

"D'joo see the size of the guy who just left?"

"Jesus H. Christ," the manager replied; "where the hell did he come from? Bought a couple DVDs and pays me with bills he must have been walking around with in his socks."

They noted the peculiar smell he gave off, not the chicken-soup smell of body odor, either. Another smell on top of that, rubbery like skunk. He hadn't smelled that kind of acidic pungency since he quit his summer job as a nurse's aide at the looney bin. One of the shrinks said it was the smell of schizophrenia.

"Guy didn't look too good either," the assistant manager said, "Really green around the gills."

"This place used to be family-oriented," the assistant store manager said. "Now look at it. Weirdos, freaks, bikers that wear sheephead they pick up on the shore around their necks to scare the citizens. Come to think of it, that's what he smelled of. Rotten fish."

Nelson knew he shouldn't have gone in there, the one big grocery store in town with its middle-class townspeople. He felt naked under the fluorescent lighting. But he was desperate to lift again; he had to get the rock-hard feeling in his biceps, chest, thighs again. He was starving. His stomach spasmed on the greasy food from last night.

Withdrawal, he knew; the toxins were flooding his system; he was literally poisoned because of his great size – losing weight too abruptly made his filtration system collapse.

He drove to the nearest Gold's Gym franchise at a shopping mall ten miles away and hoped he could flush it out of his body before he got too weak. The air was sweet with the styrene smell of plastic from one of the local polluting factories; he almost flashbacked to the slaughterhouse, almost lost it right there in the parking lot.

He went in. No one tending the front, so he hit the bell on the counter.

A diminutive blonde with square shoulders in blue spandex got the call; she would escort him throughout his visit and answer questions he may have. She fisheyed him once or twice, cutting her eyes to his girth; she asked him did he know there was a special introductory offer this month. . .

He found what he wanted. He was too cramped and shivery to use the bench press, so he backed himself into a kind of machine for developing the triceps and shoulders. She kept talking but he wasn't listening, just aching to get it on.

She set it high and he went to work – crisp, smooth over the shoulder punches like a boxer's right cross – left, then right, faster.

He looked around and saw the normal assemblage of bored housewives and puny businessmen you'd get on a Tuesday afternoon. He got into his rhythm, canceled everything else out, broke a sweat.

Too quiet. He focused his eyes and saw everyone in the place looking at him. The blonde was looking at the cotter pins in the struts that braced the machine to the wall. He had loosened them. She was looking at him hard now. His chest had filled up the slack in his muscle shirt like a self-inflating tire. She didn't say anything.

Stupid, stupid of me . . . The System told him time and time again to think of ways he could be trapped, *never stop thinking of what could go wrong.* The angel sidled near him; he felt the presence breathing in his ear and Nelson's eyelids burned with salt. He heard the delicate words nuzzling his ears like a lover's kiss: *They'll strap you onto a steel table, put a plug in your ass, then they'll put a burning chemical mix into your veins. You'll take hours to die. You'll go away forever* . . .

No! Nelson wanted to scream. *I'll be good from now on! You'll see! No more mistakes!*

Just to make sure he got the message, the angel reaches into his jock and grips his testicles and twists them. He smiled through the searing pain at the blonde staring down at him.

~ ~ ~

Phil could be prickly at work, even arrogant; get him out for a brew and he was the world's friendliest guy – a good drunk. He had his work face on now, so Haftmann has to tread lightly. Lately, Phil's been making jokes about being Haftmann's manservant, his fuckboy—not good because Phil is his best source in the manhunt.

"Goddammit, Tom, you can't convict on the circumstantiality of handwriting alone. This is block letter, not italic, certainly not Spenserian, and any way you want to take it, this is not science. It's educated guesswork. Understand?"

Fuck it.

"Look. He may have dyslexia or something. You see the way he makes the *e*'s look the same, as if he can't help it, but he changes the pattern of the other letters significantly. No way you can get him on this alone. You better find him with a machete dripping blood – "

"Phil, he's going to keep doing it. You know sociopaths have to kill, like to. The shrinks make too much out of them. Maybe they like the way blood looks when they're throwing it around."

"Thomas, I don't know shit from Shinola about psychology. I'm just a cop."

Haftmann was already in the door, gathering a full head of steam for his confrontation with Millimaki. He had to get into the investigation. And get someone in authority to begin to look seriously at Lonnie Dale Nelson. Plaster his face across a million TV sets, feature him on crime shows . . .

"Haftmann, listen, for once in your life. You were a good cop. Everybody but Millimaki knows that. But you ain't got a shred of evidence to connect him with this cassette."

"He found me! He picked me! You know these psychos well enough to know they need trophies, they brag . . ."

"Why you, Haftmann, why you?"

"Because I busted him."

"You collared boneheads worse than him every week back in Cleveland. You told me you never tangled assholes with him. He just sat in the back of the cruiser – "

"I know it's him, Phil. Help me. Help me connect him. Everybody's treating me like I'm a leper."

Jesus, years ago they sent cops to talk to school kids in the D.A.R.E. program about "Just Say No." The last dealer he'd busted on the Lake had a fist-sized wad of fifties and twenties in his jeans and a Just-Say-No button sticking waggishly from his belt. The asshole country was drowning in prescription drugs, illegal drugs, and meth labs. *Fuckola*.

Haftmann recalls his last conversation with the Lake's chief: "Millimaki, you fucking bonehead." It had come to tangling assholes too soon; the biggest case the state had ever seen and his career was in the hands of this spineless numbnuts.

"You've got orders from Agent Booth to let me in on what's going on."

Millimaki's face reddens as he points a Swisher Sweet inches from Haftmann's nose: "Fuck the F.B.I. and fuck you. Go home. Go back to your peeping-tom business. Go home."

MacDuff gave him that sideways look and a thumbs-up as he came out of Millimaki's office. "That Finn slob is one dumb sonofabitch," he said as Haftmann passed.

"I heard he was twice the cop you are, MacDuff."

MacDuff lisps his gay imitation: "Ooo, Mister Coffee Nerves!"

Haftmann's living room is filled with paperwork from the investigation, books he's ordered on criminal psychology, forensics, pathology, and even the occult; they're scattered and left lying where they've fallen out of his hands. One moment he's awake and the next he's asleep. He has the night habits and nervous tics of the insomniac. He sleeps an hour before dawn and when he's near exhaustion, he calms his nerves and stills the tremors in his hand with a tumbler of Jack Daniels with a beer back.

He has three letters in his mailbox: one from the cryptanalysis division of the C.I.A.; another from the American Cryptographers Society, and a third from a Kent State University professor of physics who was a code-breaking expert used by the National Security Agency.

Two zeroes . . . Then bingo. *God Almighty . . .*

The professor's letter said he wasn't using cypher in any obviously detectable way, but it was not what it purported to be: an old-time lyric; in fact, he'd sung it himself when he was a kid. Sung to the tune of "The Farmer in the Dell." The professor said it is more like chess if you take the middle of the board and transpose the alphabet to it in rows of six across and four down. "A child could memorize it easily if he had to," he wrote.

The numbers matched up to a chessboard. But you have to account for his phonetic spelling to see what he's doing. "Those labored *e*'s of his, for instance, aren't consistent. Note that he puts the superscripts to the left of the number when he means up and to the right for down." Then, the stunner: it's a tapping code used by prisoners in isolation during WWII. It was brought back from the eastern front by Germans in Russian prisons. British SIS knew of it; no doubt, it's still being taught to CIA trainees at Langley. But it's antiquated, obsolete . . ."

Haftmann cuts his eyes to the end of the letter:

". . . arranged in three sequential blocks of numerals, it spells HAFMANIMHEER."

"I trust this will mean something to you. Best of luck."

Chess? German prisoner of war? Isolation? What the unholy fuck was this?

HAFTMANN, I'M HERE.

Jesus upon the Jesus Christ.

Those broken-arrow *e*'s of his: . . . "as if he couldn't help himself" . . . *sweet barbecued Jesus, there's more than handwriting he can't help himself with.*

Micah called him a monster that time he raised his hand, but it was her throat he was thinking of in that nanosecond of purest rage: *choke the bitch.* End it. She *knew.* She touched her throat instinctively. *Was his mind collapsing now*? The more he read about aberrant psychology, the more he was convinced that his every random thought was schizophrenia blossoming, putting its insidious roots deeper into his psyche. *In all idealization,* Freud wrote, *there is aggression.*

Another thought: himself as spectacle, drooling in a corner, locked away in one of those facilities like the Sagamore Hills place.

"I'll eat my gun first," he says defiantly to the empty room.

He suddenly wants sex. Death, the aphrodisiac at work in his cabeza. Just get outside his own skin for a while – *Shawna.*

Instead he called the Clit Woman.

Used his oiliest voice on her, the one he used to cajole kiddie rapers into confessions in countless interrogation rooms, he lathers her with charm. *Of course, she'd heard of the Warren massacre, who hadn't in this state?* She didn't live in a cave, she said, and she knew how to read. The next part of the conversation took twenty minutes to get to. They both knew what they were talking about.

No dice. Her sex life wasn't for public retail. Haftmann wonders how she squares that with the explicit ad she used to pen for the swingers' mag online and in every porno shop in the state for every swinging dick to ogle.

He thinks of all those dating sites on the web for the sex-seekers of our society: the religiously horny, the conservative horny, and just-plain-horny. Lonely people using social networking get lonelier, not happier, said his psych textbooks.

Alienation, they also said: *disconnection, hostility, dysfunction—*

Schizophrenia.

Chapter 7

Ides of March

Lonnie Dale Nelson came awake too soon at false dawn, when the wind currents shift, the creeping black of night gives way to the coming light, and the body's fluids settle in preparation for the new day's assault. Nursing homes all over the county yield their dead then, the oldest and weakest who give up the struggle for life.

He had never been this sick since the ether fog had lifted at the Massillon State Hospital, and he'd remembered where he was and how he got there.

He was years past weeping, but the waves of anguish build toward nausea. His breath has a foul stench.

There were no mirrors in the cottage for him to see what he looked like. The little jizzbag real-estate agent had said the place was short on amenities, but cozy; it was damp, drafty, and a film of grease covered everything inside.

It was right on the lake. He guessed that two or three more years of wave-pounding action would put it in the lake. He had one back window from which he could see hillocks of dirty ice, like the King-of-the-Hill mounds of memory, dotting the shoreline as far as the eye could see. A slash of slate-blue water on the horizon coming to meet the thaw from shore.

He had to meet a man who owned a nightclub on the Jefferson-on-the-Lake Strip about a job as bouncer; he had no walking-around money left. He'd eaten garbage from a restaurant's bin last night. He might have to kill a stray cat like those poor fuckers in Syria.

His ninja tail was gone, the peroxide faded; his hair restored to its original field mouse brown. The real-estate dink had scoped out his garb and asked him if he was from the circus; gave him his pick of the low-rent cottages a mile or so from the Strip. "You come here in late spring, early summer," the pot-bellied manager said, "you won't find a thing to rent anywhere. The place'll be packed from one end to the other."

He finally shut his big bazoo and walked off with the last of Nelson's money and his signature on a piece of paper.

Even if it wasn't his real name, the angel wouldn't like it a bit.

~ ~ ~

The upside-down postcard on Haftmann's desk said two words: RANK AMATEUR. The card had been mailed from the post office where the Youngstown prison mail went.

Shawna was avoiding him, no eye contact at work even. He'd stood her in front of him, her arms akimbo; he'd pointed her chin up to see her eyes, and she'd shivered at his touch – *his touch, Christ. What did he do to women?*

He knew she knew: this homicidal maniac he was chasing was whispering to him. He had even used her to abet the evil by making her his messenger to Haftmann, the killer's slime on the messages she sensed like an infection she could almost feel in her blood.

Another warning sign: Oscar chatting him up yesterday. No wisecrack when he put a yard on a triple, a real cockteaser bet he'd never hit before in his life: Cavs over Celtics, Bulls over Knicks, Trailblazers over Nuggets – a wet-dream bet. The investigation by then had become a bloodless giant; it boomed with paperwork and nothing else. Every wacko, nut-case outpatient in the state was being investigated who fit the bill. Sex offenders were given a double-take by the best hard boys the investigators could muster: rapos, short-eyed freaks, crossdressers, *frotteurs*, transsexuals, and peepers. Every dirtbag ever busted on mopery with intention to gawk was looked at, double-checked and cross-checked by teams of investigators. Lawsuits charging harassment were pending all over the state.

A priority-one item was cons with violent rap sheets released or furloughed within fifty miles of Warren. The theory was simpler than it looked: what do cons have to do all day but eat starchy food, lift weights, and have sex? Maybe he got big from lifting iron in the prison yard. "Past or current members of Aryan Brotherhood," Booth's latest communiqué, passed on from Phil, read, "must be given special attention."

The Warren victims were literally an open book, their life stories from birth to death were compiled by a separate team of investigators. Possible drug connection because they were known recreational drug users – marijuana, coke. Loose-knit street gangs in Cleveland were checked out, Crips in Akron had to be checked into. The cartels of Northern Mexico and Ciudad Juárez were even investigated for possible connections, given the sensational violence down there. Somebody at Quantico theorized that Zetas who could leave thirty-eight victims beneath an overpass and decapitated heads on bar tops might have migrated north with their special skill set.

Thousands of names and hundreds of manpower hours had already gone into the investigation. The state's accountants were complaining that they'd need to import barrels of red ink if the investigation went on much longer. The budget-happy governor waffled on his pronouncement to the press that every rock in the state would be turned over to find the killer.

Haftmann begged for permission to check out some of the people who engaged in Internet liaisons. One couple had agreed to be interviewed if their names were kept out of the investigation. They lived in Fostoria, a town that had gained national media attention when the face of Jesus had appeared on the side of an oil storage tank in the summer twilight.

"Hey, big shot," MacDuff hollers over to him while he's brooding over his fifth beer. "The Cavs going to cover the line this Saturday?"

Haftmann sees MacDuff in his familiar scarlet-and-gray Ohio State sweatshirt with Brutus Buckeye going at it doggie-style behind a Michigan cheerleader.

"What if I told you I quit gambling," Haftmann says while staring at his own face in the cracked mirror.

"Uh-huh, right, and if my aunt had balls, she'd be my uncle."

Haftmann says nothing; he thinks that makes sense.

~ ~ ~

Lonnie Dale Nelson was given the job and fifty dollars in advance from the manager, a balding, droopy-eyed owner of several bars on the Strip. He guessed that it was difficult to keep a bouncer on because he asked very few questions about his post, didn't even require the fictitious references he carried in his coat pocket.

The bar never closed, except legal hours, of course, and, to put it bluntly, "an unsavory element, uh, had been around lately but that was no big thing, you know what I mean?" He said he knew. "Uh, blacks, that bother you? Cause I'm not prejudice myself."

"No," he said. "Money's only one color."

"Well, you get a lot of others too," he added. "Bikers, bull dykes, fag hags and their boyfriends, redneck rowdies from here and there" – the sort of drifters and losers a place like his could sometimes attract, even if he did run an up-and-up establishment, which he insisted "was the case."

"No guns, knuckles, sawed off bats – none of that heavy stuff," the manager warned. "You don't look like you need it anyway."

Nelson nodded his head.

"Just pick 'em up and put 'em out, gentle-like," the owner repeated.

"Sure, man, no sweat." He nodded, polite for the man.

"I can't afford no more trouble with these Lake cops."

"Uh-huh."

"Shouldn't be no trouble at all."

He agreed.

"One other thing . . ."

"Hmmm."

"Take a fuckin' shower, man. You smell like you been shoveling manure."

While Nelson was looking over the bar with his new employer, Haftmann was three hours' drive away, sitting in a comfortable, middle-class home admiring a print of Henry Osawa Tanner's *The Banjo Lesson*. Haftmann had to prissify his tactics for the couple. They were having second thoughts, apparently, and found him a tad disconcerting in the flesh, sitting right there on their expensive leather couch, one of their bone china coffee cups in his thick mitt.

Easy does it, he thinks. *Just a push.*

"It's extraordinarily kind of you both to assist in the investigation. I promise you utter confidentiality and discretion." (Buzz words from having waded through sleazy porn sites and picked up their jargon. He would never again use an ATM card without thinking Ass-to-Mouth.)

"You will not be made to repeat anything you might say to me here,"

Haftmann flashes the husband a badge taken from his office drawer. Booth absolutely refused to issue him a special investigator's badge. "I assure you no lawyers, depositions, police officers, besides me, of course – (he gave them his friendliest, if slightly crooked smile) – will ever come to your door."

Husband and wife, a thirty-something couple, gave a collective sigh; looked at each other in one of those meaningful glances outsiders pretend not to see.

Then they told their story; bits and pieces at first, chronology askew, but Haftmann is used to that. They help each other out, first one, then the other pitches in to fill in a gap, to correct or provide a detail.

It was almost a shock for Haftmann to perceive in a flash that they loved each other.

But they give their bodies to strangers. Like Micah.

I'll never forgive her. The mean-spirited, twisted homunculus lurking near his back brain nods happily. *Fuck that bitch anyway . . .*

First, the husband talks; he says they'd met him through an ad they placed in February two years ago. A guy between thirty-five and forty, what they were looking for.

"See," she says, "Fostoria's a small town and everybody knows everybody else's business." They were too discreet to swing with friends or locals, they affirm.

They used to belong to a small circle of friends in Toledo, where they had moved from when his mill closed down. Good people, they say – doctors, dentists, a lawyer or two. Haftmann winces here but covers it with a gesture. And wives, naturally, whose husbands didn't swing but gave their permission. That really makes him fidget in his seat. She has dimples, he notices for the first time. "But it started to get around," she adds, "we were these awful wife swappers in their midst, orgies – "

"Yeah, like we were sacrificing to pagan gods or something," the husband says.

134

He tells Haftmann some in the group got emotionally involved with each other; it got nasty, a divorce resulted. Somebody's wife and a pediatrician got together. "Ugly rumors, you know?"

Haftmann tells them he knows what they mean, he being one of the sexually liberated himself, *wink, wink*.

It was the wife who said she initiated it, the whole idea. They thought swinging was the answer: pick who you want, choose your partners without pressure, meet in neutral places like Denny's, see if everybody liked each other.

"We don't like one-nighters. We like friendly people and, well, the sex is exciting."

She was one of those redheads you'd call perky, but there was none of the ditzy redhead stereotype coming through.

"He was big," the husband said very suddenly.

"Bigger than the photo he sent us," she says.

Haftmann's spine cracks as he shifts on the sofa, waiting patiently, trying to still the uptick of his heartbeats.

"We didn't know how to tell him that he smelled," the husband says.

"Rank," she adds.

Through cajolery and sex talk, they got him clean and into their bed.

"I'm not a jealous man, you know."

Haftmann slurped some coffee to avoid reacting to the colossal understatement there. "I share my wife with other men because it gives us both great pleasure. But he was a wrong number, man. Right from the start," hubbie adds.

Haftmann thinks he's going to grab someone by the neck if they don't get to it NOW.

"We should never have opened our door to him," she said.

"Uhh-hmm." Haftmann crushes out an image of her legs around her ears, auburn muff and pouting lips. His cock is growing tumescent. He despises himself but the harsh male phobias slip their leash and form across his mind – "gash, "cunt," "hatchet wound," "split-tail," "bang hole," fuck hole."

"He tried to arrange us," the husband says. "Like, like . . ."

"Like he was acting out some fantasy of his," she finishes.

"He wanted us both to perform fellatio on him at the same time. My husband's not bi, I'm not bi, and our ad was pretty specific about our likes and dislikes."

She holds out a copy for him to see, done from their printer next to the computer. *No photo, thank God.*

"His interests," she says, "seemed to be altogether Greek."

Rimming—was that the word, Haftmann tried to remember the glossary.

"I prefer french to completion," she said. "But he wanted the other too. Insisted on it. In our own house, our bedroom . . ."

The husband interjects, wants him to *know*. "I'm no coward. But I'm not ever going to forget how he looked. I want you to know that I stopped it right there."

Told him to get out. The husband said he felt scared to death. The man was bigger than a bull, and he rose to his feet, face flushed, penis engorged with blood, eyes flicking from one to the other, muttering incoherently.

"Can you remember what he might have said?"

"No," she said, "it was gibberish."

"Something about – something about an angel," the husband said.

"An angel?"

The husband was ready to reach for his cell phone on the nightstand at that point. But the man turned and left without another word.

"Well, not quite," she said. For the first time, she looked uneasy, embarrassed.

"What do you mean?" Haftmann asked.

The husband explained. He jerked himself off in the living room on our coffee table. Haftmann barely avoided looking down at the coffee cup before him. "Showed his contempt for us, I suppose," the wife says.

"He demanded I get his letter and photo he'd sent us, I got it. I was afraid to leave her alone with him for the moments it took me to get it from the chifferobe," the husband said.

Haftmann thinks in empathy: *That must have been one of the longest walks of your life.*

"He had handwriting like a child's. Big block letters. Not educated quite obviously. Spelling was atrocious. I almost refused to give it back," the husband adds in retrospect.

That, Haftmann knows beyond a doubt, *would have been the biggest mistake of your life.*

He used the name Roger Howard. You didn't put much faith in names, anyway, they said together, if you practiced their lifestyle.

No photo. No handwriting sample. *God damn it to hell.*

But the details are coming together, a picture forms that transforms the big loutish kid sitting morosely in the back of his cruiser to this—this, whatever it was he was assuming in his bizarre physical appearance now with his California surfer's hair – the frizzy blond kind you got from Lady Clairol – big calloused lumps at the balls of his thumbs.

But no tattoos. That was strange. Psychos love to decorate themselves.

Old surgery scars around his hindquarters, above his anus.

The cut and definition of a body builder; the biceps were easily twenty inches around.

Thick uncircumcised penis. A foreskin that could hold a shot glass of water (She was playful with him in the shower at first, she said, to coax him in.)

Haftmann writes manically, the tremors garbling the letters.

"His eyes are blue," she says at last.

~ ~ ~

Lonnie Dale Nelson had a bluebottle fly pinned against the pane; its hysterical buzz crescendoing off the glass in the still night.

A crescent moon hung over the water; its blue sheen gone to putrid gray in the light. The sky was speckled with high, cold stars.

He would not see the night sky after this: tomorrow night he started work. He said the name Donald Jackson aloud dozens of times to get used to its sound. "Don . . . Donald . . . Donnie." Jackson was the name of the lecherous priest who used to come to help the boys pray and then masturbate them for a dollar. Nelson/Jackson sobbed and threw a left hook that stopped an inch short of fracturing the buzzing glass.

The next morning he awoke to sunlight in his eyes. He saw a dozen Canadian soldiers had gotten through a hole in the screen. A freakish warm spell brought them out. Then he dropped to the floor and began his push-ups. Flesh was sagging on his bones. He had to get food soon.

That afternoon, he walked into the pharmacy at the end of the Strip. A young man in his twenties eyed him back. "Help you?"

"Y-youse in l-l-luck," the stuttering, gap-toothed trash had said; "new is-issues just come in today."

He looks over the rack behind the newsie. *Asian Babes, Gent, Score, Hustler, Playboy* were at eye level. A single rack off to the side contained some G-rated beefcake and below that he noted the hardcore gay magazines, such as *JustUsBoys* and *Black Inches*. Even one for the lezzies: *On Our Backs*. He bought a selection of five and left. He left them open to the centerfolds in a circle around his bed as if he were laying out ceremonial flowers. In a way, that's exactly what he was doing. It was one way, he knew, to entice the angel to come back.

~ ~ ~

Haftmann lies on the couch with his eyes wide open, practically bulging. His one bad eye throbs from late-night reading of the material he has placed in a Xerox box. A memory comes flooding back – he had taken a domestic call on a spring day like this one. The dispatcher was confused: it seemed to be a dispute in progress, migrant workers, in broken English, the caller wouldn't stay on the line after giving the address twice. A low-rent place, one of dozens slapped up by an outfit in Cleveland that never bothered to do more than collect rent and evict.

The Mex was telling Haftmann that *the bebe was sick con un catarro*. Colicky, he guessed, and for that reason no one in the house could sleep.

"Why did your wife, *su esposa*, try to strangle *the bebe*?"

Because the baby was "possessed," he finally manages to explain. When Haftmann told his friend Tico about this part, he said: "El que quire peces que se moja el culo."

"English, Tico."

"That's the fuck the way it is, man, with these people."

Haftmann almost reminded him that he was one of "these people" not so long ago. He had crawled his way out

139

of that vast mountain of a burning garbage pit in "Gaute" – Guatemala – to come here. Haftmann never wearies of teasing his only true friend: "Of all the goddamned places in America, Tico, you came *here*." It's a ritual with them that Tico's wife Marta doesn't approve. But, then, anything involving Haftmann and her husband warrants a frown.

The husband and wife believed they next-door people had put the curse on the baby to make it cry so much. "Como se dice, por mucho que – que, the bebe, you pick up, it is crying. They put voodoo into her milk. It-it poison the bebe."

"Tell me why. *Digame.*"

"Habia enemistad! Go to Hay-suss! Go to Hay-suss!"

She screamed something about "bad blood," "going to Hay-suss."

Hay-suss: Jesus.

While walking him downstairs at the station for booking, Haftmann overhears the watch commander scowled at them and muttered to another lieutenant, "I don't give two motherfucks for all the greasers or towelheads in this country."

That night Haftmann dreams he was talking to Tico about the Hispanic whose baby was dead and that Tico was telling him of these *Flying Dutchman* stories. Tico's mocha eyes were steel-gray, somber, cold.

"*Esa es la historia mas fantastica que he oido y no creo una palabra de ella,*" he says to Tico in his clumsy Spanish: *I don't believe a word of it.*

Verdad, said Tico. *The truth.*

He's on the deck of the doomed *Edmund Fitzgerald*. Something in him knew it all along. Tidal-wave-sized combers arc over the hatches amidships, a storm at night. Nothing worse than a gale at night to terrify Haftmann, a summer sailor, unhinged by the dream's crazy transition of time and space. In a hideous cacophony of noise, he steps through a door and goes up a metal stairway into murky light.

The crew were walking around like casting extras on the set of some zombie film with bloodless faces, black, staring eyes. Some had been savaged by wild animals fresh from their graves. There, in the midst of this surging flow, was the Mex father cradling his dead baby. Only he's throttling it –

Before Haftmann can reach him, babies are being dropped into the icy waves by demons holding them by their ankles. Haftmann loses his sea legs, rolls helplessly on the deck, drenched by the water's wallop and bone-chilling cold. Two Finn brothers he and his cousins knew wave to him from the Texas deck; then they, too, are gone over the side in the curl of a mountainous wave.

The ship, heavy with taconite, pops rivets all around him like gunshots. He can see the afterend with lifeboats smashed to pulp hanging from the davits. When the lakeboat split open, the sound ripped through the sonic boom of waves and made him heartsick for the drowning men in the engine room. He raced up the stairs to the pilothouse deck: one chance: get the painter attached to the life-raft and spring it free, jump –

Water freezing; it'll stop my heart.

Haftmann dives headfirst; the shock is like an electric current from his balls to his brain. The six-person inflatable raft pops up between waves, hunter-orange against the tops of the filth-dark water; he strokes to it, a natural swimmer and hauls himself gasping into the raft. Bodies are lying about the floor – the mates, deckhands, the Captain. He's so cold his limbic brain is calling the shots now. He covers himself with their corpses to keep the cold off. The relentless shellacking of waves against the *Fitz* amidships sends it to the bottom in an earsplitting scream of ripping steel.

He's alone, but he's alive . . . His dreaming self rolls about in the raft's bottom with the bodies pressing him down in the toss of the waves. He tries to tuck his hands under him before they go numb. He looks at his hand and sees it's wet with blood. He feels sudden movement beneath him and stares down into the black eyes of Lonnie Dale Nelson. Not the boy he was but the man he became and before Haftmann can explain why he arrested him for the weed in his possession, Nelson puts a shiv under his heart with cobra speed. He feels the knife go in under his heart; he can't believe it. *Oh God, it hurts.*

He says the last word murder victims say to their murderers: *Please.*

Chapter 8

Vernal Equinox

She looked around, unfamiliar with the inside of Tico's Place or maybe it was because she was with him after such long silence at work.

"My friend Tico's a strange bird, all right," he said. "Bought this place. It was nickel-and-dime for a long time until the few families that own everything else on this Strip accepted him – tolerated him, really. He doesn't get invited to the chamber of commerce meetings."

"Nothing in here reminds me of anything," Shawna says.

"That's why I like it," Haftmann replies.

"Who's that, the guy in the photo with the pencil moustache?"

Haftmann strains his good eye to see where she's pointing. He zooms on the top row of Four Roses and finds it next to the framed print of Primo Carnera getting KO'd out of the ring by Dempsey. "That's Gilbert Roland. He was an actor in the nineteen-fifties. Marta – that's Tico's wife – said he used to look like that. Personally, I disagree."

Haftmann told her about a movie star who was passing through JOTL last summer. This guy must have said something to Tico's wife while he was signing an autograph for her because two seconds later the guy's on the floor with a bloody lip and his bodyguard's wrestling Tico with Marta on top of the bodyguard. Lord, how we tease Marta about that."

"Do you want to be with me because I'm a married woman? I hear some men like to date married women because there's a thrill to it. Some macho thing."

"No, but I don't want to lie to you and tell you there's no thrill to it. About your being married? I don't think about that. Maybe I should."

"Maybe I shouldn't have asked," Shawna says. She grimaces at that and her eyes are lighter in the half-darkened space where Haftmann is leading her to a table.

"I don't want to talk about my marriage or yours," he says.

Shawna sips her beer and looks at him. "The cops at the station say you gamble on sports."

"I've laid a few bucks down on a game or two."

She gives him a mocking smile and says, "So they say."

Off this subject pronto, he thinks. He has butterflies in his stomach like a teenager on his first date. He goes to the bar and orders her a mixed drink he's never heard of. He half-expects Tico to burst out in Spanish curses, but he makes the drink efficiently and hands it to Haftmann along with his beer.

Haftmann watches her smile at Tico as he heads back to their table; he can feel her pleasure as Tico's gold incisor catches the bar's dim light, his hands rolling around on his serving apron.

There was hubbub going on at the other end of the bar. Every few seconds one of the patrons jumps up from his stool and shouts.

The men laugh, say something they can't hear.

She turns to Haftmann. "What are those guys saying?"

Haftmann looks over and recognizes one of them from his high school days. *You age*, he thinks, *but your past keeps you the trapped.*

"They keep repeating it," she says.

"Sounds like . . . 'This town needs an enema' . . . Some line from a movie, I think."

It dawns on him he has just given a pretty good imitation of Jack Nicholson without trying to.

She turns her face upward to him and claps; the soft light captures her prettiness and her vulnerability at once. He feels the blood rushing south. *Women are perfect*, he realizes. They have all that going for them – face, full lips, hair, legs, ass, tits, and pussy – compared to men. He remembers Micah talking about "penis envy" or some such nonsense. That triple business between a guy's legs causes more trouble than greed in this world. But then, if it were a logical world, we'd ride sidesaddle. He thinks of salmon swimming upstream past a gauntlet of grizzlies, all to shoot goo in a river bottom and die. *Nature should have put a kill-switch in men.*

"What are you thinking about right now?" Shawna asks him. "Be honest."

"I'm thinking that happiness is a personal choice," he says.

"You're a gambler and philosopher, too." She sips her drink. Haftmann worries that Tico might have made it wrong. This is a shot-and-beer joint.

"That's me, Haftmann the multitasker. I should have that written on my office window."

"You joke but I'm serious," she says.

"I've read some Camus," he says, and hopes he pronounces the Frog name correctly this time. Micah had told everyone at the courthouse how he had picked up her book off the kitchen table one morning. It was about French existentialism and he asked her who *Cay-muss* was.

Look at me now, bitch, his inner homunculus says to her lurking phantom, always in Haftmann's brain.

~ ~ ~

He had seen sea gulls but never this many.

From behind his house in East Palestine, he'd had a clear view of the river in summer; the gulls would hover over the sand tugs and barges. You could tell a garbage

145

scow without any trouble: a spiraling flock circled in the warm air currents, getting high on the smell. Like white buzzards, eat and shit, eat and shit.

He wondered how they got through the winters up here. From his window he could see the phallic outline of a containment building ten miles away. They had them on the Ohio River too, Edison Light & Power, he seemed to know.

He had the skills of a pipefitter but not the training.

Years and years of shop-work at Massillon: his therapy.

He wondered if it would be very difficult to sabotage a nuclear power plant. Too many back-up systems, he supposed. He had bought a *Plain Dealer* that morning outside a coffee shop on the Strip. His first night of work dull, quiet with a few stares beamed at the new bouncer. You can only slump so much if you were his size; people noticed him.

That night, during a lull, he asked an older biker with a full beard and a head of white hair what "C-H-O-R-N-B-L" meant.

"Man, I can't spell it either but that sure ain't right," he said looking at Nelson's scrawl on the napkin. "But that Jew, Einstein, was behind it all."

The biker said that everyone between Cleveland and Erie would die right off if that nuclear reactor went up. "Vaporize you, man. Just like fuckin' Wile E. Coyote running through a brick wall."

Nelson stared at him. He had never heard of that name.

"'Beep, beep, your ass' . . . you know, man, a fuckin' cartoon."

Later, he thought about it. He smiled at the beauty of it: Light and Power. So many people would die. He thought of cars jammed on freeways, mothers screaming for their kids, men killing and running over each other to escape the blast.

The angel, of course. The System, their doings, all of it.

Lonnie Dale Nelson, the angel's scourge.

After work, the manager put on the TV set in his office and they watched CNN talking about terrorists who had shot up a building in Paris and killed a dozen people.

"Shitheads," said the manager.

"Sand niggers," said the old biker. "Goat fuckers."

"Why do you call them that?" Nelson asked.

"Who gives a fuck about fags drawing cartoons, man?" Nelson brooded on the way back unable to rid himself of an itchy feeling. He had reversed his hygiene and was showering every day, scrubbing himself with a fanatical attention.

Why won't you talk to me? The dark didn't answer back.

Tulips and daffodils popped their heads through the last clumps of dirty snow behind his cottage. He kicked the heads off them imagining they were people buried to their necks.

Not like that, the angel said, appearing out of nowhere. *There's a way to get them all.*

"How?" Nelson cried out against the wind's shriek. "Tell me!"

I'll show you.

~ ~ ~

"So how come you don't hello me when you know me so well?"

Cute as a bug's ass. The vain, grinning octoroon was putting on the dog for him, making with the old-buddy shit.

"Thomas, I know this is a pleasure for us both, but I must get down to business. I am a businessman, as you know, and I've always lived by the precept that time is precious. Do you know why?"

"Get to it, Artiss. What do you want?"

"Because, you know, time is finite. It exists in limited quantities."

The asshole and his convict education. "And you've got two more years of it to do here, is that it?"

"In a nutshell. Do you know *Hamlet*, Detective Haftmann – er, excuse me, *Mis*-ter Haftmann. I forgot about your demotion from the civil service ranks. Self-selected, was it? Or did they kick you out after learning of your . . . proclivities?"

"No, I left. And no, Artiss, I must have missed that day in high school."

"Too bad. There is so much time here for reading."

"Whose punk are you now, Artiss? The Brand's supposed to be big here. You some lifer's old lady?"

"Speaking of old ladies, Thomas, I heard that the lawyer who was boning that pretty wife of yours did the right thing and married the slut. You should have known."

"Known what?" *How the fuck did he know about that from here?* A Haftmann rule, however: *Show a con nothing, ever.*

"You know."

"Get to the point or I'm gone. It's a long drive back."

"What makes you think you can—"

Haftmann stands, walks to the door; he makes a motion with his fingers to the guard.

"Wait, wait! Come back. Let's start over."

Haftmann turns and stares at him.

Artiss made little *tsk*-ing noises with his tongue and palate. "That shows no respect for our, how shall I say, otherwise mutually respected, though adversarial, relationship."

The little man was fonder of his own eloquence than Matrooshian.

"I didn't drive fifty miles," Haftmann says, "because I like you."

"Oh, dear me, may one ask . . . if you used your real name?"

Artiss' look leaves no doubt: he knows.

Haftmann's stomach roils. *Artiss could have meant what name he had used for the visitor pass. Not that other thing. No, he isn't that lucky.*

"Bye, Artiss. Great chatting with you."

"Sit, sit, Thomas. One must indulge one's baser motives from time to time. It is the beast within us all." Artiss looked at him beneath his hooded eyes. *He's half-lizard*, Haftmann thinks.

"See the prison shrink. That's what they're here for."

"Oh, I do. He's going to arrange to get me some cosmetic surgery next month." Artiss taps his chin with his pinkie. The zircon winks at him. "A dimple right here. I'll look just like Brad Pitt."

You'll look like a chocolate Shirley Temple, you asshole. You'll be servicing the entire cellblock.

Artiss vamping was one thing, but he had other talents. He was a classic sociopath: remorseless, narcissistic, and manipulative. He was the kind to plaster himself all over Facebook and clamor for likes, friending people, strangers by the hundreds, taking over discussion boards. He had the first and best sign of the pathological personality: he tortured animals when he was a boy. His jacket started with a crime when he was seven years old; liked to stick pins in the testicles of his cousins. Shut drawers on their fingers while they screamed . . .

"My point, Thomas – Oh, you upset me so! This is not going right! I could learn to hate you so easily." Artiss batted his eyes at Haftmann and showed the tip off a pink tongue.

"Goodbye, Artiss. Have a nice life."

Haftmann got up, heels clacking loudly on the tile.

"Wait just one more fucking minute, you white scum-sucking, nigger-hating cop – "

Haftmann turns; the little weasel is fussing with himself, picking lint off his crotch, shooting his denim cuffs. "Listen. I've been getting visitors besides yourself these days. I love company, Haftmann. It helps to pass the time."

Haftmann's face is granite, gives nothing to the slime.

"Yesss. Well, these gentlemen, ahem, are more interested in me than you are. They like to hear me talk."

"About what?"

"Stories. Oh, my checkered past mostly."

Big dramatic sigh. "They are postal inspectors. They're kind of secret service-y, if you know what I mean. Well, it seems there's a copycat out there, and he's using one of my best scams."

"The feds know you'll snitch anybody off for a reduced sentence."

"What I do know, my man, is that they are very interested in Artiss Poole's techniques, Artiss Poole's friends. They don't know yet about Artiss Poole's enemies. But they'll be back. They promised me, and I may have something to tell them."

Haftmann hopes there is no telltale sheen of perspiration on his brow for him to see.

"They've got part of an Ohio license plate from the security man in Albany."

The little man's eyes are cold. "What they don't know is that the former officer who caused me to delay my career was more than a little curious about how Artiss does what he does."

"Everybody's got a style, fool – a way of doing things special to that person only. It's like fingerprints with all those teeny-tiny whorls you studied in police school." Artiss pronounces it ghetto-style: *po-leece.*

Haftmann laughs in his face.

"Don't laugh at me, motherfucker."

"Bye, Artiss, ta-ta."

Artiss' eyes are light; he's a racial mix. He's even passed himself off as a Melungeon, that Appalachian mix of Scots-Irish, Cherokee, and African-American. Scammed money passing himself off as Elvis Presley's cousin once. His eyes blaze with suppressed fury and greed; Haftmann is pinned like a butterfly to the wall. He can't leave but he can't stay; he's in quicksand in this tiny visiting cell.

"I'm forty-three years old," Artiss says, much calmer now, sensing the shift of power in his direction. "I got no more time to give to this shit. My B.O.T.—excuse me, prison parlance, my balance of time is a two-spot. That's a long way from the short-and-shitty.

Two years left . . . not little enough to feel like a short timer or acquire the diarrhea convicts get as freedom looms after so many years behind bars.

"You'll be back to your scams in no time. Don't look for a break from me."

"Haftmann, I'm getting M.F.C'd in my pod. By the A.B., no less."

Goddamned convict slang. "M.F.C." finally dawned: measured for coffin. "A B," of course, was the Aryan Brotherhood, real bad-asses.

"You stupid little fuck," Haftmann says. "Why would you try to run one of your games in here with those assholes in charge? Get yourself chalked up, get into SHU, isolation, whatever gets you out of general population."

"I'll lose my good time," Artiss says. "No fucking way."

"Maybe they'll let you off with a beating."

"These dudes, motherfucker, only deal one way," Artiss said. "I'm in the hat."

If true, he wasn't going to make it a month outside segregation and Artiss would sell out his sainted mother first. If he had a mother and if she were a saint . . . Haftmann knows Artiss has no evidence and hearsay doesn't get you convicted. But he can't afford the heat right now. Booth can cut him loose with one dirty look in his direction.

"Go to the gang intelligence officer. Tell him you need out of general population."

"I'm trying to cut a deal with you here, man."

Haftmann wonders if Artiss is wired up. There's no attorney-client confidentiality involved here anyway. *But who knows?*

"Next time, phone. Better yet, don't."

"I ain't suckin' no more dick for you, cop."

Artiss grin as he looks back, a rabid ferret, not a lizard, his long menacing teeth just out of sight.

He found his car in the guest lot; the afternoon sun had taken care of the snow. *Warmer up north*, he thinks, but it doesn't matter; his head is spinning with alarm. He sees pinprick holes where the road salt has eaten through the Neon's metal. He'd give it another year before it turns completely into a pile of rust.

But how much time would Artiss give him before he talked?

He half-listens to the Tribe playing a Cactus League game before spring training ends. The Diamondbacks win a laugher against the White Sox and he loses two hundred to Oscar.

~ ~ ~

Between the Darvon and the fizzy pink drinks she gave him, Nelson was mildly zoned. "Bellinis," it was, something she and her ex-husband drank in Venice, the city by the sea. *Big fucking deal, peaches and champagne.*

He'd made a solid connection on his second week at the shitkicker bar: "'Ludes, tranks, grass, speed, Mexican brown – you name it, dude." Just like that asshole he'd snuffed—when was it? Nelson forgot. It seemed like a lifetime ago.

"Steroids?"

"Pill or liquid? Vial or by the gross? Hurry up, man, I got customers waiting."

A light buzz for the drive – take no chances. Everywhere you looked there seemed to be cops. The state boys on Route 11 shot him twice with their radar guns on the way.

What a kick, if they'd known. He never had a driver's license for his last three aliases. But he had a .44 Magnum Python with copper-point Federals. Under the seat where his left hand could find it; a speedloader next to it. Stole them out of a pickup in the bar's lot. The guy came back inside swearing about "killing the motherfucker," but he declined to call the cops. That made it even better.

Maybe it would come to that someday sooner or later anyway – a bloody shootout on the highway. Over a traffic ticket.

"I don't give a shit about dying," he muttered and realized that he had spoken right over something she was saying.

"I'm sorry, hon, what did you say just now?"

The way she craned her neck made him think of a house sparrow looking in a window.

"Nothing. Go ahead with what you were saying, uh, Connie."

He almost forgot her name. He smiled and stretched back enough to let her see the folds and lumps at his crotch, willing her to look at it.

He was putting back some of the weight he'd lost from the move. The mystery meat sandwich, the only item on the menu at the bar, was okay once you got past the smell. *Like eating bad pussy. Good pussy had no smell . . .*

She nattered on, refilled their drinks. Brought him his. He grabbed her wrist with his free hand and began stroking her chest.

She moaned softly.

She tried to pull his hands from her blouse, but he popped the buttons getting it off – and stared. Her teats came off in his hands. The bra cups were all Styrofoam. Then he realized why she'd been talking him to death about operations and hospitals: double mastectomy.

Good; she'd be hard up. He'd get money he needed to do what he needed to get back on track. Surviving was time-consuming and expensive. He needed freedom to think, to plan, to get back into the groove, stop the voices shouting at him all the time –

The angel must have sent her. Some she-male cunt on the FM station kept singing about angels in a whiny falsetto all the way to Canton. He couldn't get the song off the radio.

She led him into the bedroom by his cock.

He didn't sweat as much during sex as he had before; his feet were dry too. He'd been off steroids and his binge eating had subsided. He hoped the angel wouldn't make him shoot the yogurt too quickly. He'd do sums in his head while he poked away at her.

She must have learned her style from porno films; she was moaning and telling him to "fuck my pussy" over and over. He had her doggie style and her ass cheeks were quivering as he bucked into her. In and out, slow, then faster.

She had a floppy box just like his foster mother so many years before. When he wasn't eating her, she kept saying for him to stick it in her hard, *stick me oh oh oh—stick me*, even though his penis stayed semihard through it all.

He held her by the haunches and rammed it in deep until his balls were right up against her anus; his pubic ruff meeting the hair curling up behind her.

He turned her over and got on. While he stroked, he looked down at his glistening cock as he took it slowly out of her snatch and put it back all the way in, moving it around some for her. His cock must think it's in a storm.

He tuned out the nonsense of her sexual moaning, and for a change of pace, he pulled it out with his left hand, peeled the foreskin all the way back over the glans' blood helmet. He whapped her vagina with it, hitting her clitoris, and called her his "fuck-bitch" until she orgasmed in jets, her tongue lolling out of her mouth like a dog's. Their bodies steamed with it, and the air was thick with the smell of cum.

She came again. Her bosomless torso dripped sweat and she black pubic hair matted from her belly button to her anus. "My pubis bone needs a rest," she said. "Let's sixty-nine."

While she was brushing her teeth with it, he made calculations about the worth of everything in her bedroom. *Solid middle-class lady.* She'd be good for at least a hundred. More, if he talked nice.

Lick me, she crooned around the head of his cock.

"Yes, Mother," he said, slipping back into his boyhood.

~ ~ ~

There are half-moons of sweat under Haftmann's arms – damned caffeine; he drinks a dozen cups a day and anything under gives him a blinding headache.

He can't think straight. His mind's pinwheeling in all directions. Most of the time, the bar helps him think, not now, though. Artiss is haunting him and any minute he expects to see a couple cops come through the door to take him in for a little questioning.

"Who you like for tonight, Half-Man?"

"Get bent, MacDuff. I'm trying to think here."

Haftmann checks him out in the mirror for the Brutus Buckeye sweater, but sees MacDuff is sporting a clipped, Errol Flynn mustache. "You're actually trying to look like Adolph Hitler now, aren't you?"

Haftmann has lost three hundred in two nights. He took a flyer on this ferocious little UFC fight. A tough little banty-weight Scotsman said he intended to clean out his division and he started with Haftmann's opponent.

Haftmann sees MacDuff in the mirror picking his nose. A quiet black man sits at the other end of the bar. Haftmann knows him.

He remembers the day he had to tell Cecil McQuone's father that his son, a Golden Gloves welterweight champ, had succumbed to gun-shot wounds. He was shot outside a bar on the Strip by a man whose description he can recall verbatim from memory: short-haired, medium-complected, early thirties, about five-foot, seven inches wearing a light-colored, long-sleeved shirt with a dark overcoat draped over his left arm. The killer never said a word, according to witnesses, simply fired four times and hit Cecil three out of four in the head. The case was still open.

His father was a shoeshine boy for thirty-five years at a saloon on the Strip; sold popcorn from a homemade cart in the summers. He still does.

Haftmann looks over at MacDuff. "Stop pointing at your brain, MacDuff."

"Fuck you, Haftmann."

Haftmann stands up, whips out the two-inch Smith & Wesson he almost never takes out of his office desk, much less brings into a cop bar, and taps the bridge of MacDuff's nose. Then he puts the gun back in his pants, returns to his stool and sits staring at the mirror.

The low hum of cop chatter hasn't increased a decibel. No one saw it.

Haftmann shuffles the papers he brought in to look over. His fingers shake as he riffles pages.

He catches MacDuff's eyes in the mirror – big as dinner plates.

Fuck it, Haftmann realizes. *Let it come . . .*

"You. Crazy. Psycho. SONOFABITCH – "

MacDuff's roundhouse haymaker knocks Haftmann off his stool. It wasn't much of a fight. None of the fancy stuff fight fans appreciate.

MacDuff is younger, quicker. Haftmann's left cheek bloomed a rosette, and his lip was cut, blood drips down his shirt. A group of detectives and patrolmen pull them apart almost as soon as it begins.

He threw only one punch with leverage, but it connected with MacDuff's eyebrow, which was growing a cartoon goose egg by the second.

Elise, a detective third on loan from Jefferson for the coming summer holidays, came over during the scuffle, righted the stools and set the tables back up; she picked up his papers that had flown all over. Haftmann likes her. He'd partnered with her that one year when she arrived, a good cop, a cool head.

"You asshole, Haftmann," she says without malice. "I see you've managed to pick-up the shattered pieces of your life since the divorce and move on."

Some cop Haftmann doesn't know wants them to shake hands as if they were kids on a schoolyard. There's MacDuff with his hand out, offering to kiss and make up. He's no worse for wear except for the puffed eyebrow. Haftmann still wants to kill him, but he's old, fat, whipped.

The men talk about the tussle for a while and then things go back to normal. Tico serves drinks on the house. He's grateful Marta's in Youngstown visiting their son tonight.

At home, Haftmann sits on his red couch with a can of beer pressing against his swollen cheek. His right hand is sore; the knuckles bruised. *Dumb, dumb . . . why can't he get things right?* He grabs the remote and turned to CNN. Nothing there. He finds the Cleveland and Erie stations and hears the same re-hash as yesterday and the day before. Newscasters are desperate for any new detail in Ohio's manhunt but nobody's saying "serial killer" officially. The F.B.I.'s Cleveland office issues a statement about "forming a task force," which Haftmann translates into "clusterfuck." He's worried because, lately, Phil's material via Booth is drying up like a waterhole in the Gobi.

It was at a standstill despite the press releases from Columbus and the paperwork it generated. Forests might not be cut down for the paper but bits of light in cyberspace – what was that? A small, compact investigation was the solution, but you'd be pissing into the wind if you were to try to convince the bureaucrats.

He still has the homicide cop's ambivalent instincts, half-wishing the psycho would kill again, so they could start over. The inertia of this investigation was spinning wheels: 292 separate exhibits had been tagged from the Warren house, according to one of Phil's copies. All for nothing if you had nothing besides a case number to log them with.

Haftmann *knows* he'll kill again, or like that Zodiac sociopath, he'll take his bloody secrets to the grave.

Vanderhyden isn't returning calls. Booth is always in conference when he calls.

Where are you, though, you crazy bastard?

He wakes up as if ice water had been poured down his back snapping to and in the middle of a conversation he can't remember with somebody he doesn't know. He loses things right in front of him, throws things around at home. His thoughts are bloody, dark but an inch-deep. Except where she's concerned.

He often drives by Shawna's house on South Road, hoping to see her silhouette against the curtains. He's a lovesick fool past caring. He doesn't want any more semi-respectable luncheon dates at Tico's. He wants to take her places, show her things, talk to her about—what, exactly? Haftmann doesn't know but the loneliness is eating at him.

What else? Be honest.

Fuck her. Fuck another man's wife. He hates the irony of it. He's a dog returneth to his vomit.

Sometimes he thinks he's being followed. Paranoid schizophrenia, that.

But (his inner voice says) *that doesn't mean somebody isn't trying to get you, homes.*

He prefers to think of it as one of his psych texts had phrased: "heightened awareness."

Fuck Freud, too. And that other guy, he thinks. *The one who says we come into consciousness out of some ancestral swimming pool. Fuck me, is nothing ever simple?*

He sees that dating ad invoking God, the terrestrial matchmaker, and thinks: *Why not a matchmaker? He's a jokester, after all. He made a psychotic asshole like Jack-in-the-Box. He makes them by the hundreds and thousands. New killers every day. Life is a swill bucket and God rattles the stick. Let's give Him the credit he deserves.*

~ ~ ~

The days were longer; the sky would show a cerulean blue from time to time, and the afternoon light was full of promise. He saw chickweed sprouting: robins fought over it despite the cars whizzing past. There were strays, dogs and cats, meandering along the highway, too far from any house or farm: drop-offs of the shameless and those for whom pets were conversation pieces.

She still moaned for him like one of those seventies' porn flicks with the organ music, *Debbie Does Hollywood*, or something, but Lonnie Dale Nelson knew a few tricks from watching porno films himself. She didn't like it up the ass much; said he was too big and it hurt—"like taking a poop backwards," she said. "The AIDS thing, baby. Too risky. I know where I've been, but . . . *what strange places have you been sticking it* is what she left unsaid.

Besides, she cooed, much better like this, "Huh, sweetie. Ah, God, that's it."

He still didn't know how he was going to do her, but it would come to him in dreams.

She was jibber-jabbering after sex the way she always did, and he wasn't listening to her. He thought he heard it, the word, *that place*. She was saying something about the Rocky actor, and a film in Massillon, some kind of prison film, years ago, she said it was. They used the boys' reformatory . . .

He thought if he had been forced to give another drop of blood or tears more than they took from him there, he would have slashed his throat. Instead here he was, lying on a four-poster below a pink canopy with his dick at half-mast.

He lay back, eyes closed. Waiting for her to finish douching so she could treat him to a meal at a good restaurant. He'd order one meal only; something with fuck energy like clams or fish. Scrod in garlic butter, langoustines. Good for the brain and the balls.

This bed was like a cloud compared to the piss- and cum-stained mattress that came with his cottage.

Like the bunks; the springs are lashed to your spine when you wake in the morning. Radios going on all over the place.

Everybody synchronized to the King; boys gyrating skinny hips and pelvis the way they saw it on an old Ed Sullivan show. One boy said the blackout over her face was done by the network because she had her muzzle ground into his crotch, trying to give him head in front of millions. "'Don' chew – Step on my – Blue suede shoes.'"

Senses alert; his eyes open and he catches her staring at him: "Why, baby, what a beautiful, lovely voice you have. I thought I was hearing the radio . . ."

He never heard her creep up on him like that. Her eyes go down to his penis; its snout going from three-quarters to full mast in an angry cockstand.

She was pink from the shower; her skin clean and sweet. He kisses the knife scars on her chest, which excite her. She's wet again.

He slips behind her, biting her nape. Pins her down on her belly over the bed.

Oh, God, not that – she starts to say, but he's already halfway home, and he's not using any lubricant this time.

He knew where she kept her stash: a bag of grass, some twenties, fifties, and a couple Ben Franklins in a silver money clip.

He stopped at a shopping mall in Niles and bought some items: manila envelopes, business-sized, plain white stationery, ten dollars postage. At a True-Valu he bought a ball-peen hammer, large aluminum nails, a hacksaw, twenty feet of nylon rope, two gallons of Silver Brite, a roller with attachment handle, and a four-inch brush.

The salesman told him the nylon brushes were just as good as the old horsehair ones. "And, unless you were painting a mural or something, you didn't need camel-hair to paint a house, for Gosh sakes. Them are good, first-class brushes, he said with the passion of all bow-tie salesman. Give you good value for your dollar."

"Whatever," he said.

~ ~ ~

The place was jumping. Bikers' music: Stones and Guns 'n Roses. They lived in a bubble except for their drug business. Axel Rose belted out "Sweet Child O' Mine" in his epicene voice. He had been challenged once, but the word got out fast after that, and he was accepted in the place as a fixture. *Don't mess with the new bouncer.* Spring fever in the air; the chill of winter not altogether gone, but you could feel summer out there somewhere. "Then," the locals said, "the place'll really rock."

The guy he hit in the stomach was a hick with a beard and an attitude problem. One of those crybaby vets who want you to know, by God, what it was really like out there in the sand or in the mountains of Helmand Province or whatever shithole his outpost was situated in. He had puked his beer up before he could rush him outside, but he would get the new barmaid with the butterfly tattoo to mop it up.

She asked him if he wanted to come to her place after work, snort a little, mellow out.

He said some other time maybe. She asked him if he was "like, fag, or something." Then she ignored him.

The noise in the place was such that it covered his brief hesitation whenever his name was called . . . *Sorry, man, couldn't hear you with that music blasting.* There were times when he could not remember his names, real or fake. He knew the System would not abandon him. He knew he was being prepared. Tears rolled down his face. Too close to it be making simple mistakes like that.

They were talking about the Warren murders. The bitch with the tattoo said they should give him to the other family members to torture and kill, slowly, just the way he did to the man and wife he killed.

"Can you fuckin' believe it?" she laughed, "cut off the dude's thing, stuffed it into the woman's mouth."

That generated about ten minutes of a lewd chorus of invitations from all corners of the bar about whether she'd like to have them put their things into her mouth.

Someone, a small but dangerous biker who rode up from West Virginia, says that the Jack-killer's "a fuckin' fairy or something."

The owner asks him, "Hey, what do you think they oughta do to him?"

"Kill him fast," some drunk at the bar answers instead, "or kill him slow. Just make sure he's dead when you're done."

"Hey," the owner says, doing a little shuffle, "that's fuckin' poetry. You could put that to music."

Chapter 9

Easter

They find Haftmann's missing girl Easter Sunday morning. Rather, the caretaker of the Jefferson-on-the-Lake State Park did who followed a family of raccoons into the bush. He thought they were foraging until he saw the white bones sticking through, a hank of white-blonde hair. The tattered clothes were those she wore the day she disappeared. Doc Harris would have to complete the identification.

Haftmann drives to the station from the park; the rest of the forensics team has gone home to shower off the stink and change clothes.

Methane probes had been used nearby in the search's early days but failed to turn up the girl's body, dead for a year. Her killing, like a few "unattended deaths" anywhere in Ohio, are checked for traits of their "Jack" killer.

"Let me go with her to the morgue," he pleads with Mook Brown who had caught the call.

"I can't allow that, Tom. You're civvie street. Riding patrol's one thing – "

The growl comes from Haftmann's stomach this time and he has Mookie's string tie with its turquoise longhorn clasp in his fist. Haftmann says through gritted teeth, "I'm riding along now."

~ ~ ~

Sometimes a fact or a trivial detail can become part of the apocrypha of a con's life and makes catching him difficult.

Haftmann has only that single, blurry, ancient memory of Nelson sitting in the back of the prowler: Nelson's eyes were so dilated they looked black.

Psychopaths changed known associates like socks. What they never changed was fantasy: that film inside their heads clicked on until the sprockets tore the celluloid.

The detective who liked to dress up for the holidays stopped by Haftmann's bar stool and offered him some chocolates; this time he was a six-foot rabbit with eyeholes in a fur hood.

"Fuck off, asshole."

MacDuff shouts from the pool table he'll take some female chocolates, without the nuts, haw. He's a notorious muff-diver, talks about it constantly, and loves to gas it up in the muster room about letting "their juices dry on his face so he can pick it off like a potato chip and eat it later."

Haftmann doesn't look up when he hears Millimaki's bear-shuffle approach. The same unlit cigar in his mouth as at the autopsy when he made a brief appearance. He looked at Haftmann for a long moment but didn't say anything. Haftmann glares at him from the mirror. His rage keeps notching one more level, one more level, until he thinks his head will explode.

"No reason to be a prick to Johnson there, gumshoe," the chief says. "He's doing all the elementary schools in the county in the Easter bunny costume."

"What assholery." Haftmann doesn't acknowledge him, keeps reading his latest report from Phil.

"The county commissioners liked the idea."

Haftmann can't make his way through the jargon. It's in F.B.I. lingo on regressive sociopaths. To Millimaki's image in the mirror, he says, "Why don't you take your boys to the Haze?"

"Funny boy," Millimaki says. The Purple Haze is a notorious biker bar. No cop would venture in there out of uniform – at least, not alone.

Haftmann sighs, burps, puts the report away, and swivels to face him. Millimaki's cheeks are spotted, his nose a cluster of burst capillaries. Haftmann feels a tiny pop of joy. Millimaki will die before he does, that's almost certain. *Everybody in the world*, he thinks, *has either a pig face or a fox face.*

"You notice what's been going on around you lately? You've become obsessed with the killer, and you aren't allowed to come within ten miles of the investigation."

"I know that. Booth promised me – "

"He's jerking your chain, dummy."

"Go take a flying fuck at the moon, Chief."

The characteristics of psychosis in remission were a penance for the most jargon-loving readers, but Haftmann, never the academic, saw confirmed in otiose, polysyllabic prose what his intuition told him all along. The killer has a discernible pattern that he is acting out subconsciously, even though he might have motives and rationales presented to him by other parts of his psyche: the logic of schizophrenia, the crazy logic of dreams, those voices in the pipes urging him on . . .

He hadn't completely alienated the federal cops, who were ever desirous of good rapport with state police; 17,000 law enforcement agencies in the country was a good reason to curtail inter-agency rivalry; you'd need them someday.

Haftmann knows, although he wasn't told this by Columbus, that the investigation is being quietly dismantled across the state, a mouse tip-toeing around a cat named Public Opinion.

Jesus Shit Fuck.

His eyes blear from reading too many sentences that begin: "In reference to . . ." Worse than academics, worse even than lawyers.

He has gone through a boxcar-load of transcripts; interviews collected and collated via central terminals at F.B.I. for quantitative analysis. The statistical probability suggests "Jack" is behind bars for some other crime, and that's the reason for the current silence.

Yesterday he spoke to the lead-team investigator of the unit in charge of Class A suspects, a B.C.I. stranger-crimes expert, and he agreed:

"We'll hear from him when he's paroled or some kike lawyer gets him a furlough . . ."

He wouldn't stop even in prison now.

He has to kill; he likes it.

The next go-round will be worse. *Jesus, worse than Warren.*

"Then we'd better get the women and children off the streets," his expert said.

Chief Millimaki was quick to remind everyone that every meth cook, drifter, runaway teen, and psycho in three states comes through the Strip between Memorial Day and Labor Day.

"Won't we have fun," says MacDuff from the pool table.

Mantooth from downstairs brings daily rumors of budget cuts – no more two-man patrols, no dope-sniffing dogs they promised us last year; the Pagans and Angels were supposed to square off at the Strip this summer.

Hey, Haftmann, Stel says, you remember 1989? Christ . . .

Haftmann moves out the rest of his pick-up furniture to get more space between rooms for his files and boxes. He's swiped some olive-green filing cabinets from the basement; the paper flood might have subsided statewide, but his own grows exponentially with every detail he gloms from the feds, from Phil, from the newspapers. More grist for its hungry maw. But no new leads.

He builds elaborate theories like a man building a house of cards under strobe lighting and watches them collapse in the cold light of logic. There is no link as yet between Lonnie Dale Nelson and the Warren killings. A small-time dope bust was little better than an obsolete vagrancy charge.

And waits.

"*Es gibt einen Weg,*" his grandmother used to say. *There is a way.* Killers and private eyes walk alone. Like lepers. Like losers and misfits, of which he is clearly one now.

He finishes up by two o'clock so that he can get some time for his own work and catch a glimpse of Shawna leaving for home after her shift. He hasn't talked to her in ten days. Today he will, he must see her. He sits in his junk car and waits . . .

"Hello, Slim, long time no see."

"Hello, you. You've been busy lately."

A reproof? But she's been avoiding me, he thinks.

"I want . . . to see you, Shawna," he said.

The VICAP material from Quantico expanded outward and bumfuzzled him with its complex terminology. All Ohio violent crimes are logged for characteristics that have parameters like Warren and Painesville. They take out the temporal distance factor. They comb through a densely populated state sifting through carnage, looking, checking, sniffing like dogs for small prey. The prey happens to be infinitesimally small, buried within a cascading minutiae of electronic blips and flashes.

Haftmann asks them to add suicides on a hunch.

"Shit, no, they are hundreds of them," B.C.I. tells him.

"The macabre ones, then. Think like a loony who wants to die."

He's gone through scores by now. Made another short list he'll try to push past Vanderhyden.

Another hunch: physical distance factor, shorten it up; he's zigzagging, but a man lost in the woods of his own mind may be like the lost hiker; your right foot being stronger brings you back to where you started: Jefferson-on-the-Lake.

He's got a baker's dozen of these. It's four o'clock in the afternoon and the light is serene, what he can get of it through his dirty windows. He sees green creeping up and taking over from the mustard-yellow scrub. A Micah-word pops into his neocortex: the desuetude of winter.

I've missed spring, he thinks.

He calls East Palestine PD on his last hunch of the day and asks for the investigating officer of . . . let's see, he finds it in the scrap pile in front of him, case number 262-12-05.

The Cavs are playing tonight without LeBron. He's hurt his back again. He laid down his last hundred with Oscar. "Are you stupid, Haftmann?" shouts one of the card players from the shadowy corner. "You better take points tonight on those Cleveland Cadavers . . ."

His dreams. Always water in them lately. Flies and music. Weights and contraptions on an oak beam ceiling. Nothing makes sense but the pieces are there for him to see.

He sees a man surrounded by flies sitting at a table in the corner of a dim bar. He laughs in his dream. It's that Al Capp character with the unpronounceable name and a horde of flies over his head. Read it when he was a kid. Showed his grandmother the character's name in print, a cartoon balloon about his head, flies. "Dat's not English, liebchen," she said.

Ashamed of her, of her accent.

The man surrounded by flies stands up. He's big. A baby spot shows how broad he is in the chest. *Like some weightlifter freaks Cleveland Vice used to bust for drugs.*

He walks toward Haftmann. His strides are slow, measured, unhurried.

THE BIG BASTARD IS COMING TO KILL HIM.

He reaches for his gun – pulls back a stump of wrist, the white bones showing through the red. Veins spout blood like a garden sprinkler.

His phone recorder in his office on the Strip is at capacity with calls. He listens to some, deletes most, and jots down some notes for later.

Call T. P. Matrooshian at the Cleveland Clinic. Billing dept. wants to discuss bill. Check bounced.

Call Artiss.

Call Agent-in-Charge Booth, Cleveland office. *Why here?* He wonders. It was Booth who put the arm on Millimaki to get him a few lousy updates, even though the cops treat him like a pariah. Call Vanderhyden, Columbus.

Shit, the riot act. What now?

Someone put a hollow point, business end up, in his mailbox.

A man's voice, garbled or drunk, wants to meet me. Client? Doesn't leave name, number, or reason for calling. Creepy but private eye draws them out of the woodwork.

Judge Stevens, clear those tickets by three o'clock, or bench warrant.

The call back to Booth was pay dirt. A dead woman in Canton. A household misadventure with soap and a slippery tub in that most dangerous place in America – the bathroom. Broken neck. Thermostats turned way up. *Get on it.*

Booth had greased his path with a call to Canton PD and arranges for a black-and-white to bring him out to the house. He doesn't know what brought Booth around, but he's going to be on his best behavior.

Scoping it out, he notes middle-class respectability: neat house, raised-bed flower garden; grackles poking around in the yard.

For a second, he believes he can smell blood inside this house, but he knows there's no spatter from a broken neck.

The autopsy report has been copied to the same VICAP profiler by directive from SAC Booth. Haftmann can't believe it: a crime scene warm, if not hot.

Ligatures, like the Painesville Woman. Sucker bites on buttocks. Anal bruising. No flies. But the heat had affected post-mortem lividity.

Haftmann no longer believed the killer used heat to damage forensics. Was this something out of his control? As Artiss liked to say about himself, "It's his style." He had a thing about heat. Maybe he'd write his name and address on the walls next time.

How long was Warren after Painesville? Is this the pattern he's operating out of?

He has a dozen questions but Booth is reticent over the phone.

They found the sex photos in the freezer wrapped in foil. A couple dozen, about half with her in them. Some with faces. Different men. No other women, just her, in lace panties or bottomless; her vagina an open wound in the split beaver shots.

Haftmann knew the reason for the bra always on and wondered if that was something that attracted her killer. A breastless woman. Like a man; latent gay possibly?

None of the men in the photo were right; all looked past their thirties. Not nearly big enough in size to have done Warren. Maybe the killer wasn't a big man. Could be one of those guys with a freakish muscle density, small in physique yet powerful.

There were no sex magazines or letters in the house. There was no indication that anyone but a single, middle-aged woman lived here. The freezer was full of diet microwave dinners with continental cuisine appeal.

The fiber analysis team was still busy, but a dozen cops had been in the room by the time he got there.

No cash in her purse except a few ones and some change. *That's odd.* Her checkbook and savings account book intact. Master Card and Visa were being checked for purchases. Maybe she bought lover boy something in his size. It would help, although he didn't count on it.

The stereo and TVs left behind, not a petty thief at heart. A mahogany tower of CDs next to the nightstand. No classical music, but a lot of Andrea Bocelli, Sarah Brightman, Celine Dion, and a Canadian, Monica Schroeder.

Normal, very normal.

After the forensics specialists had left, he went into her bedroom. Splotches of dusting talc everywhere you'd think a person might put prints and forget to wipe off later.

Haftmann hadn't been a cop for very long before he knew how misleading the business of fingerprints in the public's mind. Now and then you got a good partial with enough points to convict; even the F.B.I.'s gee-whiz technology was overrated.

They spent a lot of the public's money on informers. Their snouts went deep into the public trough.

He knew two dangerous felons with rap sheets as long as his arm hanging around the Lake with new I.D.s and walking-around money, courtesy of Uncle Sam.

He busted one rapo last summer – only to see him disappear into the Federal Witness Protection program.

"Like polishing turds," as Frank used to say. The word of scum for the most part, even though the public saw its money well spent, good citizens taking a bold stand against crime.

He lay on her bed, stared at the pink canopy overhead. Was this what it looked like while he was enjoying her?

The phone rings on the table next to him. He almost jumps from fright; his stomach churns with acid. He picks it up.

"Hello."

"Is this Private Investigator Thomas Haftmann? I've got a call for you from F.B.I. Special Agent Booth. I'll patch him through."

"Haftmann? Your cup runneth over. New Philadelphia. A man and a woman. I'm sending a unit for you now. Stay put."

Christ, look at me, he thought, *I'm shaking with excitement like a shrew.*

If you were German in Haftmann's boyhood neighborhood, you were a "Nazi." He learned to fistfight because he wouldn't be the Nazi; it was an American G.I. or nothing. The windows of his house were broken once. Some idiot bully confused him with German Jew and Nazi thuggery once by calling him a Nazi kike. "Here comes *Iky, Iky Eichmann,*" they shouted at him. *Eichmann, man of oak in name only.* A pencil pusher, a bureaucrat.

His buddies went into the factories, such as Union Carbide, El-Kem Metals, Reactive Metals, Incorporated; he went into the merchant marine. Haftmann did not believe in God, although his grandmother was a strict German Catholic. The instruction he go convinced him in later years that hell and heaven were ideas borne of lunacy and bad passions. But he could see himself suspended over a lake of Erie's size, molten fire like the sun's surface, and clinging to a spider web of rope above the consuming flames.

He felt hot anguish for himself, for the hordes of people who wound up in places like Dachau, Auschwitz, Bergen-Belsen, Treblinka. Men and women and children pressed together like shad. All to die. Some to the right, to

174

work until they dropped; others to the left, to the smoking chimneys of the crematoria.

The books said it was one of the characteristic signs of the psychopathic personality, a thing with languages. The most disturbed would talk in rhymes.

Micah: "Freud said you act out the destiny of your name."

Freud said a lot of things, Micah. "Don't trust so much in books," he says.

The officer who's driving him looks him over hard in the rearview mirror. He knows I'm not a cop, Haftmann realizes. Booth has saved him – but for what, exactly? He doesn't know what he'll find down there among the cornfields of New Philadelphia.

~ ~ ~

What he found on the walls of the farmhouse in New Philadelphia was, in the hieroglyphics of insanity, the killer's own name.

Writ large. In blood and silver-brite paint.

The old cop said the baby died, starved to death, because it had no food. Cried itself to sleep, then died. Nobody near enough to hear it bawl. "It's a real shame," he said.

It made him think of a funhouse at first: interior walls in silver dabbed in red; the blood spatters all in one direction.

He tortured them first.

Had them tied facing each other across the kitchen table. They were fresh; the autopsies were being done right now. It looked as though he'd sodomized them both with a broom handle.

Congealed vomit, very rank in odor, obviously booze mixed up with the stomach contents of their last meal – see? Ponies of beer, Genesee Creme Ale, and those other ones with the pastel labels, California Coolers.

175

What information did they have that he wanted so badly?

They could see horror in each other's face across the table. What courage, not to give him what he wanted right away.

Information about him, maybe. Something we could trace backwards to him. Probably he had it all planned out when he knocked on their door.

The newspapers would be happy. You wouldn't be able to tell the difference between a big-city paper and a supermarket tabloid in two days. A feeding frenzy over this much blood.

There wouldn't be a private moment in their lives left secret.

He stares in fascination at the silver walls and the scarlet rosettes of blood; their outlines in chalk where they'd slumped in final repose against the far wall. He touches the sticky paint with his fingers; boiler-room heat would keep it tacky. Someone opened a window to clear out some of the noxious fumes.

He could hear the drone of springtime flies awakened to the scent of blood.

He takes Interstate 77 home, decides to hit Canton for some food even though his stomach is queasy by the time he pulls into the parking lot of an all-night Mr. Happy's Donuts.

He closes his eyes and sleeps upright in his car until a unit of the Canton police rousted him with a searchlight in his face.

The cop is set to do a Breathalyzer on him right there, but his P.I. license and a letter from Booth attesting his credential halt the proceedings. He sits in the patrol car behind the wire mesh while the officer checks his identification card. His partner stands off casually at the just the right angle while the transaction occurs, his right hand not exactly on the butt of his service automatic, but he doesn't like the way Haftmann looks no matter what cards he presents. Haftmann doesn't blame him. He's running on fumes and alcohol nowadays, rarely shaves, and his swollen cheek from the fight is still yellow-black. His bad eye, too. Besides private-eye badges are almost a cereal box gimmick. His spooky F.B.I. letter doesn't strike either cop as kosher. *Better check*. He and Frank would have done the same thing in this situation.

At home, three o'clock in the morning, he finds the latest paper in a moldy pile where the others have been tossed: city utilities were going up 7.5%, it said.

He drops into his unmade bed. The sheets smell sour but he doesn't care. It's as close to bliss as he's been in years just to be allowed to sleep. He dreams again of the Man with Flies, a viscous black halo over his head. This time he got the knife blade into Haftmann's jugular before he wakes in a greasy sweat of fear and whimpering.

Shit, shower, shave—just like the merchant marine or the armed services.

Phil calls with news: "You know that fucko that blew the kid's head off last winter?"

"You've got him?" Haftmann anticipates.

"He got picked up on the Strip. Drunk out of his gourd, big as life. Can you believe it?"

Haftmann said it sounded about right.

"Can I talk to him?"

"Put your crackpipe down, Thomas."

"Then let me see him for one minute," he pleads.

~ ~ ~

The man in prison coveralls bends over the washbowl in the holding cage. He was still trying to grow out a beard but it didn't hide him from the drinking buddy who dropped a dime on him. His eyes were bloodshot from his three-day bender. His lips, pulled back from his brown teeth, looked like red worms.

"I got really drunk last night. I'm really hung over, man."

From the next room, Haftmann watches Phil work him in the interrogation room with a list of Haftmann's hastily written questions. Phil's no slouch at interrogating suspects, but today he's Mister Efficiency, no doubt fearing Millimaki's return from a meeting in Columbus. "Where's Lonnie Nelson?"

"I dunno, man."

"When did you last see him?"

"About a year, two years ago. He visited me at my old lady's trailer."

"Why?"

"Fuck, I dunno. We rode bikes together in Toledo for a while. "

"Were you dealing at the time?"

"In Toledo? Yeah, a little."

"What?"

"Grass, crank – a little smack when I could get it."

"What did Nelson do?"

"None of that shit, man. He didn't deal or use. He was talkin' weird-like. He wanted one thing. Steroids, man. He said he wanted to get big."

Chapter 10

Memorial Day

The crowds lining the Strip, awaiting the start of the chintzy parade that the Chamber of Commerce put on every Memorial Day, weren't the motley crew the JOTL police department liked to think.

In fact, they were closer to the dead Libyan dictator Muammar Qaddafi's list of Nine Enemies than anyone realized: Capitalists, The Idle Rich, Exploiters, Those Who Cooperate with Foreigners, Corrupt People, Shepherds Who Consider People as Herds of Animals, Selfish People, Rumormongers, and Lazy People.

Principally, the first and the last.

By two o'clock in the afternoon, traffic had slowed to five miles per hour between Lake Road (the business spur of 531) and Shillingham. By dusk, pedestrians crossing back and forth from one side of the Strip to the other would be unimpeded by the snail's pace traffic.

Canadian soldiers, midges, and black flies so tasty to trout were on hand to harass the visitors, sampling them as they in turn sampled hot dogs with green tips, greasy French fries, cotton candy, and other syrupy concoctions bad for the stomach, kidneys, heart, and liver.

On Memorial Day prices everywhere rocketed.

The real estate man had stopped by at ten o'clock in the morning to explain to Mister Jackson that, regrettably, his rent was doubled. He was a sagacious, trim man who had given various versions of his explanation to dozens of the cottage's occupants in years gone by and had rather come to relish the awkward looks and protestations his explanations produced. They were drifters, dopers, and losers one and all.

This one just stared, though, and that was scary.

Not to mention this guy looked strong enough to eat apples off his head.

The realtor decided to cut this explanation short. Despite the lake breeze, the realtor was sweating, and the words that rolled so felicitously off his tongue in his business with a customer in front of him weren't coming now at all. There was a smell, too, that lay under the big fellow's soap-smell, but he couldn't say what that was. Maybe dead fish from the shoreline.

He looked at the metal bars and configurations bolted to the walls that were clearly impermissible under the terms of the lease.

He decided not to mention the infraction to the lessee at this time, but a letter of reprimand was certainly called for later on.

Nelson had been doing preacher curls when the real-estate man knocked on the door. He recalled opening the door, and he seemed to remember sounds coming out of the hole in the little man's face. He had no idea what had been said to him or how long the man had stood there. He must be more careful to observe and listen to people.

He'd been slipping at work. Not hearing people talking to him, even when the noise wasn't that bad. Staring blankly and, worst of all, talking to voices in the air. The System was getting more demanding, and he was having trouble separating all the voices coming at him.

The bitch with the tattoo was openly mocking him now. Last night he saw her make the cuckoo sign, twirling her finger in loopy circles by her temple just because he didn't hear what she said.

Maybe if he fucked her she'd shut her mouth. No – he had no time for that. He knew deep inside that he was on the right course, but why were the voices nagging at him so much? So hard to think when they're droning on and on with their impossible demands.

I did it right. The last time was perfect, exactly as it was supposed to be. Couldn't they see that?

Why did they send him here if they weren't satisfied with the way he was doing it?

He was getting back into the lifting groove, and that was helping some; his confidence was coming back.

New Philadelphia should have been a triumph, should have brought him some recognition from the System. They were keeping the angel back, punishing him as if he were the organ grinder's monkey instead of the one playing the tune.

He looked at the Cleveland paper's headline, mocking his puny effort.

Plane Crash at Sioux City, Iowa, Kills 109.

If he'd known there was a baby upstairs, he'd have done that one too.

The papers were screaming for his blood. That was exhilarating – and frightening, too.

He suddenly noticed the real-estate man was gone.

He smashed his left fist through the drywall. "Eat me," he said.

He meant the world.

~ ~ ~

Haftmann has the insert faxed him from the F.B.I.'s Behavioral Sciences Unit's Latent Descriptor Index. He sucks air into his chest and slowly exhales: *This could be it.*

He wants New Philadelphia to be seen differently from Warren with its attention-getting, awesome spectacle. The silver paint was no less theatrical to the sane mind, of course, but you have to see him from the inside of his own delusions.

What is senseless to the antagonist is understandable to the sympathizer.

Like terrorism.

He may be on a crusade; widening his scope; more enthralled by dementia.

With psychosis, you never know.

Haftmann knows criminals, not crazies or crusaders.

But this one he wants more than ever.

He's acting out something, but what? Booth doesn't give much. He's got all the current intel, but he keeps it under his hat – or his shiny silver hair.

He's gone over the police report and the autopsy report a dozen times. The killer battered their brains, literally, out of their heads and onto the walls; around150 to 200 blows to each head and set them side-by-side in the corner. Moderate rigidity, the coroner estimated. He wasn't running amok as he did at the Warren house. He had a purpose, which he accomplished with the silver paint and the hammer. The frenzied bashing notwithstanding, he was creating an artwork in gore that only he understood.

For a break, he rides with Elise. Haftmann used to hate parade route duty. There'd be the fights to break up, crowds of rubberneckers to disperse, pickpockets to eyeball until dusk. Then the drunks and disorderlies come out at night. Three bars on the Strip always did a brisk business in mayhem and random violence: Mickey's Lounge, Roger's Rec Room, and that other shithole, the Purple Haze, a redneck-biker-misfit watering hole that carried over its original psychedelic name despite the kind of music played inside. He'd been in there once on a case involving a young teen girl runaway he later found in Florida. That sole visit earned a gob of spit on the back of his neck. When he turned around to confront the spitter, twenty angry faces confronted him. He walked out and you could have heard a whisper in the place.

Elise jabs the ACK button: "Three-Three-Seven,

Michael. Westbound on Beach. Where's the traffic tie-up?"

"Three-Three-Seven, Michael. No further information at this time. Do you see a vehicle on fire at Beach Boulevard and Walnut? Informant advises a vehicle on fire eastbound lane."

"Three-Three-Seven, Michael. No sign of a vehicle on fire."

"Roger that. Ten-four, Three-Three-Seven, Michael."

Shawna dispatching: her voice.

He has met her husband, finally. He turned out to be the strange caller who had asked him for a meeting but left no contact info. Because Haftmann likes him, he feels all the more ashamed.

Yet he'd punched her in the eye, *fucking coward*. A man who hits a woman – but, then, he had hit Micah after confronting her with her adultery, hit her so hard she bounced around the walls of the kitchen and ended up on her back in the living room. He thought he'd dislocated her jaw. Then he wept like a baby holding her in his arms, she too dazed to know where she was, coming to, being smothered, fearing he was going to kill her, finish it.

Stupid, stupid, trying to make his love erase the vileness of it . . .

Never wanted sex so bad with anyone in his life. The sickness of it overwhelming him.

"I gave her up out of grief and shame," he said.

"What – Haftmann, what are you doing? You're talking to yourself now," said Elise.

"Sorry," he said. "Just thinking aloud."

"No, Tom, you're talking aloud and that's creepy. Stop it."

Shawna's husband is late thirties, handsome enough, slender but muscular, an Amish-style beard Haftmann finds creep. Said he'd never struck her before. Haftmann remembers a sense of disconnection at the time. Two guys having a chat about one guy's wife. Then her husband somehow got onto talking about cars. He was good at restoring cars apparently. *Had Haftmann ever seen that candy-apple red 'Vette, 1965, cruising the Strip?* Well, he did the finish on that. Stripped it to the metal and put on five separate coats. You ever see that car under a light, he told Haftmann proudly, you'll see a rose design on the hood that shows up; it's three layers deep. The guy who owned it turned down $55,000 for it at an auto show in Erie one time. Silly bastard won't sell it, even though he hasn't got a pot to piss in. Lives on peanut butter sandwiches so he can drive that car up and down the Strip all summer long.

Then Haftmann, itchy and bored, interjects. *Play the hand you're given.*

She, your wife, Shawna (finally said her name), *is my . . .* (he can't say it, *lover*)

"I know," he said.

"So what do we do about it?"

"I don't know."

"Do you love her?"

"Now . . . right now, man, I just don't know," he said. "It would be easier to know if *you* loved her."

"I wish I could say," Haftmann said.

"I don't want to give her up," he said.

"Well," Haftmann said, weak-voiced, "I understand that."

Awful, just awful.

It went on like that for another twenty-five minutes. When they parted in front of Tico's Place, he felt confused, disgusted. The last thing the man said was that he hoped it would be a hot summer like last year. We had too much rain this spring. Haftmann had agreed to that.

They had shaken hands. Another stupid, male ritual to mask feelings.

"I just wanted you to know," he said.

"I understand," Haftmann said to him, lying through his teeth. "Believe me, I do."

Haftmann thought of his crazy grandmother and her fanatical sense of justice: *Liars roast in hell on one of Satan's special tines*. He was a boy. He had to look the word up.

~ ~ ~

There had to be a key to it somewhere: he had no known proclivities with other serial killers in the F.B.I. files. God knows, numbers of them drenched themselves in blood, bayed at the moon, covered themselves in it.

What was his dirty little secret that he kept locked inside until those moments when he went out of control with it? Did he like to hear them cry and beg for their lives first?

The New Philadelphia couple had been swingers for only six months. At this stage in the investigation with its vastly accelerated inertia, no one was holding out anything; the taint of bad publicity was much feared, so everyone cooperated, as if a dam had burst.

A special team of unproductive agents had been picked to deal with the wackos who confessed to the murders. So far, 375 had confessed to Warren; the New Philadelphia count was already 219 and growing.

Incredibly, they'd managed to keep back a little something only the murderer and they would know. The broomstick sodomies were one thing; fortunately, it was overshadowed by the grotesque interior decorating job done by the killer in his frenzy.

But not the sex angle, which played up big. Fornication in the farmland, in the midst of a quiet silo-town burgh was rocking the Midwest, giving Ohio another black eye. Preachers were defying the decorum of the pulpit off camera to scold their congregations. Wavy-haired TV evangelists with Oklahoma accents were flaying the fornicator to the delight of their sponsors. The nation was sickened by its debunking of one of its favorite myths: New York and LA? Sure, Sodom and Gomorrah. But those sweet, crossroad villages with the hokey biblical names you saw traveling down Interstate 90? "Hey, wasn't Ohio where all them Ay-mish people lived?" Sure, it was . . .

The governor was apoplectic. The hounding was unabated despite promises for a speedy end to the most insidious evil it had been the misfortune of his tenure to witness . . .

In private conversations to Booth and Vanderhyden he was less Latinate, more Anglo-Saxon. Yet the message was the same: "Get that God-damned animal off the street."

What had a twenty-three-year-old man with a six-acre farm, a pretty, brown-haired nineteen-year-old wife, and a six-month-old son been doing in the clutches of a raving maniac in the first place? No one, Haftmann knew from his reading, knew the answer to that one yet.

Haftmann had seen the couple's ad, and he wondered if either one had had a prevision that they would be inscribing their own death certificate. It looked ominous in hindsight:

WANTED ALIVE, NOT DEAD

Very sexy, attractive, slim, young married white couple. Seek white, open-minded, young, horny, well-hung, super-clean, disease-free single or married males for friendship and sex! Want hot times, not dead ends. She's 19, very petite, 5'4, very pretty, 103 lbs., sexy legs, 34-21-32, beautiful ass, very tight, multi-orgasmic and gets very, very wet. She enjoys dressing sexy. What would you like to see her wearing? She loves wearing miniskirts, stockings, garter belt, sexy, tight panties and going braless! Love giving and receiving French to completion, acting out fantasies, maybe gentle gang bangs, photography, videos and homemade videos, VHS. Love meeting on a regular basis, dining, dancing. He's 23, 5'10 and very good looking. Not interested in pain, drugs, drunks, S/M, B/D, one-night stands or phonies! He makes all arrangements. How would you like to meet? Entertain only. Must send explicit photo, letter, stating your desires and fantasies, phone, SASE. All photos returned upon request. If hot, give us a try! We are honest and for real and expect same. TUSCARAWAS COUNTY.

~ ~ ~

Her photo was placed above the ad. She was taken from behind, her ass crack covered by panties that bisected can. Garter belt, net hose, a black filigree ensemble with frilly shoulder straps. She had obviously checked the Block My Face option; there was the white circle covering her face on the screen image. Haftmann had seen that face after the ball-peen hammer had worked it over. Scrapings of nose cartilage and bone were found on the ceiling.

Haftmann had no doubt that the persuasive powers of the combined police forces of the state and the national government, throw in the IRS and the Treasury for good measure, met with little resistance in prying the photo and form loose. *Make My Day, Punk*: cops loved it.

Figure on six to eight weeks before the couple had advertised on the site, and you had cut a tiny niche in the avalanche of investigative paperwork. There it was: a new start with fresh leads.

Haftmann had seen the farmhouse ripped apart by three teams of forensics; it was exhilarating to watch pros at work: like chop-shop artists he and Frank used to bust in the Flats before it became overpriced. Junk food on the same Boardwalk, as tasteless and joyless as the Strip's cuisine, but you paid quadruple prices.

No stash of sex photos or DVDs. It was a long shot, but

you had to try it. He thought of the pretty little wife with her ass reamed out at her kitchen table and shook with rage. Their hands were bloody from the rope burns; only unbearable pain does that. If they had photos, a letter from the killer, they'd have given him anything he asked for to stop the terror and the hurt. Haftmann knew that no one's threshold of pain is that high.

Every dustbin and garbage can was being examined in the county; highway rest stops were combed on the off chance that he decided to dump his bloody clothes en route to whatever crib this monster lay in. VICAP said he did all his murders naked.

The F.B.I. was still running tests on the paint; they'd get it within a hundred miles of its purchase point, but preliminary tests said it was from a batch of pigment mixed at Plant No. 2 of SCM, Incorporated on Middle Road in Ashtabula. He was either staying within a couple hundred miles radius of New Philadelphia – or he'd vanished forever.

Haftmann felt the maniac's presence; could even smell him at night in his dreams. He sometimes awoke with the taste of ash in his mouth.

As he had done with a slew of ads compatible with the Warren couple's composite ad based on psychological profiles of the couple's lifestyle, he knew the New Philadelphia couple's ad was being dissected by the same shrinks for internal clues to be added to the Latent Descriptor Index. More dust motes added to the pile.

WANTED ALIVE, NOT DEAD.

The cryptanalysis section at Quantico was playing with that: recombining it for every possible suggestive hint. Maybe the trigger is in the caption.

Meanwhile, he has more material shipped via UPS and Federal Express every day, and every day he has to plead with Millimaki to take more cops off the duty roster, get confirmation of his status from Booth, stop taking up time with bullshit stuff.

So far, he hasn't been reimbursed a dime for travel or mileage, and because he knows something about the gargantuan incompetence of bureaucracies, he knows he probably never will be. He can't even do what ninety-seven percent of Americans did every day: use plastic to pay for meals and motels on the road. VISA and Master Card cancelled his cards; his credit in town rescinded everywhere. Oscar squawked so loud about the last rubber check that he'd drawn on the rest of his credit line to pay him off.

Chief Millimaki is covering his wide ass with a compromise until the orders assigning Haftmann to the state's investigation came through; forms in triplicate, signed and countersigned by F.B.I./Cleveland, B.C.I., and everyone else who sad a partial interest in his life or who has something to do with how he gets paid. Even Micah, it seemed, wants her pound of flesh: he'd been notified two days ago by a clerk for Judge Stevens that she's slapped a garnishment on his wages until he can pay her half of the house.

Yet he's never felt so committed to anything in his life.

Right now, though, he's falling through the cracks and forced to wait on the paperwork that will get him free of Millimaki and the two-way parade of human flesh that began on Memorial Day weekend and would peak at Fourth of July, then slowly dwindle down to a last gasp on Labor Day.

Jesus God, I'm tired of doing the backstroke in this cesspool town . . .

WANTED DEAD OR ALIVE

Steve McQueen's black-and-white TV series in the 1950s about a bounty hunter . . .He lives in fantasies.

Or he likes to escape. Same thing.

What else makes you tick, monster? Sex with pain?

Only they don't know that right away, do they? You can get in their doors. How, how, do you manage to keep a lid on those twisting worms in your head long enough?

Artiss' bragging words from his first interrogation: *Con them, blitz them, surprise them.*

Wouldn't he come up with the photo or the letter you sent him fast enough?

Wait a minute . . .

Haftmann flips through the file on the seat in front of him and gets a blast of horn from an oncoming vehicle hugging the centerline.

The irony of it: Haftmann can't move on the investigation in any significant capacity until he has signed off in triplicate. But the killer's moving all over the state, passing through the webs of the netting laid out to catch him.

Maybe the monster couldn't be got to that way. Impossible. No one's invisible. Everybody's on somebody's disk. Find which one.

Haftmann takes a call from Booth at Roland's Cafe. Two Cleveland women, housewives, members of the same clubby social set that frequented an on-premise swing club while their husbands played poker and golfed, had contracted the AIDS virus. The killer's fetish for sodomy was shared by hundreds of thousands, he supposed, but it pointed broadly in the direction of institutionalized homosexuality. His size and strength made it unlikely that he learned to like it as a catcher while a guest of the state. Pussies like Artiss filled that bill. He was a pitcher.

But what if he weren't always that big?

Some state reformatories were worse than prisons on that score. They had the same grapevine, the same argot for dealing with new arrivals. How many packs of cigarettes for the cute car thief due in tomorrow? If printed, despite his youthful offender status, a mug shot of the new arrival would be scarfed from files to assist the barter.

Get Booth on it. And that lazy fuck Vanderhyden, who spent most of his time writing reports and goosing the man-hours his CID boys were putting in.

Careerism and getting ahead. When had that stopped to mean anything to him? This one was going to put him in the big time, and he could wipe the steaming pile of ordure that was Jefferson-on-the-Lake off his shoes forever.

Got to. My last chance. The circuits are overloaded. I'm not going to make it too much longer.

On the other hand, who would know if he flipped out? The whole bizarre culture was being dragged down in front of his eyes.

Some of the night-shift women were going to a party at a rental cottage on the Strip. Women paid a male stripper fifty bucks apiece to take them on. Husbands could watch but not interfere; orgasms were counted. Cover charge at the door for the house.

Something clicked; something he had read last night before he collapsed on his sofa in ballooning swirls of dust and exhaustion.

A summary of a two-man investigation south of here. The police report noted suspicious circumstances to warrant inclusion in the state's hunt for the Jack-in-the-Box Killer.

A deadbeat found in the rubble of a charred house; owner apprised police that the house was unrented and should have been unoccupied. Probably, some winehead found his way in, immolated himself with a cigarette and a bottle of Mad Dog.

When the team followed up a lead, they discovered that the manager of a nightclub had been renting out the place under the table and pocketing the money.

Besides, they noted, the state's arson investigator told them from the description given by the local fire department that the accelerator had to be kerosene or gasoline.

One other tidbit: two locals disappeared right after the fire. Both had connections with the nightclub. One was a small-time pusher. The other was the club's bouncer and bartender, who may have dipped his hands in the till before he quit.

Bouncers tended to be aggressive with a pronounced machismo syndrome: burly, no-neck types.

He scrawled a note to have Vanderhyden check into it further when Elise got a call from base about a fight in front of Roger's Rec Room. "Wonderful," she said; "eight o'clock at night, and we've got our first tavern brawl of the silly season."

He tries out a John Barrymore line from *Key Largo* on her. "Oh, God, send a big wave and drown us all . . ."

"Haftmann, you're an asshole."

~ ~ ~

The dust-up at Roger's turned out to be all smoke, no fire. Two welterweights were mixing it up to the hoots of the crowd; a couple bets got down before Haftmann and a JOTL blue on crowd control got there to break it up.

Haftmann knew them both: a couple sorry-asses from sparsely populated New Lyme Township, where Mike Tyson used to own a fancy house with an ironwork grill of his name over the entrance. These two shitbirds were shirttail cousins, but he no longer remembers the convoluted family history that brought a whole tribe of these ridge-runners up to Ohio. They found a quiet patch of turf in New Lyme, bred, intermarried, and periodically killed one another. You go down one of those switchbacks off Tompkins Road and you'll see the same name on all the mailboxes just like the hollow they left where five families did all the screwing. Like the inbred idiot savant in *Deliverance*. Only real.

Haftmann had driven out to one of their homesteads years ago to break up a pit bull breeding and fighting ring. One of these mean bastards had devised a new wrinkle on the sport: drive railroad spikes through an old, blind swayback horse and bet how long it took Harley's or Cleese's dogs to kill it.

Haftmann saw dead dogs in the yard, and a pile of blue intestines that had pulled out of a living horse.

Cleese went to court, pulled out a thick roll of bills and paid the fine, around ninety bucks, and told everyone that day to kiss his rosy-red ass.

Elise told the Lake cop to take them in. She wasn't sure if he'd be able to drive that many miles with those two in a vehicle with a gun under his arm.

"Some fucking fun," said Harley; "You fucking cops make me fucking sick." He spits near Elise's shoe. Haftmann tries to communicate telepathically with her: *Go ahead; take them both down a side road, tie them to a tree, and fire away.*

The remainder of the shift is quiet except for the concussive bursts of waves of noise from the bars along the Strip. Drunks wander desultorily out of bars and into other bars.

Haftmann can't eat, and the odors of fried meat and grease make him nauseated. He has been passing some blood lately – too much coffee, beer, and cigarettes in his system. Not enough rest.

The shank of the evening sees the replacement of the factory workers and steelworkers from Youngstown and Pittsburgh who go back to their cottages to rest up for tomorrow's fun. Younger blood takes over the streets. There's a more frenetic pace to the crowd now; the night air is redolent with perfume that draws mosquitoes to flesh and males to females: the never-ending promise of sex.

Haftmann drove by Shawna's before returning to his empty house. He kicks over a three-foot stack of papers and texts, and without picking up anything, negotiates his way in the dark to the kitchen, opens the fridge, and grabs a can of beer. He has enough acid in his stomach to dissolve ten yards of railroad track.

He sits on the sofa and can't remember at once whether he still has a working television.

He takes the gun out. *Just do it*, says the little man in his head.

He holds the gun in his lap, nothing strange in that, he thinks, and closes his eyes. He's so damned tired lately . . .

He drives to the Strip instead and checks out the action. He's sitting in a corner of a cabaret that he'd forgotten existed.

The routine on stage presents two bosomy fräuleins mug it up with a skinny comic in lederhosen and Alpine cap. Lots of fanny pinching and butt wriggling; breasts threaten to spill loose from blouses.

But no one was laughing. The place is nearly empty except for a few customers and three old men playing dominoes in the back corner. They could have been transplanted Cubans, although Haftmann can't see their faces.

He does see the pockmarked face of the scumbag he rousted on the Strip years ago. The man's face was the closest thing to evil Haftmann had ever seen. He noted the pitchfork tattoo on his left hand and the heart with daggers on the right. He moves on out of sight. Dominoes clicked in the corner. The sound is menacing. Haftmann sees Shawna, of all people, sitting at a table near the front alone. Where had she come from? He's almost unhinged by the surprise of seeing her here at this crazy hour of the night.

He tells her he's in love with her. She smiles at him.

Her eyes are gorgeous and yellow like a cat's.

He's in such a hurry to get her to his house and get her clothes off that he puts the come-along on her. She gives a little yip of pain, then laughs.

She's a mix of surprises for him – blonde hair on her snatch, red hair on top. He's wild with happiness.

He's eating her, and she's blowing him with the most exquisite tongue action he's ever felt. She's sopping wet where he's been licking her, salty-sweet pussy juice dribbling off his chin, and she just can't stop orgasming.

He's insane for her. He rolls her off and forearms her into position, but her knees spread willingly. Their sex is perfect give-and-take until he feels himself coming again.

She moans and rolls upright to get it into her mouth, but it just shoots and spatters her on the stomach and throat; he's helpless to control it now.

He's never had sex like this before, not even in the early days of his marriage to Micah; Haftmann's no sexual athlete and sex is either good or it's better, but this is supernatural.

Out of the dark comes a voice.

That voice.

His voice, the Jack-killer.

Haftmann is fully awake now, soiled with his wet dream. He feels the pain where the material of his pants has stuck to the prepuce, but he unsticks it and feels the ooze. His heart is pounding wildly.

Haftmann's mother drank poison in America, the land of dreams. But Berlin was always with her, and her shame of the rapes by Russian soldiers and what she did to survive never left her.

His grandmother wouldn't talk about it, and slapped his face hard when he asked her about his mother. Then she held him to her chest and the tears dripped down her face onto his.

Haftmann rolls over to wait for dawn, unable to stop the bitter tears from falling.

~ ~ ~

By the time Lonnie Dale Nelson helped the barmaids, Diesel Dyke and Tattoo Bitch, clear tables, put the cans into garbage bags, stow trash outside, and secure the cash, it was almost five o'clock in the morning.

He walked from the bar to his cottage; Erie's water getting just warm enough to create wisps of fog, like low-scudding clouds, across the Strip. Here and there, lights were still on in a few bars cleaning up, and some restaurants and outdoor cafes were just preparing for the early risers.

The street held the greasy odor of food from last night. He saw puddles of vomit on the curb and sidewalk, a black dog mounting another dog, carnival garbage waiting to be swept away for the coming day and the next batch of tourists.

He had nothing to eat at home except Worcester sauce, which he poured on saltines, and a small jar of mayonnaise, sugar, and some bread. He'd been eating sugared mayonnaise sandwiches for the last three days because the rent was eating the money he made at the dive.

He tried stealing car parts for extra money. One of the chop shops paid top dollar for any Chevy part between '48 and '72. He also siphoned gas from cars parked along the shady side streets off the Strip. He found a hairline fracture in his distributor head that could have meant serious trouble on the highway. He'd heard talk at the bar from some of the scuzzbags that right now is not a particularly good time to get stopped if you broke down. "The state cops come right up to your fuckin' window with their hands on their guns. That goddamn killer, betcha any amount."

Tattoo Bitch bragged to Diesel Dyke while cleaning up she made a sign that said FREE BLOWJOBS when she was in New Orleans for Mardi Gras last year.

"No shit," said the dyke. "You give head to anything with a zipper anyways, who you shittin'"? Tattoo Bitch laughs and told her a crowd of people followed her around with their smartphones and then put a couple on a few sites, including YouTube.

"How many you give?"

"Dunno," said the tattooed slut, "but at least twelve, maybe fifteen."

Trash, all of them. Human shit.

~ ~ ~

The red ball of morning sun rising from the lake startled him and filled him with a vision of beauty and terror that rocked him to his knees. He fell to the ground weeping, unable to comprehend its meaning, but he knew the angel had touched him to the very depths of his soul. He saw curtains moved aside in the newly occupied cabins, checking out the spectacle: a morning drunk still rolling in his boots from last night's festivities. No big deal.

He knew then that his last house call had been right, found good by the System at last, and that he had passed some kind of rite of passage.

It would not stop now; he would kill them all. The very sun in the sky was the greatest of the messages that he had been chosen to receive.

There would be a new plan, and he need only wait to receive his orders. Keep himself pure from the contamination all around him. They didn't matter. He was beyond them, becoming something so great that nothing had been seen like it on earth.

Tell me.

He heard the water lapping offshore, the beat of the waves. Gulls shrieking as they clustered above a school of shad out in the gun-muzzle gray depths of Erie. He saw the dark blue patch and the careering birds above it. Just like the gulls on the Ohio River, not as graceful as these silver-tipped birds which didn't have to feed on the toxic garbage of raw sewage. The cool morning air passed through him.

Silence.

The din of voices ceased completely.

He felt as if some blessed release had been granted him from the memories that transfixed him and made him the single spectator at their grisly sideshow.

He thought, for a solitary lovely moment, he could see himself watching himself, as if he had acquired the flight and vision of one of the birds.

Please tell me.

He saw the vast ribbon of light, glittering above the wave's surface, as the disc of sun arced above the water's edge.

Then he heard the angel speak to him: *Kill them. Kill them all.*

Rising from the distant shoreline, the concavity of its base of a giant's phallus, he saw the outline of the nuclear power plant's containment building stretching through the mist: proud and clear in the light.

To him, at that moment, it became the answer to the troubled mystery of his existence. It seemed to bulge with a secret life, shimmering in the morning light.

Kill them all.

Power and Light.

Redness, like the explosion of blood from pumping arteries. There was nothing like it on earth. He trembled in awe of the enormity of his revelation.

Kill them all.

Oh, yes.

How? He begged.
Power and Light.
 "I don't understand," he said.
You will, said the angel.

Chapter 11

Summer

The riot on the Strip that year cost the Chamber of Commerce seven million dollars in lost revenue by their reckoning. Factor in inflation, adjust for current numbers, and it's more like ten million now.

One tourist died of a heart attack when rioters overturned his car. After that, the Lake fizzled as the premier vacation spot for families on what locals pretentiously began to call the North Coast. The lean years lasted until the late-eighties; by then, eighty percent of the land and sixty-five percent of the concessions were in the hands of a few families.

Three key positions – mayor, fire chief, and police chief – were rotated among minions of the powerful families to ensure an equitable distribution of the spoils.

Now that the Lake was back on its feet, it was amusing to watch the sharpies and hustlers scramble for the crumbs from the table. No idea was stupid enough, no scheme crassly obvious enough in rattling the stick inside the swill bucket, that it would not prove remunerative enough for the freebooters and small-change artists to fight over. People came to the Strip from three states and thirty-five Ohio counties for the express purpose of enjoying themselves by dropping money into the coffers of the richest families.

The rubberneckers kept on coming with their families, the college kids lined up outside bars to pay $5.00 to get inside where they could buy bottles of beer for $3.25, if they were fortunate enough to get seats, and the rest milled up and down the streets to be serviced by the hawkers and gypsters and purveyors of amusement.

Haftmann had been there when thirteen teenagers were pried from a smash-up at Larkspur and DayLily with the Jaws of Life.

In the riot year, as locals call it, your worst element was the biker gangs, particularly the Cleveland Chapter of the Angels and the Pagans from Wheeling, West Virginia, who no sooner agreed to turf rules at the start of the season than they were getting it on after somebody's chick got raped or somebody's hog got pawed by the wrong low-riding slug. Those were the days of the so-called 3%ers: when 97% of the bikers were decent types whose colors antagonized no one, simply stated where they hailed from or announced some kind of insipid slogan about their home towns or states.

One of the popular exhibits at the county fair at the Jefferson campgrounds was always the weaponry taken off these dangerous rebels: knuckles, sticks, pig stickers, stilettos and switch blades drew gasps from Ma and Pa Kettle from Hicksville.

Before the sun worshippers had acquired the red bronze glow that they could show off to unfortunate neighbors in New Antioch and Mineral Ridge, the JOTL police department had detained 176 perps, all but sixteen males, indicted 154 on counts ranging from vehicular homicide, aggravated homicide, manslaughter second and third, assaults, assaults with battery, aggravated menacing, arson, thefts galore – petty and felony, possession, possession with intent to sell, DUIs (Millimaki had a quota system set in accord with the restaurant owners at the start of the season), public drunk, vandalism, vagrancy, receiving stolen goods, harboring a fugitive, selling alcohol to minors, moving violations that paid half the budget, concealed weapons, public nuisance, filing false reports to police and fire departments (a popular gag with the out-of-town frat rats, those little fascists-in-training), child molestation, and oral sodomy.

The domestic violence calls tripled. The accident reports rose exponentially. The loonies, in effect, took over the insane asylum for the summer.

By the end of June, the storage space for seized weapons was packed to capacity with enough sidearms and rifles to make John Brown spin dizzily in his urn over there in nearby Austinburg where locals claimed to see his ghost walking about the farmlands, awaiting the next racial ruckus. Sightings after Ferguson were more frequent.

The semiautomatics were a popular item this year; so were the ever-popular sawed-offs. Last year they found an Uzi in the back of a Trans Am with New York license plates.

The handguns were the most varied; all the P Series from Glocks, Berettas, Rugers, Brownings were represented in the evidence room. Home defenders, by and large still traditionalists, favored the Colt Python or .357 Magnum. These were usually picked up during domestic violence calls. This year, automatics were running 2 to 1 favorites over revolvers. Silencers, laser sights, Tasers by the score, two new night scopes used by Immigration on the border, a luger, a Walther PPK, a Rossi .357 mag carbine, a Magtech 586-P 12-ga. shotgun, stun guns, cattle prods, and a set of surgical knives in a bag with a doctor's name and address in Parma rounded out the special collections.

Witches from Vermont had shown up, and an alert was sent out to the Cattleman's Association and Granges in all surrounding counties to set watches on herds. Five whiteface Herefords were found last summer with their innards surgically removed.

Skinheads from Akron, Dayton, and Cleveland; punks from Detroit and Cincinnati. Bikers, Hare Krishnas chanting their Maha Mantra (with their website IKSON) from Buffalo and Moundsville, NV, drifters, geeks, and down-and-outers from all points of the compass were tossed into the Strip's slumgullion, but nothing would prepare the locals for the visitor to come, that product of Ohio's reformatory system; he was proving an *amuse-bouche* for a meal they would never forget.

Before long, enterprising individuals would set up as entrepreneurs of skin flicks, orgies, crack houses, and any vice you could lay claim to and provide the jack to finance. Capitalism at its grimmest. Dope was usually a second currency on the Strip by August.

Booth had been unable to get Haftmann officially assigned to the state's investigation, so he had to put time in at his office to draw a paycheck. Last week he combed the impound lot to locate three missing vehicles for out-of-state clients. The thieves, usually locals, left them lying around for pickup because the new season meant newer cars. When Haftmann described the condition of their cars after a season's joyriding, the owners usually preferred to collect on the insurance; as a result, Haftmann often got stiffed. Fortunately, the three he claimed from the lot were in good condition, a little dinged here and there; the RICO statutes were proving an unexpected boon: three Bay Liners sat at their berths in the marina surrounded by plastic yellow ribbon that said POLICE CRIME SCENE KEEP OUT.

This afternoon he rode security with Elise, unable to sit still at his desk, and too obviously aware that he had no part in the hunt for the "Jack." Former congressman and ex-jailbird Jimmy Trafficant was back in the news. Only this time he wasn't promoting his harebrained notion of an Ohio Canal to run parallel to Route 11 all the way from

Jefferson-on-the-Lake to Youngstown, which would leave most of the farmers in Ashtabula and Trumbull counties under water. A classic antique tractor he was driving back into the barn on his property turned over on him and killed him.

It seemed to Haftmann that he has gone past mere tiredness of mind and body into a zone of ratiocination he's never experienced. Things were in slow motion or double time. He lost the knack of enticing clients wasn't taking routine calls about his services.

This is hell. No escape from it.

Phil picks him up. He's showered and shaved. Wearing his old blue suit and a tie too skinny for fashion, but he hasn't been to Cleveland in years – and this is an invitation from Booth himself. On the way, Phil hands him the latest copies from Booth's task force. Phil's starts telling him about a joke where a drunk stands on a street corner and hears a suave man address passing women with what sounds like an obscene invitation. Phil ends the joke with the drunk's slurry falsetto: "'Tickle yer ass with a feather.'"

Haftmann smiles but not at the joke; he's looking over the latest Booth papers and he finds something for the East Pal PD to follow up. Somebody, a bar pick-up, was seen talking to the bouncer a week before the fire. She might know something.

He tells him that Booth is following a lead, but it looks thin. They've run the East Palestine club manager's license through DMV and, standard procedure all the way, through the F.B.I. and NCIC computers. He was dirty: left an early-release work program prematurely, a mere two weeks, but he was back in the slammer in Massachusetts.

The arson report filed with the state described a lot of burned metal in the basement. The follow-up team had a guy from Scandinavia Club check it out; he said the guy was a mechanical genius. It wasn't that easy to duplicate the Nautilus's cam principle.

A strong bastard, Phil said. Five, six hundred pounds of weights, judging from the melted plastic and sand after the fire.

The crispy one must have been fairly big too. The druggie's license said 6'2, 223. But was he big enough to lift a man by the ankles and attach him to the ceiling? Haftmann barely heard Phil:

"God damn! U-turned right in front of me, the peckerhead. Charles-Four-Four-One, base. Gimme a DMV check on an eight-five Chevy Malibu, license Tango-Alpha-Baker-Six-Six-Two, over."

"What about Immigration and Naturalization?" Haftmann asks. Phil's whipsawing to get the U-turner doesn't interest him in the slightest. "Zippo," Phil says and hits the flashers.

"How about the Dutch and German embassies?" Haftmann asks. He's perked up now even if it isn't that much.

"Forty-one Hauers or Howers checked out through military service records, no native sons, all clean."

The Malibu has pulled over, its big souped-up engine idling.

"What about the Howards?" Haftmann asks.

"They got the phonebook – but Booth is checking every one of them."

The Malibu driver taps the horn, impatient to get his ticket and get going.

Haftmann says, "Quit fucking the dog, Phil. Let's get this show on the road."

~ ~ ~

"I want to thank Private Investigator Haftmann for coming here today," Booth begins, eyeing the men and women assembled for him in the muster room. He's brought in his entire task force together for this meeting. Haftmann sees Cleveland PD, Highway Patrol, B.C.I. and several of his own handpicked agents who are introduced from the Cleveland, Youngstown, and Columbus field offices.

"As you men and women may already know, Thomas Haftmann is a former homicide detective of many years' standing with Cleveland Homicide and your own precinct before deciding to go into private practice." (That ensures a tight-lipped smirk in Haftmann's direction). This bit is for the team, Haftmann knows. Cops respect other cops – a private investigator is barely above a vagrant, a notch above bounty hunter.

"Mister Haftmann made the initial contact with the man we believe is a suspect in the slayings that the papers having been calling the Jack-in-the-Box murders. The station parking lot at Jefferson-on-the-Lake has been surveilled since contact was made. No one, not even Mister Haftmann here was told, nor the police chiefs of Jefferson or Jefferson-on-the-Lake."

Haftmann barely suppresses a groan. If they'd surveilled the lot, they'd have nailed him. "Mister Haftmann has parked his car at a place where our camera can see it at all times. We had to go to the CIA to get this stuff but it's the best surveillance gear on the market. If he tries to leave another note, or drop off a package – do anything in that parking lot, we'll have him.

"We are bringing a trained civilian in on this part. The fact that he used Mister Haftmann has made this necessary.

"I asked Mister Haftmann to speak to you this morning before we conference today because he is the one who pointed us in the direction of the single lead that may yield something toward identifying this man."

Haftmann steps around the lectern Booth used to speak from. It makes him feel awkward, like a college lecturer. "Special Agent Booth tells me that many of you have volunteered to pose as swinging couples and try to attract him on the basis of the New Philadelphia couple's physical descriptions." (Some open laughter around the room, a few fingers get poked through holes made by circling the thumb and forefingers.) It's a long shot, according to Booth, but the decoy ads in swingers' and BDSM websites and phony addresses might lure him out.

"He likes middle-aged women who live alone," Haftmann says. "Your reports make that fact clear. The similarities between the Canton and the Painesville women are too striking to be coincidental. We know that there may be as many as fifteen deaths by misadventure in the last two years in Ohio that look suspicious." Haftmann has marked these JDLR on the reports Phil gives him: Just Doesn't Look Right. Cops, like criminals, have their own slang.

Haftmann summarizes what they already know: These women are without family or divorced or widowed, no one questions a dubious autopsy. Every one of those women suffered some kind of trauma before death – ligature marks, abrasions, and so forth – that can't be easily accounted for. He offers a theory: "I think he's widened his circle from single women victims to couples."

A Cleveland detective he doesn't know says, "We know that. What else can you tell us?"

"He's losing what little control he has."

The same detective, clearly no fan of amateurs like him being involved, asks: "That's easy to say, isn't it, considering what he's done lately?"

Booth interjects, "Remember, there's been no evidentiary link to connect Haftmann's man with our suspect."

Haftmann relaxes a bit. At least acknowledging him means he's not completely invisible.

"Your own experts say that isn't likely for this kind of psychotic behavior," Haftmann notes. "There's a good possibility he's fighting two impulses simultaneously. He wants to enjoy the exhibitionism of his crimes and he wants someone to stop him."

Haftmann is thanks and shunted aside, his Andy Warhol fifteen minutes are up. Booth resumes control and Haftmann admires his cool aplomb.

"We know this much. He can't use an exercise club in Ohio without us finding out. Every body builder in the state in the heavyweight division down to middleweight is being checked out. If he's using any a.k.a.'s with Thomas Hauer or Hower or Howard, we'll see him in a database. If Nelson is the man Thomas or Roger Hauer, he may be using the same habits and patterns he acquired years ago. You have Nelson's rap sheet. We're looking into bartenders and bouncers who fit his description and who live in Northeast Ohio. And if he's being paid under the table we'll have to sniff him out the hard way. Every dew-drop inn, every shitkicker's bar, every low-life hangout will be inspected by a team member and accompanied by the local PD for backup. Let's get him. There's no grandstanding on this one. We just want to stop him. There's credit for all when we do."

Before Booth sends them off into their "focus groups," Haftmann points out something the experts have missed: "One other thing. He works nights. He has to. He uses the daylight hours for killing."

This time, the Cleveland detective gives him a look of grudging respect.

~ ~ ~

Haftmann takes the innerbelt section known as Dead Man's Curve at 55 MPH and boosts it to 75 behind a white pimpmobile that got off at Martin Luther King, Jr. Circle. At the East 72nd Street overpass, he looks up to see if any pedestrians on the walkway hold bricks or chunks of cement in their hands – an old habit from his Cleveland patrol days before the curved fence was installed. He tromps the accelerator home on I 90. The air blasts him from the side vents is moist and hot despite the speed. A damp, chilly spring has turned into a muggy green summer in a few weeks. His tie has come off as soon as he was out of the Federal Building on East Ninth.

He pulls into his reserved spot at the station at three o' clock in the afternoon, sweat-soaked and itchy. He was passed on the way in by two men in brown suits carrying Xerox boxes out the door. "Hotter'n a bitch," one of the men said.

Although Millimaki's door is shut, he can hear the bellowing before he cleared the top of the stairs.

"Phil, who put a quarter in him today?"

"I don't know for sure, but I think they're Internal Affairs guys from Cleveland. They requisitioned all our old records from the basement."

"What the hell for?"

"Who knows?"

A dim hope but he tosses it out: "What records are those?"

"All that old larceny and fraud stuff that Millimaki was supposed to get transferred over to computer disk or outsource for digitizing. He didn't because he used the money somewhere else. Thinks they're here to prove malfeasance or something bigger."

Larceny and fraud. Oh shit . . .

You just get in from Cleveland? Go see Van Scyoc about the pool for next week's game.

Fraud, Artiss. Dropped a dime on him, finally.

"Yeah. I'll do that."

Haftmann wheels and heads back down the stairs.
Phil shouts: "Now where the hell you going?
"East Palestine."

~ ~ ~

He locates her house from directions given by a mongoloid boy on a red bike. She's at the end of a row of five identical white houses with flaking paint.

She's got a boyfriend hanging around, muscle shirt and tattoos, and he asks him to leave in a tone that policeman haven't been allowed to use in years.

He's done this before, so often, so many places that looked the same. The smell of Pampers in the kitchen is an invisible cloud of noxious fumes. She doesn't notice or doesn't mind.

"I told them other cops that was here then the same motherfuckin' thing I'm telling you. Why don't you ask them what I said? I don't know his name or where he lives. He just come over for drinks one time, is all. 'Zat a crime? I gotta tell them welfare people ever' thing I do, it seems. Now you cops come hasslin' me about some dude I hardly know."

Haftmann sees that she needs dental care badly, but she's attractive enough in a dingy way and exudes a dirty sensuality. He remembers how the last one had tried to claw his eyes.

Haftmann asks her to remember anything she can about him, any small detail at all.

"Well," she says, "he acts like he's in a big goddam hurry to leave when he gets here. We drank a few mixed drinks, right here. He sat where you're sitting."

"Anything else?"

"Shit, no. He just kept looking at his watch like he's fuckin' bored, ya know."

Remember it, he wills her.

"Like this," she says.

Got it: he's a southpaw.

"What else?"

Coulda used a bath.

Haftmann takes his hand off the table top: a fifty dollar bill. She wipes sweat beads from her forehead, shrugs, picks up the bill and stares at it while she says in a low monotone so the boyfriend in the other room won't hear:

"I thought he was some kind of religious nut. He kept mumbling about somebody named "Dustin." Kept calling me his angel over and over. Kinda sweet, really."

That would qualify as the understatement of the century, Haftmann thinks.

"Guilty of dust and sin." Dustin.

LOVE BADE ME WELCOME.

~ ~ ~

There were more fights now; the nights were hotter. More beer went into the bellies of the swine and clouded their tiny minds faster. Nelson was either disciplining a customer or escorting one out the door. Sometimes kidney punch on the way helped to resolve the troublemaker's problems without inviting reprisal – or bringing the cops around.

He was losing muscle tone; the bad diet and lack of sleep was taking off the cut ripped-muscle look. One of the bike trash surprised him with an uppercut to the ribs as his buddy was being walked to the door. The punch had good leverage and rocked him; he still had a purplish yellow patch of broken blood vessels to show for it.

The songs from the jukebox were getting more urgent in their messages to him, but when he tried to concentrate his mind, convinced that the angel was at last revealing his will, the words would scatter like ants under a baseboard.

The heat and humidity stifled until early evening when it was time to go to work.

He fell into long periods of stupor awakened by the sound of his own voice singing Mendelssohn's "Scheidend" or by the cramp of his muscles and his tongue extending obscenely out of his mouth in the Lion Pose.

Cops everywhere lately. Two of them down the street at the cottage where he had seen white broads bringing black men inside. He could be pinned where he was easily, like a rat in a hole, unless he went over the bank into the lake. He was surrounded on three sides by water.

What had happened at the farmhouse was bad, very bad. He took sex from them too soon, not as he had planned it, and it all went bad, too fast, too soon.

He tried to focus his mind, but he saw the woman screaming, the husband trying to interpose, as formidable as a rabbit without teeth. He felt the blood pound in his veins at the runt's attempt to take him on. He could not remember what he had said or done to make it erupt so fast, but he finally got it right and they were there in the room he had prepared for them.

He had burgled one of the cottages yesterday afternoon and taken the dope stash he found taped behind a bureau mirror. Going through drawers, working from the bottom up, he saw several pairs of panties.

He held them around his cock and masturbated into them.

He had not had sex since the Canton woman; none of his emails sent from the Internet cafe in Ashtabula Harbor were answered. It took him hours to prepare each one with a pocket dictionary.

The number of women advertising for single males had fallen off to almost nothing. He had written that he "had his wife's approval," but nothing was working.

He had a very bad feeling about mailing out the last batch of emails. The police could be monitoring these; he knew was leaving electronic footprints back to himself.

Somehow that rat fuck Haftmann was going beyond what he had intended for him. He was to receive the angel's messages and squirm before it was time to die. Lonnie Dale had seen him with a woman from the police station. He had followed her home.

He had called the man's house one time and hung up. He caught himself just in time.

Something was really wrong —

He unfolded the printout.

She was petite, young, and brown-haired like the New Philadelphia wife.

She wore the same kind of lingerie.

Had an ass like an upside-down valentine and even stuck it out in the same way.

The ad was similar. Too similar. He suspected a trap.

He looked out his back window at the cottage; the sky was opaque, the water calm and oily — a ribbon of haze on the horizon.

His head was throbbing again; he was muzzy with fatigue. He had driven to Cleveland that morning and had arrived at a bar on the west side; it was a known swinger's hangout, but no women showed up. He drank three tequilas at inflated prices and left by the middle of the afternoon.

He did not know how long he would be able to stay away from the cottage. He wanted to catch them fucking.

If the angel didn't come soon, he was afraid he would bring disaster down on himself.

He stared at the western edge of the shoreline, surprised that he could see the reactor building from this distance.

He felt his penis stiffen in his pants: three long hours until work. There was no point in trying to sleep in the hot afternoon sunlight boring holes through his cottage, so he drove south through Jefferson on 46, all farm country baking in the heat, corn stalks stunted and barely knee-high to Route 422. He drove through conservative McKinley Township, a cemetery without headstones on his left, and found the Girves Brown Derby, just like she said, midway between Niles and Girard; AMOCO and BP stations catercornered on the intersection, three Chinese restaurants advertising Hunan, Polynesian, and Shanghai specialties, and an adult book store sandwiched between a realtor's office and a Kirby Vacuum Kleener Center. The sign over the entrance didn't say Red Masque's Lounge anymore; it had been replaced by an elaborate neon panel with six-foot letters in fancy scrollwork. The sign was unlit. It said Suite Judy's.

Inside he found the tacky black-and-red decor preferred by aging lounge lizards. There was a plush Naugahyde padding for resting your elbows that ran the bar's length, which touted artsy-deco, 1920's. The middle of the bar straightened out and seemed to loop around the rear of the building. No mirrors. Bright bottles caught the light and winked at you with the slightest movement. Francis Cugat's print of Gatsby's Daisy, carrying a convenient green tear over neon cityscape, hung on one wall. The place was dark and cool.

Freddie Sateriale's Big Band was coming over the speakers mounted on the walls, but he couldn't see the stereo system. He recognized it right away: "Yama, Yama Man Rhumba." His grandmother often had often sung the lyrics to him; it was an operetta in German, she said. She said Karl and Otto wrote it for her, but that American nobody, Bessie McCoy, became a star overnight because of it. His grandmother would prance around their kitchen to the meringue beat and then subside into a sputtering rage at how she had been cheated of fame that was hers. Sometimes she would find him and flail her skinny arms at

215

his head; once she tore a strip of skin from his cheek with her long yellow nails.

Frankie Carlel's piano took over after that, and he listened to a medley of *South Pacific*, *Oklahoma!* and *Carousel*. He knew all the lyrics. He drank Campari and soda at five dollars a whack. An hour to drink and scan the room.

He saw a few couples scattered around the booths in the back and a few business types at the bar sipping exotic drinks. There was laughter and loud whispering from time to time as one of the booths filled the hiatus between plangent notes.

He heard a voice next to him call the bartender over. Her breath competed with her perfume; he didn't move while she gave him the once over. The bartender came over and when he stepped into the light, he could see a handsome mahogany face with planes that Hollywood liked to call ruggedly handsome. She ordered two Black Russians. When he left to make the drinks, she turned to him and said in slow, lush articulation: "He's got one that will stretch across this bar top. Can yours do that?"

He lighted up the fury of his eyes and made a mask for her. She was on the downside of her forties, big boned, frosted blonde, her cleavage a good seven inches. "No," he said with a big smile.

"Can you drive a railroad spike with it?"

"Not yet," he said.

She smiled, liked that. He looked around to where her husband was toasting them with his glass, a friendly nod back.

"There's a motel near here we like to use. My husband's a crossdresser, do you mind?"

"Does he join or watch?"

"Watches, takes pictures. But no face shots, unless you don't mind. He'll join if we ask him."

"I have to be to work in an hour-and-a-half."

"Honey, if I can't get any man's rocks off in twenty minutes, I'll pack these big old tits of mine in the closet for good."

Just like her ad said it would be: "Order a Campari and put your keys inside the sweat ring on the bar, and I'll find you." He licked the perspiration off his upper lip, picked his drink up, and slid off the stool. There they were, smiling as he approached their table . . .

Chapter 12

Midsummer Night

It's a truism that serious crimes rise with the temperature. The siroccos of southern Europe and the Santa Ana have acquired a romantic mythos that, despite a babel of tongues, unite people in a common misery; hot, dry desert winds that burnish the edges of stop signs to metallic silver and put grit in your teeth.

True, the notorious lake effect does wreak a little havoc with your digestive system at times and you never lose the clammy feeling of your shirt stuck to your back; you get sick of watching beads of sweat pop out on your skin at only seventy degrees.

Ask any beat cop on duty summers at Jefferson-on-the-Lake if there is some magic number like ninety-three degrees that will make people go berserk. He'll tell you there are more rapes, aggravated assaults, and, certainly, more homicides in the summer simply because there are simply more people walking around without that much tolerance, compassion, or respect for their fellow man.

And as every good cop will swear: sex, drugs, rock-'n'-roll, and TV have more to do with violence than the rise and fall of sap.

By midsummer, the worst of it seemed to have peaked; but there was still a rumor on the Strip of the biggest rumble in a decade. The relentless drought had set records all over the state, and while the farmers in the hinterlands bellyached and shot out the windows and sometimes the hearts of the bankers holding their mortgages, Jefferson-on-the-Lake was having the most successful season since Glenn Miller opened a set with "In the Mood" at the Bavarian Chalet.

Young women in string bikinis sashayed along the boardwalk licking ice-cream cones and it wasn't hard to imagine what the young men watching them were substituting for the cones.

The heat was a bit much for some people: a teenager working for his old man at a burger joint threw hot french-fry grease at his father's eyes, and, in despair at what he had just done, stuck his own head in it. The old men who couldn't bum a ride anywhere else, and who weren't dirty enough to annoy the Chamber of Commerce into having them removed, were dying of heat stroke at a rate of one per diem. Cops would find them dead on the beach under lifeboats, under piles of newspaper behind Kimpel's Eatery and under trees along shady side streets. There was always a betting pool, some lackluster brainstorm of a desk sergeant or timeserver in the department, between the All-Star game and the World Series in the fall. This year, beat cops were bet on according to the number of dead bodies claimed.

Haftmann's dreams were getting more vivid as the days of summer expanded the translucent light of the solstice; in fact, he had acquired the gift of dreaming in Dolby stereo. Colors were twice as intense; sounds rippled outward from the source of his dreaming self or contracted to pinpricks of vibration along bands he had never heard before. He was like a newcomer to African heat, doped on mefloquine and subject to dreams of violent sex.

He was terrified of his own consciousness. He took pills to short-circuit the dreams, which would put them into abeyance until the wrong chemistry won out and favored the dreams.

Last night's, for instance: he dreamed of a white wolf looking down on him from frozen rocks. He turned his head and it was gone, a blond boy in its place with eyes as fierce and yellow as the wolf's.

Then he's on the job, in patrolman's uniform, himself a rookie cop again, and in this wasteland his job is to give mouth-to-mouth to all the old men and women who have fallen, exhausted and crying, unable to breathe. He gives them back the breath of life: it's his duty. But he's giving up his own air that cannot replenish itself. He trod further and finds his job worsened by the misshapen and diseased forms ahead in the snow. They look dead, but they are desperate for his air, which he gives until he comes to one old woman.

She's hideous; a bag lady without peer: foul, smelly, crooked teeth and all. He can't do it; put his mouth on those blue lips. Her eyes beg him. So he does. He's near death from giving up the last of his oxygen. He can feel the outline of his lungs when he draws back to see the horrible transformation complete itself. The mouth he has clamped with his own a moment ago is jetting its bodily fluids all over his hands; a yellow bile gushes from the nostrils he has pinched shut; every body orifice opens and feces, urine, and blood soak his uniform and stain the snow all around him. He vomits, sickened and disgusted over the corpse's face. The eyes stare at him.

He has forgotten the boy who has tracked him and turns in time to see the mad wolf eyes, as the knife, the long-bladed Finnish *puuka*, goes in under his heart.

"Please," he says.

Drops of sweat rolled off his brow at a steady drip, drip, drip per ten seconds, spotting the B.C.I.'s latest memorandum on the killer. The air conditioning was on the fritz again; it was ninety degrees and only ten in the morning.

He read the morning paper and his ex-wife's husband had just been made a partner in his firms, and felt the grip of burning shame jolt through him the way a retriever shakes a muskrat's neck.

Vanderhyden's addendum to the memo referred to instructions for each lead investigator's area of responsibility. Vanderhyden must have crossed Booth because his role in the investigation was reduced to penning harmless, cover-your-ass memos. Haftmann wasn't formally acknowledge anywhere in reports. B.C.I.'s own administrative flunkies had all the communication and coordinating posts, although the momentum had clearly shifted to the F.B.I., and Haftmann wondered if the killer could feel the noose drawing tighter.

Those Crimes Against Persons (not all murders) that could not pass the list of criteria consisting of a redaction of characteristics, psychological and physical, were itemized by townships in the northern part of the state; you couldn't expect MOM (motive/ opportunity/means) to work anyway with a serial killer mentality, but these as-yet-unsolved murders could not pass go:

AKRON 3   JEFFERSON (JOTL)1
ASHTABULA 1   MANSFIELD1
AUSTINBURG1   MASSILLON2
BARBERTON 1   MESOPOTAMIA1
BRISTOLVILLE1   NEWBERRY 1
CANTON4   NILES2
CHARDON 1   ORWELL3
CLEVELAND 10   PAINESVILLE 2
EAST CLEVELAND 3   ROCK CREEK 1
EAST PALESTINE 2   ROME 1
EAST LIVERPOOL 2   SALEM1
EUCLID3   STONEVILLE1
GRIGG'S CORNERS1   WARREN 2
JEFFERSON1   YOUNGSTOWN4

Haftmann doubted the monster either started at or passed through a place called Grigg's Corners. It was more likely some barkeep broke some farmer's nose and got himself sprung into the state's investigation. Orwell's disproportionate number surprises Haftmann because Don King's Training Camp ran smack through the town on Route 45, but America's most famous promoter with electro-shock hair (and a pair of murder convictions) isn't using it these days. What about Mesopotamia? Amish country. The pull of the blood: *Blutbruderschaft*: blood brotherhood. Hardly a place where you could run around with a dripping meat cleaver without somebody finding out. State institutions in Mansfield and Massillon; unemployed steelworkers in Youngstown, rubber workers in Akron, and that old newscaster joke about Cleveland as the Mistake on the Lake. Those were the key places. Cockroaches prefer big cities.

He knew three of the likeliest candidates on his own turf without having to think twice: those biker and metal-head bars had to have muscle to control their clientele. Haftmann took one of them off every now and then on a fugitive warrant. A good reference for Roger's was a long rap sheet of criminal violence. He'd seen harder customers in there on a Tuesday morning for their eye-openers than he saw going into that sleazoid tattoo parlor next door, where the macho thing was to have your dick tattooed and a photo taken of it for display on the wall.

Haftmann picked up the paper and turned to the sports. A rookie was on the mound for Cleveland tonight. He'd cleaned out his savings and credit bureau balance back when the house still held his wife's scent, even though he'd thrown out or burned every scrap of hers he could find.

He had fifty dollars in the checking account – enough to feed him until payday. He'd have to take eight-to-five odds, even though Cleveland was under .500 as usual.

He felt jittery about taking his car under the long-distance eyes of the camera's lens, but this was money, and he was due. He took the fire lane in front of the Chalet and went inside; nothing wrong with Oscar's air conditioner and he felt the drops of sweat gel inside his shirt as his pores contracted.

Oscar was in close conference with Augie at the bar. *A red letter day*, he thought, *when the best brains in town put their heads together.*

Oscar fixes him with his eyes and looks at the twenties and ten on the bar top. "Haftmann, you're getting to be a piker."

"You'd crawl over your dying grandmother and pull the money out of her hands if she got behind on the vig. Give me the Tribe tonight, over-under and seven."

"Ten. Verlander's pitching tonight."

"Give me my money back."

"Take it easy, sport. I'm just having a little fun."

Haftmann pivots from their laughter, his shirt stuck to his back despite the cooled and scrubbed air. But he wonders why and out of what abyss he had to pull that grandmother crack.

She used to sing softly to him in her German a child's song that would embarrass him because he was too old, but she laughed and stroked his forehead, crooning: *Ich bin hier; Da bist du.* Over and over until he stopped fighting it, let her fold him in her arms. The day she died, when she no longer knew who he was, he lifted her from her sickbed and sang her song back to her in her language.

And here I am, he thought, stepping into the glare. *And where the fuck is that?*

His cop instinct pricks him into alertness: *Trouble.*

Suits in sunglasses in a white Prism three cars back. Scoping him out.

Take your pick: federal cops, postal inspectors, gun thugs, Internal Affairs – he should keep a list of people who would like to see him with his ass in a sling.

~ ~ ~

She smelled like sex. She had an ovine face, wore cut-up Levi shorts and her dirty blonde cunt hairs were peeking through every time she shifted her legs.

She told him that she saw him walk past their cottage on the way to his every morning. "Must lead some kind of wild night life, huh?" He told her what he did. "Oh," she said. She'd heard about the place from the guys who shared the rent, but they didn't go there because they said the place was prejudiced against blacks.

She asked him what he did all day; he said he slept.

She said it was pretty hot for sleeping and popped her gum. She said she knew that because she grew up not too far from here. Liked to spend her summers out here as much as she could. She lost her rental house in Jefferson, she said, because the landlord was also "prejudice against blacks." She had some black friends; he should come over some time and meet them. "Really great guys," she said.

He said he's "love to sometime soon," and smiled at her. Right now, though, he said he'd like to have a drink with her. Maybe she'd like to have a drink with him at his cottage.

"Great," she said. "Just be a minute; check on the baby first."

She was admiring the configuration of bars and devices he had arc-welded to the inside while he explained the purpose of each one. Smelling her close. She said some of these looked like stuff she'd seen on websites where they – *you know* – *tied each other up for sex and stuff.* He explained how you had to concentrate the effort you wanted to expend so that you could get maximum results. He flexed a bicep in front of her and showed her the difference between tricep and bicep muscles. "Ooh," she sang, "what's this little number do?"

He reached from behind her and his breath was hot on her neck. His hands had her cup-sized tits easily and she made noises with her mouth and turned into him.

He had her naked in three swift movements and his cock was sliding in and out of her sopping crotch before he could get her to the bed. Cum boiled out of him as he lay over her, almost completely hidden under his bulk.

She said afterward that she once made it with an entire band after a set behind the stage at The Hideaway Lounge. Seven guys. The band was pretty famous too. Had he heard this tune and then she hummed a few bars of it off-key.

He sang the next passage for her, and she said, "Hey, you got a great voice. You should be a – one of them, whatchamacallits, opera singers."

He did a cockstand for her. "Suck it or I'll beat the shit out of you."

She didn't know if he was kidding or serious, but she went down on him just to be safe.

~ ~ ~

"I thought it would be – "

"Different?" She asked him.

"Yes," he said, drawing out the *s* like Matrooshian.

"Better?"

"Yes," he admitted.

"I know," she said.

Haftmann had trouble getting hard; trouble finding her when he did get it stiff enough, and winced with pain when she scissored her legs and bent him.

He had tried to make a joke of it. "Like a piece of spaghetti with a crook in the middle of it."

Terrible, terrible. Just kill me now, God.

He wanted her badly, so he had blocked the treachery to her husband out of his mind. But she had startled

226

Haftmann when she got in the car by announcing that her husband knew she was with him.

"OK," he said and didn't know what else to say to her. It didn't sound like an open marriage, and his single meeting with her husband didn't give him that vibe.

"I told him," Shawna said.

"OK," he clucked.

Jesus, shit, fuck.

He drove her to a motel on the Strip; you had a choice of thousands, it seemed, and he wanted to be sure no one could recognize him. Like a teenager with his first motel date and a boner.

He knew she was unhappy too; both had tried to make the sex good. She faked her orgasm; offered to relieve him with her hand. Which, of course, made his failure complete. The television had sex movies, if you rang the office and gave them your room number. WE ACCEPT VISA, MASTER CARD, AND DINER'S CLUB said the sign.

She cuddled up to him on the bed. Then he drew the sheet up to his chest, ashamed, and wondered if she were making comparisons between him and her husband.

She kissed him on the cheek.

"It's okay, baby," she said.

Baby is right, he thought. Flaccid. He'll never mock one of those erectile dysfunction commercials again, ever.

Then it happened. They began to talk. He couldn't stop himself, his words came halting; his voice broke, rusty and unused to conversations like this. He moved an arm under her neck and held her face up to his to be kissed. She was not beautiful, never would be by standards of today. Her yellow eyes, held him with a deeper, questioning look. Then he kissed her. She kissed him back. Suddenly they were talking and kissing, and he felt the sordidness of adultery and betrayal move off somewhere else in his mind. She helped him with her hand find her and they made love with slow movements until he felt the dam of filth break within, a light burst free in his head. She moaned softly to his coming inside her – real now, no faking this one, and he felt her coming too.

Both were reluctant to be the first to get up and dress. She eventually did, saying that she had afternoon shift. He knew that, but he let her say it anyhow.

She had a little bit of belly; some cellulite on the backs of her thighs, some gray coming through the auburn. When she looked at him, he felt the surge of love and pity and desire he had when he saw her that day wearing the shiner.

Jesus God, I think I really love her, he thought.

She had to jiggle her shorts over her panties in that practiced way he'd seen women do on the beach. "I'm sticky," she said.

"Yes," he thought happily, "with my come in you."

"Tom, we have to go."

He got up and dressed and thought about her yellow eyes drilling him in the back. He didn't know where this was going to go, but it seemed to have a life of its own.

~ ~ ~

Four new guys at the table in the back. Near the door in case the place gets too wild for them. Slumming. Something in italic script on the back of the jacket of one of the men, but he couldn't read the red letters from this distance.

He sidled over, curious, a whisper in his head beginning to stir. He read it moving his lips: PIPEFITTERS LOCAL 306. What did a pipefitter want in a biker shithole like the Haze?

Under it, smaller letters, block print in gold silk: RICHLAND NUCLEAR POWER PLANT.

Nuclear. Power. Plant. *Power and light . . .*

Lonnie Dale Nelson felt something move through him. The angel, at last.

He barely heard anything spoken to him that night. There were two fights that could have been stopped before they got past the name-calling bullshit, but he didn't get to them in time.

Flashbacks of Massillon were rip-sawing his brain all night. He had to get out of there, get away from the smoke and noise and confusion. Figure it out.

Tattoo Bitch was on the rag, half-moons of sweat under her arms thanks to that Gray Goose Vodka she slipped into her Coke cans, more foul-mouthed than ever. She'd called him *cocksucker* three times so far. She'd been nagging him all night when he told her to go fuck herself, clean up the cans herself. She'd been using him as her private eunuch too long. He'd have snuffed her long ago, but there was no way to avoid being questioned by cops if he did. They'd have to ask him questions: she was as safe from him as if she were wearing sequins preening in front of the knife thrower at the circus.

The flies were buzzing on every table, sipping spilled brew at the edges and even getting into the jar of pickled sausages.

"Yo, yo, yo!"

"Yo' name Jackson, motherfuckah?"

Not a question.

"Yes."

Two of them bracing him in front of his cottage. Not big enough to threaten in that tone and mean it, but two of them all the same.

"That white pussy belong to us, motherfucker."

"Get the fuck away from me while you can, nigger."

One of the black men, the six-footer with bronzed, sweaty arms and a Seahawks hoodie, smiled and looked over to his sidekick. They moved in on him at the same

229

time, good fighter's stance both, but the bigger one more casual about it, as if to say, "This shouldn't take long."

He'd have to take two for one. No choice. Make his hurt more than theirs.

He took two right off: one to the temple, one to the cheek. He felt blood inside and out his mouth. Just a jab, but he cut: rings.

He took three more – neck, face, shoulder – before he connected with a right to the smaller one's throat. They could be pros. The smaller one made gagging sounds and forgot about looking cool; he was choking from the blow to his trachea.

The bigger one launched two before he could recover: left eye, stomach.

He threw three: two lefts and a roundhouse right and caught air all three times. He wasn't going to win this fight, even though the smaller one was sitting on his ass dazed.

Lights were popping on at the nearest cottages.

Cops'll be here soon.

Do it now: he walked into the man's next punch – a wide-arcing left hook he had telegraphed with too much body English and took it high up to deflect some of the energy. It hurt, but it couldn't put him down. He dropped the way he'd seen fighters do on TV, especially Ohio stiffs who practiced looking poleaxed for $500.00 a dive against up-and-coming fighters.

It convinced the bigger man, who looked over to his wheezing friend to see if he had an audience. "I'll come back here and kill you, white boy."

He got a kick in the back while he was lying there waiting for them to move off.

"James," the victor said to his friend. "Ya'll OK? We got to go, man."

More lights flickered on: James is hoisted to his feet and Nelson hears them scuttle into the shadows.

If the cops should see him, write him up . . .

Nelson stood up, spat out a gob of bloody pulp and a tooth and jabbed a finger inside his mouth to see if any more were loose.

Inside his cottage he dabbed cold water, the only kind he had in the place, on the cuts and swelling. He had the consolation that no one would notice him and be curious at work; bruises came with his occupation. He'd stay out of sight in the daytime until he healed; he knew most of the occupants of the other cottages by sight: they weren't the type to call police.

Something glorious had happened to him today.

He had to have time to sort it out.

He had been playing with the idea of killing himself after the next one.

But not now.

He felt good about himself again; the way he did when he discovered that his big arms had become his weapons against the world, and he could talk to them the way a ragtag warrior whispered secret words to his spear before battle.

KILL THEM ALL.

He watched the sun explode out of Lake Erie, a fireball that was a blood orange he could touch with his hand.

Something was wrong with the red disc: it was pulsing. He could see its corona of gaseous flames with hideous accuracy.

The sun was going to nova very soon. They would become a scorched cinder. That was the angel's message.

He saw flocks of gulls fall into the lake, blackened wings aflame. Thousands of silver fish burst through the water's surface; he saw them flopping helplessly on the beach: big sheephead with their nigger lips, carp the size of small tuna, and pike and muskelunge, dying – all dying in the incandescent light.

The noise was like thunder but a thunder of celestial bodies spinning out of orbit. The sky grew murky within a second as clouds and vapor forms materialized across the skyline. He thought he was seeing some kind of freakish time-lapse phenomenon. Tornadoes spun off the wild air. From extraordinary heat and light there grew waterspouts of black coils like monstrous snakes. He was weeping.

"I'll do it," he said to the angel. "I'll kill them all."

The angel said: Do you understand?

Thank you. I know how.

~ ~ ~

Haftmann beats off for days afterward, hating the ignominy of it, the shame and degradation he felt. He was frenzied and obsessed with driving her image out of his mind. His tormented imagination saw Shawna gaping, licking her lips and lolling her tongue around like a porn actress taking stage directions. He drew jism out of his swollen balls; jerked off until nothing but air came out and he could not even stand on his feet.

Whore. Cunt. Bitch.

Yet he couldn't exorcise her face and how she had looked at him in the motel room; she pitied him. Her eyes said it.

"I'm alone too much," he said to the walls of his house. "I can't live right anymore."

Work was getting beyond his ability to separate the important from the trivia.

The Jack-killer was appearing to him in dreams, surrounded by his halo of flies, leaking madness out of his pores.

He awoke during a storm and thought he saw a face outside his window.

He arrived late at his desk avoiding all eyes but hoping to see hers.

At home he couldn't bring himself to clean anything: he threw all his dishes out the door, sailing them like Frisbees into the field, as soon as he had eaten from them.

Flies were getting into the house because he left windows open, and every time he made a motion to go shut one, he promptly forgot and thought about something else.

He wouldn't even bend down to pick up loose change that had dropped from his pockets and rolled off the sofa.

He thought about his gun too much, but it was a balm to take it out and press the barrel against his temple.

He took out the Federal Specials and put dum-dums in. *To hell with it*, he told himself, as if that were the proper, lucid explanation.

Only Phil speaks to him now. Elise offers to take him on ride-alongs. He thinks Phil is putting her up to it.

He was too busy trying to patch his practice together, get solvent again. He knew that he was back in the doghouse with Booth and Vanderhyden again: no one returned his calls.

Booth nonetheless continued to send him updates and memoranda on the investigation. He tore them up without reading them. "Fuck that psycho motherfucker," he said to Elise one day, when she asked him if he wanted to ride with her.

The drought worsened; fifteen consecutive days of one hundred degree weather; even the cloudburst on occasion was too short-lived to bring down the heat; the sidewalks smoked after a rain.

He was out in his yard throwing seed to the grackles when he had a flashback to his last murder case in Cleveland. The guy was a religious freak and he cut all the kids' throats with a serrated steak knife. He shot the wife in the brains and did himself in.

Haftmann felt his stomach churn at the memory. Blood spatters: the Painesville schoolteacher, the Warren couple, New Philadelphia. *How many more don't we know about? How much blood will there be before he's through?*

He walks out of his house and turns left down the driveway at the moment an Escalade with four white-haired men in bright tourist clothes drove past and gaping at him, open-mouthed like cadavers. Before they roar off, he sees the frozen look of one old man with egg salad stuck to the corner of his mouth.

He drives to his office on the Strip and realizes he's too agitated to work. He kicks over his desk and pulls out all of his files and throws them around the room. He walks out into the suffocating heat, sweat-soaked and shivering.

From his driveway he could see the flap of his mailbox hanging open like a big silver tongue. *That Shithead mailman.*

He opens it: sees a single sheet of paper and the block letters; the 'e,' as two times before, a child's effort, backwards and slanted.

This is what it said:

THEY FLEE FROM ME WHO SOMETIME DID ME SEKE

Chapter 13

Dog Days

Tico called him at home: "Why don' you call me back, homes?"

"I've been working on a few things."

Haftmann translates part of it: ". . . *es una chorrado. That's a lot of crap.*

"Listen-a-me. The word on the street is that a guy who is well known to both a us has got himself into trouble. You the only guy I know that fucks up more than me. I don' know what the trouble is, but you better watch you back."

"Thanks."

"Anything I can do, Tomás?"

No, I'm okay. *Estoy hasta los cojones*, just fed up.

Tico laughs: "Okay. *Como se dice*, you suit yourself."

Click.

Not good, not good.

The Canton postmark on Haftmann's message from "Jack" was worthless as information. Even Booth had come around fast after Haftmann's call. The F.B.I. shrinks had said Haftmann's man, Lonnie Dale Nelson, would not stay in one place too long and was probably out of state. Serial killers were known to drive a couple hundred thousand miles a year when they went trawling. Compare that to Joe Sixpack's ten thousand.

Haftmann wanted to be their stalking horse. Booth said no. "We don't work that way, cowboy."

So close. He chose a city where he left a corpse we knew about; playing it safe was playing it dumb in this case: now we knew he knew. Unless he pulled something stupid, not an often-made choice of serial killers, he would be like the man on the Quaker Oats box holding up a box of Quaker Oats with a man on it into infinity. We could stay behind him and never make the move that gets him.

He had stirred the investigation up again, no doubt about that. A rogue wave beating itself against the rocks.

The F.B.I. brains sent back new data about the message, which turned out to be a line of verse: the title of an Elizabethan sonnet by Sir Thomas Wyatt. The analysts waffled about the implications for the psychological profile: psychotic killers were a bloody lot, but a few were borderline genius; some like dashing Ted Bundy were pretentious.

"After all, Mister Haftmann," said one of the four-eyes, "you thought he was a functional illiterate because of the spelling of *seek*."

"Kiss my ass," said Haftmann.

"Yes, well—"

The number the pointy-heads did on the possibilities of who the "they" might be were amplified in psychiatric jargon and covered five single-spaced word-processed pages.

"Who do you think 'they' refers to here, Haftmann?"

"Same as this Wyatt's. Women he's had sex with and knows he's going to kill. Maybe the couples he does, too. He likes to work in pairs. As you guys are so fond of saying, "It's a pattern.""

Pissing on my pant legs and calling it rain, Haftmann thinks.

He couldn't stop them from staking out his house. All the teams were drawn off the rest of the state and concentrated on northeast Ohio. The suspect list had so far resulted in seven extra deaths: two investigators were shot to death outside a bar in Youngstown, and five men on the list died under circumstances provoked by the interrogation or the fear of it. Grand juries were tying up some of the team for other litigious matters that resulted from the renewed effort.

None of the papers knew of the third contact so far.

"I'll tell you one thing," Haftmann informed Booth; "he's bragging now. He's gone past this catch-me-if-you-can bullshit at the start."

"He still likes you, though," Booth observed.

Haftmann arranged with Elise to cover his messages for the weekend. He drove to Morgana and Richmond on the Strip to check out the action. They called it Little Minnesota because of the number of teen runaways who wound up there over the summer from all over the country. Chickenhawks from Cleveland cruised by the Strip for the boys; no one knew how many girls would wind up permanently missing. Vice couldn't keep up with it; the court dockets were overloaded with major crime cases, so officially it didn't exist. Haftmann had seen more than one county big shot chatting it up with teens of either sex, probably negotiating prices.

Sex equals money and money equals drugs – a simple equation.

They were getting younger every year, he thought, *I can't be aging that fast.*

The girls looked about fifteen, jet-black hair or dyed blondes, some rainbow-colored, their hair spritzed and moussed about their faces like wet cotton candy. They looked frazzled in the heat; their young laughter too high-pitched, as if they were strung too tight on a single chord.

He thought that looking at them would bring on desire, let him follow the trouser snake's lead. He felt old and worn and out of touch with life.

At the intersection traffic slowed to a crawl; girls went up to car windows and looked in. They looked like demons in a Hieronymus Bosch painting from one of Micah's art books, their faces catching the reflected neon colors all around them, shimmering from the cars' hoods.

"Hey, mister, want to have a party?"

"Not tonight, sweetheart."

"Fuck off, faggot."

It took him forty-five minutes to find a place to turn around and make the trip back down the Strip.

The same girl, the same sweat-streaked face with desperate eyes and dimple: "Hey, mister, suck you off for ten dollars?"

He showed her the badge this time. She disappeared like smoke.

That night, unable to sleep, she went down on him in his dreams and he kept filling her pretty red mouth up with his cum.

~ ~ ~

The little pipefitter with the mustache who had worn the silk jacket the first time was calling him all the time now. Lonnie Dale Nelson didn't mind. He sent them beers, about four Heineken every forty-five minutes or so.

Everyone could see that he was pals with the guy and knew not to fuck with him. On Fridays and Saturdays it was too busy, so he gave him a grin and a wave from time to time: reassured him he was there, looking out for him. "This isn't the armpit of drinking establishments you think it is, pal," he once said to him. He hoped the beers would addle him to keep him happy; make him want to come back again soon and shoot the shit.

The little guy was a loudmouthed, braggart greaseball who saw himself as macho enough to drink in a dangerous dive like the Purple Haze so that he could tell the guys on his shift where he had a few when he felt like drinking.

The Heinekens were his private stock, and he told the bitches to keep their mitts off. An investment, as he saw it.

The little man liked to knock them back okay. He was slow to draw when his turn to buy came round. That's when he showed up at their table with the primo stuff. Made friends easy, he did. A real glad-hander. But he was the man with the plan, and they'd learn that too late.

They talked mostly about work and sports and pussy in that order. Bragged about all the poontang they picked up on the Strip. He figured they must be including their entire sexual lives, but they wanted it to sound as if it all happened last weekend. *Goddam, they were boring as hell.*

He was happy knowing that, no matter where they went, they were going to die too. No one was getting out alive. Those towelheads must have felt this happy strapping on the bombs.

He watched the little man all night out of the corner of his eye, afraid one of the bikers might hassle him out of sheer meanness; he didn't want his little man hurt or frightened off.

There was a right way to get to him and there were many wrong ways. You coaxed people in the way they wanted to go anyhow; find the right button and jab it once you were sure: sex, he guessed, but there was money and drugs and ego to consider. Maybe he wanted to be a real tough guy. He was amazed at how nature managed to blunt the self-awareness of stupid people, who thought they were smart, of ugly people, who thought they were good-looking, of cowards who thought they were brave.

You stupid little fuckhole nothing. I am going to kill you . . .

You want to be brave? Be dead first; then they can't hurt you.

He had learned that at Massillon, but you couldn't teach it.

They got up to leave; must be midnight shift this week.

Half-tanked and working in a nuclear power plant. It's a wonder we're all still here.

He got to them at the door and made a lot of sounds and gestures as though he owned the joint. See you again, guys; thanks for stopping by. To him he said: "C'mon by when you get a chance to chat. I've got something you might be interested in knowing about."

"Sure, sure." His brown eyes are hot and his breath is sour. "Hey, tell me something?"

"Name it."

That broad with the long black hair and those silver loops in her ears –

"I know which one." *Tattoo Bitch.* "The one with the big lungs," he said.

"She suck the chrome off a trailer hitch, or what?" He opens his mouth and his jaw works up and down, yet no sound comes out except a whiny screech that sounds like nails being ripped out of planks. *Heart attack*, he thought, and then realized it was a joke.

Having a joke for the boys. They all stand around laughing like disturbed hyenas. He pats his man on the back, buddy slaps between the shoulder blades.

Now he knows: it's sex.

Back at the bar Tattoo Bitch says to him: "What the fuck are you doing with those jerkoffs, Jackson?"

He snarls: "Mind your own business, cunt."

Later on, he comes up behind her and lays his tumescence against her backside.

"I may be setting up a little deal," he said. "You want in on it?"

"Do I get to fuck you as part of the deal?"

"I can see that as a definite possibility."

"Which hole you want first?"

~ ~ ~

She was coming on too strong all the same, but he thought his luck was about to break. She was a newcomer to the Strip, or so she said, a local girl, who named the high school that Haftmann had gone to; about six years in difference from what she said.

The dress was all wrong, too formal, but with Hispanic women you didn't know. The liberated ones were the biggest puzzle.

When Micah left him, he went wild for a few months – a real tear with the booze and some heavy sport fucking. He'd never had three women in three days before in his life, one coming in the front while the other one was just leaving by the back door.

Maria was the strangest of all; she'd go through this moaning and weeping prayer routine off by herself at the corner of the bed while he's lying there with a hard-on. Then, all done with the incantations, she'd devour his cock and suck him dry. Sometimes he'd mouth-fuck her: just hold her head back and stroke himself in and out of her painted mouth; her eyes shut the whole time.

This one was like that too, but her slyness wasn't because she had religious scruples about sex. There was something off. Maybe a husband, kids somewhere.

Nevertheless she had come on to him, right there in Tico's. Picked the stool next to his and started chattering away. Let him whiff her perfume, check out her cleavage. Big rolling hips. *Lots of fur down there,* he hoped. *That bald-pussy look isn't sexy.*

They got down to the my-place, your-place *schtick* as soon as she came back from the ladies' room. All the Latinos in the place ogling her walk. Tico gives him a wink you could see from the end of the Strip.

She takes his arm as they walk out. Chitters away about a lot of nothing and pinches her dress at the top of her tits; he knows she's sweating there.

By the time his brain takes in the parked LTD, he knows it's too late. She's off his arm and running. Two guys brace him front and back, and before he can do much about it, he's in the one alley on the whole fucking Strip where there's a good chance no one will notice any commotion.

He gets ready for it; his stupidity with the *chica* something he wants to redeem.

The bigger guy stands guard at the alley with his arms crossed in front of him.

What the hell, only one, and a cruiserweight at that. Haftmann is starting to feel good about it when the beating commences with two jabs to his face that knock his head back. There's a snap at the ends of the arms and from the shoulders on, he's a blur.

He gets Haftmann to drop his guard with one to the midsection that he knows is turning his face green and then the left comes in high on the cheekbone.

Some stinging rights follow up, and Haftmann is covering up, covering up, but the punches find him. The combinations are professional looking and they hurt like electric shocks. He can't get off a punch, and he doesn't intend to try; the man is unhurried and methodical – getting damage in with each stroke.

Haftmann's clothes are ripped and the sweat is blinding him. There's blood from two cuts on his face and one eye is shut. He has to spit out pink froth or he'll choke to death. He can't think about anything but surviving; he might die in this alley if that's what the man's instructions are.

He wants to drop, but he's afraid he'll get stomped to death, and the last thought he'll have is dying in his own yellow-shit cowardice.

Haftmann feints and the man doesn't bother to block, but the jab with the right hand moves him into target range for the left; he uncorks and catches the fleshy part of his opponent's ribs: a whoosh of air surprises the big man standing guard and he looks jittery, as if he's going to have to get involved.

But no –

The smaller man regroups, gives Haftmann the tiniest smile of acknowledgment, or sadistic pleasure, and then explodes with jabs to his face, neck, and shoulders. He comes in with the right hand two more times – Haftmann so out of it he's semiconscious – to straighten him up with a juddering uppercut followed by the one to the center of his stomach that has him convinced for a moment they shoved a lit silver tube down his throat; all the nerves in the pit of his stomach are in shock . . .

He thinks about vomiting. He has to roll over to keep from swallowing it, and he's even pleased that he went down without knowing how he got there.

There's so much blood on his face that he can't see where they went, but he's far enough in the alley's shadows that no one walking by can see him. He's not able to call, although he awakens from time to time to hear people walking past.

He comes to one more time before passing out for hours: no one is there, but it's later than it was because the light has that golden tint of late afternoon.

He doesn't care about dying, he realizes. *It's life you got to watch out for.* It's the ones walking around that cause all the trouble. Where had he heard that before? He's sleepy. Somehow the blood and sere of his facial wounds have failed to coagulate the hole in his cheek; he sticks a dirty finger through the sheen of fluids and feels a bone chip.

Then it's all blackness sucking him down . . .

~ ~ ~

He needs a special doctor. Word on the Strip is that there are three to choose from, the best costs $2,000 for a complete package: new I.D., employment history, references. A credit doctor. He's got the hacker's name and a way to get in touch with him. This outlay cost him fifty dollars, but whoever said life in the information age is cheap?

Money is getting to be a problem. He's turned down offers from some of the bikers who frequent the place because leg-breaking stuff is too risky now.

And he's afraid that he might antagonize the System again; they'll drown him in white noise if he hesitates. They were in the bars of the bench press he had built from scrap metal and pieces he had scrounged and stolen: telling him to get strong again, change his diet for power. Lift, lift.

He found a place that sells vitamins and Super Tea, but he's got to have the ready cash.

He found her on Craigslist. He chose her over two others on intuition; actually he preferred the blonde businesswoman posing next to a Jacuzzi with her breasts in profile. She wanted no emotional entanglements; huge built males for discreet one-on-one; between thirty and forty; drink and high times okay; no blacks. Nylon stockings and net lace garter hose on; her asshole and pussy lips pink and gaping at the camera lens. NORTH CENTRAL OH and WELL-HUNG MALES in boldface.

Those were the kinds of ads from single women that had all but completely disappeared since the Jack-in-the-Box Killer was coined by the tabloids. One of theirs.

The one he had emailed and received a reply from had said: NYMPHO NEEDS THICK COCKS at the top and "Don't measure up? Don't bother" at the bottom. Sandusky, one-and-a-half hours on Interstate 90.

She was a big shapely woman with jug-sized, floppy tits. She showed an expressionless interest in the camera snapping her, but she had exposed one mammoth breast by pulling down her nightie strap; it looked like a pancake at the end with a fried egg on it.

Her photo included the name Joyce and had a number and a convenient time to call. Her hair was prettier in this one: done up and parted in the middle. Her skin was olive and the labial lips were outlined in dark pigment. Her breasts hung down over her stomach and nearly obscured her crotch, but she had an untrimmed bush with black curly hair that veed out from her pudendum.

He could smell her cunt and her money from where he stood.

She would get his photo in today's mail at the latest: an old shot of him holding it out in front of him with a ruler next to it for scale. No face. His body hair shaved for the photo, a little kink of his he explained away by saying it heightened pleasure. If she balked at seeing hair where she expected none, she'd be the first one who did.

His friend Gino is coming by tonight. Gino is more than a pipefitter at the power plant; he's a union rep and foreman of a crew of sixteen in the feedwater section of the containment building. Better and better.

Grease the little wop a little more each time. He'd rubbed the back of Gino's neck while he was telling the table of men Gino brought in the latest joke from Tattoo Bitch; yukking it up and all the while methodically massaging Gino's neck, the curly hairs like wire between his fingers; touching the carotid artery, letting his fingers learn the contours so that, when it became necessary, he could break it like a chicken's.

After weeks of dry skin from the toxic afterburn of drugs, he began sweating freely again. He had to have three shirts to get through the night; already sweat was pouring from his hands.

Some of the bike trash were talking about a big rumble between the Angels and Pagans by late summer. He had to have things in motion by then.

Maybe pick Gino's brains a little bit tonight; it would have to be security or pipefitting. He might not stand up against a thorough check on the one, but he knew that the company didn't train its own: they contracted rent-a-cops who were themselves vetted by Department of Energy.

It's all timing, he thought; even so, the angel controls time.

He had never tested his powers of recall adequately; he had a simple set piece ready for her if she answered or one for her answering machine, a hair less assertive.

He mentally rehearsed it while standing in front of the pay phone on the corner of Morgana and Beach. Some bearded fool in a Foo Fighters Tour T-shirt steps up to the phone in front of him as if he were invisible, makes a drug connection in ten seconds' worth of speech.

He barked a sound from his throat in what was his first laugh in years: the angel had made him disappear from sight for a few moments of time. He could never be caught now.

He'd mail the cop something nice from Sandusky too.

He hummed *Magic Fire* Music from the Ring saga.

~ ~ ~

Haftmann was furious because his ass was hanging out of his nightshirt and he had to walk up and down the hallways looking for a nurse on duty.

The intercom was ceaseless tonight with its STAT commands and cryptic code designations for every color of the spectrum except magenta. No black, the absorption of all color – or white, the absence of all color. Colors to terrify.

The heat wave was blitzing the generators: he was reminded of the Psychedelic Lounge of his youth with its strobe and black lights that made for dazzling white teeth, bronzed skin, and the incense reek that reminded him of going to mass on Sundays as a boy. Torched by an owner in one of those frequent cases of Jewish lightning, the infamous Haze now stood on its spot earmarking a new age for slobs. Woodstock, Micah once told him, died at the Stones' concert in Altamont with the Hell's Angels.

Where the fuck were they now? Wouldn't let you sleep at six in the morning, buzzing all around you like flies, but when you have someone dying in the bed next to you –

"Fuck what the insurance said, he was out of here tomorrow." Couldn't take another day of it; he was alone with his thoughts enough as it was. Now with immobility pressing him down through the bed and every grim thought he'd ever had multiplied tenfold, he just wanted out, to get back to some kind of activity, even if it all amounted to pushing more rocks up bureaucratic hills.

A repo man left a calling card about his being in arrears on the stereo set he had thrown out the second story of his house when Micah's husband called to ask him for it.

Shawna sent flowers. Tico sent a get-well card with an obscene limerick. Booth's flunkey dropped by with summaries and précis of the Great Bouncer Chase all over Northeast Ohio. The Jefferson suspect had slipped south a few miles to a roadside tavern in Mechanicsville and was so far unavailable for interrogation.

Cleveland F.B.I. wanted a deposition from him at the Federal Building with a lawyer representing him about a matter pertaining to Dumont Nathan Jones, a.k.a. Raymond Artiss or Artiss Raymond III.

The crackerjack prize, however, was tucked within the attachments appended to the Niles team investigation of a bartender/ bouncer named Averill "Hulk" Dubois, a relocated citizen of Baton Rouge. The team had cleared him but had noted the suspicious circumstances of one large-built Cauc male's visit to a Niles Gold's Gym franchise in early spring. This male had impressed a few customers in the place and the young woman, Donna V. Healy, 27, WF 63421 N. Minneola Dr., of the city, on duty that afternoon.

Niles was due south of Jefferson on Route 11, about sixty minutes away.

He didn't match the mug shot of the Mechanicsville bouncer. "Bigger," she had told Dets. Bradford and Wheystone of Columbus B.C.I., "but not balding."

"This one, the one who worked over the weights, had crazy eyes – "

"What else?"

"A sharp odor, like, he gave off with his sweat – "

"And," she recalled, "he reached out with his left hand first."

They were sixty minutes and about as many miles from a sketch artist's rendering of the Jack-in-the-Box Killer.

The merciless bastard had made his first stupid mistake.

~ ~ ~

He was good at this part, but he never quite understood its reason for being. He knew that most fights were preceded by name-calling. Most bouncers who were any good ignored that part or got their punches in first: a maxim of his trade was, The One Who Hits First Wins. He lived by that rule.

While he didn't care much for the talking-before-sex part, he understood that it had a part too, and it might help to set the right tone for later. Couples talked less than single women, who wanted reassurance from a prospective partner who had the musculature to pin them down and physically dominate them; that's why neutral ground was ordinarily preferred: *you like what you see, you take it home with you*. He was blown once by a woman under the table who liked the kinkiness of sex in public.

He was never crudely suggestive in his remarks unless he had the ones who liked dirty talk. Almost always these were women who had their husband's company and approval on hand; they usually liked women or jigaboos, too. *Coalburners, muffdivers.*

This one had the overweight complex in spades, avoided the subject and returned to it offhandedly without realizing that she had done so. He nodded and smiled at everything she said. Talked about himself easily and convincingly. The fact that nothing he said was true had no bearing on either of their motives or aspirations. He could say, for example, that his penis would go from five inches to ten within a minute's time. But if he had said that he wanted to make a baby deep inside her, she would run screaming from the room.

The same boring lies, deceit, and hypocrisy everywhere. He'd scoped out many websites where college-aged girls gave random blowjobs at girls'-night-out events. Some Chippendale fool walking around with his dick out in front of him and girls who never saw him before in their lives are on their knees or bent over tables, all in public view, all accompanied by the cheers of their equally slutty girlfriends. The most amazing thing, he thought, they were all being videoed to wind up on the internet forever where the current boyfriends or future husbands would see them and their kids would be taunted on playgrounds forever.

When they took him from behind at Massillon, they beat him and called him names and said he deserved it, had it coming, or wanted them to do it.

The names and faces of his tormentors popped in front of his vision and he nearly snapped the goblet of Beefeater's she'd given him. *Control, timing,* he told himself.

She asked him if he had tattoos.

He said no, told her that was low-class.

She agreed. "Gauche," she said. "Tacky."

"Well, I think I know you a lot better now that we've talked and, well, we've had a chance to look each other over. Nowadays . . ."

"Yeah," he said, "You can't be too careful with strangers."

"Oh yes," she said, "I know exactly what you mean – I can't bear to think about it – those people . . . sickening."

"Don't think about it," he said; "it's a . . . tragedy."

"Well, I think the weather's been unbearable, don't you?"

Phony cunt with your wide-open box. He's tired of this.

"I can get a full erection in eight seconds," he said.

"Ooo," she said. "Show me."

For a large-boned and hugely titted woman, she had graceful, swift movements. He knew she'd never had a man with his strength of body, so he slung her around, positioning her where he wanted. She liked that.

He moved under her, got between her legs and began nibbling the folds of her labia. She hesitated awhile but got the message he intended and deep-throated him once she had the foreskin tight against the shaft. Her hand was very big and her feet were square-shaped, but the toes were almost delicate by contrast.

He inhaled the clean smell of her cunt deep into his lungs and felt a hair catch at the back of his throat. He'd see if he could get her to shave it for him before he broke her neck.

~ ~ ~

Mother McCree. Were these assholes kidding?

"I've swallowed tequila worms in my day, Booth, but I'm not swallowing this!"

"We've got his likeness and it's gone to seventeen-thousand law enforcement agencies."

"But we don't have the manpower to shut down one resort town, is that what you're telling me?"

"That's exactly what I'm telling you."

Jumping Jesus.

"The only plausible explanation for this mindlessness has got to be greed. The Chamber of Commerce got to you through the governor's office. Something like that, right?"

"Haftmann, shut up. I've heard you say that to your former colleagues all over that precinct. Now you follow your own advice and just shut up."

"Okay, he said, I'm all ears. Thrill me."

"It can't be done," said Booth.

Haftmann still drew stares on the street, but the station personnel were used to the rainbow apparition of a human face. One of the clerks ran into the women's rest room and got sick on her first day back at work when she saw him loping up to his borrowed carrel.

He still had the crimson, bloodshot eyes like a vampire and one bandage on his cheek had to be changed every day; he had squeezed about a pint of pus out of his cheek wound in the hospital after he'd come around on drugs. Two teenagers had found him. They were going to use the alley for sex.

"Listen to me, you thickheaded, flannel-mouth Irish – "

"German, Booth. I'm German."

"Whatever. You cannot isolate an area between Cleveland and Erie with a traffic volume on major arteries and interstates in the millions."

"Jesus, Booth, we know what he looks like. Cordon it off with the 101st Airborne if you have to."

"We'll fax you as soon as we get anything solid."

"I know a kiss-off when I hear it, Booth. He's here, right here! Don't you see?"

Haftmann jabs a finger at his desk, as if the Jack-killer were crouched in the leg space.

"We can't operate on that assumption just because he used that lot out there as a mail drop to communicate with you."

"Bullshit."

"For once, listen to the experts. He won't kill in his backyard."

"The Zodiac did. Gacy did."

"The Zodiac's the exception that proves the rule," Booth said. "Besides, Gacy hunted in Chicago."

Micah, ever the lawyer, once told him that if you have an exception to the rule, the rule itself is no good.

~ ~ ~

He gave her a royal tit-fucking for twenty minutes by the clock on the wall – kept pumping it up through her fleshy boobs and let her get a bite on it once in a while. Her cleavage turned pink where he had greased a channel up and down with it.

"Let me have it," he said and plopped it out of her mouth.

"Fuck my big tits with your cock."

How original. Her big porno line, apparently.

"No," he said. "Get off your knees and get on your stomach. On the bed, like this."

Her teats were spread out on either side under her armpits like brick-colored water balloons. "Oooh, what are you going to do to me?"

His first slap caught her left buttock just right; the flesh quivered. He cupped his hand slightly to take most of the sting out. Slap! Slap! Slap! His hand fell back and forth on her backside; "like Jell-O," he thought, nauseated.

She moaned something that sounded like *Unnnh* each time his hand fell.

When she came, he was showered with it; her aroma was atomized in the room. She kept making that gurgling noise. Soon, it would be a real death rattle.

While she showered, he went through her drawers and found a dozen pairs of crotchless panties from Frederick's of Hollywood, size: full-figured – but no money or jewelry.

She was evasive about their next date, a bit dizzy from the sex and slow on the uptake in responding to his questions.

Finally, she agreed to four days from now, and he said that would be him knocking at her door at noon.

"Great," she said.

"Guess what I'll be knocking with," he said.

"Oooh," she crooned, "I can't wait."

He made it back in time for work with fifteen minutes to spare; he called the credit doctor and made an appointment for three weeks from that day. He had Gino's number, wormed it out of him with his Heinekens at the bar, and he gave him a call.

"Gino. This is Jackson from the Purple Haze."

"Hey, man, what's up?"

Giving it a coon topspin. He'd give the little man a different kind of spin soon. *They're all on my list now*, he thought happily.

"I need a small favor," he said.

Pause, thinking. "Okay, lay it on me, bro," Gino said.

"I got you a date with Silver Earrings tonight, but she says if you come in her mouth, she'll cut your dick off."

"Oh . . . my . . . God."

Said it like the little fairy bitch he was.

Chapter 14

Labor Day

Jefferson-on-the-Lake hasn't always been a resort haven for tired factory workers and their families, or lounge lizards on the make.

John Brown made it famous simply because he was a local wacko who made good in the history books. There is still a farm where he used to plot his mayhem, and as the County Historical Society has ably documented, Highway 45 was once a wagon road that took slaves to freedom. Brown used its scattered farms and homesteads as places to stockpile weapons.

There were other figures of note who earned themselves state plaques along the county highways for their trouble; the man who designed Spenserian handwriting used to come down to the beach at Geneva-on-the-Lake (A JOTL knockoff which plays to the family values side of North Coast entertainment) and practice writing his newfangled script in the sand.

There were Joshua Giddings and Benjamin Wade, the latter famous for not becoming our nation's president. And novelist Albion Tourgee, carpetbagger and judge. The most famous man of letters that the area boasts is William Dean Howells, friend of Mark Twain, and founder of the *Jefferson Gazette*, still printed today. Howells may not count, however, because he was only a boy of seventeen when he got out for good, a victim of his father's wanderlust who dragged the family up from Martin's Ferry on the Ohio River.

The ghosts of those abolitionist scourges rest easily in their graves and tombs, their job done, their dream of freedom for black Americans achieved. Many tourists still come to gaze over the limitless expanse of Lake Erie and know that history happened here: black men and their families arrived at the northernmost terminus of the Underground Railroad and were shipped across the lake to Canada, to freedom. Although the houses that once sheltered them, as they awaited ships to carry them, creak and groan with age, a few still stand: Hubbard House in Ashtabula, atop a hill overlooking Walnut Beach, and here the McDonough House and the Stone Homestead are testimony to that courageous epoch.

There was a slight problem with the follow-up, however: Canada was not an especially hospitable place for settlers at this time in its rugged history. Nearly every black man who got safely to Canada froze or starved to death in the winter. The Arctic wind called the Siberian Express was a railroad of another kind of metaphor. Today blacks are not forgotten in the stride toward progress. All along the Strip you can see the effects of target marketing; Schlitz Malt Liquor signs are abundant and H. L. Heilmann's new 7.5 proof brew PowerMaster has found the Strip an ideal place to test market its latest beverage aimed at low-income, urban-style blacks. No crusading preachers have shown up with a pack of high-minded citizens to whitewash the billboards that show blacks how to live right and be in control; instead you see the effects of such control all along the street in high summer in the dazed and ravaged faces, cirrhotic livers, and escalating homicide rates among the black and Hispanic males drawn to the lights and promise. Everything looks fine at night and it's, well, just business.

When the duty sergeant at the station got the word from the State Highway Patrol in Pittsburgh that the Pagans were riding long and strong out of Wheeling, West Virginia, headed north on Interstate 79, his first question was, "How many?" "Oh," said the dispatcher after a long pause, "we make it about a hundred. Another thirty coming from the Youngstown chapter."

"Oh shit," said the desk sergeant.

"God damn it to hell," said Chief Millimaki.

"Here we go again," said the public relations director for the Chamber of Commerce.

"Good," said Haftmann to his image in the mirror when he got the word in Tico's. He was nursing a cold beer and brooding in the half-light. "I hope they burn it all down and piss on the ashes," he told Tico.

Haftmann could use the distraction; he had, he was certain, dodged one bullet already. The deposition he gave at the Federal Building two weeks ago was an obvious sham. No one had accused him – yet – even though they were circling him like buzzards over a roadkill.

Two postal inspectors, an F.B.I. agent, and two stenographers discussed Haftmann's former career as a homicide cop amiably for an hour over coffee and donuts, the F.B.I.'s treat.

Haftmann was certain that one of the stenographers, the one who kept fidgeting and gawking at him when she thought he wasn't looking. He remembered faces. She may have been one of the postal workers in Albany who had a good look at his mug when he dropped off the bags. One thing was certain because he hadn't been bothered since: she didn't recognize him.

How could she, she must have wondered, *when his face looked more like a basket of eggplants than a human countenance?*

The Man with Flies was getting deeper into his dream life. "Fugue state" (*Merck Manual* said): dissociative flight from reality. "Depersonalization Disorder" (*DSM-V* said): "Confusion about personal identity under stress or impairment." One of the Afghan vets Haftmann saw in Tico's said: "PTSD." Tico said: "He just loco, man."

Haftmann used up another perk to bill the county for another fifteen-minute call to Quantico and was put through to one of the consulting psychiatrists at the Behavioral Sciences Unit.

Dr. Brittany Trask, a University professor at U of Virginia, said there was a discernible pattern that might yet establish the psychic motives of the Jack-in-the-Box Killer, but she couldn't say why the killer is unable to realize he's in the grip of his fixation. "Sometimes," she told Haftmann, "you pass through states of lucidity but the obsession to re-enact powerful scenes through violence and disorder is too strong." The shrink adds: "It's a bit like creativity itself."

"I don't understand, "Haftmann interjected, "how creativity is aligned with this kind of balls-to-the-walls destruction."

"It's the way were built," the professor said; "it's how nature designed us as a species. A man's face is shaped and designed for taking punches."

Haftmann asked her when he'd make the mistake that gave him away.

"What do you mean?"

"Will he ever get so psychotic he'll write his phone number on the wall in blood?"

"You mean like 'Stop-Me-Before-I-Kill-Again'? Oh, it happens but the chances he'll betray himself aren't that good really. You'll just have to catch him through police work," responded the voice from Quantico.

Haftmann knew the average criminal was generally stupid in intelligence, but she informed him psychotics operate without inhibitions and have a compartmentalized ability to protect them from self-incriminating acts during the time they're acting out phases.

"Doctor, what about what the papers have been saying about his getting his ideas from newspapers, TV – "

"Categorically, I'd say no." She told him the killer's derangement is so advanced beyond what we normally mean by schizophrenia that he's able to function in society. "Obviously."

"Why 'obviously,' Doctor?"

"Because you'd have caught him by now."

"I'm afraid you're alone in the opinion, Doctor."

"The average educated layperson doesn't understand the dilemma of trying to apprehend a man who, if he stays mobile and acts sane, is virtually uncapturable in a society like ours."

"Will he get cured, do you think?"

"Remission of the psychosis is always possible. Unlikely, however. A recent Dutch study implies that sociopaths can acquire empathy in tiny increments. I'm skeptical. He may become dangerous intermittently, but right now it has to be inferred that he's not going to stop."

"Do your people there have a better theory?"

"Well, here's mine. He's duplicating scenes from his past. Some occurrence, some important, to him, event he's fixated upon. It's not to be confused with the classic suicide's cry for attention."

"What event do you think he's reliving?" *Fucking English, please*, Haftmann hoped.

"I'd say he's recreating . . . evil," the psychiatrist said.

"Wh-what? Why would he do that?"

"The key is your New Philadelphia couple. They might have provoked him to act out of his intended pattern somehow. Your focus should be the red blood on silver walls."

"It sounds like a wreck—a car crash, or, maybe a plane crash?

"No one can tell you that with certainty. Jung said famously that the mind cannot confront evil directly. It circles closer, in spirals, so to speak, getting closer by gradations."

"I see." Haftmann absolutely didn't.

"Are you a hunter, Mister Haftmann?"

"No. I just like guns."

"Yes, well. Do you know Tennyson, 'Nature red in tooth and claw'?"

Here we go. Asshole poetry, Haftmann thinks.

"The normal person works out his or her fears in dreams. It's healthy, for the most part. But the schizoid individual doesn't know a real difference between dream and reality. Dreams are reality. More real, in fact. That's what they listen to. That's why they go over the edge."

"One more question, Doctor. Who's he blaming for this evil?" *Haftmann remembers Micah telling him psychologists aren't supposed to believe in evil. Biological determinism, she said. No such thing as free will when it comes right down to it.*

"The truth, Mister Haftmann, sad or not, is that a so-called 'monster' is finally just the distortion of what makes us all human."

Red blood on silver walls. Torsos hanging from the ceiling.

They wash them out with steam hoses. Flies and blood. Guts in the corner of the carpet in Warren. The husband's head in the box. Like meat wrapped in cellophane to be stored in the freezer.

But not a supermarket . . . a side of beef hanging on a hook.

He gets it in a flash. His smart-aleck ex called it a sarong—no, that's a dress or something. He's got it . . . a satori:

. . . a slaughterhouse.

~ ~ ~

"Who the fuckin' hell ever heard of nigger cowboy? Ain't no such thing, girl."

Tattoo Bitch is watching the bikers pass, two-by-two, with their colors stitched by their women on their denims.

"Some things don't change," he reflects, watching the parade of Harleys tool down the Strip, cruising speed for the gawkers to behold. Tattoo Bitch says there are twenty, thirty Angels in town right now.

"Well," said a barfly from his favorite stool in the Haze, "They's gonna be a whole lot more real goddam soon, I can tell you."

~ ~ ~

Haftmann on another ride-along with Elise, clientless and adrift as usual these days, watched the chrome-and-steel parade of the big engines passing down the street with their bearded, riders in formation. Micah once told him that in England the aristocratic men of the seventeenth century had long flowing hair and made "dashing" appearances on their steeds. Opposing them, she said, were the godly-minded Puritans who despised their fornicating and gambling ways.

He explained that bit of history to Elise, who said, "These guys sell dope and women. I doubt they write any poetry unless it's on bathroom walls."

He told Elise that it confirmed somebody's theory that everything happens twice. "There's going to be a lot of shit hitting the fan then," she said, "if the next one's anything like nineteen-eighty-nine."

"You know it, babe."

"Watch it, you chauvinist pig," Elise responded. "You hear some guy was stopped last night on the Strip for driving with a noose hanging from his cab windows?"

"Micah was right. The more things change, the more they stay the same."

"I've heard that before," she said, "but I think she was talking about you, idiot."

~ ~ ~

The owner's in the bar tonight, and Nelson knows he's waiting for the cop to show, always the same one, according to him. Pays him off over the counter. The cop bullshits a little with the broads, then leaves.

Gino is supposed to have them with him tonight. He's so nervous his palms are wet. He has devoted all his free time to preparation and study. His ability to perceive spatial relations and comprehend design principles was untutored, yet, like his voice, a gift that couldn't be taught. When one of the volunteers at the boys' dorm in Massillon brought a chessboard and said he'd teach him to play, Nelson wiped him out in three consecutive games. The man was angry and said he knew damned well how to play. He himself was a club champion, played blitz chess in many tournaments and no untutored kid like Nelson, a ward of the state, could possibly have beaten him like that unless . . .

. . . *unless he was a prodigy.*

Nelson mumbled the word to himself all day and even into the night from his bunk. He had no idea what the word meant but it sounded good. He, Lonnie Dale Nelson, castoff, retard, reject, fuckboy, ass bandit – and all the other derogatory terms they bullied him with – was a *prodigy*, too.

The credit doctor said it was going to cost him another five Ben Franklins because he was choosy. His woman in Sandusky was loaning him money steadily in small amounts and taking less explanation than it took to get the first few hundred.

How much time did he have? He wondered. He had not been visited by the angel in days and it was worrying him. He did not think he could do it without the angel's guidance.

"Jackson, c'mere, man," Tattoo Bitch calling him over like he's her private manservant.

I'll fucking rip your face off and eat it in front of you, slimy-cunted whore.

"Yes?"

"He wants you." She thumbs in the direction of the dickwad owner.

"Stand right here, Jackson. Yeah, like that – closer to me. Now put your work face on."

"What do you want me to do?"

"Nothing, damn it. Just stand there like that. Don't say a fuckin' word."

"What's my work face?"

"The one I seen you wearing that time you took that wrestler outside, that Indian guy was in here two, three weeks back," he said. He recalled it: an Ojibway from Michigan, an ironworker turned TV wrestler for a small network in Cleveland.

The cop came in; he blinked from the contrast of light to dark. The owner, blowing his stinking breath into Nelson's face, whispered from the dimly lit corner where he had Nelson stand still like a cigar store Indian:

"Look at the prick, thinks he's a fucking Jew in a junkyard. Just walks right up to the counter for his money."

The cop looked around, blinked like an owl, eyes adjusting to the dark. He approached.

When he saw Nelson, he jerked to a sudden halt, put a hand out in front of him.

"Don't believe I ever saw you before, big guy. The new bouncer, huh?"

"Yeah."

"What do you go?"

"What?"

"How much you weigh – two-ninety, three hundred? I used to play some ball myself."

The owner piped in: "Cut the shit, bag man. I got work to do in here. Take it."

The owner held out the banded cash in his hand and Nelson watched the cop eat the pasted-on smile.

The cop looked once more at the towering bulk next to the potbellied owner and then changes his mind about what he was going to say. To Nelson, extending his hand to shake, he said: "Name's MacDuff, by the way. Friends call me Duffy."

"You ain't got no friends in here, MacDuff," said the owner.

He watched the cop's retreat into daylight. He turned to his bouncer and said, "Shit, Jackson, move away. You give me the willies, too."

~ ~ ~

Haftmann sent his slaughterhouse theory down to Vanderhyden and got the usual noise from his staff. "We'll pass on your message ASAP," said the last flunky in line.

Haftmann knew the doctor was half-right about one thing: he might not be a copycat, but he's spawned them. They always do.

Every pimp who offed a whore in Cleveland nowadays tried to give credit to "Jack." Downtown female office workers kept their hands around the pistols in their purses and paid the parking lot attendants with their left hands. "You get too close," they told them, "you'll see the gun." There were three cases of copycat murders, two by suburban husbands bored with their marriages or seeking the insurance payouts.

The loonies who confessed realized this was a golden opportunity, and scores of them wanted credit for Warren and New Philadelphia. You name it, they did it. Social networking proved a nightmare with accusations hurled throughout cyberspace by everyone with a grudge or a desire for gossip. Some of it had to be checked out.

Macabre humor sprang up and entered the culture in a variety of ways: soreheads sent jack-in-the-boxes to their employers, bosses gave them to employees about to be canned, and greeting cards even found a way to incorporate the grisly theme: "Don't lose your heart to anyone but me!" A jack-in-the-box clown with a butcher knife holds out a dripping heart toward a pretty girl.

Haftmann called Shawna but never got her at home, and the second time he called he faked a message for her from the station. He knew her husband would know his voice; the degradation was eating out his stomach lining. He vowed not to call her again. Her move now.

The mood in the station was anxious; on the Strip, tense, palpable. Something was going to happen soon. You could feel it on your skin.

The last of summer was looming and, next to the mania of the Fourth of July, Labor Day is the biggest of the holidays at the Lake. Now was the time to take the vacation before the weather turned because autumn was the true season of death up North. Nothing but a barbed-wire fence and a lobo wolf separating the U.S. from Canada.

So far, no new Angels had ridden in and the Pagans were avoiding confrontations, although they had their enemies outnumbered. Their presence in town was minimal, uneventful, except for a public drunk and a couple urinating-in-public citations. The calm before the storm, Haftmann said to Elise.

One thing it did was to resurrect bars that were barely getting by. Beer trucks were tripling their stops to some of the worst hole-in-the-wall places like Eli's Bar and Grill, The Jamaican Lounge, Harry Beard's, Annie's, the Pit

Stop, Slipper Inn, Skinny Dick's, and a couple of nameless cement block jobs at the end, where the owners drank along with the customers and the cops issued citation every week. Some of these would have vanished at the end of a single season, but they were all booming now.

The drought was unabated by the few cloudbursts that sizzled the parking lots and streets and sent more condensation up in the air to form clouds the size of skyscrapers in Rorschach shapes that made you think God was testing Northeast Ohio's sanity all at once. Seventy-foot oaks all over the county, planted by second-generation immigrants from Europe's farthest corners, were in such stress they wouldn't last out another summer.

A rogue biker gang rode into town: the Forgotten Few, mavericks from one of their few chapters in San Jose, La Jolla, or San Ysidro (famed for the McDonald's shooting spree). They were hanging out at Roger's Rec Room. Haftmann got word from the street that they'd come for the celebration of the anniversary of their chapter founding. Haftmann didn't think so.

"What celebration?" bellowed an exasperated Millimaki. "We got enough to worry about with that other low-riding human garbage." The detective Who Dressed Up was given surveillance duty with three vice cops: find out when the Akron-Cleveland-Youngstown Angel chapters were going to ride; get word to the state cops. Right now, they sat quiet around Ohio waiting for push to come to shove; so far, so good. The few Angels in town meanwhile kept giving the Pagans a wide berth.

The street was quiet. Nobody knew when, or if, it was going to happen. Labor Day was favored by those who were teens or college kids when the summer of 1989 blew up in their faces.

Haftmann remembered it. He had arrived home to bury his grandmother. She had declined into a total religious dementia by then, called her grandson "the spawn of Satan" from her hospice bed in the county. He saw the street after one mini-riot that barely made the six o'clock news in Cleveland. It looked no more devastating in its wake than one of the frequent gale-force winds that kicked up off the lake every now and then. Debris in the street, people standing around scratching their asses, telling lies about what they did while it was happening. Haftmann's own grief and guilt for abandoning the old lady were too much for him at that time, so he was indifferent to the locals' tall tales.

He was going to cop school in the fall; marry Micah, if she'd have him.

He remembered how Micah used to try to explain one of those artsy-fartsy Ingmar Bergman films they'd seen at Case Western's foreign film program—or was it Fellini? *No, he was the happy one.* Haftmann knew only that if his life were going to be filmed now, it would be Brian DePalma who should get the job.

* * *

Lonnie Dale Nelson's massive frame was drained by the heat, and he sagged exhausted against a column of books stacked against the corner out of sight of the doorway's angle of vision. Bouncers weren't supposed to be up on the principles of fission and fusion.

Most of the technical stuff he ordered from the campus library of the Kent State branch in Ashtabula and was shown how to access any volume in the twelve-story library on the main campus. Kent State was one of two universities in the world that held a patent on liquid crystals, so its technical library was amply stocked. What they didn't have, Google did. You could get anything on the web.

He couldn't build a detonable nuclear device, no way, like the physics student at Princeton a few years back, but he might be able to figure out how a nuclear power plant operated. Not so much operated, but where it was vulnerable. He discovered the government had apparently censored anything involving power-plant schematics that might be useful to terrorists flying a crop duster or driving a ten-ton truck. Snooping with a library card would have drawn Homeland Security's attention to him and he'd be known to every NSA, F.B.I., C.I.A. and Secret Service database. Gino, his chatty source, told him the government had hundreds of buildings all over the country strictly for gathering intelligence.

"Won't it be too late when that happens," he asked him.

"Won't what be too late?" Gino replied. Fortunately he was too drunk at the time to be suspicious of Nelson's motives for asking all these questions. The promise of pussy and the booze kept him in line.

Gino supplied him with technical manuals swiped from production and control. Safety manuals, evacuation charts, daily work sheets, and, riskiest of all, the schematics for the main feedwater loop. These were kept in supply in a locked cupboard because the entire system and its backup were on computers.

To Nelson, it was like an array that resembled a roller coaster where circuits tripped red lights on the board to show where the tram cars were. Only this time the chain reaction was going to be the train.

He could not process the technical information, although he could recall all of it and, if he had to, recite whole passages of it. But they concepts were beyond his comprehension.

He instinctively understood the beast's great beating heart, however, and he knew that the right trigger would cause this chain reaction. The key was somewhere, lying, waiting to be found in the tangled web of crisscrossing pipes.

Fortunately, Cleveland Electric Illuminating Company, which owned the reactor, had a privileged position in Lake County, where millions in tax revenues benefited schools and hospitals. Its corporate officers were tired of comparisons to Chernobyl by every yellow journalist in the state. Its record number of safety violations had the NRC breathing down its neck again.

The Lake County sheriff's department had sent word that those assholes from Greenpeace were going to be snooping around in the fall with their fucking upside-down smiley faces on black flags stuck in every homeowner's lot within ten miles of the reactor. What's a little cancer or a small leak compared to prosperity and jobs anyway, the authorities contended.

Reasonable restraint was all that's necessary when you're trying to work out intra-company problems. Morale was bad enough on the floor; the pipefitters were going for a new contract in October, so some farmer is blowing smoke up the nineteenth district's Congressman's ass about how come all his neighbors come down with cancer of the back and why can't his cattle get good conception wasn't news.

When the kiddies get ready to go back to school in a couple of days there was bound to be that same old stink about the elementary school evacuation plan; all because those low-life bus drivers won't fulfill their obligation to pick up somebody else's children and drive their prearranged routes in an emergency.

Nelson had to get the cocky little wop to cough up more good, but all Gino wanted was get his skin flute tuned and Tattoo bitch was demanding more money, more favors for every blow job. "Teach me how the water loop works," he said to him; "show me the way the main feedwater pump kicks in" . . .

Gino was getting nervous. He didn't understand the most basic principles, apparently, because Lonnie Dale had to explain to him what the diagrams said but got nothing but blank stares.

Gino knew safety, though. He gave rousing speeches to his men.

"That's how you put your face on the map," he told the bouncer.

At night he would study the diagrams and imagine himself inside the pipes, invisible like the isotopes he read of, traveling around the loops of pipe big enough in diameter that a man could walk upright in one section, and a particle in the next, around and around, until he came to a tiny pinprick hole in the flange of a pipe – then around and around the screw threads of pipe, silent, invisible, deadly.

"Would badges pick up the difference?"

"No," Gino said. Pipefitters don't wear badges in the containment building. "You can't smoke in there," he added, as though a lit cigarette could precipitate a nuclear reaction.

"Would the radiation detectors pick it up?" Nelson asked.

"Sure," he answered.

"But not if you clipped or soldered the resistors first, right?"

Gino stared at him. "What-what are you up to, Jackson?"

"I want a job out there." He wrapped a heavy arm around Gino's shoulders. "I'm a pipefitter, too, remember? A union man like you."

The System had better find a way.

One of the books said: "There's enough energy in a drop of water no thicker in diameter than a dime to power a city like Chicago for ten months."

Power. Light.

The nuclear flash.

His cock twitched at the thought of it.

Some blacks had come in with some white girls.

Three Pagans at the back left table and two Angels up front looked on. He tensed. This could get ugly despite the calm between these gangs. The owner explained the history of the Strip to him. Bab blood, 1989. He didn't care. A lot of chickens would be coming home to roost very soon and motorcycle gangs would be the last thing on their minds. He smiled. Just like Gino's stupid joke: What's the last thing going through a bug's mind when it hits the windshield? It's asshole. People were bugs to Nelson. Some had their uses. That was all.

He admired Tattoo Bitch's phoniness; she was a nigger-fucking hillbilly who came out of one of those forlorn shacks on North Bend, where the old man shaves in his boxer trunks in front of a doorless living room, but she's all tits and buckteeth for the customers. "Nasty bitch," Nelson thought. He knew she'd shit out a couple halfies that her mother back in the hills was raising. Mothers who abandoned their children were the lowest form of life to Nelson.

So far, no trouble; neither table regarded the other; it was the same all over the Strip where Pagans and Angels drank at the same watering hole.

During break, Tattoo Bitch came over for her money, the same toothy grin and cleavage. "He coming in tonight?" She asked, propping her boobs up so he could see down to her kneecaps.

"I think so," Nelson said.

Gino came in an hour later. Hitching his pants high up his belly, he did his usual banty walk down front with his buddies from the plant in tow. He knows the bouncer Jackson, it's cool. Gino waved Nelson over: he's a big noise in here now.

They fist-bumped. Gino pulled down Tattoo Bitch onto his lap, played with her blouse as she took the order. The other two ogle the tits and Gino's stock went up a big notch.

She told Nelson last night after work he had a mushroom cap for a cock, and he should bring his own tweezers.

"Keep him happy," he told her.

"Make me happy, tough guy," she replied.

"I'll make you happy," Nelson said but he thought: *Blood on the moon, bitch.*

The Angels stopped talking to witness the machismo display from the power-plant workers, not liking it one bit. They don't control the bar because Jackson's always visible whenever they start goosing the waitress or shortchanging the bar tab.

This is different. There are citizens now, locals, and some wimps who think they own the bar. *Showtime.* He can feel it coming.

One of the Pagans got up to play a tune and punched in some change. One of the Angels, a bald and bearded pig-eyed giant, says: "Hey, shut that nigger music the fuck off."

Gino and his group stopped speaking, each man began eyeing the door.

The Pagan was about six foot, rangy, all whipcord muscle and sunburned skin. Drank seven, eight beers a night and didn't get fat or drunk. *He's trouble all over,* Nelson figured.

He jumped onto the bar top like a water moccasin and began a slow dance down the bar. As he came to a drink, he kicked it over. Glass and booze flying in all directions. Tattoo Bitch, for once, was speechless. Nelson watched.

"Hey, Huey, lookee here," the Pagan says to one of his Angel brothers. "I'm doing the Owner's Shuffle. You can't kick me out because I own the place."

He danced over to Nelson and said: "Hey, fuckface. You let nigger trash in here. You let them other assholes in here. What the fuck kinda bouncer are you?"

"Get off the bar, please."

"You look like a big pussy to me."

The Angel did his shuffle back up the other end, gyrating his hips and pelvis in what he thought was black rhythm. "Hey, coons, you got one this big?"

Nelson swiveled his head to see the Angel holding his long, thin penis out of his Levi's.

All the Pagans rose to their feet. Then they turned as one and walked out the door.

No bar fight, nothing busted up. *Now he knows it's close . . .*

He walked calmly over to the Angel with the wagging cock. He moved slowly but in measured strides, calculating distance to the strike like a cat on the Savanna cat measuring a rodent in the brush. He reached out, fingers splayed, and bunched his hand around the base of the Angel's bobbing penis. Nobody in the place moved or breathed.

Huey jumped to his feet in an agony of indecision; he looked at the Pagan who wasn't able to talk or move or even scream. Everyone stayed rooted in the same spot, as if turned to stone. Droplets beaded the Angel's brow and he shook hard, twice, like a man with malaria, but didn't cry out. His lips were bloodless and his eyes rolled back in his head.

As he fell, Nelson reached out his fist and collared him, took his balled fist out of the Angel's crotch and thrust it into the belt. Then he did presses with him, all the time watching Huey, who's still stuck to the floor, unable to comprehend what the fuck was going on.

The Angel's cock looked like curly pasta as it flopped with the motion of the man's horizontal body. Nelson did two sets of him and then set him right-side up on the floor. The Angel fell to the floor in a heap.

He told Tattoo Bitch to come over and tuck it in, which she started to do, and the place awoke from its trance, hoots of glee split other night sounds from the Strip. Someone put more money in the jukebox, and a frenzied headbanger number sent jolts of sound booming through everyone's ribcage and up the spinal cord. Huey watched her zip him up, and a big smile crossed his face. *Hey, some fun.*

Gino's eyes were big with admiration for Jackson, his man, and he pinched each girl's that came within reach. "Drinks on the house," he yells. To Nelson, he bawled out: "Here's to a man with balls the size of basketballs!"

Lonnie Dale pasted a grin to his face, tipped a bottle he held by the neck in Gino's direction. In the cynosure of madness and hooting going on all around him, the Haze in a chaos of lust and barely suppressed violence, anybody walking into the place would have said there's a riot going on in here. Inside, Nelson was calm, alert, aware, calculating new odds.

He knew the smiling cop would hear of it.

Soon, got to be soon.

* * *

When Haftmann got the call, he couldn't shake off the dream that easily. When he did manage coherence, he recognized Booth's voice and part of what he said:

" – left you a message."

"Where?"

"Sandusky," said Booth.

It's after midnight when he arrived. Booth had left sufficient notice around the crime scene for him to get past the beat cops. She lived in a house like the last one; the side of the house facing north had taken a beating from the weather. You could smell the lake water from here: rotten fish under the pilings. Coal dust left black grit in the cracks of the house; Haftmann felt it in his hair.

Inside, he found the state's lab team going over the house again. No one's taking anything on faith this time. The Sandusky cops are brooding in the corner about the implied insult, and there's silver-haired Booth, an old F.B.I. smoothie, pouring oil on the waters.

"Take a look," says Booth.

He had filleted her torso. Her teat flesh was a soggy red mess.

Look what he did with them. Booth leads him through an alcove to the kitchen where her breasts lie on a plate; a knife and fork on the left, a spoon on the right.

"He don't know how to serve at table," cracks a young cop, pointing. "The spoon should be on the left." Haftmann glared at the cop. "Suck shit through a straw, sonny."

Haftmann walked straight at it, stared for a long time at the words misspelled or spelled in text-English like a teenager on a cell phone. He was prepared, somewhere in his limbic brain, he supposed, but it's a four-star, revolving shock all the same. The killer's message on the white walls in her blood, the same 'e' like the skewed arrow from the first message:

i SAveD THiS 1 4 U HaFMaN

The other men in the room are suddenly embarrassed. One of the techs, a woman with a doughy face and red lipstick, looked away abruptly, as though he had something to do with the outrage in the house. Haftmann felt his skin prickle the way it did when he found his name linked to some obscene graffiti in the stalls of the station crapper.

Haftmann found the head honcho from B.C.I. at an actual crime scene. Out of the corner of his eye, he noted the paramedics with the gurney were hanging around. A detective told them that body wasn't going anywhere for a while.

Haftmann asked a forensics tech, "Did he know what he was doing with the knife?"

"What do you mean?"

"His technique, God damn it."

"No good. He's a butcher."

"Where'd he put her eyes?"

"Nobody's found 'em yet."

The M.O. looked similar. Heat jacked up. Windows shut. Flies busy on the corpse, burrowing into cavities and wound channels. But he left her head alone.

Booth's F.B.I. liaison from Sandusky was a veteran but his face was white. Booth had asked him to fill Haftmann in, which he seemed to do grudgingly enough and Haftmann couldn't be sure whether it was the agent's distaste for him as somebody outside law enforcement or whether the crime scene had affected him.

He used the woman for money, apparently. "The bank she uses—used, will tell us tomorrow, but she's got receipts for withdrawals on her credit card checks in a drawer in the dining room."

"How much?"

"So far, about fifteen hundred."

Now the fucker is after money. That doesn't make sense. This Jack the Ripper shit is just smoke . . .

"Why the look? You're looking for sense from this loony ax murderer?"

"No, sir," Haftmann said. "But he's not a criminal. He's not a thief."

"Excuse me, but when we catch him—"

"He's been making sense and now he resorts to a copycat killing of himself. Do you buy that?"

"I let the experts worry about his motives," the agent said.

Haftmann thought, *We're supposed to be the experts.*

"Do us a favor, Mister Haftmann. Stay out of people's way," the agent said and walked off.

Haftmann felt like a mongoloid child underfoot.

Vanderhyden, weary from the long day, still had a publicity piece to do for public consumption. He left Haftmann standing in the middle of the room staring at the message.

He saw the state's best blood man packing up his gear.

"Don't fucking say it," Haftmann scowled at the man's crooked smile.

He says it anyway, with a leer, "We've got to stop meeting like this."

~ ~ ~

The riots started at ten o'clock in the morning on Labor Day. Eight Angels were riding go-carts and tearing up the machines and dragging each other into the bales of tire buffers. The owner came out of his shack with a shotgun and blew off a round of buckshot overhead.

After that it was complete madness: cops came and arrested the man for his own protection; besides, the cop wasn't stupid enough to arrest eight Angels.

They savaged his place when he was gone and burned up the go-carts while a crowd of mostly teens watched and cheered them on. Ten minutes later the rest of the Angels arrived: 125 strong. The crowd went crazy, as if they had been held captive by an alien army and the besiegers had come to the rescue on their shiny black mounts.

Haftmann spent the night in a motel in Sandusky rather than make the trip back in the early hours of morning. The morning sun was cooking the inside of his car, and he smelled ripe; he'd forgotten to bring a change of clothes.

As he cleared the Willoughby exit on 90, he got the first dispatch of rioting at the Lake from his scanner. Besides a high-tech laser mic for eavesdropping, it was his most expensive p.i. gadget, the same radar used by the drivers who made the annual Cannonball Express run from New York to California in a little over a day, which meant an average speed of 90 mph. You needed to know where the staties were hiding.

He felt a surge of panic, although he knew that was irrational.

He got off at the Geneva-on-the-Lake exit and took the one access road he believed would stand a chance of remaining open. Within minutes, the panic of vacationers getting off the Strip would create bottlenecks at both ends and nothing would move on wheels except the big Harleys.

By 11:29 on the Strip, it was all assholes and elbows. People ran in all directions without a sense of purpose. So far, it was all a big lark. Minor damage, except for the go-carts, and the usual bruises and lacerations caused by frenetic crowd action.

By noon, the situation had worsened because people had begun to drift in and out of little pockets, havens of safety for some, congeries of troublemakers in others.

At this time there was still a mixed bag of people on the streets. Young and old alike were scattered among the roving packs of young males of every social class and description. Even so, you could still find a vendor to sell you a bag of popcorn or cotton candy.

It was as if the crowd wanted something else to happen to give it the license it secretly wished for to set its powerful force in motion. That came at 12:45 when a 300-pound Hell's Angel appeared in the middle of the Strip without clothes on.

Fights broke out, old scores that wanted settling, but mostly it was a matter of where you happened to be in the crowd. The teens, the youngest, best dressed, gravitated toward the video arcades, which were already in the possession of a mixed bag of Goths, punks, and heavy metal set.

The contrast was inflammatory. Rocks, fists, and sticks acquired from trash bins along the beach had found their way into hands as if by providential design.

Up to that point it may have been possible to contain the riot with the presence of the JOTL police alone. But no one will know for sure because the motel and restaurant owners had long since been assured by Chief Millimaki that his force would be deployed along sections of the Strip where most of the money and property was.

In any event, it amounted to a Band-Aid on a sucking chest wound because the National Guard was the only force sufficient to contain the riot once it got cooking.

A compilation of eyewitness reports and field interviews gathered later revealed:

An officer of fifteen years' service attempted to separate the skirmish in front of the video arcade. He was clubbed behind by a burly teen, a rocker type with shoulder-length surfer hair. The cop died on the street of cerebral concussion, and it seemed for a moment as though the crowd's shock and horror would accept one man's death and bring its own momentum to a halt. But there was too much activity going on up and down the Strip for the guilt of one part of the crowd to affect the rest of it with any kind of shame or hesitation.

That's when the blood flew.

People jumped out of cars wherever they were and fled on foot. Fathers had their children in their hands and ran toward the beach, if they could, or just back off the street as far as they could get. One family of four was later found ten miles in the brush, dehydrated and filthy, grateful to be alive.

The greediest of the concession stand owners stayed in business as long as they dared; most, however, felt the tug of personal safety with slightly more resilience than greed and shut their doors as soon as the crowd began to smell ugly. But no vendor who boarded up was spared.

It was as though the angel who passed overhead looking for the mark on the lintel to spare this one's business or that one's life acted with the caprice of a tornado at its peak.

A push-cart popcorn stand was untouched by the crowd milling all around it, but a family restaurant, sheltered in the lee of the poplars that gave it its name and disguised by the houses bordering it, was trashed so badly that even the plumbing was torn up and the brass fittings stolen. Piles of human feces were left as calling cards on the tables.

The smashing went on unabated all through the ebb and flow of the riot. Sometimes you could walk by an establishment and see a gang in the act of demolishing the place and you might think they were a paid work crew; a few guys swinging wrecking bars and makeshift axes, some standing around watching and smoking cigarettes.

The worst part of it wasn't the looting, although the news telecasts from Erie and Cleveland made the millions lost in property damage seem a state tragedy; to the insurance companies, no doubt, it was. They gamble on someone having an accident: you believe you won't, and when they win, you lose.

Two children, an eight-year-old boy and his six-year-old sister, were crushed to death by a panicking crowd inside a funhouse; their own parents were part of the crowd and thought their children were being tended by an older child at another part of the rides park.

One fifteen-year-old girl lay with her dress hiked over her thighs, beaten unconscious on one of the busiest intersections of the Strip. She died there, probably of shock, because no one came to her aid.

Twenty other violent rapes occurred during this period, but the actual figures will never be known; the girls who were beaten senseless and mauled by roving gangs were all brought in after the riot by friends or family.

The actual number was probably three times as high, and the casual raping that went on against buildings and those antique lamp posts that the Chamber of Commerce thought so quaint lent an eerie grotesquerie to the violence.

Little Minnesota did a brisk business, however: it seemed to be the one place on the entire Strip that, at first anyhow, provided a neutral, if not exactly safe, harbor for all factions of the crowd.

Young whores of both sexes performed fellatio right on the Strip in open sight of passersby. Some bull dykes came along to capitalize on it, and one plump sixteen-year-old girl, a local, it turned out, was made to perform cunnilingus on all of them. Pagans and Angels mingled harmlessly, but elsewhere on the Strip there were serious fights with weapons brought along for protection.

Although the bikers got the blame for nearly all the raping and looting that went on, there were surprisingly few deaths; most of the violence was directed against the old and the young and, of course, those who owned property.

One biker was shot through the eye and the throat and lived. One Angel was shot to death by his friend inside the shooting gallery. They had peppered the dummy piano player and decided to shoot beer cans off each other's head.

Mostly the two gangs stayed away from each other and drank beer on their hogs or smoked joints. They made drug sales when they felt like it, but otherwise existed calmly in the eye of the storm, unperturbed by the action except when they were participating.

The worst violence in one spot over the duration of the riot had to come from Ollie's, a frou-frou bar of shabby gentility mostly frequented by fraternity boys from private colleges in upstate New York. The stray biker would walk in and out of the place just to check it out, yet for the most part it remained intact.

No girl who walked in there wasn't, however, raped, some with bottles. They took a few sorority girls under their wings, if they happened to know them or their daddies. These girls spent the riot getting moodily drunk, watching the action, and taking the occasional frat rat off into a corner for a quickie.

Old people who sought shelter with them were beaten and robbed and kicked back out into the street. One elderly man, a lifelong member of the fraternity whose pin he spied or one young man, tried to give the old passwords and secret handshakes, but he was punched in the mouth so hard his dentures flew out and he, too, found himself back in the street.

Some Hispanics were lured into the bar by a concerned young man who offered them safety inside. Once inside they were kicked and beaten over the heads with empty liquor bottles. One man, separated from his family, remains in a coma; two others were found brain-dead stuffed into a trash bin in back of the bar.

Haftmann had to ditch his car at Lupine and Rosalind, a good mile and a half from the midpoint of the Strip. He grew up here, so he knew the right alleys and shortcuts.

He was dressed right for the occasion, for once: T-shirt (suit coat, tie, and dress shirt peeled off on the run), pants off the rack, and a Glock23 with a .40 mag capacity. The leather shoulder holster he had saved up for last Christmas was hanging from a branch of a Japanese dwarf tree in an empty lot two hundred yards back. He was panting, sucking in great gulps of air.

By the time he got to the first of the abandoned cars at Bolsterli and Ohio, he was wet and dripping; his pants were dark with perspiration at the crotch. It was ninety-three degrees with eighty-seven percent humidity. Summer's brutal last gasp before fall.

It looks bad . . .

He runs into the nearest cottage and is met by an elderly woman with her mouth completely open, her cell phone clamped to her ear, leading an old man with a strawberry nose and plaid pants up to his nipples. Out the door, he can hear the noise of the crowd in the near distance, a blue haze settles over the Strip at its farthest point, tiny specks running at the edges, gunshots, sirens. There's a plume of black smoke billowing above the Strip. He's almost certain Tico's Place is ablaze.

He sees blues and Lake cops in the distance. Up close he sees Elise giving them commands, her badge pinned outside her blouse, so no one makes any mistakes.

"Haftmann, you picked a great time to run off."

"What're we doing? Who's in charge?"

"Nobody, as far as I know. Look for wounded. We have to get the paramedics and the fire department in before they burn the whole thing down."

"Elise, I'm not a cop anymore – "

"Just help out, Haftmann!" she ordered.

The worst of the riot has subsided in parts, but there is commotion wherever you look. All the children and old people have disappeared by this time, a few limping and praying or weeping as they hold on to one another's arms heading to the fringes.

Winos had found the liquor stores and are calmly sitting around the front in the broken glass, some unconscious from the windfall, others weaving in or out the door, more bottles cradled in their arms than they could possibly carry.

Devastation everywhere. Like Berlin after the war.

When anyone approaches them who doesn't have blood streaming down his or her face, or who looks like a wrong number, Elise sticks a gun in his face.

They move farther up the Strip into the thickest part of the crowd, parting the action as they go like Israelites and the Red Sea. At Little Minnesota, the sex action is raunchy and disturbing. Haftmann notes Elise flush with anger. She's the toughest cop he's known since Frank, and she has a white-hot hatred for sleaze.

At one burned-down shell of a nightclub, a middle-aged woman comes running out to them with her midriff bared, breasts bouncing through holes in her blouse. Two Pagans lope after her like a pair of Rottweilers stalking a rabbit. They stop dead when they see Elise's weapon drawn and pointing at them. Neither makes any effort to move off; one grabs his crotch and makes kissing noises at the hysterical woman.

"Get on the horn, Elise."

She has the two-way out while Haftmann covers her side and his so she can talk.

Millimaki's staccato comes over; the woman Haftmann is gripping by a flabby tricep is making burbling noises.

"What'd he say?"

"He said MacDuff must have got caught in the riot. He went to check out the bouncer at the Purple Haze around noon."

"What for? We checked that list out weeks ago."

"MacDuff said he wasn't on the list. He just saw him last night."

They meet the team coming the other way. Elise gives the EMTs and stretcher units the okay to move in but they seem reluctant. Like working for the Red Cross in Syria, she says.

Haftmann peels off from the blues who've joined them and take the woman, who is still babbling in shock.

Haftmann picks his way through the street to the side where he finds the door of the Purple Haze. He slips his gun into his pants, not sure he should, but he doesn't want to walk into a dimly lit biker bar with glinting metal over his heart to guide somebody's aim. He hears a noise, as if people were mumbling or whispering . . .

He finds MacDuff propped against a wall with his brains blown out the back of his head.

Haftmann gets his gun into his hand fast. It feels light as he swings it around the room in the stiff-jointed Weaver stance you practiced in the academy. He knows he's beginning to hyperventilate. The air is rank with the gaseous smells of cordite and evacuated bowels.

Other shapes against the wall. He hovers above each body, cuts his eyes down long enough to ascertain dead or alive, then moves on to the next one.

Six of them, a bullet apiece.

MacDuff got his first through the mouth and out the back of the skull; white brains stuck on the wall. Flies alive and everywhere in clouds all over the room; he'd heard their feasting when he entered. Sandusky was merely appetizer to the entrée. He'd never seen this much horror up close. He didn't understand what had caused this place to explode and turn people into savages like this.

Haftmann knows Nelson couldn't be far away: the blood from a Hell's Angel nostril is still oozing out fat drops, no rigor.

His sweat has turned to ice, but he doesn't have the shakes anymore. A sob catches in his throat. He moves into the back of the bar; checked out the door, entered the walk-in cooler, flips light switches wherever he can find them.

Back inside the bar he checked wounds and notes the victims' positions, tries to reconstruct because he knows the killer's got to be close; the blood stench mixed with the fear and the suffocating heat to make one putrid, nauseating vapor in his nostrils.

He's looking at a bar waitress with silver loops in her ears; she didn't get a bullet, didn't need one, because her trachea is smashed and her head lolls to the back to look behind her. The other bar girl was shot: her right eye was a hole where the blowflies have made a home. The stippling around the crater told Haftmann he'd placed the gun right on her eyeball.

All the men are shot in the head except a short, chubby man who doesn't fit the clientele of the place; he's wearing a polo shirt and Nike High Tops. Haftmann doesn't see a head or chest wound.

When he turns him onto his stomach, he smells defecation, a head shot symptom. But something else: greasy blood, the sere separated in the heat, smears his hand. He looks at the man's open fly, sees the raw wound. His heel crunches broken glass—maybe the weapon used to castrate him.

Haftmann doesn't want to know more. It's too much and the killer is gone.

I'd have felt him, he realizes and shivers from that knowledge of this connection.

At the door he slips on something greasy and does a pratfall; his Glock spins out of his hand and clatters against a table leg, and he's just had the perception that goofy stuff like this only happens to TV detectives. Three large figures fill up the shaft of light from the open doorway.

Angels.

Two pin him while the third stomps him; the seventh or eighth kick to his head and guts puts him out.

When he comes back up into the light, he sees boots and legs surrounding him like a forest. "What you say, cop?"

Haftmann's first sense to recover was the jukebox playing one of those godawful country-western tunes about blue eyes crying in the rain and his mind jumped to that crime scene note with the lyrics about blue eyes, a mix of country western lyrics and some corny Jazz Age tune. Everything was funneled into a mashup of sense and nonsense in his confused state. Even his limbic brain was firing mixed messages: Flee, Run, Fight, Flee, Run, Fight, Run, Run . . .

"Cossacks," he says. His scrambled brain is reaching for the word *cocksuckers*.

"What the fuck," an Angel says; "fucking stomp that fucking motherfucker."

Later, recovering in ICU, he'll attribute the word confusion to his grandmother. She used to scare him as a boy with stories of Cossacks riding into villages out of the steppes, light dazzling the villagers' eyes as they rode down at them with the sun at their backs; men, women, and children butchered with those curved swords that hacked and bit into flesh. Once she caught him out in the yard whooping and hollering and asked him what he was doing.

She slapped him across the face and, without a word, took her linen handkerchief and licked the corner of it, and wiped the tear tracks and dirt from his face. "Cossacks are bad men," she said.

The beating goes on for a while, but fortunately for him, the Angels are like kids in a candy store: there's just too much looting, screwing, pillaging and raping, to be wasting time on one middle-aged nobody.

One of them delivers a final kick to his liver and they adjourn to greener pastures. Haftmann hears music again. A soprano is singing an Italian opera. He is past pain at this point and thanks to that squirt of enzyme from his amygdala, he's being prepared for his own death. One-third of our brainpower is devoted to sight, and Haftmann is desperately trying to see right then. He's going down these ever-narrowing cellar steps in the dark – he doesn't know why or where he is anymore but it feels right. Then he misses a step, slips, his body twists in black air, and he falls into a deep pit. It's a mile-long fall, the same distance his grandmother told him as boy that Lucifer took in falling from heaven.

Chapter 15

Aftermath

In the end, Haftmann did get his wish: the Ohio National Guard, the same unit that had made Kent State University a household name in May of 1970, came to "quell the hostilities," as the major in charge of public relations put it. They were calling it a gang war between the two biker clubs, and that seemed to explain it—the drought, the heat, the rumormongering all summer; it was inevitable, the Chamber of Commerce claimed, already busy in the act of wiping the shit off their fingers.

The entire Strip was cordoned off, and nobody who wasn't law enforcement, a relative of the dead or wounded, or part of the state disaster emergency crew got anywhere within ten miles of the resort town.

The bodies were carted off any place that had storage room. Doc Harris suffered a mild heart attack and was spelled by pathologists and interns from University Hospital and the Cleveland Clinic.

All Purple Haze victims were posted at Cleveland Metro General at the governor's request.

The Jack-in-the-Box Killer was still loose.

For the second time in a single month, Haftmann was packed in ice. Two fractured ribs, chipped teeth, a broken finger, and a pair of *circumorbital haematomae*, which was the medico's lingo for two black eyes. They took out his spleen first thing. His brain was concussed and neurological damage might show up later but there was no bleeding of the brain.

Lucky, considering.

They told him what the risks of colonic cancer were for men his age and wanted to go to work on his piles. He said he'd let Doc Harris do brain surgery on him first.

Millimaki didn't know whether Haftmann should be put up for a citation or a formal reprimand for lone-wolfing it in that kind of emergency. So he did nothing, and for once, Haftmann was grateful to him.

The state team and forensics people did what they could but there was so much carnage and confusion in the street that day, nothing was resolved.

He gave them everything he could recall until the moment he went out; the Angels who stomped him weren't caught, not that many arrests were made overall, and were about as likely to be Haftmann was to be invited to lecture on mannerism versus rococo in the seventeenth century at the Cleveland Museum.

"C'est le guerre," as Phil quaintly put it when he visited Haftmann after his transfer from ICU. When asked how he felt, Haftmann told him to get the hospital to stop playing Frankie Yankovic's polka tune "Roll Out the Barrel" through the speakers.

"You're joking," Phil said. "That's a good sign. It means you're healing."

Haftmann's CT scan came back normal, but it took the neurologist ten minutes of talking and pointing to the different colors on the colored printout from his computer to say that. "You can get punch drunk from too many blows on the head," he said while adjusting his bifocals.

Haftmann learns that Elise had tangled with a couple bikers later on but had come out okay – a sprained wrist and some facial bruises. "You know," she told Haftmann later, "I had to get a tetanus shot because who knows where those dirty animals have been."

Haftmann still couldn't believe it. *What timing that lucky bastard possessed.*

* * *

Lonnie Dale Nelson was born Albert Manfred Schmidt in Steubenville, Ohio. He was six pounds, five ounces at birth and his eyes were blue. All babies eyes are blue.

Besides being birthplace to Rat-packer Dean Martin, his hometown is the largest city of Jefferson County, looks across the Ohio River at Weirton, West Virginia, and is typical of most manufacturing, blue-collar towns of its size. The river freezes in November, and June bugs thunk against window panes until August.

Last year, a national scandal involving high-school teenagers and a drunk 16-yearold girl made national news when two members of the football team were indicted for raping her and dragging her unconscious body from party to party. When they dropped her off at her girlfriend's back in West Virginia, the deed was finished off with a final act of urinating on her. Every avenue of social networking via Facebook, blogging, tweeting, re-tweeting, trolling with false posts, and online posting the high-schoolers frequented was filled with obscene references in the days afterward. A teammate, not one of the participants, sent his indicted classmate an encouraging message after the police came to school that Monday to arrest him: "We got your back, bro. Some girls deserve to be pissed on." The big joke at school that week was to download Nirvana's "Rape Me" for Mp3 players and ringtones. All of this, text and video, was being subpoenaed as evidence by the DA's office. Every cell phone ping was going to leave a lovely trail right back to these boneheads like bread crumbs in Hansel and Gretel's fairy tale.

Nelson/Schmidt's mother remained a shadowy figure who had never fit in with the placid, stolid townsfolk and their ways, a good portion of whom were second- and third-generation Germans.

All that is known about her after she abandoned her family is that she moved north to East Palestine and soon after acquired the reputation as a roundheels and slattern; she moved on but no one knows where. The last informant, an elderly man in his eighties, said that she intended to get her son back and go to California.

The father is unknown, according to the birth certificate filed at the Probate Court Division of Summit County. Teenaged pregnant girls were commonly ensconced with distant relatives during the final months of parturition in those days before crying rooms as add-ons in high-school building construction, out of earshot of the town gossips.

The boy was partially raised by his grandmother – partially because she apparently suffered some sort of derangement during her final years that resulted in virtual neglect of the child. They both ate cat food out of cans. The nutritional value was sufficient.

When the county stepped in after neighbors reported seeing the child running around, half-starved and filthy, he was years behind in physical and mental growth for a boy his age. The consensus was that he was retarded.

The grandmother had no income to speak of and was too proud to accept charity. She had once sung solo soprano for the church and had been a local beauty in her day. There is one photo of her, a daguerreotype, in which she poses in the haughty look of a debutante, the set of her mouth so fashionable among young beauties at that time. She was bilingual; spoke German fluently and had once lent her voice as a Valkyrie at the Cleveland Metropolitan Opera in the *Niebelungenlied* saga.

When the boy was taken off, she didn't appear to know who he was. His former foster parents were all dispersed to different cities and lives by the time the state's investigators found the records.

All but one: a middle-aged barfly, thrice divorced, who used too much rouge and whose prominent bosom belied her age. She told them that the boy had been a complete nuisance and had made lewd advances toward her. Her husband, a gray-faced mechanic named the boy "Lonnie" after a dead twin brother. When she ended their marriage, she didn't have any idea what happened to her husband or her son thereafter.

There is a gap here and there in the chronological reconstruction of the boy's early life, but once the state had custody of him, he's fixed in place.

The Massillon Reformatory for Boys has long since been closed down for economic reasons, and the newer facility at Mansfield now houses most of the recalcitrant state's teenaged males.

It isn't clearly known why he wound up there. Normally, court records regarding adolescents are sealed by law, and that's that. In this case, the records are simply vague or cryptic. There was no crime, misdemeanor or felony, that got him incarcerated with the j.d. sticker, sanitized to "youthful offenders" in today's p.c. jargon. Lonnie Nelson was the name mistakenly used from this point on because, like any third- or fourth-world orphan in the world, he was guilty of lacking influence, protection, or family support.

The state's investigators consulted the Attorney General's Office to see whether the woman's husband's letter would have been sufficient grounds for the state to bypass the intervening remedies that would keep the boy a ward of the state but out of Massillon, which had a reputation prior to its closing as one of the toughest hard-core facilities in the state. Its graduates more often than not wound up doing serious time at its big brother institution where Artiss Poole was doing his time, the Ohio State Penitentiary in Youngstown.

There was no record of extraordinary behavior while he was at Massillon. His confinement appeared to have been routine, if you disregard the obvious fact of his having come of age in a state disciplinary facility for wayward youth; at that time, they were not referred to by any state agency as YAO's – Young Adult Offenders.

Naturally, the cops who had to clean up after them referred to the acronym differently: "Yahoos" and "Young Assholes," mainly.

Records show the boy had surgery for reconstruction of part of his colonic passage. It could have been acute hemorrhoids due to his stressful environment, or, more likely, he was sodomized so brutishly that tissue repair was necessary. The state records and the medical officer retained at that time cannot say because he's been dead for nine years. None of the nurses who may have assisted in the operation can be located because of the hiatus. Too much time came and went.

There is one other interesting observation to make on the record: the boy had been complaining of headaches shortly after his admission and a brain tumor was feared. They took him to a specialist at the Cleveland Clinic, then the only institution in the state that could give you the option of peeling your head back or shrinking it. The doctor is deceased, although there is a notation on the extant report in the Clinic's archives or library, as they call it.

The boy got the whole nine yards: the biopsy showed nothing, so the examining physician recommended a psychiatric evaluation. He was booked in for three days. The state's team found the records and had them evaluated by the present Clinic psychiatric staff.

They gave him a complete battery of exams, such as they were at that time, and had him draw pictures of houses, trees, and figures. None of these could be located, however. Basically, they discovered the boy's unusual talents lying dormant where he was currently living, not surprising. At first, they thought he might be one of those *idiots savant* with an extraordinary gift for music. But he was no idiot; in fact, his genius potential in every category they measured got around the hallways and more staff psychiatrists and psychological researchers came up to have a peek at him. He shook with the palsied movements of one afflicted with chorea, but the diagnosis records the abbreviation *idiopat*: unknown.

He had learned English, and a smattering of German, from his feeble-minded grandmother, who frequently traversed casually between tongues during her dementia. He even used clicks of the tongue for certain expressions, apparently imitating her there, too. He could sing arias and bits of opera in a voice they at first thought had been trained, and, in a sense, they were right: the grandmother made him sing for his supper, literally, and with such exactitude that if he did not meet her standards of pitch and tone, at the moment, he was not fed.

His total recall went beyond musical pitch. He could look at a page of print from the most abstruse psychiatric journal and recite it back at ninety-seven per cent perfection. Like most such gifted individuals, he did not know what he could flawlessly recite.

His spatial perception, an intuitive ability to measure angles and see objects in three dimensions, was not measurable by any standards of the day.

Yet he could barely write English. The Rorschach was the biggest indicator of all. Because no one can reconstruct the test from this late date, the investigators have no access to a second opinion. Simple autism, they thought at first. "Schizophrenia," they all finally agreed; "with delusions." The boy heard voices inside his head that were like the images on the pages he was looking at.

"Whose voices?"

"The System," was all he would say about it.

It was a word he could have picked up anywhere, once he fell into the hands of the state.

Haftmann didn't give a rat's ass about any of it. This was all going backwards in time and had no bearing on finding him at this moment. He told Booth, "I don't want to write his biography. I want to kill him."

"We all want that," said Booth.

The synopses of reports and details gleaned from seventeen separate teams of state's investigators get murky very fast after that.

At seventeen he's made eligible for the state's helping hands pre-release program, practically a duplicate of the state's work-release program for eligible cons.

He went to work in a slaughterhouse on the outskirts of Massillon; left the facility at six in the morning to get the first bus and arrived back by six in the evening on the same bus.

There is a notation here that registers a complaint from someone named Janice Sherbourne who complained that Nelson boarded the bus with blood-spattered Levi's and work boots. Thereafter he was requested to sit at the very rear of the bus due to the stench of blood that was offensive to the other passengers. There is a signature affixed to the copy of the bus driver's complaint and above it the words: "So Noted."

Then, the remarkable circumstance of his releasing himself occurred, an unorthodox but not uncommon occurrence for boys who have the scent of freedom in their nostrils. The state chose not to pursue the investigation after his eighteenth birthday because he was legally an adult by that time. He was, of course, a strong suspect by Massillon police in the stolen car from the facility's lot. Grand Theft Auto, if they caught him. Hard time guaranteed for an adult with the stench of Massillon trailing behind him.

It picks up again in different cities with gaps in his young manhood. Everyone in Ohio has had a look at his face by now, and men with large physiques have taken to jogging in the morning with t-shirts saying, "I'm Not the Jack-in-the-Box Killer" stenciled on the chest.

It's difficult to separate unsubstantiated reports from reliable testimony because of the numbers of places that have claimed the Jack-in-the-Box Killer once worked there. That, too, had become a commonplace joke and like every other inanity of our culture found its way onto t-shirts and placards and even, inspired a grim wrinkle on the Baby-on-Board stupidity of some years back, a yellow hazard sign with thumb-stickers that sits on a back window and says "Help! The Jack-in-the-Box Killer Is Hiding in my Trunk." Latex arms, legs, feet, and hands were purchasable in every department store. The Jeffrey Dahmer jokes from years ago had given way to more enterprising ways to satisfy the public's appetite of bottom-feeding consumption.

Everyone now knew what he looked like, but nobody knew where he was. Every *Crimestoppers* segment between Toledo-Cleveland and south to Dayton-Cincinnati exploited the newsworthiness of his last sighting; he was getting around the state like the ghost of Elvis and Bigfoot.

They were certain that he had worked a bar in Wooster for eight months; another in Macedonia for six. He worked bar and bounced, maybe for the first time, at a tavern in Berea. Then Solon had him. Cleveland had him for a while. He drifted eastward to the state border and worked a teen bar in Conneaut called Dr. Feelgood's. Then south again to East Palestine, where he had faked his own death. Back to square one.

Everyone who saw him or knew him came forward for the notoriety and the possibility of reward money, which had topped $150,000 during September's end.

The cottage where he stayed on the Lake was disassembled for clues; every bar he had soldered and welded was cut up and examined in the event he used them as niches for storing items. They had photographed these first and sent them to the Quantico shrinks who might be able to tell something from the odd configuration of crisscrossing bars.

"Goddamn it," said Haftmann when he found out; "it isn't Stonehenge."

They did get the kinesthetic opinion from a Ph.D. in Phys. Ed. at The Ohio University that he had devised the arrangement so that several muscle groups could be worked simultaneously with concentrated bursts. A mechanical engineer was looking into the possibility of a patent for Scandinavia House, Inc.

They had his prints, all fingers, both thumbs, twelve-pointers, all. "Great if they catch him with his mitts around a glass," Elise quipped.

"More likely, they'll find him with his mitts around somebody's throat," said Haftmann.

"And his weenie up their dirt chute," added Mookie.

The two black guys who had beat him up were local heroes. The bigger one said he was thinking of turning pro. The young woman who had sex with the killer became the most famous of all. Tabloids featured her three times as often as Jennifer Aniston, Brangelina, or KK of the gorgeous ass with headline banners like LOVE INTEREST OF PSYCHO KILLER IN OHIO TELLS ALL.

Hollywood sent a team of scriptwriters to interview her to see if there was a film to be got out of it. That got yuks from the cops at the station; one of the female patrol officers made a hit pantomiming gagging on a big one for the biggest laugh of all.

"It's a fucking circus, Haftmann," Millimaki growled to him.

"I didn't do it," Haftmann snapped.

Now what the hell? Haftmann read that a secret grand jury was being convened next week according to courthouse scuttlebutt and indictments would be handed down; not all of them on dope charges or the riot-related crimes of Labor Day. He had heard that Artiss had a parole hearing scheduled after the grand jury. *Timing too neat not to be real.*

His reputation around the department was at an all-time low: he'd refused to attend MacDuff's burial ceremony with full police honors and a caisson. The governor had sent the lieutenant governor in his stead, not wanting to call too much attention to the ineptitude of the state's investigation.

"He was a hero, plain and simple," said the lieutenant governor to the crowd of mourners.

"He was a grafter, a dirty cop, and a fuck-up," said Haftmann to anybody at the station house who repeated that nonsense. "I'm amazed they didn't corkscrew him into the dirt."

He writhed with a paralysis of the heart and mind; it gripped him especially at night with claw fingers that squeezed the air out of his esophagus. Limping around the precinct, he moaned aloud: "Why didn't I see him during those weeks before the Riot?" He had worn out the muscles around his eyes with continual staring from patrol cars into neon and sunbaked crowds parading past. *Here, all the time, right under our noses . . .*

When he saw Mookie coming up the stairs with his arm around Shawna, just a notch above the swell of her ass cheek, he almost went out of his mind with jealousy.

Their laughter echoed back to him like a volley of thunder, and it was all he could do to concentrate on his report writing for the rest of the day. Mookie's lewd tongue in Shawna's ear and his hand exploring her ass was the image he returned to. Haftmann put mental pins in a Mookie doll and real pins in the state map he tacked to the ceiling above his sofa. He wanted to be able to see it and track him in his mind before he closed his eyes and when he opened them again. Each pin was a victim or a bar where the Jack-in-the-Box Killer had worked.

He doodled Albert Manfred Schmidt and Lonnie Dale Nelson on memo pads and accidentally inserted it into two letters he wrote to clients requesting his services.

"You're cracking up, Haftmann," said Millimaki, puffing on a Garcia y Vega out in the lot.

"Smoking out here is a violation," Haftmann said as he passed by.

Millimaki smiled at him. "You're on borrowed time now. As soon as your F.B.I. pal gets a new assignment, a lot of people are gonna want to square things up with you. You remember what Hoffa said about Bobby Kennedy after JFK got shot?"

"Who cares, Chief?"

"'He's just another lawyer.' You'll be just another third-rate snooper."

Haftmann learned that Millimaki had nearly succeeded in arranging a transfer to an office at the Jefferson Precinct, but MacDuff's death had put an end to that. The Lake cops were shorthanded worse than ever; more than one cop had had enough of the cop's life after The Riot, as it was called everywhere to distinguish it from that picayune affair of 1969, and all two-man patrols were reduced by half. It was back to twelve-hour shifts for all detectives; leaves cancelled until further notice. The Fraternal Order of Policemen was urging blue flu among its Lake Chapter until certain work conditions were improved.

Part-time cops were hired on as a temporary expedient to solve the manpower shortage.

"What the fuck," Haftmann said to Stel. "You guys were arresting some of them and chasing them off the street before Labor Day. Now you're giving them badges and guns." It was like those Miami cops after the cocaine invasion of the seventies. Or New Orleans cops in the nineties. Millimaki handpicked the new-hires himself and was building a new power base from their ranks.

One day he got maudlin drunk and called Shawna at two in the morning.

"I miss you," he said. "Don't," she said, and hung up.

Her image was so sharp in his mind that he was in agony and couldn't sleep until dawn. When he wasn't being chased by the Man with Flies, he saw her copulating with strangers, her naked back dripping sweat down to the crack, and when she turned her head he could see she had Micah's face in profile.

He woke up screaming *Wo bist du*? Yet had no idea he was speaking German or who, of the many people lost in his life, he meant by *you*.

"Your breath smells like a tomb," said Elise. He'd picked up his two-pack-a-day Marlboro habit again.

At night he lay on the sofa with all the lights on in the house and stared at the pins on his ceiling map trying to figure out the pinball-logic of the killer's movements.

One thing stood out clearly: he gravitated toward water. "Nice," Haftmann thought sardonically, a psychopath with a recreational bent. *I know you're somewhere close*, he said to the ceiling. He practiced the old drill of snapping in his speedloader as he lay prone. He was torn between asking Booth to put more men on surveillance or take them all off and let the killer find him.

301

There were sightings in California and Oregon. He was said to be living in the woods like one of those crazed Iraqi war vets.

Haftmann had lost $200 on both of the Browns preseason games and had to sell Mookie his four-shot derringer with the lacquered mother-of-pearl grips. Haftmann later sold him the store for $300, including his favorite gun, a Browning with a twelve-round clip. "This'll stop any Cossack in his tracks," he told him.

"I'm not shooting homos, for Chrissake," Mookie replied. "Give you a C-note for your old service piece."

"No," Haftmann said. "I've got plans for that gun."

It was only a rumor, locals said, that Oscar was giving odds to any takers that Haftmann was going to blow his own brains out before the year was out. Still, another rumor said Mookie got down for $300 that Haftmann would last until New Year's.

One day Elise stopped by during her shift, the dogwatch, and she found Haftmann lying in a room of filth-beer cans and papers scattered everywhere, holding an intense conversation with himself in the dead air. She heard the name *Micah.* Haftmann never heard her come in or go out.

"It's like the last days of Howard Hughes," she told Phil sadly back at the station.

"Yeah," Phil cracked, "except no money."

Chapter 16

Fall

Those little biting flies with the black bodies and red, mullioned eyes that pester you all summer long are gone by the end of September in the northern counties of Ohio. "Deer flies," "midges," "sand flies, "Canadian soldiers" – Ohioans have a hard time distinguishing among them. If the summer has been hot enough, you can get two breedings of several species of these insects that form into huge buzzing clouds high in the air at dusk. Their drone is soothing to Haftmann who drives down to the water's edge at times to watch them blowing in the offshore breezes in massive black ribbons that appear and disappear in seconds. *A magic time, autumn*, he thinks, *not the season of death at all.*

Autumn arrives later and stays longer here than down by Columbus, and even Youngstown and the Mahoning Valley, that Jimmy Traficant used to call home base, has a shorter life. Lake Erie's slow-to-wane temperature protects the northern parts from killing frosts a bit longer. Even so, the trees' colors are brilliant. The air is soft and golden, often hazy, and even the most hardened succumb to bouts of nostalgia. Haftmann who always believed that things happened twice, not three times, as in the common folk wisdom, hated autumn with a passion.

When had he returned home from burying his grandmother in Kingsville, near the Christian Academy founded by Albion Tourgée, where the slate headstones are so worn you think of New England, he picked up the paper at the kitchen table, still warm with the scent of cinnamon and baked apples.

If he were ever asked, Haftmann would say he didn't believe in God. "You'd have to be a lunatic to believe this is the best of all possible worlds," he said to Micah, whose Jewish God was alive and well somewhere despite her husband's blasphemy. Yet, each autumn, Haftmann wasn't as certain. The world still had evil in it, but sometimes he could look at the colors on display from his window and not feel too bad about being sentimental.

When he and Micah were married, he used to drive her out to an apple orchard on Johnnycake Ridge and pick a bushel of McIntosh, a bushel of Rome, and one of Red Delicious. Micah couldn't bake worth a damn, however, so the apples rotted in their baskets, wafting their sweet smell of corruption all through the house.

This autumn was different; his solitude had deepened but rarefied itself and become almost monastic. The Jack-in-the-Box Killer had come to monopolize his mind to such an extent that it refused to heel, attend to the moment, when he needed to concentrate on something he was reading or doing.

One thing that helped him focus was the knowledge that MacDuff's gun was in the hands of the killer. The killer had the stones or the sheer stupidity to remove MacDuff's ammo and speedloader after he had wasted all the clientele in that bar that stank of cordite and blood. He'd become a cop killer now, the most hated of men.

He couldn't register in a motel without looking as conspicuous as a rat screwing a grapefruit. He couldn't hire on as day labor for union or non-union outfits. He couldn't work harvest alongside the Mexicans. Nor could he take out a license, sign a paper, or go to a hospital. He couldn't do one thing a normal person could without calling attention to himself. But he had to eat, sleep, wash up, excrete, yawn, stretch, burp, walk, and, unless he were living and shitting berries in the woods, he had to talk to people every now and then.

Why, then, was he still at large?

The incumbent governor dropped three points in approval on the basis of his law enforcement's failure to bring in the killer. The opposition party had already contracted for manufacture of 150,000 campaign buttons with a jack-in-the-box logo, one smiling with vampire-sharp incisors.

The Riot cost thirty million in property damage alone and would mean reduced revenue next year of an estimated sixty percent normal gross intake. Or, as Haftmann translated it from his nasty couch, "They'll be hiring balloon-blowing goats for cops before this place recovers."

Haftmann read everything he could get his hands on pertaining to the killer. He was bored to distraction with speculations about serial killers and their labyrinthine ratiocinative patterns. He read Elizabethan literature because the killer's musical tastes ran that way; he knew the killer's songs by heart.

Jack was an Elizabethan in the same way that a devil worshiper was a Christian backwards: it was still belief, only upside-down, perverted, misanthropic.

The Elizabethans believed in a chain of being, a single world where all meaning was reducible to one ethos. Everything in nature and on earth, all things above and below the moon, were linked by a single thread, and your place – your existence and your destiny – was permanent, fixed forever, and changeless in time.

He read *Hamlet* for the sheer hell of it: he felt like that dumbfuck Rosencrantz (or was it the other one, Guildenstern?) coming between a great man and his destiny.

He found Artiss' line about being "bound in a nutshell".

"... 'king of infinite space' ... 'If only I didn't have bad dreams.'

The blood-spattered walls. 'Something is rotten – '

The Jacuzzi Woman. Rotting in her whirlpool with flies living and breeding in her mouth.

A six-by-ten prison cell. *Love Bade Me Welcome.*

The dead baby in its crib

'Ripeness is all' ... 'on heaven and earth.'

The little pipefitter shouldn't have been in there, a definite wrongo. The autopsy report said that one biker's dick was mashed to a pulp. *What the fuck.*

MacDuff from the grave: "Does the Pope shit in the woods?"

A one-eyed man in the kingdom –

A chain of being –

'One for all . . .'

'The dog returneth to his vomit.'

'You jig, you amble, you lisp, you nickname God's creatures – '

'What monsters you make of us then.'

You like power over them before you kill them.

If they made it disappear, the hurt and pain, the loneliness –

"You'd still do it," he said to the ceiling.

~ ~ ~

Lonnie Dale Nelson got into line with the other guys from USX and moped around the snack food aisle, his stomach an absolute torment because he couldn't get enough food in his belly, too dangerous.

He didn't look as bad in their midst, but he knew he looked like death eating a sandwich on the street in daylight. His stomach growled looking at all the food, but he had reserves of discipline left and the memories of the Purple Haze were enough to get him erect.

He ambled into line, shuffled from foot to foot like a working stiff who's just come off shift, tired and dirty from the steel mill, the company supervisors ragging you constantly.

Dipshit Arab running the store spoke broken English and took forever at that dinosaur of a cash register. Sometimes his wife ran the store at night; maybe he was in the back counting the money on an abacus.

If he used up the last of his money, he'd come in here and kill them all, the pretty daughter, too, with her black eyes and long black hair. She was hairy on her arms to her wrists.

The one-block walk was like crossing the Mohave under the open sky; he knew his luck couldn't hold out.

Why, he asks the angel, *have you abandoned me now?*

The little corner store run by the Arabs catered to a working-class clientele at night and pot-smoking black teenagers skipping school in the daytime. The baby gangbangers all tried to mean-mug him, but he ignored them. A few of them demanded money from them but he simply stepped right up to them, got in their faces, and dared them to reach for the piece they might not even be carrying in their pants. It made him almost laugh. His own face, a crude artist's sketch, and his description were plastered on every other newspaper. *Couldn't these assholes read?*

Every day for a week he went to the same pay phone on the opposite corner of the street and made the call to Personnel. And every day it was the same formulaic piffle he heard from a different receptionist's voice. He would make them pay as they would all pay.

But time was running out. He had to get in there soon.

His voice almost betrayed him last time, a quaver.

Must not sound desperate; must sound like the professional your application says you are; years of experience as a technician on the floor of a mold-design factory in Utah. "A God-fearing man, not a Mormon, nossir," he'd say to the man – if he ever got a chance to speak to him.

"We'll both benefit, sir. You'll have skill at the pipefitter position and I'll have . . ."

I'll have –

I'll have access to your water loop and coolant system, your back-up in case one of your six seismographs tells you there's a quake bigger than the dynamos can handle, your feed pump and every pipe that goes into and out of the one nuclear power plant that has the magnitude of a fifty megaton bomb at ground zero, which, in this case, as you must know, is between Cleveland and Erie, Pennsylvania, and will snuff out the lives of three-and-a-half million citizens immediately and, after fallout, of all the rest who stay behind in this state. The others will go like falling dominoes, once the winds start to walk the dust east.

And everything will die, Mr. Personnel Supervisor.
NOW STOP FUCKING AROUND AND CALL ME.
IT CANNOT BE STOPPED.

"Ah, Twinkies and pop again, sir? You must try to eat better . . ."

"Yes, ha, I'll try to do that." He smiles big for the camel jockey.

"That'll be four dollars and forty-five cents, please."

"How much for the Moon Pie, too?"

~ ~ ~

"Hello."

"Who is this?"

"Thomas Haftmann, right? I'm a friend of a certain mutual, uh, acquaintance to us both."

"And who might this friend be?

"Artiss Poole."

"Fuck off."

That told Haftmann more than obvious entrapment, this ruse. If they had him, Millimaki or some other clown around here would be Mirandizing him at the precinct right now. But it was close, too close . . .

~ ~ ~

Nelson lay curled like a huge jungle cat in the patch of autumn sunshine pouring through the upstairs window, calmly watching the dust motes twist and turn in the heated air. They were like thousands of bodies uprooted and thrust into the sky, only to fall back to earth in the tug of gravity.

Would he kill as many?

Oh, yes. Just behold me.

He felt the stirrings of eroticism in his blood and he squeezed his thickening penis between his legs and rocked, worm-like, on the floor. He was sure that she had driven by last night and stopped. He couldn't see her from the darkened car, but he knew what she looked like.

He practiced for her: "Would you care for a drink? I have some white wine chilling."

Sometimes his mind would play back the scenes for hours on end, and he could hear every word spoken and the tones of each expression. What sort he was playing at the time: young, professional, a lover of the classics or theatre; a good old boy, working-class stiff with a taste for brew and pussy and don't mind telling you, you sure are one good-looking woman, the bicep-flexing macho man, the big yet soft man, vulgar or delicate sensibilities – he played them all and they played for him, their roles, and their single purpose in life, as he saw it, their deaths for him.

He thought that he was more a witness to their deaths than their killer; that sordid epithet from the papers, the Jack-in-the-Box Killer.

Who was he this time?

Sometimes he forgot that his real name wasn't a made-up name that he gave himself.

The dye job was shitty. He stoppered the Jacuzzi and filled it with water from the Grand River that ran through the gully behind the house.

Climbing down and back up in the early hours of the morning was exhausting and risky, but it let him sleep in the daytime. There were two vantage points where a neighbor's back window exposed him and a passing car might see him from the bridge. Yet these were negligible risks.

He was truly at risk in the Arab store on the corner and at the pay phone. But he did what he could to lay protective coloring around himself. The steel plant sent hundreds onto the highways at the same time every night; the little store was crowded with big men in dirty clothes.

But one cop in the place, and it would be over.

The greatest triumph he could imagine. They would all know his true name. His fame would live forever.

They had his name, so there was no need to leave credentials behind. He had a plan to take care of that, a signature that, unfortunately, the Lake's private eye, that Kraut-fuck Haftmann, would never see because he was in the radius of the blast.

He did not need Gino's manuals any longer; those had gone into the trash and some had been ripped page by page and set adrift on the wind behind his cottage where no one would see them. His photographic memory could call them up at any time.

He opened his fly just in time –

Coming. He holds his juddering cock over the sink, the milky ejaculate demanding release.

Wouldn't look right to walk in there with pecker tracks.

~ ~ ~

"One thing the guy wasn't was a thief, Mister Hoffmann. We got guys around here that'd steal the whole plant if it wasn't bolted down. And Gino, he never stole nothing before."

"That's Haftmann. How sure are you, Mister Matthews?"

He laughed and scratched his chin. "You can't ever be sure, you know? Gino's night-shift foreman, and he's the only one with access to the locker room, storage room, certain sections of the building. I mean, hell, guys'll take directional spigots and stuff like that just because they're layin' around. Midnight requisitions, ya know?"

"Yes, I understand." His standing order apparently: stop employee theft.

"It's not like they're valuable or anything like that."

"Why is that?"

"You know. The place is mostly younger guys who knew somebody, their father and all, and you gotta be in the local. Those old guys are mostly gone now, dead or retired. There's nobody here now who was around when the place was built."

"I don't understand, Mister Matthews."

"Well, it's like this. If Gino, just saying for instance, sold those schematics to those Greenpeace nuts or to one of the papers, there could be some bad publicity over it."

"Not sure. Aren't the design specifications accurate according to what they're supposed to be?"

Long pause, thinking. "Somethin' like that, yes."

It had to be an NRC violation of some sort, but he didn't see what it had to do with Gino, who seemed the ideal company man until now.

"Tell me, sir, and I assure you this won't come back on you. What difference could those designs make?"

"I'm not a technical man, myself, Mister Hoffmann. I just pick up things here and there, you know? I don't think you could have a use for those unless you had a college degree in engineering."

"Thanks, Mister Matthews."

"Glad to help, Mister Hoffmann. I hope you fellows catch that evil sonofabitch."

One thing any investigator didn't have to do much of anymore in this state was explain the reason for asking questions. Thanks to "Jack," we're all on the same wavelength for once.

When the power plant tested its sirens, you'd hear it all the way to Ashtabula Harbor if the wind was right. Like the old Cold War era joke about what to do in the event of a nuclear attack: "Put your head between your legs and kiss your ass goodbye."

Who else was in that bar?

Bikers, hangers on, misfits, the women tough with long histories of abusive men. Autopsies said both had brain shots, temple and right eye.

The mangled dick, Jesus.

Gino should have been drinking at the Chalet with his sort, the Johnny Walker Red and mixed-drink type. Those piss concoctions served up in the Purple Haze would take enamel off your teeth. "Boilermakers from hell," Phil called them.

The bar girls: smashed throat and bullets from MacDuff's gun. Copper jackets made a mess. The head with loop earrings had to be lifted at the same time as the rest of her because the neck muscles were shredded wheat after fragments ricocheted off the skull bone.

Castration was so personal—and time-consuming, yet he took the time to do it.

Why not cut off the biker's penis too?

Just Gino Calteforte, pipefitter foreman at a nuke plant.

Revenge? What could the little man do to him?

No, no – not possible.

Jesus, no. Not that.

~ ~ ~

The elevator music was irritating. The hiss of traffic unnerved him. Seconds in the open like this became minutes. The risk of using the Duke & Duchess payphone like this was barely worth it, but he'd never be one of those idiots caught by using a cell phone pinging off towers and leading cops right to him. Gino told him one night in the bar the government had a secret agency that scooped up every phone call in America, a billion every day, he said, and every email and text message ever sent from every iPhone, and stored it all in these factory-sized warehouses full of servers all over the world.

They put him on hold and made him listen to a canned female vocalist for five long minutes while cars passed at a steady clip. A man in his late twenties went by – earbuds, sunglasses, knitted skullcap – does a double take when he sees Nelson.

"What are you looking at, punk?"

Nelson couldn't take a chance on walking any farther to find a pay phone that either worked or wasn't being manned by some black pimp or dope dealer who used it for his business. The guy removes the earbuds, gawks at him. A riff from *Phallus in Wonderland* blasts free from the guy's Mp3 player.

"Nothin', dude, nothin'. Just passin' by. No sweat."

"Keep moving, asshole."

Nelson watched him cross the street. He knew he cut a swathe through crowds too easily. He breathed deeply from his chest through his nose to calm himself. This call was fate itself.

"Thank you for waiting, Mister Cole."

"No problem, sir."

"I've looked over your application portfolio, and I'm most impressed. You do know, at the moment, we aren't hiring design engineers?"

"Yes, sir. I'm interested in the pipefitter's position you advertised recently, and if at some time you should be hiring engineers, I would certainly be interested in applying."

"You say here you are licensed, is that correct?"

"Yes, sir."

"Very good. I'd say around nine tomorrow would be good for me. Let my check my calendar. Yes. Can you be here at that time?"

"Yes, sir."

"I'll leave your name at the guardhouse. Use the visitor's lot in the southwest corner and be sure to get a pass from the guard. My office is in C-wing, Room one-one-three. That's the east corridor facing the lake. Too fast for you?"

"No, sir, I have it exactly."

"See you tomorrow—oh, say, ninish."

"Thank you for talking to me, sir. I really appreciate it. As I said on my application, I've relocated to Ohio from California with my wife and child, so I'm eager to begin working in my field in any capacity."

"That's great. See you tomorrow." *Click, gone.* Nelson listens to dead air.

'Ninish.' You asshole.

He hangs up and turns to cross the street; a Navigator SUV with two kids and an elderly couple pass him. The kids ogle. One of them yells "Jack-in-the-Box!" Blood pounds in his temples; he rocks on his feet, ready to bolt until he realizes it's a game kids in cars play like spotting VW's. "Drinks on a coke," the boys used to say in dorm. He almost gags from the adrenalin jolt.

Five more miles to trek from the abandoned cottage to the power plant. He'll have to hoof it in the dark; use the beaches and scrub as much as possible. Keep Interstate 90 on his right shoulder, but not too close.

Right now he has a bigger problem: he has no clothes except what he's wearing on his back. He's made it back to the cottage's street but not in time. There are cops and paramedics coming up behind the cruisers. He has eighteen hours to find clothes that look presentable for his job interview and shopping in a Big and Tall Man's store is out even if he had the cash.

I know a place, the angel says.

~ ~ ~

Haftmann is informed by a Vanderhyden memo his "unofficial role" as state's investigator in the hunt is "hereby and forthwith terminated." No reasons given. He called Booth, who's in New York City for an F.B.I. seminar, and discovered he's terminated as far as the state's investigation is concerned.

Booth didn't know. He suspected Millimaki put the kibosh on him.

There was no street to sift for information anymore, so he sampled the right places. Tico didn't know anything and no cops or courthouse types were running loose at the mouth so far as he knew.

Haftmann knew the system: it's okay to be dirty if you're a cop on the take, a bagman for the graft-takers, and even smalltime pushing. The property room leaks like

315

a sieve after a dope bust, and everybody's got a good idea who's on the arm. Rookies have to learn fast; some toes you don't step on here. Some kids that get into major-league trouble are too well connected to roust. You have to know the score or you can figure on spending your career handing out parking tickets and littering citations.

The Browns were playing their last exhibition game before the new season against the Giants in a London soccer stadium. Haftmann can't process soccer-loving Europeans and American football yet.

He dials a number and gets Oscar on the second ring.

"Three C's on the Brownies tonight. What's the spread?

"Cleveland plus seven-and-a-half. Cleveland's got quarterback problems."

"Tell me something I don't know."

They thought Hamlet was crazy too for talking to his father's ghost. What would they have made of him, he wonders, for talking to his bookie while the *Titanic* is going down?

Chapter 17

Walpürgisnacht

The beach is deserted, yet that only doubles its attraction for Haftmann. He asks Shawna if she's chilly as the late afternoon breeze off the lake is batting loose wisps of hair in front of her eyes so that she had to keep pushing it back as they walk.

Her hair had gold highlights; a strawberry blonde when she was a little girl, he guessed. She links her arm in his.

He has to resist the childish urge to skip stones and he seems unable to keep from eyeing the smooth, flat-surfaced ones so ideal for it. When he was a really young boy, he tells her, he thought that the coin-shaped stones tossed ashore by the waves possessed magic.

"What kind of magic?"

"The good kind," he says, "the kind that turns your wishes true."

"You mean, like, 'I wish for a billion dollars'?"

He laughs. That would be my wish now," he says. "Back then, I think I only wanted to be happy and to see other people happy."

She stops dead in her tracks and pinches his bicep. "You've changed a bit since then."

He teases her about the black armband she wore on her uniform shirt. We can take them off at the end of the month, she told him, and he said that was appropriate since it was All Hallow's Eve, a day for the dead. He just wasn't sure if MacDuff's ghost qualified for the "hallowed" part.

He knew that everyone from Millimaki on down to the maintenance staff gave him the evil eye for his blatant refusal to wear the black ribbon band in homage to a slain fellow officer. The Lake had settled into its autumn mode at last – both the water and the Strip. The water temperature dropped a degree a day now, and those businesses which had insurance claims were busy remodeling outside while the good weather lasted. Sometimes it snowed by Halloween, and the last of the high-school football games were haloed in the bright lights by the thick flakes of snow dropping from the heavens.

Some of the uninsured have For Sale signs placarded against their boarded-up windows or corkboard battened against the gaping holes torn out by rioters. A few have called it quits and were gone south for good.

"I love this place, Shawna," he says.

"You mean the Strip?"

He smiles. "No, not that, although I don't hate it as much as I pretend. I meant the water and the light, the way it looks now."

She asks him why he left Cleveland; her grip is tighter on his arm.

She knows the rumors: some said he didn't like being a bagman for the remnant of the mob that blew Irish Danny Greene to bits as he opened his car. Others said he was yellow; let his partner down on a shoot one time, got him wounded. Or he was caught dirty with drugs in his system. Haftmann is always surprised when one of these stories is passed along to him by Phil or Tico. For one thing, he doesn't care about other people.

"I don't know. I suppose I wanted to see if I could come home. I was tired of being in high gear on patrol, then downshifting to low. Chasing the same losers into and out of the system. Nothing changes, writing reports, sitting on my ass for hours outside a court hearing."

"I don't think there'll be much complaint about lack of excitement from now on after what happened on Labor Day," she said.

"Our fifteen minutes of celebrity. Isn't that what that Campbell Soup painter guy said we all get?" *Something Micah laid on him, one of her many educated factoids.*

"Hmmm," she eyed him, "I never heard that."

"I felt good being a cop for a while," he said. "Then one day I didn't . . ."

Shawna says, "My mother used to say that God never gives you more than He thinks you can handle." She pushes another red-gold lock out of her face.

Haftmann nearly chokes on that but coughs into his hand. *Oh, yes, He does, my girl.*

"She and my old grandma would have hit it off," he says.

"Somehow I don't think you and your grandmother share the same beliefs," she said.

"I believe in God the same way I believe the Browns are going to make me a multimillionaire and the State of Ohio is going to choose my six numbers next week."

They walk on; two perfect skipping rocks lay at the water's edge the perfect size to fit within the circumference of his hand. He picks one up and gives it a hurl just to dissipate the nervous energy of being with her, touching her again, imagining her body pressed against his. He tells her he's all over the motel fiasco, blocked that out of his mind, just to get it out of the way. She never refers to it.

Across the lake, Canada geese fly in a ragged vee; their honking frightens a covey of killdeer along the shore.

They walk on. She leans her head over but his shoulder is too high for comfort. She wraps an arm around his back and smiles up at him. They kiss easily and with passion. *Lovers' play*, he thinks.

"Oh," she says. "Look how those birds run with their funny legs." She does a piano-playing imitation to show him.

Haftmann's mind is content for the first time in weeks, maybe months. His thoughts drift to stories of his mother and grandmother's escape from Berlin. She said that some of the Russian soldiers were peasants who had never seen buildings before. They stole water faucets because they thought that the water came out of them, so they were taking them back to their villages.

"What are you think about?" Shawna asked.

"My grandmother," he said. "She told me pregnant women who had just given birth were raped in their hospital beds. I heard my grandmother talking to an old neighbor woman once. She said, 'How many times did it happen to you?'"

"How sickening human beings are at times," Shawna said, frowning.

"Yes," he said, giving her hand a squeeze. "It's called civilization."

"Was your mother – "

"I don't know. Neither one talked about it much. My mother killed herself when I was young. She was hospitalized for a long time. My grandmother used to take me to visit her in Lima. I never knew my father."

They saw a Norwegian elkhound wearing a collar trotting across the dunes, poking his head into the saber grass. Sniffing, his tail arced like the letter C. Then he flops onto his back and begins rolling, his long pink tongue lolling out of his mouth.

Haftmann ground his teeth at the spectacle; it seemed an obscene intrusion. He never talked about his family to anyone before, not even to the little Cleveland shrink.

"What's he doing?" Shawna asked.

"Rolling on the exposed vertebrae of the rotting fish. They scratch their backs that way. Maybe the oil from the feels good on their skin. He'll stink like a Chinese egg. He'll be lucky if they let him in the house tonight," Haftmann tells her.

They've gone far enough down the shoreline; the sun is a huge red balloon about to sink into the water. As if by instinct, they turn around at the same time.

A speckled gull, young for the lateness of the season, is squabbling with an older, larger bird with a snowy chest. The young bird is caught from behind by the nape and the bigger bird is pushing its head under the water.

"My God, will that bird drown?"

"I don't know. I've seen grackles do it to sparrows. Hold their heads under at a birdbath and drown them. For the food. Birds hate to share."

"Awful."

He laughs at her. "Not much of a country girl, are you?"

'Nature red in tooth and claw.'

Haftmann hears scurrying in the brush and sees a mother opossum leading her young to the water's edge.

They walk silently back to the wooden steps that lead up from the beach. Their time together in these last weeks has erased all confusion and misunderstanding. He's finally at peace with himself. When he isn't with her, Haftmann feels his mind reel into blackness; his fears about his sanity intensify.

Finally, at their cars, where they were parting, she says: "He won't divorce me."

"I know, love."

~ ~ ~

His heart hammered in his chest. The pipes were so intricate, so many; there had to be hundreds of miles of them. They wove themselves into loops into and out of cavernous rooms, loomed overhead like the barrels of warships, disappeared into that holy of holies: the concave maw of the containment building.

He had so little time left and every waking moment was agony for him. He could hear wolves baying in the distance, getting closer to him. He almost sniffed the air to see if they had his scent in his nostrils.

His job was mindless tedium; a skeleton crew operated at night until the reactor was brought back up. He heard the foreman, Gino's replacement, probably, say that they were at sixty-five percent full throttle and would go to full the following week. Bingo, he thought.

His Cole papers were sifted through the computer in Personnel, and he had signed the signature of Martin Albert Cole so many times he was cross-eyed and his hand shook.

He could not write italic script easily, but he dared not block print. He hoped what he had practiced would suffice. The arrogant weasel who had interviewed him two days ago seemed to buy it. *Mister Big Shot, telling me I was hired on as a second-class pipefitter. You'd think we were on a nuclear submarine.*

Much to do first: the pipes were not simple, and although he could mentally impose the schematics over any section at will, he could not match up several sections in the steam loop. Too complex even for his visual imagination. The valve casings could be got at, but he was afraid of compromising the pressure, get his arms shaved off by radioactive steam. The water loop gave him fits: it was too intricate. No one, he realized with a shock, actually knew this section well enough; it was all asymmetrical; racks of piping traversed other sections as though some mischievous child wizard had been turned loose with tinker toys.

He needed to find out exactly what happened when the plant depressurized, what each section of pipe's role was. It was like being inside a great rumbling belly; the pipes were like veins. Now he himself was inside the bloodstream. He would find a way to burst this giant heart and boil every man, woman, and child in a fifteen-mile radius to screaming death in hot radioactive shit.

He stared at the huge concrete walls of the giant's belly and saw the radioactive phosphorescence ooze through the fissures and cracks. . .

"It could eat through titanium," the books said. He thought of the ice-blue lake water just beyond the containment building's walls. The China Syndrome.

That ought to be enough to do it, he thought.

~ ~ ~

The night is steamy, incandescent over the lake. Haftmann keeps scratching himself but the itch is on the inside. He has a thought in his head that won't go away.

He calls Painesville homicide and asks for Lieutenant Mondine. "C'mon, swing shift, be there," he prays.

"Homicide, Mondine."

"Thomas Haftmann, Lieutenant. Remember me?"

"Sure do, Haftmann. Your friends from Columbus gave us a working over. We never figured her for the psycho."

"Nobody did, Lieutenant."

"Your floater come up?"

"Yes, early-spring thaw. Listen, it's about the daughter I wanted to ask you. Do me a favor and give her a call right now."

"It's nine o'clock here, Haftmann. What time you got where you are?"

"Tell me this. Did she sell her mother's house?"

"Nope. There's a real-estate sign on the front lawn. Been there since the murder. People are a little

323

superstitious about buying houses where people got slaughtered in them."

Droll, Mondine, thinks Haftmann, but he says, "Lieutenant, as a favor to me, would you order a drive-by? I'd appreciate a call when your unit clears the house."

"What're you thinking, Haftmann?"

"What's going on in Painesville these days? You getting the same Jack-in-the-Box sightings we are here?"

"Christ, he's as popular as a flying saucer around here. Everybody's seen him on one street corner or other. One old woman calls in every other day, claims she's married to him. Another old bat claims he's sleeping in her basement. We can't keep the Nine-One-Ones clear for the real emergencies."

"Send the unit, Lieutenant. Here's my cell number."

He paces. Before the first four notes of his phone go off, he answers.

"There's a unit outside right now. One of the neighbors down the road comes over, says that he saw a light flick on inside the house three days ago. He says nobody's supposed to be in the place. Everybody with a vacant house is afraid the place will turn into a needle academy if they turn their backs too long."

"Listen to me. I've got a bad feeling. Just tell me nothing's been happening in Lake County these days that looks unusual for this time of year."

Same stuff you got probably. B & E's, shitloads of dopers, carrying, same old shit. Fistfights after the football games –

"Have your men go inside."

"No way."

"Why not?"

"You know better. You haven't told me why yet."

"It's a – feeling, a hunch. Just humor me. Check it out."

"You better have the juice, Haftmann. I don't want that woman's daughter suing us for because you got a hunch in the middle of the night."

"Call me right back, OK?"

Timeserver, he says to the dead air in the room.

While he willed the callback, he sees a small vampire come up to his front door and knock. Even though his house is off the main drag, trick or treaters find him. He gives away money he found lying around on the floor or in the sofa cushions. He forgot it was Halloween. He gives the vampire a five-dollar bill just to get him the fuck off his porch when Beethoven's *Ninth*'s ringtones signal Mondine calling back.

"You better get over here," the lieutenant says. *Not good. He sounds grim.*

It's bad.

"Tell me."

"A mother and her two kids."

The line goes dead.

Haftmann looks out his window and sees the departing vampire meet up with some friends in costumes. One of them is dressed like an Ebola doctor in a Hazmat outfit. His mind is on idle. He wonders if it's like athletes being in the zone where alpha and theta waves intersect, in a perfect sine and cosine synchronicity (Micah info stored away for use and how she had explained it to him). Time slows, you see things clearly; the mind is calm, deliberate, unhurried.

Haftmann's brain triggers an old memory of a silent film he'd seen with Micah when they were dating: *Nosferatu*. He saw the words flash across his mind: 'That night in Bremen in a somnambulistic dream' and didn't realize he knew the face of evil so well.

He calls Booth but almost thumbed Shawna's number from the directory before he catches himself. He decides to take a change of clothes this time.

The place inside and out is swarming with cops. He tries to convince Mondine and his superior to call the men out of the house, kill the arc lights, and set a trap for him: *He's coming back. He killed them in a hurry . . .*

"No dice." Mondine looks at him as if he's carrying Black Death, the sequel.

They take out the mother and the children. He tossed her into the Jacuzzi, rimed from recent use. Her forehead is split open to expose the skull bone.

The Lake County M.E.'s assistant tells Mondine she might have been dead at the time because there was very little blood. Some of the younger techs are holding handkerchiefs to their noses. The deaths are recent but the humid, airless upstairs is rank and suffocating.

He put each one in a different room. The children died of simple asphyxiation; he covered their mouths with his hands and cut off their air. Probably after he got the woman upstairs and broke her neck.

Haftmann tries to grab the men passing to and fro with their cases and klieg lights, tries to speak reasonably to anyone who'll listen. *This isn't it, this isn't what he's here for.*

He finds the lieutenant in the yard giving commands to some blues. Houses up and down the street are lit for Halloween, even though most of them have shut down for the night.

Mondine sends out a canvassing team: "Get that neighbor who saw the light."

To Haftmann: "She was planning on moving into the place after she sold her house. She just got divorced."

Mondine knows Booth and the state team would take over as soon as Booth has mustered the forensics people out of bed and onto the Cleveland Memorial Shoreway. "Twenty-five minutes," he told Mondine. Not realizing Haftmann was standing right next to the lieutenant, Booth says: "Keep that private eye at arm's length, Lieutenant. He's off the team."

Booth's silver SUV pulls up. Haftmann counts six cars in his entourage and a van from the Cuyahoga County Criminal Task Force. SWAT teams are positioned below the house, in the gully, and on the highway. If he crosses the bridge, he'll put himself into a cul-de-sac at every point.

"He'll be trapped," Booth says. The rooftops across the street have silhouettes assuming fixed positions. Lights in the houses across the street began to blink off as cops go door to door.

Booth grimaced when he found Haftmann at the crime scene, but he's adjusted to his presence. *Cool Hand Booth*, Haftmann thinks, but he doesn't trust the dapper fed as far as he can throw him. He's just grateful they're all on the same page, for once – *surprise him when he returns to the house*. Booth orders him to stay put: no one in or out of the house at this point. The F.B.I.'s crack shot and three of the best SWAT marksmen occupy the upper floor.

Haftmann and Booth remain in the kitchen, out of harm's way, but Haftmann has no doubt how many shots he plans to get off when the maniac shows: *I won't stop until I hear dry fire.*

Haftmann doesn't see the children because they were bagged by the time he got there. He imagines their last moments on earth, absolute stark terror, and his heartbeats against his rib cage.

He's got to be taken out. This can't go on.

Haftmann and the cops inside settle into the darkness. There's the occasional scrape of a foot or a hushed whisper in the steamy house, but the house settles slowly into the night's quiet while the stink of death grows in intensity.

He feels a mosquito bite his face, then an ear lobe; black flies are in the room now. One walks across the back of his neck, seeking a place to draw blood for its eggs.

A half hour goes by: tick-tock, tick-tock . . . .

Street noises. Dogs bark in the distance. A normal house in a normal, middle-class residential neighborhood. Haftmann has always imagined him homeless, sleeping under bridges, squatting in derelict houses.

A rush of wings from out back in the humid air makes both of them jump at the table. Just mallards hitting the water, out for a late night cruise. Haftmann has never known them to roost so late.

Everything's off kilter in this heat, he thinks.

It turns out Booth's speedy response was inspired by an incident. He tells Haftmann Painesville PD got a report of a break-in. A thief broke into the Cleveland Browns' locker room out there at Lakeland Community College where the team has its summer camp and ripped off some clothes. A defensive tackle had his locker cleaned out. No one else's stuff was taken, although plenty of expensive equipment lay around.

"What makes you sure it's him?" Haftmann asks.

"How many people you know running around this state wear size thirteen, triple-E shoes and a fifty-four long sport coat and don't play inside linebacker or defensive tackle?"

They hear somebody big walking around on the porch haltingly, as if uncertain; there is enough light from the last-quarter moon to show a large figure in dark clothes and what could be blood smears looking in the far window. Guns are cocked everywhere, in the alleys, down at the river, on rooftops.

Click. Click. Click. Click. Click.

Lights go on all over the street. The front doors of houses swing wide open and discharge black-clad men in combat gear. They head toward the house in a rapid single file like ants moving head-to-butt at a picnic basket.

Haftmann races into the living room where he's memorized the position of the wall switch and catches it with a swipe of his hand.

Guns point in all directions at a very large, flustered teenager who'd had a recent Bela Lugosi makeover, which he's sweated through. His black cape is pimpled with a dozen red laser dots. He looks about to burst into tears at the mayhem surrounding him.

"Trick or treat!" He gasps out at the cops flying at him in all directions.

Chapter 18

Gotterdammerüng

Haftmann awoke at the Bide-A-Wee Motel and remembered what got him there. His brain felt insulted, he was badly hung over, and his stomach was off. He made it to the toilet in time with fiery spurts of his insides.

He heard a crow cawing somewhere in the cedar trees, and traffic sounded as if it picked up volume in the sulfurous haze of chemicals following traffic west to Cleveland. The phone went off, an uncouth motel phone, with a shrill burr.

"Haftmann, get dressed. I'm having coffee at your motel in what they refer to as a lounge."

Booth. He doesn't want to tangle assholes with him now; last night was bad enough. Booth screaming in his ear to put down the gun. Cops regarded him with that look, the one you give people whose elevators don't go all the way to the top.

The morning light outside is still autumn even if it was the first of November, yet the chill is unmistakable: winter's coming. Getting dressed, Haftmann cut his eyes to the mirror and surveyed his flesh: nicks of scars from too many Lake punch-ups, a starburst of damaged tissue on his neck and inside the crook of his elbow, there's a hash mark where a biker's beer bottle caught him from behind. Tears in flesh heal but not the memories of the wounds. He saw the pale flesh, not so muscled now, big hands and arms, and finally, he gazed at the apparition of a worried and anxious stranger, someone he almost didn't know anymore wearing a face he didn't like. But he had earned it all, he knew – the broken career and failed marriage, the

331

dead-end life of a private detective doing the backstroke in a cesspool. Too many memories of guilt and sorrow and dying love.

Shawna, he prayed to the mirror, *save me from this man who's hijacked my soul.*

In the parking lot he saw a grosbeak; its red breast startling in a dingy, downtown Painesville motel. He checked out the licenses of the cars: mostly local, an occasional Pennsylvania plate with the Quaker State slogan: YOU'VE GOT A FRIEND IN PENNSYLVANIA. He figured the place for a seedy fuck palace for adulterers on the prowl. He willed away the images of his miserable tryst with Shawna at a similar place in Jefferson-on-the-Lake.

Booth was his usual dapper self, couth and kempt: "You want breakfast? The toast looks good."

"No, I don't want breakfast."

"Listen, Haftmann – "

Booth paused. "I'll bet those two words have been used a lot together in your lifetime because it seems to be a habit for people to say it around you."

"What have you been doing since last night?"

"You're still off the case if that's what you're intimating by the question. That's official. I'll get the governor to sign a proclamation if necessary."

"Consider it necessary."

"You were going to shoot a boy in a vampire suit."

"I noticed everybody else was drawing a weapon or were those slide rules?"

"I don't intend to exchange barbs with you. I'm afraid that if I try to come down to your level, I'll find the descent too abrupt. Go home. Stay out of it."

"Go home?"

"Yes, go home."

"What about the APB on her car? He's out there trolling for his next victim." Haftmann was too ashamed to mention his latest theory. *He must be losing his grip like everybody said.*

"Don't be obtuse. We have every cop, state, local, federal, every trucker with a CB, you name it, watching for a powder-blue Taurus."

"He's eluded you so far. You keep making the mistakes you made before and he keeps getting away. You aren't thinking like him. He's pissing on your little traps by the highway." Haftmann knew the killer wasn't going near any highway or interstate. Since Nine-Eleven, every city in the country had to have a lockdown plan for terrorists: every bus station, train terminal, airport, highway, or tunnel could be secured within a fifteen-mile perimeter of a call-out in thirty minutes. Some cities like DC could do it in fifteen.

"Booth, he's not going anywhere near a major road. He knows he's stuck here," Haftmann said but his voice lacked confidence. *The truth was*, he told himself, *I'm too old. I'm past it.*

"Haftmann, I'm all through talking to you. Coffee's on me."

Haftmann stopped home to change socks and put on a shirt; there were bags under his eyes and a two-day beard. On his way out the door, he remembered he had to start buying seed again: *juncos will be leaving Canada soon.*

Then, an odd moment of déjà vu, a feeling of detachment as he was about to get into the car. He knew it was the combination of stress and diet, a double-thrust of neurons down the wrong path. He knew somehow, too, that it was more than chemistry of the brain: he felt an empathetic bonding with all that's hideous and repulsive in the Jack-in-the-Box killer.

The station house buzzed with the rumor that some members of the Benevolent Order of Policemen were going to burn down the Purple Haze. His stomach spasmed, so he headed for the can downstairs. He found a stall and sat with his head in his hands.

He heard the door open and footsteps, loud talking by the washbasins. Two policemen named Orris and Whitlow. He had his hand on the latch when he heard the black cop, Orris, speak her name, and it froze him to stone. He didn't want to hear her name in the crapper, so he was about to clear his throat, announce his presence when it registered. What they said. The horror of it:

" – shot her in the face and put it to his head right after."

"Haftmann was supposed to be fooling around with that broad," Whitlow said.

"Nobody trusts that fucker. He ain't right in the head."

"Tell that to the chick," Whitlow said.

They laugh together and go out the door.

Haftmann has not done this trick since he was a nineteen-year-old ordinary seaman on a Great Lakes ore carrier and discovered why five shots of Bushmills Irish and five drafts are called boilermakers. He gushed from both ends. Dry heaves followed the coffee he had with Booth a couple hours ago. He is so wracked by the spasms shaking his body that he cannot see through the tears. "Shawna, NO!" He howls. Even his sinuses open and he has the added ignominy of rivulets of snot pouring down his chin dripping onto the dirty tile floor. His body is no more his friend, it's in full revolt rejecting him and everything he stands for as a man.

It takes an hour to get himself right, clean up. His brain numbs the pain; it's all too fresh. Somehow he finds himself at the morgue. Doc Harris has just finished posting the husband and was about to start on the woman. He makes Harris jump when the pathologist turns to see him there, see his face.

"Detec – What are doing here?"

Maybe Harris has heard the same rumors.

Haftmann can't find words. He just stands there gaping like a fool and staring at the form under the sheet.

"What is it, son?" Harris asked with more gentleness than he's ever shown Haftmann.

"Nothing, Doc. I don't know why I'm here."

"She's not here anymore. You have to let her go . . ."

Haftmann walks away before Harris removes the sheet. He drives out to the cottage and looks inside. The door's off the hinges; the exercise bars and paraphernalia he'd used are stacked in back like cordwood. The cottage is a foul-smelling husk; nothing but open sky and exposed joists. He can see the shoreline from here. Lake Erie is brilliantine blue through the fissures in the bedroom wall.

The daybed is spotted and moldy where the October rains got to it from the ceiling cracks.

He kept nothing personal in the place besides the few clothes that were taken off for analysis. Nothing to show he'd ever been there.

He must have looked out at the water from time to time, Haftmann thinks, watched the gulls wheel and plummet. Haftmann can see the spot ahead in the distance where he and Shawna had gone for their walk. He sees the nuclear power plant's stack concave silhouette and the vapor clouds above it; so familiar from the shoreline, it looks hellish to him at that awful moment.

Something tickles its way through his bone-aching grief.

The woman's house in Painesville is fifteen miles from where he's standing; you could walk it, if you were in a big hurry. *After the riot, who wasn't?*

The practice field of the Browns for their summer camp was just the other side of the power plant across Interstate 90. If you took the power plant as the fixed leg of a compass, you would see that his orbit in the last half year is the merest crescent of Lake Erie's edge that stretches from Painesville to the west to Jefferson-on-the-Lake in the east.

Haftmann's latest theory, more proof he's losing it as those two cops said. Jack's not trying to get away, Haftmann wearies of telling them – even the barflies at Tico's are bored with him – he's not hiding. He didn't want to kill that woman and her children. *He had to.* They must have surprised him at the house.

The little pipefitter and his designs – a nuclear power plant.

One human being, no matter how strong he is, and even if he has the berserk strength of a psychopath, can't cause a –

. . . meltdown?

Jesus. Shit. Fuck.

Haftmann roared back to his old desk at the precinct to call the guardhouse at but was told Matthews had graveyard shift: four to midnight. He got his home phone number from Personnel and dialed. I'm not allowed to wake up my grandfather when he's sleeping. A child of eight, like the girl Lonnie Dale Nelson had smothered in his powerful hands: choked off the carotid the way you'd pick a strand of spaghetti from a plate.

"Please, this is an emergency."

"No. Goodbye."

His mind pinwheeled, but he knew he couldn't let himself think of Shawna. He looked around and it was all normal activity for early afternoon: cops talking and sitting in front of their computer screens, some of them with a phone clamped to their ears while they hunt and peck out the letters. Time stopped: surreal, slow motion.

He felt moronic, but he decided to call Personnel back.

"Administration and Records, please."

Haftmann explained who he was and gave his old badge number. He was coy about the reasons for his request, although he put the right tone into it so they didn't shine him on. Then a man named Miller got on the line:

"Nineteen new hires since Labor Day," he said. "Three administration . . . four production . . . two maintenance . . . one engineering . . . let's see, one payroll . . . three electricians. Hang on, five more, Christ is this necessary, Officer? Two security and three computer programmers. That's it."

"Give me the names and medical stats on production, maintenance, security, engineering, and electricity."

Miller gave him seven names and descriptions.

All too old or too small physically.

"What about the other three?"

"Their names have not yet been transferred over from Personnel," Miller said.

"Would you please check their names and vital statistics for me?

"Is this an emergency, Officer?"

"Get the fucking records, now."

"Blica, Cole, Kennedy. All pipefitters."

His skin crawls up the back of his neck like a baby spider when Miller told him that one pipefitter, Cole, weighed around two-seventy, two-eighty.

He is amazed to see the office around him exactly as it was before he picked up the phone; he can almost hear the sentence Stel is mouthing over the phone; nothing has altered its position in the moments since he was aware of them.

He had a prevision of all of them caught in a nuclear flash: they looked like x-ray images of themselves in his mind's eye. He imagined a kaleidoscope of dazzling colors of the spectrum rippling in fiery oranges, crimson-reds, butter-yellows cascading across the sky. Then the all-consuming black of nothingness.

Normal sounds erupted all around him again. Chattering and clacking away at their computers.

Mother of God. Was it possible?

They all said he was crazier than a two-headed dog in a meat market, *non compos mentis*, loony, couldn't write or spell, dumber than a bag of dicks – and yet . . .

"Fuck me," Haftmann said aloud. "He can do it. *He knows how.*"

~ ~ ~

Nelson has found it at last: the flaw.

There's even a bright red wheel valve at the very juncture he needed. Like a mathematician doing logarithms in his head, he takes a last mental inventory of the whole process as far as he can go, from the moment the water entered the plant from Lake Erie to the steps whereby it became a coolant for the reactor core.

He smiles.

Every drop of water that was ever on earth is still there. The permanence of life and his place in the scheme of things enthralls him. "I was born for this," he says to one of the other new guys, Kennedy, his new partner on swing shift.

"Fuck," says Cody Mayhew into his cell. He had just been called by Miller in HR. The new guy on his shift is terminated; he's responsible for giving him the news.

Mayhew didn't understand because the big ox was working out OK, but somebody in administration found out he violated security clearance. "Kennedy," he mutters to himself, "couldn't pour piss out of a boot if the directions were on the heel." "No," he said to Mayhew. "Cole. It's Cole you terminate and that's an order."

There was nothing to be done about it, but he knew that the night crew were already scattered around the plant.

Cody, bull foreman of the skeleton crew at night, feels he has more problems than he can cope with – especially since Gino had left things all fucked to hell when he got himself killed in the riot on the Lake. He has to give the guy a negative rating on his New Employee Evaluation Report. The goddam guy is always gawking at the pipes like some kind of booger-eating retard with his head in the air. "Hellfire," Mayhew mutters, "he didn't smell too good neither."

Mayhew looks around the coolant section where he finds the new man.

Nelson starts to pass him by, ignoring his foreman, a man he deems an amiable idiot, unworthy of his attention, like the rest of the crew. But because he's so close now, he doesn't want to waste time. The angel had warned him about overdoing the "new-guy" thing anyway. "Big men don't make small talk," the angel said as if the ghost of Dale Carnegie were speaking through the voice.

Then as the foreman repeats what he said, it registers in his neocortex.

He blinks at the foreman. "Did you say . . . did you just say I was fired?"

Before Mayhew can rephrase it, take some of the sting out of it, Nelson has the foreman's windpipe in both hands. The wiry little man begins to kick loose, so he lifts him up in the air and tilts his body off to one side to keep from getting a booted foot in his groin. Mayhew fights hard, fights for his very life. Nelson squeezes so hard he brings bloody sputum out of the foreman's mouth. He draws back his right fist and hits him on the temple, using his calloused hand's knot of flesh; he can't afford broken fingers at this moment.

The little foreman won't stop struggling, though. A dark stain spreads out across the front of his pants. Nelson bangs his head against the wall twice, hard, then a third time. Mayhew's eyes roll back into his head.

Nelson has planned it for the shift change at midnight, but the Angel screamed NOW. He feels greatness enveloping him. He looks down at the body of his foreman and understands his destiny is now. The calm he feels is supernatural. *So be it.*

He picks the foreman's body up and slings him into a storage closet locker and kicks the door shut hard enough to jam it. A dim memory of having thrust a girl's body into some weeds many years ago crosses the threshold of the memory. He smiles. He has the Lake cop's gun taped to his leg.

He needs exact timing for this part; between turning the red valve, a quaint vestige of the plant's origins, and allowing for the computer to read the drop in feedwater, he has eight minutes, no more. The backup won't trip at twelve minutes. He learned that part from Gino who told him about testing sirens when the reactor was decompressing.

If no one in the control room reacts to the pulse before that time, he will have the only chance he would ever get. He could send a surge of contaminated water into the water loop by rerouting the normal path.

He has to have the help of the computer. He doesn't know if the person he gave his order to would respond the right way. He might know what would happen, might even try to be a hero, circumvent his plan somehow. A gun to his head might not work; you just didn't know. After Nine-Eleven, nuclear power plants In America were reinforced to be ensured against airplane attacks. He recalls how some men had gotten over their terror and fought him to save their women.

He maneuvers himself into position and strains at the valve. It has probably never been turned since the plant was built in the seventies. He clasps his powerful forearms through the spokes to give himself more leverage and thrusts the entire weight of his body's strength against the wheel.

Nothing, not an inch.

"Hey! What the hell you doing? Get away from that, you fucking moron!"

He sees a Quality Circle man wearing an aluminum hardhat approach with his clipboard swinging.

"Help me," he grunts, to the angel. He picks up a large pipe wrench and swings it bolo style so that it comes down on the hard-hat with maximum velocity. It opens up the head beneath like a can opener going into stewed tomatoes – a jagged hole in the center imprints the metal in starburst pattern through the blasted-open skull. The momentum of his swing has enough torque to unhinge the man's jawbone.

He goes back to the red valve and throws enough strength into it to have jerked four hundred pounds. It won't give. More leverage, more. He has an iron bar about eight feet long and five inches in diameter secreted in a spot near the maintenance room. He jogs for it, losing precious seconds. He breathes through his nostrils, sweating, still comfortable – a man of destiny at peace with himself.

The bar does the trick, but he has to expend so much energy that he collapses to the floor and almost vomits from the superhuman effort. Living off junk food, he was losing three pounds of muscle a day since making it safely to Painesville. His mouth tastes of copper, and he has had very little to eat in three days.

He staggers in a loping run while sweat pours off him. When he comes within sight of anyone, he slows to a stride that he hopes won't cause concern if anyone should see him. He has to have six minutes to operate without interruption and half that time is gone.

At the control room, he's almost sick enough to puke again, the stakes are so high now, but the adrenaline pumps him back up. He sees a worried-looking security guard approach him to see what the trouble was. No pipefitters ever came this far into the admin section or the control room. Nine-Eleven enforced new and stricter policies on internal movements among all employees. The guard must have seen a look in his eyes.

"The feedwater pump—" Nelson begins to say – then draws the gun from the slit in his jumpsuit and shoots the man in the forehead. He's deafened by the ringing shot in this cavernous building even with the other noises, but now he has the guard's own security card ready for the laser scanner slot.

They must have heard the shot because the men in the control room look as though they know something is about to happen when he enters the room and stands in their midst.

He checks his watch: not even two minutes left.

"You," he says to one of the programmers in a white coat. "Stand there."

Then Nelson shots him in the ear.

The one closest to the door whimpers "Oh no oh no oh no" and tries to run.

Nelson centers on the man's back and squeezes, missing, blowing the man's elbow apart in a haze of red mist. His dying body's inertia sends him crashing into a row of computer gauges at the far end of the room.

He puts the gun at the mouth of an older man and says to the younger man next to him, "If you don't do what I say, I'll kill him first and you next. Shut down the water loop when I tell you."

"I don't understand – "

"Shut it down NOW!"

Moments later, he can see the board lights behind the terminals rising as the sensors pick up a surge in the system. He takes a chance and swings the gun from the older man to the younger one and sets the gun on his lower lip. As the man's eyes open wide in horror, he fires; the bullet caroms off the skull and fractures the thick plate glass window into a spider's web. He looks calmly at the older man, whose face blanches from pink to gray.

"Don't fuck with me," Nelson says.

"I-I know who you are," says the man. "You're . . . him!"

"Everybody is going to know that," he says calmly. "Shut it down."

"All right, all right."

As soon as he touches the right switches and turns to face Nelson, he sees the bore's black hole about to rest on the tip of his nose.

He starts to say the words *No Please* but his brain isn't receiving messages anymore because a slug has already chewed a burrowing comet trail through the cerebral cortex and is en route to the corpus callosum.

Nelson wants to weep from the sheer joy of it. There's no one left to kill in the control room.

"Well done," says the angel.

Sirens and bells are being tripped all over the power plant.

It doesn't matter now. *Let them come or flee as they choose,* thinks Nelson.

He has only to reclose the valve and send contaminated water into the loop. The sensors will override the failure of control, and in the curious doublethink of computers, actually guarantee that his plan will succeed. The reactor core will be exposed. The nuclear chain reaction will result in an explosion that will shatter windows twenty miles away and be seen like a ball of fire from outer space.

No one will live, no one can escape. It is final – and glorious. His power, his light.

He feels bulletproof as he walks out of the control room. He hears people running in all directions.

Bolting around the corner at that moment with a gun in his fist, a guard he's never seen in the plant turns, looking in all directions, unsure. Lonnie Dale Nelson sees the face of the man he hates more than any other human being. *It's that fucking cop who sent him back to prison on his only drug bust.*

Haftmann and he look at each other at the same time. Then Haftmann fires.

Haftmann is wheezing from the run and his eyes are blinded with sweat.

He missed from the distance, and there are too many people in panic running about. He hears the bullet clang off metal in a ferocious ricochet.

Haftmann sends the guard to phone Painesville PD, JOTL cops, Booth at F.B.I., Cleveland.

"What about the fire department?" The agitated security cop asked, goggle-eyed.

"Get everybody down here now!"

Haftmann has no idea what to do in a situation like this.

He waves back some technicians approaching, drawn to the ruckus.

"He's going to expose the core," Haftmann says to them. "Can't you do something from here?"

"He – he can't do that," one of them says. "That's not possible!"

Everybody is thinking terrorists at first. Haftmann calms them by saying it's a workplace shooting and they have an active shooter somewhere near the control room. They just have to kill him, he thought. Nothing bad can happen. BUT THEY HAVE TO KILL HIM RIGHT AWAY.

One of the men shakes his head, bewildered. "I'm not . . . so sure," he says to Haftmann.

"What do you mean? Can he or can't he?"

"Uh, maybe you should just kill him now," he says in a voice that quavers.

Haftmann follows the direction Nelson had taken, deeper into the reactor center. The sweat pops out in thick beads all over his body now. There are fewer people running past him now, escaping from the chaos, but the sirens' din is earsplitting and he wishes he had told somebody to shut the goddamn thing off.

Meltdown, he thinks. *Why wait for flak jackets and body armor?*

Haftmann sees a man with his head caved in; there's another man in a white coat sticking obscenely through a window. He sees a man's arm dangle from a rack of piping, whirls, and fires at this. It was another corpse, someone jammed into the crotch of pipes overhead the way you'd stick luggage in an overhead rack on a flight. *It's like a dream*, he thinks, but the rotten taste inside his mouth is all too real and the watery feeling in his legs says, *Flight, not Fight*. Training forces him onward. He's shaking now: it seems like perfect destruction no matter what. The shrilling of the sirens gives him goosebumps.

Lights begin to flicker on and off.

There's a metal-on-metal sound ahead; the rumbling noise from the center of the place grows a notch. Some burst pipes ahead. Hissing. Even here he has to think of the little Cleveland shrink Matrooshian.

He sees him twenty yards ahead, trying to pull at an enormous red wheel valve. Haftmann drops into a crouch and fires three shots at the moving bulk in the shadows. The lights go out. Blackness. More hissing.

He hears laughter. It's not wholesome laughter, either.

"I'll still have time enough to kill you, Haftmann," a strange voice says from the dark.

"I didn't come here to die, Lonnie."

But he feels that's exactly what he has come here for.

The laughter peels down toward Haftmann in waves through the same terror of the sirens; he stands above him on a catwalk as Haftmann whips his body around to fire upwards. *Fuck the ricochets*, he thinks.

He holds the weaver stance so long he can count his own heartbeats. It's too dark to see anything. He holds both hands out, feet spread, inching toward the voice. He feels as if his hands have touched a live wire, grabbed lightning. The gun flies out of his hand before he can do anything.

Then someone with unbelievable strength picks him up by the scruff of his neck as if he were a kitten and something hard smashes him in the side of his face. A boot, a fist – something is pressing his face into the concrete floor with massive weight behind it. Veins in his neck throb, his eyes are going to pop right out of his head, and through the din of his own soon-to-be extinction, Haftmann hears a deep male voice change into a nightingale's chirp, a falsetto, then an opera in Italian, and end, finally, before his brain will fade, into the English of Shakespeare's time. The words, those hideous words again: *Love Bade Me Welcome*

. . . *But my soul drew back*, Haftmann finishes. He's dead and he knows it.

A massive whirlpool opens in front of him or below him because somehow is above his own body looking down at the monster crushing him with his boot. The vortex won't say how this works; it simply demands him, body and soul, and he's sucked him down into the maw of its blackness before he can take a moment to resign himself to his own death.

~ ~ ~

When Haftmann comes to, his eyes are swollen to puffed slits, and there is a dead man's face staring right into his; some blood drips from the man's nose. The drops pitter-patter onto Haftmann and make him think of Chinese water torture.

He's got some of his hearing back and can make out the sound of semiautomatic rifle fire. Bullets whizz past his ears, spanking into concrete and making a strange *chirruuunging* sound in diminuendo as the ricochets double and triple like stones skipping across a pond.

The dead body has SWAT CUYAHOGA stitched over the body armor. The piping on his uniform has to mean Booth is out there directing things.

Not coherent but instinctively lying still, Haftmann knows something is wrong –

They can't flush him out but he's able to pick them off as they come forward. He twists his head to see, but the pain is so intense that he blacks out again.

This time, when he comes to, he has managed to squirm some of the dead man's body weight from his arm. He reaches out for his gun to pull the trigger, end this hideous pain, but the gun has clattered off. Instinctively, he reaches for his ankle holster, completely oblivious to the fact that he's not on patrol with Frank, he's no longer a rookie cop in Cleveland, and this reactor is going to go up like a Roman candle any second.

He can't see where Nelson's position is down the darkened building, but he guesses that the rifle fire has him in a niche pinned back there beyond the red wheel valve.

Haftmann feels the pain rush in, grateful for what it means, but knows deep down it's all hopeless now. Every time the fusillade picks up, the body over him bucks as it jerks with ricocheting slugs crisscrossing over him. He hopes Nelson is using up his ammo soon.

The lights went off and stayed off for a full minute while the orange and yellow muzzle fire defined the shooters' position. There's a cry out there somewhere as another man went down.

Haftmann frisks the corpse above him at those places where cops hide guns. The SWAT cop has what feels like a small automatic secreted at the center of his back. Haftmann slips it loose and waits for the lights to go back on.

The reactor floor rumbles. Haftmann has a moment of fear so great he wants to put the automatic to his head and end it here.

He sees a pair of black figures working their way down to him. They don't know about the catwalk in this section because they come ahead in their crouch walk. Nelson will have a near-perfect vantage.

They get a barrage of cover fire but it's all for nothing. Nelson from above puts a shot into each of their faces without exposing himself. Haftmann thought they'd never get him as long as he had guns. The two dead SWAT men just brought him two automatic rifles.

Haftmann knew he'd stay alive only as long as he can play dead and Nelson is distracted.

He wondered whether Booth, or any of them, knew whether Nelson had time to finish what he started.

Haftmann had a glimpse of Nelson's shoes moving back and forth between the pipes, never far from the wheel valve. He couldn't see the man's face.

Haftmann caught one through his arm; it cauterizes the nerve endings as it passed through, so he didn't feel the pain at once.

He had to get some of the blood out of his eyes.

Nelson grunted with strain as he put his body against the bar, still trying to move the valve. One more SWAT guy made a heroic charge down the corridor and sprayed fire as he ran. One bullet dropped him to the floor inches from the other two.

A suicide, another gun for the psycho.

They haven't got a chance, Haftmann thought.

He heard Nelson writhing and grunting like an animal under a load it can't carry. The bar falls to the floor with a great clang. Haftmann heard Nelson weeping, sobbing.

Haftmann can't get the dead cop's body weight off him. The crying from the shadows continued. *Whatever it is he wanted to do, he can't do it yet*, Haftmann realized. *We might all live.*

The scrape of shoes as Nelson moved closer to him.

Like a bull charging, there's a palpable menace rushing toward him like displaced air from a runaway diesel. Haftmann felt the dead body jerked off him and used that moment to transfer the .25 automatic from his broken right hand to his left.

He waited a second longer to find the blue eyes of his man before firing. All five shots go into him but Nelson rips and tears at Haftmann's face and neck with powerful fingers. Haftmann's eyes were blinded by blood.

Nelson staggered back and looked down at the places where the bullets had gone in, groping at them with bloodied fingers. The slavering, spittle-flecked mouth of Lonnie Dale Nelson's face is contorted in fury. *Die, fucker*, Haftmann pleaded.

Haftmann fell headfirst into blackness. This time the whirlpool kept him.

When a team of cops led by Booth cleared a path through to Nelson and Haftmann, they found no pulse in either man. Twenty minutes later a paramedic found the smallest tickle of a pulse in one of the two men, but because of the noise, cloud of cordite stench, and pandemonium all around, he got the names mixed and Haftmann went to Lake County Hospital shackled to the gurney with a police escort holding a drawn gun over his unconscious body while Nelson was sent in a zippered black bag to the Jefferson morgue.

When Doc Harris cut the tag with *Haftmann, Thomas* on it, and opened up the bag, he was not sure that the bloodied and pulped face of the decedent was, in fact, Haftmann on the slab until somebody noticed this corpse had the acid-burn scar of a Navy anchor tattoo on the left forearm. By the time Booth got the mix-up straightened out, Haftmann had been in surgery for five hours and was given a 50-50 chance to live.

Chapter 19

Aftermath
Coalton, West Virginia.
The federal penitentiary, months later.

He woke in the cell in the morning light. There was the sound of steel bars clanging, clanging; it's the one sound that never stops in a prison.

He was always frightened when he first opened his eye because it took a long while for him to remember who he is and how he got here. He's still not used to seeing out of one eye. The doctors told him when he came to in recovery that there just enough to salvage that would not be permanently damaged. Forget driving at night, they said. Lonnie Dale Nelson had gouged Haftmann's right eye and damaged the optic nerve. The surgeon said it was like mashing a cigarette in an ashtray.

He's in AdSeg, Administrative Segregation, because, they said, "They'll kill you if we put you into the general population." Sometimes he thought it was he who had killed all those people because there was so much blood on his hands. The dreams were bad every night.

He has a routine of washing down the hallway with a mop and bucket and it takes him most of the morning. He likes the way the bucket turns black after he dips the mop in it several times.

His face hurts from the surgery; he doesn't want any more of it, yet they say he'll be as good as new when they finish.

There's a plastic pin in his knee and a plate in his head. He has dizzy spells, although not as bad as at first. When he first arrived, he had to be sedated most of the time. The drugs were good for the pain but bad for the dreams.

They told him to finish the floor early because he had a visitor today.

"How's it going, Thomas?"

"It's all right."

Booth is more silvery on top, wavier. *Dapper* is just the right word for him, he thinks.

"Yeah, this is okay," Booth says, pleased, looking around. "We got you a federal joint to do your time because it's better than state. Much better than Youngstown, right?"

He agrees.

"Artiss is dead."

Artiss Poole, dead. He wonders if he should feel a certain way about that.

"They nailed him in Cleveland. He didn't want to do the time."

Haftmann remembers Artiss. *Another dapper little man.*

"Hanged himself," says Booth. "He really wanted to go because he had to keep his legs bent. He was in this little storeroom no bigger than a pantry. The doctor said by all accounts he should have passed out and that would have taken off the pressure."

"Some people want to die."

"How about you? You making it okay?"

"What brings you this way? Long way from home."

"You know how it is in government service. You move around a lot. I'm giving a gang seminar in Charleston. Thought I'd drop in on you."

Haftmann had a question to ask him but couldn't remember how to ask it. *Frustrating.*

Booth said: "I didn't know you at first. You look different. You look good."

He shrugs. "Thanks."

"How many months until parole?"

"Six." It was a question Booth already knew the answer to.

"Six? That's great. I want you to know we, that is, the Bureau will do everything we can to get you probation."

"All right."

"You made a few enemies, you know. Your police chief, for one. We couldn't budge the prosecutor. Two years, that's the best we could get for you."

"That's okay."

"You took a pounding. We showed pictures of you to the D. A.'s office, the judge – ."

"It's okay. It's over."

"You can go back into private investigation when your time is up. There won't be a problem."

"Ah, so the fix is in," Haftmann says but it doesn't come out right.

"The experts all said nothing could have happened afterward. I mean the reactor core wasn't going critical."

"Yes. I read that."

"That's the official version anyway. The truth is if Schmidt had a bit more time, well, who knows with these damn things?"

Things: nuclear annihilation. As if it were a disputed word in Scrabble.

Haftmann sees his odd stare disconcerts Booth, one eye frozen, the other not.

"Listen, I'm sorry about that woman. I heard. It isn't your fault."

"I know."

"Don't pity yourself over it or try to take personal responsibility for it. You're not Jesus Christ, you know."

"I know. I won't." *I'm not crazy, Booth*, he wants to say.

"So long, Haftmann."

~ ~ ~

On the far ridge he could see trees in full bloom. Some were gnarled by the mountain winds. Haftmann turned his back on the window. Too much view of the world –

Haftmann signed papers to have his house sold and used the money to purchase headstones for Shawna and her husband. Each grave was marked with black marble stone. He didn't know any poetry, so he wrote Phil to be sure that a nice verse was carved on them.

The prison in West Virginia was nested in hills with rounded tops as far as the eye could see, an island surrounded by green ocean. Now, in late summer, the leaves were losing color and the afternoon light shorter.

He missed the water, the clouds, the shifting bands of light over the lake.

Once an earthquake had rumbled through the area at night and shook his bunk. He woke gasping for breath, thinking he was back in the power plant.

Sometimes it was difficult for him to think clearly about anything for very long. His throat ached less and the doctors had said that his larynx was not permanently damaged.

There might, however, be evidence of slight brain damage, they said. Did he understand that the beating he took in the power plant, coupled with other recent unhealed beatings. "It's like a career in boxing: too much energy into the brain, secondary concussions, blah-blah."

He'd heard it before, he told them. "Tell me something new."

He got two letters from Phil and then he stopped writing. Tico sent money to his account that he used in the commissary for snack foods.

A deep anxiety would possess him from time to time, but he didn't know what to do except lie in his cell until it passed.

He found a desultory rhythm in the days, even though he had difficulty telling one from the next. Normal for convicts serving time everywhere.

His dream life was more real to him than his waking life. All the color and flourish and freedom from pain and anxiety would happen in the dreams. Visions of bliss would come to him at these times and he would rock himself and hum in his bunk. He told the doctors about these good dreams and they said it was a good sign that he was healing but –

"Did he dream of him at all?"

"No," he said. "Never."

That was good, too.

"Soon,' they said, he would be allowed to go outside and work in the fresh air. It was cold in the hills so he had to wear thick gloves. He dug holes and planted bushes around the perimeter with other cons also isolated from the general population.

The soughing of the wind through the pines was exactly like the wind off Lake Erie. He felt himself healing in mind and spirit.

He decided to keep the dreams to himself from now on.

He tried to exercise again and was surprised at how fast the body remembered. He could barely do ten sit-ups or pushups the first time he tried. After a few weeks, he was doing five sets of twenty-five with ease. He felt better.

He decided to try a jog around the inside perimeter of the prison. He made it, but he was gasping and sucking air hard.

His routine on the ward was varied, nothing challenging to him intellectually, just small painting and fix-it jobs using tools from the wood shop.

It was getting increasingly difficult to read at night because of his bad eye in the poor lighting and because of his inability to concentrate on the words.

He thought of Shawna and sometimes he woke in terror because *he,* not her husband, was the one who had taken her life, and the images of her dying sickened him in dreams.

Over the winter he had an operation for hemorrhoids and the doctor said he was cured, although he would be on a bland diet for the next three months. Prison food, being what it was, hadn't much appeal anyhow, so he thought little of the penance.

He thought of suicide but never to the point of beginning those small steps that lead toward its commission; it remained a strong idea with its own kind of morbid allure.

By summer he had gained his strength back; in fact, he surpassed what he had been capable of before coming to prison. "Incarceration," the warden told him one afternoon while he scraped old paint, "works differently on different men. Do your time well, the way you are."

One evening after supper a squall blew up and knocked out the prison's generators for a while. He sat on the bunk and looked out at a sky of mackerel clouds in formation: he thought of those sudden, violent storms that churned up over the lake. Summer was in full swing, and he imagined that the Strip had recovered and was back to moneymaking. He wondered if the crimes were meeting their quotas, too. Nothing really changed.

When he was a green deckhand on the Lakes, there were curtains you could put around your bunk for privacy. The deckhands called them "jack-off curtains." Haftmann rigged up a semblance of these to seclude himself even more in his cell. He lay there baking in the summer heat until he was dehydrated. It became a kind of ritual with him, a cleansing of the toxins in the food and the prison filth that seeped into your skin from the walls. Sometimes he masturbated in there while thinking of teen runaways from Little Minnesota ministering to him with their lips and tongues. He despised himself for those images.

He hardened the edges of his hand, karate-fashion, by chopping strokes against the wall. It was probable that there was a shiv out there somewhere for him but the odds were strongly against it situated where he was; nonetheless, it was insurance of a sort.

He had spells of stir-crazy behavior where he'd walk about in his bare feet all day or throw the tin serving trays around. Give the guards fish-eyed stares from time to time. In prison, you can go a long way from that before you're considered disturbed, or, as their administrators liked to call it, "maladjusted."

Haftmann received a letter from the wife of Gino Calteforte; she thanked him and ended her letter by saying she'd like to find that "psycho bastard's grave and dig him up and cut off his head." She was serious as a heart attack, she wrote. Somebody, maybe Phil, sent a postcard that said Millimaki had suffered a mild heart attack but was recovering. Elise surprised him by sending a book by Deepak Chopra. Haftmann gave it to a guard, who asked him if it was a self-help book—"ya know, one a them books by guys who liked to hug you when you've had a rotten day." Haftmann said, "No, it was a self-harm book." The guard thanked him anyway. Booth dropped a line to say he would visit after Labor Day in time for his parole board hearing. Haftmann wrote no response.

His insomnia worsened in the long summer days and nights and it would often be dawn before he found sleep. It wasn't the sleep of exhausted nerves that he welcomed as respite from his days of hunting the killer. It was more like crossing the threshold into a region where colors and noises were rarified to such extremes of excruciating precision that he often awoke from these by sobbing and thrashing about.

He would be the centerpiece of these dream trips, standing slightly to one side watching himself perform; often these were sexual and the climax would release him from its throes; more often than not, these were strange and violent performances, so darkly fascinating and steeped in bloodletting that he would snap to with his hands shaking like a palsy victim's, as if he were spraying blood from his fingers.

He tried weightlifting but it only redoubled his nervous energy. Sometimes he bought strychnine-laced grass from the daywatch guard at exorbitant prices or homemade hootch from the prison infirmary.

When prison policy about pornographic literature had to be revised in the light of a class action suit brought about by some jail-house shyster up on the second tier, claiming infringement of the First Amendment, Haftmann used the dwindling proceeds of his house sale to purchase what old-fashioned guards still called "fur magazines."

Although concentration was difficult, sometimes he would misplace objects in his cell and have to hunt for them for minutes. "Dissociation," his old psych textbooks, reminded him.

Booth came for his parole hearing in September, but Haftmann's indifferent responses to the panel's questions about his fraud blew his chances. In the hallway, Booth looked hard at him, although he didn't say anything besides wishing him luck. They shook hands again.

Finally, pus stopped weeping from his bad eye socket; the burning and itching made him feverish sometimes, yet he never thought to take himself to the infirmary to have it treated.

At the end of his issue, Haftmann found that he anticipated his release with something akin to dread. He was jumpy all the time, and there were occurrences in the prison routine that leaped out at as unexpectedly bizarre. For example, the cleaning solvent he needed to wash the floors was not where he knew it should be. He tried to explain this, patiently, to some dimwitted guard, but the man didn't seem to have the wherewithal to comprehend. He was escorted back to his cell by a second guard who tapped him below the shoulder blade with his key ring.

"Hit me again," Haftmann said to him, "and I'll stick that thing up your ass."

He earned a week in his cell on "cake and wine" rations for another infraction. Haftmann wanted the bench press and he didn't feel like waiting an hour for this white trash with idiot cartoons up and down both arms to finish. He was amused, more than distressed, to learn that bread-and-water punishments were still chalked up. He had figured that one for the fiction writers.

The last seventy-two hours of confinement were an agony so indescribable that he writhed in his bunk and vomited up his food. He had diarrhea and blood in his stool. "Ulcer, most likely," the prison medico said; "we'll have you down for a body scan tomorrow."

He paced his cell. It seemed no bigger than a poultry cage.

On his last night he lay awake and listened to the night sounds of metal on metal and men coughing, one or two sobbing. Too many fears and bad dreams. A talker would say words into the air from time to time: the kind of dream you get in lock-up.

I don't know what to do, Haftmann said quietly to himself.

Ssssshhh said a voice. "I'll take care of it."

Haftmann felt his body relax, let go; it was like death, yet sweet like the body's reward in sex.

Then the voice disappeared into some bandwidth in his brain of other noises jostling for attention, the way it was at night all the time now, and left him to fall asleep to the buzzing of flies. But he knew there were no flies in his cell. No flies—just buzzing, buzzing, the maddening BUZZBUZZBUZZ of tiny wings like the feasting of clouds of cadaver flies on a rotting animal's corpse.

THE END

Author's Afterword

The wartime song "Es Geht Alles Vorüber" Haftmann remembers his mother singing to him as a child (page 111) was composed by Fred Raymond. Born in Vienna (Raimund Friedrich Vesely (20 April 1900 – 10 January 1954), the Austrian composer's song about all things in life falling away was performed most notably by Lale Anderson (*Bums Valdera*, c. 1954) and a pair of Indonesian-born Dutch brothers known as The Blue Diamonds in the 1960's (Ruud de Wolff and Riem de Wolff).

The two poems referred to in the narrative on pages 41 ff. and 234 are noted below:

Herbert, George. "Love." *The Oxford Book of English Verse: 1250-1900*. Ed. Arthur Quiller-Couch. Oxford: Clarendon, 1923. 295. Ralph Vaughan Williams conducted this piece from *Five Mystical Songs* on Sep. 14, 1911 at the Three Choirs Festival in Worcester.

Wyatt, Thomas. "They Flee from Me." *The Oxford Book of English Verse*. 63.

A note on the "Strawberry Girls" of Cleveland, Ohio:

To date, none of the cases of the victims known as the strawberry girls has led to an arrest or indictment. The Cleveland P.D. has claimed 4 cases cleared, which does not necessarily entail an arrest, let alone a conviction. I reserve the author's traditional privilege of subject in choosing the format of a novel, although a true-crime work is someday needed to vindicate and perhaps explain how so many women could be murdered and their families affected. Yet the public has never expressed sufficient moral outrage, as Haftmann ruminates on page 123, and it was not until the bodies began to turn up in Geauga, Ashtabula, Ohio and Western Pennsylvania that a task force of F.B.I. and rural law enforcement investigators was initiated. In writing this work of fiction, I did not intend to disrespect the memories of those women and girls known in police parlance as strawberry girls nor to impugn the Cleveland P.D. and its elite homicide division. The child-like quaintness of the name *strawberry girls* belies the horror of the reality and that has always been the essence of evil– its very banality. Since the initial *Plain Dealer* article in 1994, the murders of four more Cleveland women, whose bodies turned up in rural Northeast Ohio counties, suggest the fact that the lives of the marginalized are still subject to the most horrific sort of violence by the very worst predators.

Thank you for reading.

Please review this book. Reviews help others find New Pulp Press and inspire us to keep providing these marvelous tales.

If you would like to be put on our email list to receive updates on new releases, contests, and promotions, please go to NewPulpPress.com and sign up.

About the Author

Robb White lives in Northeastern Ohio close to the house where he grew up. Many of his crime stories feature private investigator Thomas Haftmann, the protagonist of two earlier novels: *Haftmann's Rules* (2011) and *Saraband for a Runaway* (2013). A third novel, *When You Run with Wolves*, was published in 2015. He has a collection of short stories titled *Out of Breath and Other Stories* (2013) that mixes mainstream and crime fiction. Until he retired from college teaching this year, White wrote book reviews and conducted interviews for the print magazine *Boxing World*. His short story "Frotteur in the Dark" was selected by the editors of *10,000 Tons of Black Ink* of Chicago as one of 6 Best Of for 2009. *Special Collections*, an ebook crime novel featuring a female detective and an obese academic book thief, won the Electronic Book Competition of 2014 hosted by New Rivers Press (Mankato State University at Moorhead, MN).

NewPulpPress.com